HELL BENT

A ROGUE WARRIOR THRILLER

IAN LOOME

INKUBATOR
BOOKS

Published by Inkubator Books
www.inkubatorbooks.com

ISBN (eBook): 978-1-83756-351-7
ISBN (Paperback): 978-1-83756-352-4
ISBN (Hardback): 978-1-83756-353-1

1

The night air was warm, and the northeastern breeze off the Santa Catalina Mountains considerable. Martin Guevara stood on the very lip of the homeless shelter roof, three stories up, his sneaker-clad toes over the edge, his body swaying, buffeted by gusts of wind.

The booze flowing through his veins numbed him to his predicament, but only slightly. He was insensible, drunker than he had recently been while remaining conscious, of that he was certain. At least, in the few seconds that he could hold a coherent thought together.

He looked down, the pavement wobbling from side to side like the image in a funhouse mirror, farther away, then seemingly a little closer, then farther again.

Long way down.

His thoughts were muddled, fatigued, drifting. He didn't want to fall; he knew that much. He didn't want to die. He had a family in Agua Prieta whom he loved, who would miss him. At least, he hoped they would.

Ojos que no ven, corazón que no siente, he thought.

Eyes that do not see, a heart that does not feel.

Out of sight, out of mind, as the gringos would say. Will my family even miss me? After so long away, how will they even know I've died?

The evening was not supposed to end this way. He'd gone to the shelter angry, yes, but he was a danger to no one. He'd sat with his friends; he'd played cards. It had been a good day.

I was a danger to no one.

That was something they knew. They told you that before you left, stupid. Before you crossed the desert and risked everything for... what? Living in a dirty homeless shelter, no job, no money, no prospects? No love in your life?

Somewhere at street level, he could hear the faint sounds of mariachi music, a pub across the street playing "Cielito Lindo" on a jukebox, the notes interspersed with jumbled voices.

Happy, normal people.

They haven't discovered the body yet, or noticed Manny slumped in his chair.

When they do, those people will probably run screaming.

He looked down, over the edge. His former friend, Manny Ramos, lay dead just outside the shelter's front door, with two bullet holes in the back of his head. From across the street, the music drowning out the shots, they probably just thought he was sleeping. Some of them probably even judged him for it, the old narrative about the lazy Mexican, even as the man with the opinion downed another fat burger and overpriced beer.

Poor Manny.

What will they think of me? What will my mother think of

any of this? He wanted it to be over, but he didn't want her to suffer. *If she learns you bled out on a sidewalk...*

He hated that idea.

His family had practically disowned him in Agua Prieta because of his involvement with cartel members. But he still loved them. He had tried, when working, to send money home. He hadn't been a gangster himself; he'd just helped out from time to time, delivered the odd paper bag, the occasional briefcase. He'd known better than to look inside.

His mother had refused to pick up the wire transfers. They wanted him to work in one of the factories, the maquiladoras – businesses that allowed American companies access to the same manufacturing standards as across the border, but at a fraction of the daily wages.

Instead, he'd accepted the cartel's compromise, that he pay his entire life savings, that he cross the desert like anyone who owed them and wanted life in America, guided by "coyotes." That he work for them to repay his debts. Two years of manual labor, driving other migrants to illegal shelters once the coyotes' jobs were done.

His mother and sisters were ashamed of who they thought he had become. To them, he was as bad as the people smugglers. If he left, his mother had said, he should not bother to return. He'd begun drinking, been unable to do his job or find another.

It's all gone so terribly wrong, Martin thought with a sigh.

He looked down again. The street was perhaps forty feet below. Maybe it wasn't so far, he told himself. Maybe he'd survive.

Then what?

"All right, chief," a voice behind him said wearily. "Adios. Time to go."

The sole of a boot slammed into his backside. His balance lost, his body was pushed over the edge.

And then he was falling, headfirst, arms flailing to each side as the sidewalk rushed towards him, everything decided in the blink of an eye.

The screaming started just a few seconds after Martin's body slammed into the sidewalk with a thump, pub patrons shrinking back from the gore.

2

Sister Eva Morales never wore her nun's habit at the Pima Youth Center. There was something officious about it that made kids nervous, she'd found. So she usually settled for simplicity: denim overalls, a checkered working shirt, her red hair tied up in a short, frizzy ponytail.

She walked around the café area of the Pima Youth Center and nodded approvingly.

The cafe was divided into two sections, each housing eight tables and divided by swinging galley doors halfway along. The front half, which led to the building's main doors, was occupied by paying diners, proceeds from the small restaurant helping to pay for the center's operations.

The back half featured a scattering of kids aged three to ten, their parents unable to afford daycare, and some late to pick them up. They were kept busy with handheld video games, picture books and crayon drawings, all donated.

Behind the café, a short flight of steps led to the rec center lounge. It was filled by older kids, most of them watching a furious Xbox battle on the flat-screen TV on the wall. Past them, a gym area took up most of the large, open-concept room, with two universal weight machines, some free weights on suspended barbells, mats, and a basketball hoop affixed to the wall. A rear corridor led back to the offices. At the far end of the café, a kitchen supplied the kids with nutritious meals twice a day.

Sister Eva made her way to the back of the lounge. "Excellent," she said as she stopped behind a recliner and watched the gamers. "Nine kids still, at nearly six o'clock."

"Very impressive," a familiar voice suggested from her left flank. "You play video games too, or do you just hustle pool?"

She turned. Bob Fleming was in a black T-shirt and sweatpants, leaning against the back wall with his arms crossed, next to two exercise mats and racks of barbells. They'd met six months earlier, when he'd dropped a package off at the convent chapel. A few games of pool and some enjoyable company later, he'd volunteered to help at the center if she needed it.

But he'd developed a slightly disconcerting habit of just appearing, as if a moment earlier he'd been mist.

"I didn't see you come in. You look like a gym teacher," she said.

"Thanks."

"You're welcome. It's an improvement." They had an easy, dry banter, she'd found. He'd come to Tucson to get away from something, but didn't want to open up about it. So had she, many years earlier. It worked.

"Oh gee, thanks. I need fashion tips from a nun, obviously."

She nodded towards the stairs. "Sit and chat?"

"Okay."

They walked back down to the café proper and took the last table, by the galley doors. She retrieved her coffee, left a few minutes earlier, then looked around to make sure no one was watching. She took the flask out of her purse and dropped a dollop of whiskey into the coffee, then stashed the container. She took a sip, sighed contentedly, then reached into her top pocket and took out a capsule.

She popped it into her mouth and washed it down with more coffee.

Bob's gaze narrowed.

"What? A nun can't have a drink when she's taking a break?"

"You're taking your cancer meds with booze."

She took on a deadpan look. "Like it really matters."

"It'll matter when you're chucking your guts up, you know that. Makes it twice as bad. You said so yourself."

She shrugged. "I'm going out fighting. That's what everyone wants, right?"

"Sure."

"So don't begrudge a dying woman a drink. Or even two! Gosh! Perish the thought!"

"You're not dying."

"I am dying! You trying to boost my spirits by telling me I can win this, when we already know I have about a six percent chance, isn't going to change that. I'm okay with it, Bob. I wish you would be, too."

He clearly didn't even want to talk about it, which she understood. Bob had problems with emotion, handling them, seeing others disappointed. She'd seen the same general social awkwardness in him that she saw in some kids on the spectrum. When he was focused and fascinated, he was all business. When people just wanted him to relax?

That just seemed to make him more tense, like he was perpetually waiting for the other shoe to drop.

He crossed his arms and nodded towards the door. "Where's your boy?" He glanced at the clock quickly, just irritated enough for her to realize Chico was late.

"He'll be here. He has a lot of responsibilities for a sixteen-year-old. No father; mother works three jobs."

Bob considered that. "Sure. Are you... entirely sure you're cool with this idea? Teaching kids self-defense is sometimes seen as encouraging them—"

"To fight? Believe me, he doesn't need any encouragement. He's in a tough school, in a tough neighborhood. He's... well, he's headstrong, Bobby. He's got a bit of a temper, and it keeps getting him into trouble. And he says he wants to be a boxer."

"Okay then, as long as no one's expecting miracles overnight. I'll train him a little, and if he's still into it after that, we'll find him a proper trainer. He... any good at other sports?" There was a slightly plaintive tone to it, like he wasn't relishing coaching a nerd.

"Don't worry, he won't trip over his shoelaces. Geez! I mean... I'm guessing. I don't know him too well, if I'm being honest. He's working with a guy from social services and agreed to come here to convince them he's taking working on his temper seriously."

She heard steps to her right and turned to see the boy approaching. The rest of the center was obliviously engaged, kids playing air hockey on tables near the front, others gathered around the titanic video game battle.

The boy looked around self-consciously as he approached. He had jeans on and a worn leather jacket, a T-shirt.

"Uh... Hi."

Sister Eva rose. "Chico! How are you?" She moved over to his side and gestured to his new instructor. "Chico, this is Bob. He's agreed to show you some stuff. Bob learned to fight in the Army and did some boxing."

Chico frowned. "Okay. Are you a real trainer?"

"I've worked with some really good ones," he said. He leaned in and offered the kid a hand to shake. The kid did so firmly.

Bob gestured with a half-nod for Chico to join him on the mat.

He looked the kid over. "Jeans and sneakers aren't really ideal for this, kid. Maybe shorts next time? It's not like it's cool outside or anything."

The kid frowned. "Yeah, okay. Whatever, dude."

" 'Whatever, dude'?"

"It's just training, right? And you ain't even a real trainer."

Bob looked over at Sister Eva. "Is he for real?"

The nun cringed slightly. Bob was probably unaware that Chico's family were perpetually broke: a single mother left after her husband's death with three growing boys. He'd probably literally grown out of his shorts, and she probably didn't have the money for replacements yet. As he was the oldest, there was no one to hand down clothing to him.

But he was proud, and angry sometimes, and he wasn't going to admit any of that.

"It's fine, Chico," she interjected. "Right, Bob?"

He looked at her quizzically. "Sure. I'll get you some gloves, and we'll get started."

He began to cross the mats to a storage trunk in the back corner.

The nun's phone rang. The number displayed was

Sacred Heart, the men's shelter she volunteered at on week-ends. "Hello?"

"Sister Eva?"

"Hey, Jen. What's up?"

"We've got some visitors. The same officers as this morning."

Jen was one of the volunteers from the intake room, where they screened new guests and ran down the shelter's rules, including its no alcohol, no weapons policy.

"What are they looking for?"

"They said something about wrapping up, but they didn't take their tape down, and they're talking to some of the men. It's making them all really uncomfortable. I'm sort of worried one of them is going to flip out or something."

"Okay. Just leave them be; don't interfere. I'll be down there in ten minutes."

"Okay, Sister. Thank you!"

The nun ended the call. "I have to go out. Can you look after things here for me, make sure they lock up at ten if I'm not back?"

Bob looked curious once again. "Sure. Anything I can help with?"

She shook her head. "They're still investigating the incident at the Sacred Heart Home. Police want to wrap it up tonight. The regulars... they're not being helpful. Mostly they're scared of the cops."

"And you're good with handling all of that?"

She was about to put her hands on her hips and lecture him, but she recognized in the moment that it was just more concern. "I'll be fine. Nauseated as hell within a half hour, I'm sure, but this shouldn't take even that long to handle."

He nodded slowly, but didn't ask her to elaborate. The

"incident" was a murder-suicide three days earlier. It had made local headlines, but she'd asked him not to bring it up around the kids. It was another part of her world, and one the kids did not need to enter.

"I had a regular beer delivery for a local microbrew to one of the bars down the street just a few hours before it happened," Bob said absently. "Harsh way to go."

Eva noticed Chico looking puzzled. "It's nothing. Just... be good and listen to Bob! He knows what he's doing."

She took Bob by the elbow and moved him to one side, then lowered her voice. "Like I said, Bobby, he's got a temper. If he loses it, don't be too harsh on him, okay? He's had a really tough life."

"Cheers," Bob said, giving her a wink. "This squares us, by the way."

She nodded and grinned as she backed out of the room. "Until I run the table on you again."

"Never going to happen," he called out.

"You said that before, as I recall," Sister Eva chirped. Then she was gone, the front door swinging closed behind her.

Bob turned to Chico and handed him the eight-ounce boxing gloves.

"These look... smaller than on TV," the boy said.

"They are. These are lighter, less padding."

"Won't that... like... hurt more and stuff?"

"Nope. The weight of the gloves does much of the damage. It's why you have fewer traumatic head injuries in mixed martial arts than in boxing. They use lighter gloves. Until you know what you're doing and can defend yourself, we go with the less damaging option."

Chico looked over his shoulder towards the door. "Sister Eva beat you in a fight?"

"Sister Eva beat me at pool."

"You mean, like—"

"She beat me at eight-ball. Yes. She won. I lost." Even just saying it out loud irked him.

"You got beat by a *nun*?"

"Yeah! So?" Then Bob realized maybe he'd responded a

little too aggressively. "We've been playing for six months. She beat me a handful of times out of a few hundred games. It happens to everyone."

Except, it didn't happen to him, ever. Bob wasn't exactly out there daily trying to compete with other men. But on the odd occasion he'd taken someone on at pool or tennis or even just Ping-Pong, he never lost. Never. It was part of the deal, the impeccable muscle memory, the technique always being there, the perfect timing and co-ordination. As a government assassin, it had made him near unstoppable.

She'd beaten him, though.

A middle-aged nun.

She'd run the table with him having almost no shot on the eight. A middle-aged nun with multiple cancers.

He was trying not to let it bother him.

It had been four weeks, and so far, it wasn't working. His competitiveness had deep roots.

They'd been playing on and off for nearly six months, ever since he'd arrived and Bob Singleton had become "Bob Fleming," a delivery driver, intent on putting his career as Team Seven Alpha and the CIA behind him.

Something had to be off, something internal out of sync, he told himself.

Maybe this is what you need, a little humility, he reminded himself. *Maybe knowing you won't always win is good for you.*

Or maybe you're just getting old. Most pro athletes retired before forty, and that was already in the rearview mirror for Bob. It made his decision to go to ground seem that much more sensible. Old dogs were never much good at new tricks.

"Yeah..." Chico said as he slipped on the gloves. "But she's a *nun*. Like, how bad are you at shooting stick, *guey*?"

Bob laced the gloves up for him. "Terrible, I guess. Chico... I've always thought the best offense was a good defense. So today, we're going to start with how to defend against a jab."

He reached down and picked up his own gloves off the mat. He put on the left, using his teeth and his free hand to lace it, then put on the right, pulling the lace taut with his gloved left and his teeth. "Normally, we'd have tape over the laces to make sure they don't come undone during the fight. Now... hit me."

"*No se...* I... don't know if..."

"You want to learn how to fight, kid—"

"I already know how to fight, homes, believe me."

Cocky little shit. "Then you want to learn how to box, right? You're going to have to actually do it at some point. So show me what you've got: hit me."

"Yeah... but you're... like... old as shit."

Gee, thanks, kid. "You're worried you might hurt me?"

"Well... yeah, a little, I guess."

He was a big, muscular kid, nearly a match for Bob's six feet two inches. *Probably hits like a truck.* "Maybe, like Sister Eva's eight-ball game, I'll surprise you."

The boy didn't look convinced, but he squared up to Bob anyhow. "Okay..."

Bob raised his guard.

Chico weaved from side to side ever so slightly, looking for an opening. He threw a stinging jab. Bob bobbed it, moving his head out of the way at the last second. The punch missed by at least two inches. The boy frowned and tried to throw another. Bob saw the muscle flex in the boy's shoulder before he'd even extended his hand. He ducked it, natural instincts taking over, everything so slow he could practically count the hairs on the kid's arm as it sailed by.

The boy threw two more, in quick succession, stumbling forward slightly as he did. Bob weaved around both.

Chico looked irritated. "*Pinche movimiento!*" he muttered. *Fucking movement!* He threw a right jab but cut it short, a fake, trying to guess where Bob would go, following it with something Bob guessed was supposed to be a right cross.

Bob slipped both punches, the boy stumbling after missing the second. Bob restrained the urge to push him to the ground.

The kid charged in, throwing right crosses, left hooks, body shots, all in furious, quick succession. Bob leaned in low, taking away his torso as a target, crossing his arms just ahead of his face in a defense perfected by the late boxing great Archie Moore, the flurry of blows bouncing harmlessly off his forearms, elbows and shoulders.

The boy backed away a few paces. He looked frustrated and angry, his Latin complexion flushed with blood. "*Fuck this!*" he barked. He charged at Bob, lowering his head to tackle him. At the last second, Bob dropped instinctively to the ground, turning side-on and using both feet to trap one of Chico's ankles. His momentum arrested, the kid slammed face-first onto the mat.

Bob rolled to his feet. The boy rose a second later, blustering, spitting angry. "*Maricon!* Maybe I take off these gloves, go get my piece—"

Bob held up both hands, his left palm signaling a stop, his right-hand index finger aloft. "Hey! I'm trying to help you! I'm not here for my enjoyment! Now... would you *calm the fuck down*, please? You're embarrassing both of us!"

Chico stopped in his tracks. Both men realized the adjacent lounge had gone silent other than beeps from the video game. The older kids were staring wide-eyed at them over the backs of chairs.

"Sorry, everybody!" Bob called out as pleasantly as possible. "Minor disagreement, go back to your business. Go on now!"

They grudgingly turned back to the TV.

"Man... I'm sorry, okay?" Chico said. "I didn't mean that." He looked genuinely embarrassed.

"The part where you threatened to go get a gun and kill me? I certainly fucking hope not!"

"I didn't mean to scare you or nothing," Chico said. "But you was... you know—"

"Making you look bad? Feel inadequate at boxing?" Bob asked. "What?"

Chico hung his head. "Maybe both. You don't know what it's like in this city. I got a reputation to worry about, you know? It's stupid, but that's what it is."

Bob nodded. "I do. You use your 'piece' a lot? You slinging dope or something?"

The kid looked away quickly, his discomfort obvious. "No. Not really. Just... you know, we go out in the desert sometimes and shoot bottles and rocks and shit. But dudes get shot in my neighborhood all the time. You've got to be strapped and ready."

"You in a gang?"

"Sort of. I mean, we're not, like... I mean... not really."

"That's a good thing, man, not a shortcoming."

"I know. But... like I said, it's hard. You've got to be tough... or seen as it." Chico stared at his shoes, as if he knew the whole notion was beneath him, but he had no choice.

The kid needed real guidance; that much was obvious.

Bob understood why Sister Eva wanted him involved. "I'll make you a deal, okay? You let me teach you how to box, once a week for the rest of the summer. If it goes well, I'll help you find a full-time trainer and compete. Okay?"

"Okay. What do I got to do?"

"If we get to the point where you're getting proper training, you sell that piece and give the money to your mom. They don't go cheap, so you'll get some good money if you take it to the right store, probably a few hundred."

He didn't seem to like the idea, but he eventually nodded. "Okay. Deal."

"Now..." Bob backed away a few more feet. He had no idea if the kid was being honest, but it was worth a shot. So he had to hold up his end. "Let's do this again. Hit me."

Chico rushed in, targeting the body again, throwing both hands in sequence, leaving his chin unprotected. *We'll get to that next week, I guess*, Bob thought as he blocked the punches methodically. At the end of the sequence, the boy threw a quick, furious cross that Bob just managed to bob away from, a gloved fist whistling past his chin.

The boy looked disconcerted again. He let the gloves drop to his sides limply. "This is stupid. I can't do this."

You're not competing, you're teaching. Don't be an ass! Help him!

"Yes, you can," Bob said. "Anyone untrained would've had their head taken off by that cross. You're a big kid, and you're fast. Don't knock your own potential! But if an opponent can't hit you, he can't hurt you. Got it?"

"Yeah, but—"

"You said you wanted a trainer who knew what he was doing. I'm proving you can't even hit me if I don't want you to. And...?"

Chico looked puzzled. "And?"

"What did I just tell you?"

The kid took on a look of recognition. He nodded gently. "If an opponent can't hit you, he can't hurt you. Yeah. Yeah, I got it now." There was a glimmer there, too, in the kid's eye. He'd learned something, and it had been quick, and the guy in front of him thought he was fast and powerful.

He'd gained a little confidence. That would make everything that was to come a little easier.

It felt pretty good, Bob had to admit. Six months had passed, and Tucson still didn't really feel like home. But he had a decent job, he hadn't played "hero" and gotten anyone else killed, and he hadn't killed anyone himself.

It felt good to be doing right, teaching someone else to fight their own battles.

Keeping trouble in the rearview mirror.

4

The week passed quickly, a blur of delivery jobs that took him to every corner of the city and a few spots in Cochise County, besides. By Friday, Bob found himself back on Park Avenue, delivering craft beer to a pub just down the block from Sacred Heart shelter.

It was demanding work but gratifying. People nearly always enjoyed a delivery, in an age when they occurred daily. So he saw a lot of smiling faces.

He also got to see Tucson, in all its white, pink and sand-colored adobe-and-plaster glory. Aside from the downtown, Tucson was low-rise buildings built to accommodate the constant, sweltering desert heat, most three stories or less. Its green spaces were xeriscaped to accommodate the absence of water, saguaro and cacti competing with small, spiky shrubs like aloe vera. Most of the traditional grass in the city was limited to golf courses. Its streets were made of solid concrete, because asphalt would soften too much in 100-plus Fahrenheit temperatures.

The businesses he delivered to, however, were sometimes

problematic: his job was to drop items off, not move them to the owners' preferred locations. But many did not seem to understand that concept. They'd order eighteen cases of beer or six crates of porcelain pottery or three boxes of peaches, and they wanted them on a shelf in the kitchen or in a deep-freeze... or in a deep-freeze in the basement.

But Bob wasn't being paid to carry hundreds of pounds down basement stairs; in fact, his supervisor had made it clear they weren't bonded and insured to move or relocate already delivered items. So he wasn't even allowed, in those cases.

Still, as he unloaded the six cases of Copperhead Old Reserve Craft Ale and placed them on the dolly, he was glad the bars seemed to know where the dividing line was. Beer was heavy – hard work in the midday sun. The pub staff knew to show up at the back door, sign the sheet, lead his dolly back to where they wanted to unload.

And then he'd wait while they did so, to get his dolly back. Usually – and today was no exception – they offered him a coffee or tea.

"Figured you'd want it to go," the young waitress said, removing a tall Styrofoam cup from a round tray and handing it to him as he waited by the back door.

"Appreciated."

From the front of the building somewhere, past the kitchens and the bar that lay between, Bob could hear a commotion. He frowned and checked his battered old Seiko wristwatch. "It's... 11:52 in the morning. Are they actually tossing someone at this time of day?"

The waitress rolled her eyes upwards. "I swear, dude, some days they're waiting outside when we open at ten. Like, go to the liquor store, you losers, my God! I mean... I'm glad they don't, because otherwise I wouldn't have a job. And we're the only bar for a couple of blocks. So it's not surprising or nothing. But you get my drift."

"Oh, too many times," Bob said. "I used to be one of those losers."

The young woman blanched a little, and her hand shot involuntarily to cover her mouth. "Oh! I'm sorry! Really, I didn't think... I mean..." She was blushing furiously.

"It's okay. I get it. If I had to deal with drunks, I'd get pretty sick of them, too. But... ah, you know. Give it a little thought." He could tell she already had, so there was no point belaboring it.

A crash emanated from the other room. The girl's head whipped around. "That... sounded serious. Should we go see?"

Bob held up both palms. "I'm not allowed to get involved, and wouldn't anyway. Not my business," he said, backing towards the door.

"Fair enough," she said.

Bob left through the back door. His truck's diesel engine was idling; his boss insisted they cost more to restart continually than to leave in idle, and that he didn't want "another fucking discussion about the ozone layer." So Bob had learned to live with it.

The sound of glass breaking was unmistakable, shards spattering the pavement in front of the business. *Jesus H, what the hell are they up to?*

It's not your business. Get in the cab, go to the next job. Learn from your past, you idiot.

He'd decided after Memphis that his inner monologue was generally giving him an angel/devil sort of scenario; it either wanted him to do the smart thing, or it wanted him to get really, really drunk. The latter was no longer an option, and he was trying to be more conscientious about the former. Recognizing which voice deserved his attention was finally becoming second nature.

He pulled the truck out of the alley and headed north, back towards Park Avenue.

At the corner, he looked left.

The man on the sidewalk was flat on his back, bleeding. He was covered in glass. Bob couldn't see his face, but one arm was outstretched, hand gripping the remnants of a whiskey bottle jaggedly broken just below the neck.

Another man looked through the shattered front window. He was big, muscular in a black tank top, with frizzy hair and a beard. Bob thought he'd seen him before, maybe manning the door as a bouncer. He began pushing shards of broken window out of the frame, onto the sidewalk – and the prone figure – below.

Then he disappeared inside. Bob checked the rearview mirror. There were no cars behind the truck. He waited a moment, expecting the man to step outside and haul the ejected patron to his feet.

But nobody came.

You don't need to take an interest in this. This is that guy's problem, not yours.

After a minute, Bob anxiously checked the rearview mirror again. He had a car behind him, waiting patiently for him to turn at the stop sign. Bob glanced to the left again. The man was still lying there.

He hadn't moved.

Did they kill him?

Surely somebody's going to help the guy up, at least, call him an ambulance...

The car behind him honked.

"Yeah! Yeah, yeah." Bob gave them a wave. He put the truck into gear and stepped on the gas, turning left onto Park.

He was halfway up the block when he chanced one more look in the rearview mirror, across the double-wide boulevard.

The man was still lying prone, and still hadn't moved, as far as he could tell.

He pulled the truck over to the curb.

Shit.

He took out his phone and dialed emergency.

"911, what is your emergency?"

"Yeah... look, there's some guy lying on Park Avenue, in front of the bar at the corner of... Yeah. Yeah, that's it. He hasn't moved in a minute, at least."

There was a pause. "Sir, I'm just going to put you on hold—"

"*Wait!*" Bob called out. But it was too late; the call had been directed to a loop of canned orchestral string music.

An emergency line just put me on hold.

What the hell?

He waited. Another minute went by. Bob checked the rearview mirror again. The waitress he'd been talking to walked out of the bar and over to the man, then crouched beside him. After a few moments, she went back inside.

Bob remained on hold, the string music switching to a particularly bland rendition of "King of the Road," the old Frankie Lane hobo song.

The attendant came back onto the line. "911, what is your emergency?"

Eh? "I was just talking to you. There's a man on—"

"Hold, please."

The music resumed.

You've got to be freakin' kidding me.

He checked the mirror again. The man had moved a little, rolling onto one side. *He's not dead. He's not your responsibility. When you try to help, you just make things worse.*

But you've been that guy, Bobby. You've been the drunk people just walk by without even checking to see if you're dead or dying.

Fuck this.

Bob undid his seatbelt and got out of the truck.

ngel Herrera talked animatedly even as he leaned one elbow on his oversized teak desk, its cherry stain reeking of money. Dark haired, with a goatee and moustache, he was sturdy and broad-chested at five feet six inches, with a once-muscular frame that had given way to fat.

He was jabbering on the phone, proclaiming the spectacular deal he was giving a local man for a plot of land.

Detective Carter Hayes watched him from beside the office door, remaining quiet.

"So we agree on eighteen thousand, right? It's scrub. A former gas station means a remediation plan, and that is going to cost you, right? That bill could be gigantic, my friend... I mean, I'm doing you a favor, *ese*! Yeah, yeah, okay..."

He ended the call.

Hayes hated sitting and listening to him yammer. The detective was well paid to make sure Herrera's operation ran without interference, that his men weren't arrested when more competitive alternatives existed. He was tall – over six feet. He thought of himself as traditionally handsome, with sandy hair and blue eyes, a strong chin. His midsection was beginning to expand. He'd been a quarterback in high school, expected to go to a big college until a knee injury.

The first time we met, you told me I "looked like a gay." You little cockroach.

The head of the Tucson branch of the Omega Cartel struck him as a small, self-centered, and venal man. For the better part of a decade, however, he'd paid for the detective's cocaine habit, among other things.

The room was gaudy, a rich red pile carpet clashing with old oak bookshelves, each stacked with "self-improvement" titles, bro culture handbooks with titles like *The View at the Top* and *Be The Better Man*.

Clearly, Hayes thought wryly, they weren't working.

Herrera sat behind his desk and contemplated the deal he'd just made. "What a sucker! That *idiota* just gave me a parcel of commercially zoned land less than ten minutes from downtown for less than the cost of running services to it!"

The policeman nodded approvingly but said nothing. He tried to look relaxed, hands in pockets. *As if I know he can't really touch me. As if the power balance is equal.*

The owner of the Flaming Garter and four other night-clubs had a famous temper. Hayes knew that the slightest wrong word – a sound out of place, a careless remark, an interruption – could bring on the "red," where Angel's vision just clouded over and the rage took over.

Typically, when that happened, someone else paid a terrible price. Then Angel's father would call. Then someone would have to fix his mess.

As a young rich kid in Phoenix, he'd abused his privilege, with a serviceman who'd been mouthing off in one of his father's nightclubs paying the ultimate price. His father had had to arrange a surrogate to take the fall, pay off the man's family, and apologize to the cartel.

It had necessitated a move. Rather than being his father's number two and obvious successor, he had been shunted off to the much smaller city of Tucson, to run the operation there.

A decade later, he remained firmly in his father's shadow. And he hated it.

Angel gestured to the chair ahead of the desk. "Sit," he commanded.

Hayes waved a hand. "I'm good."

"Not a request. I want to show you something."

Hayes shrugged. "Sure." He sat down. His hand was below the top of the desk, and he made sure to keep it near the speed holster clipped to his belt, and his Glock 21 in .45 caliber.

"Go for your gun!" Angel said excitedly. "Go on! Draw on me!"

"What?"

"Don't shoot me, asshole! Just draw on me."

"Oookay," Hayes said.

He went for his pistol, proximity letting him pull it quickly from the speed holster. But before it could clear his belt line, Angel's hand came down on his desktop, slapping a small, round red button. In an instant, a door slid back and a gun popped out of the desk and directly into his waiting hand.

"Eh? Eh? You like?" Angel said excitedly. "You like? It's spring-loaded! You know, like *Taxi Driver*! 'You talking to me?

You talking to me, punk? Well... make my day!' Pretty cool, eh? Manolo helped me put it in."

Hayes breathed in slowly and steadily, calming his anxiety and curbing his tongue. Mixed metaphors aside, it seemed a waste of money designed to please a child.

"Nobody gets the drop on you, I guess," Hayes said.

"You got that right." Angel mimed looking down the gun's rail, one eye closed as he sighted the detective. "Ptchew! You're dead."

"Yeah. Good one." Hayes didn't bother to smile or even pretend he was impressed.

Angel seemed to notice his reticence. He sniffed loudly. "Yeah, well... it's just a backup, in case I get caught without a piece handy." He nodded Hayes's way. "So... what happened?" he demanded.

"Like I said on the phone, there was a witness: Tito Agustin."

"You're sure?"

"I saw him just before we went up the stairs. Those two were tight, always getting into shit together. Tito stayed at Sacred Heart before he found work, and he visited Martin whenever he was staying there. Pretty sure I saw them talking when I first got there that night. He was always hanging around there, wearing that stupid, grimy Dodgers cap and that equally stupid grin."

Herrera sulked at that. "I heard he was barred. How did that *maricon* get off the hook, anyhow? I never got the whole story about that. Guy like Tito, he was an asset—"

"Because he's a lunatic with muscles? There are others."

"Yeah, but they don't owe us their entire life. I mean, he don't neither, now."

"I talked to Eric, who handles books for your Nogales

coyotes. Word is Tito kept a secret stash of cash, parlayed it into some coke sales, enough to buy a brick. Sold that, and it got him enough to pay Eric off and rent a place. Eric kicks back to us, so Tito's debt is paid. Last anyone heard, he was having trouble finding work, though. Can't get off the drink long enough, and he has no proper papers, so..."

"Finding work. You mean a job? He's gone straight? Tito?"

"Yeah, you could have put long odds against it, with his rap sheet back in Meh-hee-coe. But it turns out he's got a kid—"

"I knew that. He had a wife, too. She kicked it, cancer or something."

"Donny Legs, one of the other bums at the shelter, said Tito's been straight since he crossed, other than the dope. He told me he quit before he even came down here; that's why he owed Omega. That's why Manolo couldn't convince him to stay with us once he'd paid. And I guess he's a pretty solid mechanic – and that's not a euphemism for him being a hitter. He literally rebuilds engine blocks as a hobby, so he can find work, even if it has to be under the table. Or he used to. Now, he's just three sheets to the wind half the time, living in some rented shithole in Southland Park."

"Still... Tito going straight!" Herrera scoffed. "That must have made them happy in Mexico City."

"I doubt he even worries about what he left behind in taco land."

Herrera took a stiff breath, clearly maintaining his temper with difficulty. "Yes, well, it would do you well to learn a lesson in this business, Hayes. The same thing I told Manolo: everybody knows somebody; everybody's related. The cartels are like a big, semi-functional family. You got to know who you're dealing with, because the right people have to stay happy. The *idiota* who does not learn that lesson usually pays for it."

Hayes checked his watch. "Getting late," he muttered.

Herrera took another short, sharp intake of breath, which the veteran cop recognized as his effort at warding off anger. Hayes knew how to push his buttons, by not paying attention to him, or by saying "Mexico" like he was trying to speak their language.

"That he fled across the border in the first place should have been the end of him," Herrera said. "Instead, he agreed to pay a migrant's debt, move here."

"And now, he's weaseled out of it and is making noises about Martin Guevara," Hayes continued. The detective took one hand from his pockets and fiddled with the miniature Star-Spangled Banner on Herrera's desk. "And you need me to clean up, as usual. When we find him—"

"Deal with it. This wasn't supposed to go down like this in the first place."

"Yeah, but... there's dealing with it, and there's *dealing* with it. I'd prefer a methodology that eschews extravagant spectacle. That's your crew's preferred approach, not mine."

Herrera did not allow irritation to show, to bubble to the surface. He'd been working with Hayes for nearly two years, but the man's penchant for fancy words that didn't say much was as annoying as ever. *Mierda pretenciosa.* He reminded himself to tell Manolo Marichal to get his crew ready and looking, in case Hayes failed. "Meaning what?"

"If we don't have to kill him, we don't kill him. All he needs is a good scare," the detective suggested. "Or maybe I get some proof he sold the dope in your territory. Then he's even more in debt to you than he ever was, because he owes you the deal and tribute and restitution."

Now that was an interesting proposition. Herrera nodded. "Do it. Let him know what happens when he crosses Angel Herrera. Make the message stick."

BOB WAITED for cars to pass, then crossed the street. The man was still prone, but he'd moved a couple of times. By the time he got closer, he could see his chest rising and falling.

Okay. He's alive. That's all you really needed to know. This is not your problem.

The bouncer must've seen him, as he was leaning through the front door, holding it ajar with his bulk. "Don't worry about him; he'll be fine," he said.

The callousness irritated him. A man could be sad and pathetic in his own right, but the person who mocked that guy? The ones who punched down always made Bob seethe a little; they always made him want to punch right back.

He crouched beside the figure. The man had a gash at his hairline that needed stitches, blood slicking hair around the wound. Bob didn't move him, aware that a paramedic might spot something important he'd missed that required more care. But he put his own head down to the sidewalk to look at him in perspective. He had another bad gash somewhere near the temple, probably from his head hitting the sidewalk or a jagged piece of window.

"This man needs an ambulance," he said. He turned back to the bouncer from his crouched position. "What the hell were you thinking, tossing him through a pane of glass?"

"Hey, his momentum carried him. I barely shoved."

"Sure. That's why there was enough force to almost scalp him, I guess. Call a fucking ambulance, for fuck's sake!"

The bouncer shrugged. "Not my problem, man. I've got five pounds of glass to clean up. Besides, they won't come here."

"What?"

"Too many calls over the years. Cheapest draft in this part of town, so the most problem drinkers. That's why they pay me. Dispatchers hear our address, and they put us on hold because it's always just some drunk who just needs to sleep it off, not a real emergency. Same with the shelter down the street. And that fucker... he's been a problem around here for months. Everyone on the street knows him because he used to stay at Sacred Heart, the shelter. Doesn't live around here anymore, I guess... but cabs won't pick him up, neither."

Fuck this bullshit. Bob took out his phone and dialed 911 again.

"911 emergency."

"I just called about the man on the sidewalk on Park Avenue."

"You just... Hold, please," the voice said.

"No! Don't—" But it was too late. The canned classical music resumed.

Bob looked over at the bouncer.

The man shrugged again. "Fucking told you, dude."

On the sidewalk, the prone figure stirred. He was younger than Bob, maybe in his early thirties, with a sunbaked complexion, collar-length greasy black hair slicked back, his skin pitted from teenaged acne. His right eyelid flickered a few times before opening fully. Even then, the lid drooped. He reeked of tequila, and whether it was the booze or the concussion, Bob figured he was pretty dazed.

"You fell through a window," Bob said. "Don't move, okay?"

The man ignored him, trying to push himself upright. He got as far as his left elbow half-propping his body off the ground.

"Stay still. You might have internal injuries," Bob suggested. "I'm trying to get an ambulance—"

"No ambulance!" The man's eyes widened as he shook off cobwebs. "No... I don't have no money for that. No hospital, no ambulance. No..." The man's eyes fluttered, and he passed out.

Bob turned to the bouncer again. "Why doesn't he want an ambulance?"

The bouncer crossed his arms and leaned against the door frame. "Why do you even give a shit, dude? He's some fucking wetback drunk loser. Leave him there long enough and the dehydration will probably get him. He's probably illegal, so they'll call the cops. And I'm pretty damn sure he doesn't have insurance, so... like... do you want to pay for this miserable piece of shit?"

Anger swelled inside Bob, a propulsive sensation telling him to cross the sidewalk, let the bouncer understand what it felt like to be treated like trash.

But he held it in. Helping out a drunk was one thing. Fighting was out of the question.

"At least help me up with him," Bob said. "He's dead weight."

The bouncer looked put out, but he walked over anyway. They lifted the man to his feet, his arms over their shoulders. "So... what do you want us to do with him?"

Bob nodded towards his truck. "Just help me get him into the cab of my truck. Maybe I can figure out where he came from, give him a ride home at least."

This isn't your business. This guy is trouble; this situation is trouble. And it's someone else's trouble, the internal voice said.

But Bob wasn't sure which internal voice it was, the one that tempted him to drink, the bad voice, or the one that steered him straight. *Ignoring them both seems the humane choice.*

They began to slowly carry-drag the unconscious man across the street.

6

B ob was a block from Veteran's Hospital, the truck
rolling along Ajo Way, when his passenger woke
once more.

He looked around blearily. *"Dónde...?"*

"My truck. You got thrown out of a bar and got a bad cut
to your scalp. I'm taking you to see a doctor."

The man straightened up slightly. "No! No, no," he
insisted, shaking his head. He reached for the cab door
handle.

"We're moving!" Bob used the switch panel on the
driver's door to lock the passenger side. "Don't open the
damn door while we're moving, you idiot! Look, you need
stitches."

The man frowned and pulled at the lock. "No hospital,
man, okay? I got no papers."

There was a gap at the curb ahead. Bob pulled the truck
over.

"I should go," the man said.

"Those cuts need stitches, especially at the scalp line,

and you've lost some blood. You almost certainly have a concussion. Can I at least drop you somewhere you can get help?"

The man raised his chin slightly and studied Bob. "Why are you helping me?"

Bob sighed. "Because I've been there. Look, I think it's crazy not to get help, but your life is your life. Do you want me to drop you somewhere or not?"

His passenger removed his hand from the door handle. "Okay. Sure. I live across town, though."

"I'm not due anywhere until two," Bob said. "And Tucson's not that big." He kept his left hand on the big steering wheel and held out his right. "I'm Bob."

The man shook it. "Tito. Thank you, man."

"It's nothing."

"No, it ain't nothing. You helped me, *vato,* now I got to owe you."

"You don't—"

"No, now I owe you. But that's okay." Tito took a deep breath, like he'd relaxed just a little. "Beats the shit out of walking."

TITO RENTED a one-bedroom cinderblock bungalow just off Alvord Road in Southland Park, near the city's southern limit.

Bob's hackles had gone up as soon as the truck entered South Tucson. A delivery truck was a target on just about any city street if he wasn't careful. But some parts of town were tougher than others, less privileged, leaner and meaner.

His passenger must've sensed his unease. "You got something on your mind?" he asked.

"It's nothing personal, Tito. You know there's more opportunity crime in South Tucson, and I drive a delivery truck."

"Yeah, yeah, I got you, homes. I'm just yanking your chain, is all. Take a left here. It's the third on the south side. There's a spot about five cars—"

"Yeah, I see it."

Bob parked in the spot.

Tito climbed out of the truck. "You going to come in? I owe you a beer at the least."

Bob held up a hand. "I had to quit. Bad kidneys." He liked to think he was learning, on the social front. It was a white lie, but it saved making what appeared to be a habitual drinker uncomfortable... and Tito didn't exactly seem stable.

He had a thought and frowned. "You got someone who can stitch that up for you?"

Tito squinted as he pawed at the long gash by his hairline. He was swaying in place slightly, far too drunk still to take care of it himself – assuming he even could. "*Coño...* my head hurts," he muttered.

Yeah, that's about par for the course. Bob turned off the truck's ignition and got out of the cab. He checked his watch. *Twelve fifty. I've got maybe forty-five minutes for this.*

"Come on," Bob said. "I've stitched a few people up over the years, too. And you're in no condition to try threading a needle."

The front gate was bolted and padlocked. Tito opened it and led Bob inside. "We don't got nothing to steal, really, but you never know what's going down these days. Better safe than sorry." Then he added, "I worry about my boy."

"Yeah? How come?"

Tito shrugged and closed the gate behind them. They followed the walk to the steps. "We've been here a year, and I don't think he's got no little friends, still. We lived on the other side of the city for the two years before that, so he never sees his old friends. Is probably nothing, I guess, just... you know, getting used to a new place."

He was about to open the front door when it swung inwards. The boy holding it ajar was perhaps twelve or thirteen, his dark eyes suspicious. That changed when he saw his father.

"Dad!" He looked shocked. "Ohmigod, Dad! What happened?"

"I... It's nothing." Tito was clearly too in the bag to think of an excuse.

"He got hit by a car while walking home," Bob offered. "Took a hell of a shot, too. Hospitals need insurance, so I brought him back here."

The boy was stunned. Then he glared at Bob angrily. "Did you hit my dad?"

Tito put a hand on his shoulder. *"Calmate!* Take it easy, Sean, take it easy! This dude was the only person who stopped to help me. Now, he's going to help me with some stitches. So... just cool it, okay?"

The doorway led into a small living room, bare save for an old floral-print sofa, a coffee table and a small flat-screen TV. Tito closed the door behind them. "Bob, you want a drink of water or something? I don't think we got..."

"We have Sunny Delight and apple juice," Sean said.

"Some water would be right on, thank you," Bob said. He took a seat on the edge of the sofa. Tito sat down at the far end. The boy headed into the kitchen.

Bob nodded approvingly as he looked around. Putting people at ease had been part of his tradecraft at the CIA; increasingly, it was the one positive takeaway he could transfer to civilian life. "Decent place."

"It's okay. Nicer than my mother's house in Juarez. Not by much, though, and she owns hers."

There was a picture on the end table by the couch. A young woman sat flanked by a younger Tito, standing, and an adolescent Sean. Next to it was a picture of the boy taken recently, holding up a peace sign outside Challenger Middle School.

Bob nodded towards the small display. "Your wife?"

Tito nodded. "Elizabeth. She and Sean came down six months after me. But in a transport truck. My wife and son wasn't walking across no desert."

"You can speak Spanish if you want," Bob said.

Tito glared at him, but briefly. "I like the practice, okay? Besides, I don't want to insult you or nothing, but your Spanish is kind of shit."

Bob was puzzled. "I'm completely fluent."

"Yeah, but you say things wrong, like you read it from a Spanish textbook or something."

"I guess. It's supposed to be a familiar accent in Cuba."

"Eh?"

"Long story. So... what happened?"

Tito seemed to space out for a few moments, sucking on his tongue, picking at his front teeth with the tip, staring into dead space. He looked bleak. "She died. A vein in her brain ruptured, a stroke. There wasn't nothing anyone could do. But... I don't like talking about that, okay? You lose anyone?"

"Yeah. Yeah, I get it." Bob nodded towards the bathroom. "You've got a needle and thread?"

Tito frowned and looked confused. "Eh?"

"For your stitches."

Tito looked baffled.

Bob sighed. "I've got an emergency kit in the truck. I'll be right back."

"Wait! Before you do that... you got my piece?"

Bob stifled the urge to judge. He retrieved the pistol from his waistband and handed it over.

"A man's got to protect his home," Tito offered nervously.

"No explanation necessary."

Bob headed back out into the sunny afternoon. He had to remember to leave a number for the kid, just in case, as well as instructions if his father took a turn.

Helping out Tito was completely eating up his lunch break, but he didn't mind. Everyone needed a helping hand now and then. He'd had more than a few.

Returning the favor wasn't doing anyone any harm.

I'm just here to get along.

7

"Eight ball, corner pocket." Bob leaned over the shot, lining up the cue ball. He drew the stick back just an inch before striking it, the white sphere hammering the black, the latter disappearing.

He stood up straight and studied the table with a look of contentment.

"Really? You're glowing because you ran the table on me?" Sister Eva was standing six feet away, her cue stick propped between her feet, chalk end up. "Congratulations, you potted out on a nun."

Bob gave her his best look of cynical disbelief. "Yeah, like you wouldn't be crowing from here to Phoenix if you'd kicked my ass again. On the rare occasion that you beat me, I had to hear about it for weeks each time."

"Yeah... but I'm *dying*. Would you begrudge a dying woman a few moments of happiness?" She grinned broadly.

"You're going to play that card—"

"Right up until the moment I kick the bucket, Bobby.

And, like I told you, no pity. I swear, if I thought you'd let me win, I'd never forgive you."

That caught him flat-footed. He felt a surge of morose anxiety and pushed it down. He hadn't cried in a long time, but on occasion, Sister Eva could almost manage to prompt tears. For six months, since a chance delivery meeting at the church near her priory, she'd been the one Tucsonan he could talk to, who could share his big worries and small victories.

But that wouldn't last much longer. They both knew that. She'd already lasted longer than the doctors expected.

"You don't have to joke about it all the time, for Pete's sake," he said. "I mean... you're cool with it, and I guess that's what's important—"

"But..."

"But I'm going to miss you. So are a lot of other people, I'm guessing. I..." He felt awkward, the easy banter that had developed between them suddenly breached by serious intentions. "I don't have family or many friends. It's been good having someone to talk to."

She sat down at the small round table. He took the stool across from her. "That's a problem that only has one solution," she said. "And I've told you this before, many times."

"I know: if I don't put myself out there—"

"You can't be close to people if you never talk with people. You can't find what's important to you if you have no responsibilities. You can't have a life—"

"Unless I'm actually living my life. Yeah. Anyone ever tell you that for a dying nun, you're kind of a hard-ass?"

"It's been mentioned. I wear it as a badge of pride." She held up her hand to signal the waiter. "Am I wrong?"

"No."

"So..."

"You're not wrong, you're just pushy. And for your information, I met someone new just a day ago. Nice dude named Tito. Got himself into a small bother. I got a chance to give him a ride."

"Again," she said, waving her index finger in a circle around her pint and his tea. The waiter nodded back and headed towards the bar. "Giving some dude a ride isn't being social, you know that."

"You sound almost disappointed in me," Bob said. "I'm trying. I really am."

"I know. But you've also told me enough about your incredible murky past for me to know this isn't what you deserve, this... isolation. If you keep assuming you're going to fail, the effort is always going to be half-hearted."

She made it sound even bleaker than it was, Bob thought. "Hey... I'm not totally isolated. I'm helping out at the drop-in center, and I've got you to talk to, right?"

"For now." She took another sip of beer as the weight of a couple of words hit home for Bob. "I don't worry about dying, Bob. I believe my God will take care of me. But I don't want to go out worrying about you. I don't want the last of my life to go flying by quickly, all the while worrying about you dying slowly. Because that's what it is, living alone, isolating yourself. And I don't want you to die slowly and unhappily, Bob. You never like to talk much about personal stuff, so it's always music or sports or travel, never... you. But... you're a good man, and the thought of that—"

"If you knew all the details, you'd be less forgiving," he said. "Like I told you after we first met: I did terrible, terrible things."

"You also told me why. That you believed what you were doing was protecting your country, protecting people."

"I was wrong. I got it wrong, over and over again. And people died, Eva. I'm not sure that's ever forgiven."

"And I'm not sure it's up to you," she said. She pointed up. "He's a lot better at those choices than we are, Bob."

"So maybe what I need is a sign of some sort, something that tells me He or anyone else gives a damn."

She smiled wryly. "Yeah, because having a friend who's a dying nun and who worries about you... clearly that doesn't qualify as either. Let me give you one piece of solid advice that has nothing to do with religion and everything to do with happiness: what we're doing right here – shooting the breeze, generally just being there for each other – you can do that with as many people as you like, you know. There's no rule that says you can only reach out to one person at a time, trust one person at a time."

"That's..."

"An endearing notion?"

"A lot of potential for pain."

Her head sank slightly. Then she steeled herself with a deep breath. She took a long sip of beer. "Maybe that's why He hasn't taken me yet; He wants me to help you figure this out, this notion that you have that feelings are risky. I mean... of course they are. But there is no reward without risk. It's why He gives us free agency, to make mistakes. To fight when we believe in something. Or someone. Without the bad, the good would be meaningless. And you're good, Bob. You have to know that."

He figured he must've blushed a little at that. But Bob let her have the last word.

Eventually, she'd figure out what others had: that good intentions would never fix the damage he'd done.

THE LIGHTS WERE out in the living room, but the TV was bright enough to make up for it. Sean Agustin had begun playing *Mario Kart* before the sun went down, now it was nearly ten o'clock, and the frantic gaming hadn't slowed a step.

A fist hammered the front door three times, shaking it on its hinges.

He hit pause on the game. Nobody ever visited their little house aside from the church social worker who checked up on him from time to time. His father had made it clear to him that being illegal meant staying away from the authorities, not trusting them.

He'd been eight years old when they left Mexico. Now, he was in seventh grade, almost a grown-up. He barely remembered it.

The door shook again, the knocks even louder.

His nerves fluttered.

He got up and walked over. He stood on his tiptoes to reach the spyhole.

Two men, their shapes warped by the curved glass. Sean frowned. He was sure he'd seen the taller man somewhere before. He wore an old-fashioned hat, like men in the movies his father liked, on the oldies channel.

A hand shot towards the door, the image warp making it seem huge, a 3D-movie punch that made Sean jump back slightly. The hand hammered on the door again. "*Tito!* Open up, you bum!"

Sean's heart was thumping, his breath nervous and short.

His father had been clear: never open the door to strangers. But these men clearly knew his father – one of them even seemed familiar. He knew – he suspected – that his father worked with bad people sometimes, even though he was usually a day laborer. The other day wasn't the first time he'd come home injured.

"I was stupid, boy," he'd said. "I didn't know any other way to live, and I did bad stuff. But you never want to do that; never be the bad guy. They get empty inside, full of unhappiness, anger."

Three more hammer blows shook the door. *"IF I HAVE TO DO THIS OFFICIALLY, I CAN ALWAYS BUST THE DOOR IN DUE TO THE SMELL OF MARIJUANA,"* the bigger of the two men called out. "WE HAVE THAT RIGHT."

Marijuana? What was he talking about? *I'm twelve.* His father didn't use marijuana, as far as he knew. He just drank too much.

And what did "we have that right" mean? Was this man a cop? If he was, Sean knew it could mean trouble if he was denied access. He'd seen enough of that on TV and in games to recognize the threat.

Maybe... he reached up and put the emergency chain on the door, then undid the deadbolt and opened it a crack.

The two men looked less intimidating at normal scale, a middle-aged guy in a black golf shirt and black trousers, his taller friend in a tan suit and fedora. "Where's your old man, kid?" the latter said.

"Out. But he'll be back soon."

"Yeah? How soon? Maybe we should wait."

"He didn't say."

"But... then how could you know it would be soon?" the

taller man asked. "You wouldn't be lying to us, would you, kid? You know you can't lie to police officers, right?"

"I don't see a badge," Sean said, because it sounded tough, and he felt the sudden need to show courage.

The taller man looked irritated. He reached into his jacket inside breast pocket and took out a billfold, which he flipped open. The badge was gold tone, gleaming under the porch light. It read "Tucson" at the top and "Detective" at the bottom. "I'll tell you what... what's your name?"

"Sean."

"I'll tell you what, Sean," he said, leaning over slightly to accentuate the size difference, as if talking to a toddler. "You tell your father that Detective Hayes stopped by and needs to have a word with him, and he'd better call me. Now you tell him – and make sure you get this exactly right – you tell him that I know about his little package, and he might want to think about who else he talks to. You got that?"

Sean nodded.

"Repeat it back to me."

"Now that you know about his little package..." Sean said with a puzzled squint, "... he might want to think about who he talks to."

"Good enough."

The shorter cop nodded toward a dark-colored sedan near the curb. The street was otherwise empty, quiet in the late evening. "Let's book. I've got court in the morning."

Hayes gave Sean a wink. "Keep your head down, kid. Always do what police tell you... and don't answer the door to strangers, okay?"

He turned on his heel. The two men made their way back to their car and, a few moments later, were gone.

8

B ob stood in the office doorway. His boss was a rotund, neckless figure in sweatpants and a white T-shirt, with thinning ginger hair. He sat behind a keyboard, his left leg twitching constantly, beads of sweat running down to his shirt.

Occasionally, he took long slurps from an oversized Sonic chocolate milkshake through a plastic straw before pushing his slipping steel-framed glasses back up his nose. A placard on his desk read "Dennis King, Supervisor."

He didn't even look up from his laptop. "You're fired. Drop your prox card and your keys at the front desk."

"What?"

"I heard about what happened at the bar, with the wino. You used a company vehicle for personal business, and you know the rule on that. Get your stuff and get out."

He still hadn't looked up.

Bob felt a surge of anger. He cricked his neck muscles, but let it go and began to turn towards the corridor.

"Don't know what you were thinking, picking up some greasy illegal…"

Bob stopped and turned. "Excuse me?"

"You heard me." But this time, King looked up. He saw Bob's expression, and his eyes widened in fear, a sudden realization that his title meant nothing. "Look… I don't mean nothing by it! It's the insurance. You can't have nonemployees in the vehicles. Now… go on! Y'all go on, and… I'll send you an email recommendation, make sure you don't have no troubles." He chewed on his lower lip as he said it, a worried frown etched across his sweaty forehead, as if gauging whether Bob would make an issue of it.

Instead, he just shook his head in disgust. *It's not worth it, Bob. Just… let it go.*

Outside, at the curb, he called a hire car and waited three minutes for it to arrive.

At least it was air-conditioned.

He was at home fifteen minutes later. The tiny apartment was devoid of art or decoration. It still didn't feel real, the concept of considering one place home, and he kept a go bag in the closet by the door, ten of his fifty thousand recovered in Memphis stored in a secret inner lining pocket.

This time, he knew, he hadn't done anything wrong. *Any decent person helps that guy, the condition he was in. Jesus Murphy, I couldn't just leave him there, could I?*

He thought about King slugging back milkshakes and sweating, his head and neck one long, greasy hunk of meat, not even looking up as he'd canned him. *Jagoff.*

Maybe it was like Sister Eva said: he kept expecting good deeds to be rewarded, instead of doing them for their own sake. When the exact opposite happened, it felt toxically unfair. But it didn't mean anything other than the fact that some people are bad more often than good.

"Find purpose in the moment," she'd said. "You can help others, but you can't fix them. They need to want that."

She was right about that. She was right about a lot, Bob had decided.

Who knows? Maybe... maybe she gets lucky. Maybe she gets to be the one who isn't supposed to make it and does.

Maybe we all get lucky and she's still here this time next year.

He hadn't slept well the night before, a cicada's drone irritating him well past midnight. He flopped down on the sofa and put his feet up on the coffee table.

BOB WOKE SUDDENLY. He had his feet on the coffee table, still. But through the window, the sky had darkened, evening setting in.

He checked his watch.

Six hours. I slept six hours. Stress forcing operational responses again, body telling me it was safe, no schedule to meet, an opportunity to recharge.

He tried to recall what he'd been thinking about when he fell asleep. Sister Eva. Her suggestion that he needed to rejoin civilization properly.

Maybe she was right about that.

He went to the small white computer desk in the corner of the room. He took a flip phone out of the top drawer and turned it on, then hit speed dial.

After three rings, Dawn Ellis answered.

"Hello there." Nurse Dawn would probably be at work, at the free clinic in Chicago's West Loop. They didn't use names. That hadn't been safe since the fateful event of eight months earlier, when she'd saved them both from the consequences of Bob's lengthy CIA career.

The burner phones prevented them being listened in on, but anywhere public could mean she had eyes on her. After seven months of Bob being on the run from the national security establishment, it seemed unlikely they still thought her useful. But he had to be careful.

"Sorry. I know it's been a while."

"Jackson, Mississippi, as I recall, just after you left New Orleans. Your situation in Memphis worked out?"

"It did. I'm solvent again. Sort of. I'm also unemployed, as of a few hours ago."

"Oh! You have got to be kidding me! Were you...?"

"Fired, yeah. You'll never guess why."

"You got into a fight."

He managed to hold in a large sigh of exasperation. "Nope, just trying to help someone."

"Usually, with you, that means fighting." Her tone was deep and wry. Then she added, "But I know you've been working on that."

"All I did was give a man a ride."

"So?"

"So, I don't own the delivery truck. And they have rules about using it for personal business. But the guy was pretty badly hurt, Nurse Dawn..."

"Uh-huh. Setting aside that I find it weird you still call me Nurse Dawn, as close as we are, did you know about the rule beforehand?"

"Yeah. Yeah, I guess."

"But you felt you had to help him anyway."

"Uh-huh."

"Hmm. Sounds to me like your boss is a bit of a dick."

Bob's mouth dropped open a little involuntarily. The surprise was mildly pleasant. "Nurse Dawn! That's not language I would expect from someone who once spent two weeks reminding me not to swear!"

"Well, I do know it's wrong, but it feels good to be bluntly honest sometimes about the twerps in this world. Maybe you're rubbing off on me a little. Ah! Not a bad thing, before your usual self-loathing prompts you to contradict me. You going to have trouble finding more work?"

"Probably not. I'm fit. I can drive a truck and operate heavy equipment. He claimed he's giving me a recommendation."

"Then stop worrying. You did the right thing. And if this feels like a punishment now... well, these things sometimes have silver linings. You'll get something you like more."

Bob paused for just long enough to unnerve her a little.

"What? You still there? Bob?"

"Yeah! Yeah. I was just thinking for a second. I miss you, Dawn. I miss talking to you in person. Even miss Marcus."

"I know, sweetie. We miss you too. I mean, I do; that boy is so stuck in his studies—"

"Studies?"

"He got into the Illinois Institute of Technology for a mechanical engineering course, and they have this deal where they place the students. So after his second semester, he'll get to go work somewhere with engine designers and such. He wants to design engines! That's pretty exciting, right?"

"He's going to do great," Bob said.

"Bob... thank you for calling, sweetie. I admit I was getting a little worried."

"I won't let that happen again, okay?"

"But I should go now," she said. "I've got a clinic loaded with patients..."

"I understand. You take care now. Don't do anything I wouldn't."

"That's a pretty broad set of parameters. You have nothing to worry about."

"Bye."

She ended the call.

Bob put the phone back in the drawer and closed it. And just like that, losing his driving job didn't seem quite so important.

MOPING AROUND the apartment wasn't going to help his mood, he knew. He had some money in the bank, so getting a job immediately wasn't necessary. But he figured that if he walked down to East Twenty-Second Street for dinner, he could at least keep an eye out for hiring signs.

The meal had been okay, a plain chicken breast, an egg-white omelet and a large salad, a slice of low-sugar apple pie for dessert. Bob knew he had broader tastes, buried down there somewhere, but most meals still felt perfunctory, a chance to absorb the protein and nutrients required to maintain muscle tone.

He'd then spent twenty minutes browsing at a gun store, mentally cataloguing anything new, before realizing he was doing so not with reverence or fascination, but almost professional detachment. It had been uncomfortably automatic.

He left, feeling uneasy.

It was still hot despite sunset's approach. He ambled the sidewalk at a leisurely pace. Mica Mountain, miles out of town, loomed through a dusty haze on the horizon, as if Twenty-Second Street would eventually just run into it. He passed a giant hot tub outlet store.

He'd learned to respect that the city was in a desert, and the lack of humidity could prompt dehydration quickly. He was up to eight glasses of water daily.

But he still didn't feel like he was settling in. Despite Nurse Dawn and Sister Eva offering him emotional support and advice, he remained empty, purposeless. Volunteering and holding down a day job had helped, but they were nowhere near enough. He still wasn't sociable; he still felt any time that was unproductive was wasted, off-mission.

He needed to know where he belonged. So far, it didn't feel like Tucson was that place.

It had been difficult. He'd met Sister Eva after a week in town, and she knew everyone. But he found himself unable to take advantage of her social circle, unwilling to go out and meet new people. New people meant learning about them, about their lives. That meant caring about them, hoping they'd care back. It meant all of that inevitably meaning nothing when he disappointed them or, worse, destroyed them completely. Or they just died.

So there was no new life, not yet. And without a sense of greater purpose, he felt like a shadow, drifting across an empty room as the day passed, barely noticed, without form or function.

His phone buzzed. He checked the number but didn't recognize it.

"Yeah?"

"Mr. Fleming?"

The boy. "Sean?"

"Yeah. You said if I need to call..."

"What's wrong?"

"My dad. It's my dad. He's... He had a lot to drink. He has his gun, I think. And he said he's going to kill someone."

9

The hire car driver was a twenty-something college student. An extra twenty bucks and a promise to pay any ticket was all it took for him to make a mockery of the speed limit.

The subcompact's dust-caked brake pads squealed like a smoke alarm as it ground to a halt at the curb.

"Appreciated," Bob said as he clambered out.

Tito was standing outside the front door of the Sacred Heart Home in black jeans and a T-shirt. He had a pistol in his right hand, different from the one Bob had handed back when they'd met, and people had evacuated that side of the street completely. Bob approached at a jog.

Walther PDP compact, four-inch barrel in 9mm. I just saw one of those at the store. "Yo, Tito!" he said, raising a hand to greet him.

Tito wheeled his way, raising the pistol. Then he saw who it was. He was staggering drunk. The bandage was still covering his stitched-up scalp. He waved the gun like a greeting. "Heeeey! *Hola, vato!* You come to help me kill these *putas,* eh?" Then he returned his scowling attention to the front of the building. "That's right! You'd better lock that door or..." A string of Spanish expletives followed too quickly for Bob to fully comprehend, but he caught references to mothers, dogs, and numerous unnatural acts.

A spindle-thin man in jeans and a string T-shirt scurried from between the shelter and its neighbor, as if he'd come out a side door. His eyes were bloodshot and skin sallow, a few strands of hair plastered across the top of his otherwise bald head. He had a blue ball cap in one hand. "I didn't do nothing, Tito, I swear..." he offered as he passed, turning slightly to prevent showing Tito his back.

Tito waved him off with his free hand. "Man... get fucked, Donny Legs... you fucking bum! I don't give a shit about you, *cabrón.*"

His associate nodded twice quickly, then ran, taking off down the opposite sidewalk.

Bob assessed the rest of the street for threats. He needed to get Tito out of there as soon as possible. Police would doubtless have been called already, and an active gun call meant a rapid response, usually somewhere under ten minutes if Tucson was like most cities.

He nodded towards the building. "What's going on, bud?"

"Bob!" Tito grinned drunkenly. "You're a good man, Bob." Then he frowned. "You see me talking to that guy? That's Donny Legs. Donny Ambrose, or something like that. He just about lives here."

"So... who are we shooting at today?"

Tito closed his eyes for a moment, as if trying to ward off nausea. He swayed in place, the gun dropping to his side. "They killed my best friend, Bob. He was a good man, too. A good man! And these fuckers..." He waved the pistol at the building. "Got a clean piece; cost me sixty bucks and my favorite knife. But... see? No serial number."

Bob put his right hand over the top of Tito's and lowered the gun. "Let's... just take this out of the equation for a minute, okay? Is *everyone* who works there the problem?"

Tito frowned, puzzled. "Wha...?"

"Do you think the people who work at the shelter all killed your friend? Or the guys staying there? Because if you start shooting, that's who you might hit."

The inebriated man scowled back. "Someone got to pay, Bob. Someone got to pay for what they did to Martin. I was there, that night, earlier. He wasn't hurting nobody."

"Okay, but... you don't have papers, and the cops will be coming. Let me take the pistol..."

Tito reluctantly let him take it. Bob stuffed it into the back of his waistband.

A dark-blue Mercedes SUV pulled up to the curb. A pair of men got out. A third joined them, slamming the back door.

What do we have here?

They had tattoos, wraparound shades, ball caps for the sun, sleeveless shirts over track and sweatpants, one in a Phoenix Suns jersey. *Not cops, that's for sure.*

And they're checking both ways on the street, looking for police.

"Gentlemen," Bob offered as they approached.

The man at the head of the group was heavyset, muscular, in sunglasses, tapered buzz cut and sideburns running down to a wispy goatee. "Yo, Tito, *¿qué está pasando, hombre? ¿Dónde has estado?*" *What's going on, Tito? Where've you been?*

Tito raised his chin haughtily. "*¿Qué te importa, Manolo?*" *What's it to you, Manolo?*

"Boss wants to talk to you."

"I heard. He sent his little bitch Hayes over to my house. He threatened my kid. I don't care if he is a cop. He touches my kid, I'll kill that motherfucker."

What have I stumbled into? Bob wondered.

"Angel wants to talk," Manolo said. "Now, are you going to come along quietly? Because he said if you make trouble, we're allowed to do to you whatever the fuck we want."

"Gentlemen, if I might interject," Bob offered, in Spanish, "the police are going to be here soon because Tito was waving a gun around, and as I figure you know firsthand, they don't take kindly to that. So maybe—"

"Who the fuck is this gringo?" Manolo interrupted, jerking a thumb Bob's way. "Who've you been talking to, Tito?"

"He hasn't been talking to anyone," Bob offered.

"*Hey!*" Manolo turned his way, switching to English. "Did the words 'stupid fucking gringo, I want to hear your opinion in bad Spanish' leave my lips, huh?" He turned back towards Tito. "He tell the truth? You got a piece on you?"

Tito looked Bob's way. He didn't appear happy. "I gave it to him."

"Yeah?" Manolo said. "Then maybe you" – he drew a Glock 19 from his waistband – "better give it to me. Maybe then, if you're real lucky..." He pressed the barrel against Bob's forehead. "Maybe then I won't blow your fucking brains out."

Bob reacted with instinctual speed, his right hand flashing to his forehead, grasping the barrel and ripping the pistol from Manolo's grip in the blink of an eye. He took a quick step backwards, eyes on the men throughout as he removed the slide, the firing pin and the magazine, dropping them all on the ground with the rest of the Glock.

Manolo looked at the disassembled gun, the pieces lying on the concrete pavement. "Motherfucker..." he muttered, shocked. Then his gaze shot back to Bob, his face a wrathful scowl. "*Puta*, you just made a very big mistake." He reached into his back pocket and withdrew a switchblade, popping it open.

Bob weighed the scene. *Blade is the most immediate threat; number two's going for the waistband, though. Number three's moving to flank.*

Manolo strode in on him confidently, jamming the knife towards Bob's stomach, trying to gut him. Bob kept his eyes on Manolo's face even as he struck downwards with both fists simultaneously, the double block knocking the blade free.

It clattered to the asphalt. Bob wasn't waiting for a reaction, his foot shooting out in a short front kick, catching the gangster square in the testicles. Manolo groaned and doubled over. Bob pushed past him, the second gangster's hand raised and gripping a pistol, the adrenaline zone kicking in, things slowing down.

Smith & Wesson, 9mm probably. He hammered the man's elbow joint with a flat palm punch, feeling it give backwards, the man wincing and yelping; the gun dropped. A punch flew in from the man now just to the right, and Bob bobbed his head sideways, the knuckles just grazing his ear.

He dropped to one knee and hit the third man hard in the gut with a front punch, standing abruptly as his attacker staggered forward, coming up under the man's chin with the top of his forehead, head-butting him on the mental nerve. The gangster's legs deserted him, and he collapsed, dazed.

"*Maricon!*" The second gangster was still clutching his damaged elbow to his side but retrieved a butterfly knife from his pocket and opened it with his other hand. "You're gonna bleed for that, motherfucker..."

He charged in, but Bob knew he had a reach advantage and stung the man with a jab to the nose before he could swing the blade. He hit him with another, the nose breaking, blood flowing freely even as the man's eyes teared up, blinding him. He staggered back a step. Bob took two running strides and leaped into a side kick, hammering the man in the solar plexus, driving the wind out of him even as he went down.

Bob checked the street in both directions. People were filming the fight. *Shit. Can't have that.* Police sirens were getting nearer. "We need to get out of here," Bob said.

Manolo had raised himself back to one knee, a look of agony still on his face, one hand cradling his testicles. Bob leaned in and hit him with a short right cross to the chin, the thug's legs turning to spaghetti. He collapsed, confused, onto one side.

Bob reached down and rummaged through the man's pants. He took the keys to the Mercedes.

"*¡No manches!*" *No way!* Tito muttered. "I mean... holy shit, *ese*..."

"Not exactly holy," Bob said.

"You just laid out three guys like they weren't moving."

"And you sound more sober than eight minutes ago. Cops are coming, Tito. We need to get out of here, *now*."

Bob headed for the SUV and got in. Tito followed.

"We're taking their ride?" Tito looked amused as he

slammed the door. "I have to admit, Bob, for a gringo, you've got cojones the size of a fucking car, man. Manolo... he's no weakling, and you unleashed a biiig mama on him. He's going to be real, real mad."

Bob put it into gear.

"You going to give my gun back?" Tito asked.

"Let's talk about it when we're clear, okay?"

He stepped on the gas.

10

They were halfway to Bob's place when Tito began to get agitated.

"We've got to go pick up my kid, man. He's home alone. School's out right now, and if they go there looking for me..."

"Point taken." It probably wouldn't help if he mentioned the boy's frantic call, Bob decided. Tito was already on edge. He hit the turn signal and took the next right. "Who were those dudes, anyway?"

"*Ay, ¡coño!*" Tito muttered. He reached into his pocket and drew a packet of Marlboro Reds, lighting one before Bob had a chance to protest. "Manolo, the mouthy one, he—"

"Could you crack the window, at least?" Bob said. "Jesus H."

"Hmm? Yeah, yeah, cool. My bad, my bad. Anyway, Manolo Marichal is Angel Herrera's number-two lieutenant." He glanced over at Bob to see if he understood. "That's like a right-hand-man sort of thing for gangsters."

"I got it from the context."

"Yeah... so he works for Herrera."

"And Herrera..."

He whistled softly. "Him you don't want to know, *ese*."

"A real jagoff?"

"Eh? What's this mean... jagoff?"

"A real asshole. A no-goodnik. A bad dude."

Tito found it apropos. "Yeah... well... he's that. But mostly, he's a gangster. Got a big crew operating out of the Flaming Garter, a strip club on East Drexel."

Ah, shit. That figures. "And he's pissed at you because..."

Tito tilted his head back and closed his eyes tightly, then inhaled deeply. "Damnnn, my head's already starting to hurt."

"You're probably a little dehydrated. He's pissed at you because..."

"Because I think he had my friend Martin killed, and we talked earlier that night. His flunky detective, Hayes... he saw me by Martin's cot just an hour before it happened. So he probably figures he told me all sorts of stuff. I figure he already planned on killing Martin."

"Like I said—"

"Yeah, yeah, suicide. But I don't believe it. Martin was into God; he was illegal, yeah, and he was a criminal; but he'd never hurt nobody that wasn't trying to hurt him. Mostly though, he had a lot of faith, and suicide is a mortal sin. He never jumped, man."

The murder-suicide. His friend is the guy in the papers... Shit. "They say he shot the doorman, Manuel, before he—"

"Man, that's bullshit, *vato*! Believe me, he did not have that in him. He didn't even own a gun." Tito opened his mouth wide and stretched out his tongue. "My mouth tastes furry."

They were nearing Tito's rented house. "Why?" Bob said. "What does a gangster gain by throwing a guy living in a shelter off its roof?"

Tito seemed doleful. He shook his head gently. "Martin was... man, he was tired of it all, you know? Guns and drugs and whores and illegals. He fled Mexico to get away from all that shit, same as me. Only we both got stuck owing the cartel for our freedom, at twice the rate the coyotes normally charged, and agreeing to leave Sonora."

"You still owe them money?"

Tito shook his head. "I... got lucky. I got an investment and took it, made a bunch of cash in the first year. That was nearly five years ago. They took all of it, but... I got to walk away. Martin must've had something on Herrera, maybe, or was talking to Immigration. Some reason why they did what they did. He was loud about his debt. He thought it was bullshit. He started drinking... I'm not one to judge on that."

"Who's Hayes again? You said something about a detective?"

"*Ay, chinga su madre!* He's a cop, Carter Hayes. Homicide detective. Local golden boy."

"He works with Manolo?"

"He's more crooked than a pretzel, that one. Bob... for a guy just being helpful, you ask a lot of fucking questions."

"I know, sorry. Your business is your business. But I'm sort of dragged into it now. I don't imagine those jagoffs are going to give up so easy, even though I just beat them down."

"It's true," Tito said morosely. "Ay, why did I go down there? What the fuck was I thinking?"

"No point worrying about that now. You got drunk; you blew a gasket." Bob pulled the truck over to the curb. He gestured towards the house. "Go get your kid. They'll be around soon, no doubt."

"Hang tight," Tito said as he climbed out of the cab.

Bobby, Bobby, Bobby... what have you wandered into? Everything about this dude says trouble, but still, you can't help but stick your stupid nose into other people's business.

He watched Tito mount the front steps and head inside.

Really, he figured, it was just like the incident outside the bar a day earlier: someone was in trouble. Someone had to help them. It was a moral prerogative, not a philosophical debate. Would Sister Eva or Nurse Dawn have just driven by that man lying on the sidewalk and bleeding?

Hell no. So... are you going to be more gutless than two middle-aged female caregivers? Don't ignore your best intentions. Better that and to fail than to just keep hiding from people. That's what Sister Eva was saying, right?

Besides... all you're doing is giving him a ride to someone who can help him. Then it's no longer your business.

Tito returned five minutes later, his son trailing him. Both carried a fairly full jumbo-sized black garbage bag.

"What...?" Bob wondered as they climbed into the SUV, shoving the bags onto the back seat, next to the boy.

Tito shrugged. "Clothes, *ese!* Can't wear the same thing every day until it's safe to come back here, if ever."

"I brought my PlayStation, if that's okay," Sean said.

"Believe me, we don't want him around without his games," Tito said. "He gets cranky."

"I don't get cranky!" the boy protested.

"Ah... I'm kidding you, *pequeño Rey.*" He mussed his son's hair. "You're almost a man, eh?"

"Where are we going?" Sean said as Bob put the SUV into gear and pulled away from the curb.

"Well... first, we're going to get rid of this SUV because it might have a GPS tracker in it, or a road-service subscription that can locate it. Then we're going to go visit a friend of mine."

11

The cab ride to the convent was quiet. Exhausted and with too much booze in him, Tito fell asleep almost immediately on the back seat, next to Sean.

After an uncomfortable few minutes without speaking, Bob nodded towards the radio. The driver turned it on. A female singer began to croon in Spanish.

Bob half turned to look over the back of the bench seat. "You want to pick the music or something?" he asked Sean.

"No... that's okay. You wouldn't like what I like. It's more for young people."

Ouch. But probably true. I doubt he'd be thrilled by Son Seals or B. B. King. "Sure."

The boy was quiet again, and Bob watched him for a moment in the rearview mirror. His face was riddled with anxiety, like their jobs had reversed and suddenly a twelve-year-old found himself cast in the role of a worried parent.

Eventually, he said, "He doesn't always drink like this. I mean my dad."

Bob glanced over at the driver, who he knew was probably listening. It made him squirm inside a little. "I'm sure he doesn't."

"It's been really hard for him since my mom died. When it happened – when she had her stroke, she didn't... she didn't go right away. She was in the hospital, on machines and stuff, you know, to keep her alive."

The poor kid. Bob remembered the bleak void he felt after his own parents' deaths, the sense that order had gone from all things.

"We waited at the hospital, and we waited, and waited. When they asked him about turning off the machines, he couldn't do it at first. He kept crying, leaning over her in bed and..."

The kid went silent. Bob checked the rearview mirror. He was wiping away tears, trying to put on a brave face.

"After that, he started drinking more often. Sometimes, I can see it in his eyes in the morning. He tries to be all happy and stuff for me, sends me to school with lunch and stuff. But it's like he's empty, somehow. He goes weeks where it's okay and he's not dwelling on her dying. And then it hits him, and it's like... it's like he's broken. And I know when he's like that, he's going to start drinking and just not stop until he's out."

"He's in a lot of pain," Bob said. "You both are. He probably thinks he's keeping it away from you, numbing it so that others don't have to share in his misery. He may even blame himself."

Sean sniffled and wiped his nose with the corner of his T-shirt. "That's crazy. She had... I don't remember what they said it is... but, like, it's because it runs in her family..."

"A genetic predisposition," Bob said. "Yeah. The person who was like a surrogate mom to me after my mom died had cancer that ran in the family. She and her husband fought it for years, but it killed her eventually." *Him too.*

Sean was nodding vigorously. "So he couldn't do anything. Nobody could. That's why..." He stopped talking. Bob checked the rearview mirror. The boy was crying again, this time not bothering to wipe away the twin tears tracking down his cheeks, his expression indignant and irritated.

"It's so unfair," Bob finished the thought. "Yeah... Yeah, I know that, too."

Behind the wheel, the driver sniffled. He wiped away a tear in a blink with one thumb, keeping his eyes on the road.

SISTER EVA PEERED down her nose at Bob, his obvious amusement annoying her just enough to turn it into a cut-rate glare.

She stood just ahead of the reception desk at the Sisters of Benevolence Convent, just east of Campbell Avenue, her arms crossed as a colleague sat behind the desk and tried to pretend nothing abnormal was going on.

"Okay, explain," she said. "I mean... not the stupid grin. I know that's because I'm in my habit, because you do it every time you see me outside street clothes. It's..."

"Charming?" Bob offered. "Kinda sexy?"

"Juvenile. Who are your friends?" Then she squinted and peered down her nose at Tito instead. "I know you."

He hung his head grimly for just a moment. "I stayed at Sacred Heart Home when I first got here four years ago."

She pointed at him. "And you still stop by sometimes to

see someone. Tito, right? And this is the boy you talked about."

"Yeah. His mom and he came down a year after me. She died."

"My condolences."

"They're in a little trouble," Bob said. He gave her a quick, censored rundown.

Sister Eva's eyes flitted momentarily heavenward. "Tito... the police seemed to be quite certain—"

"Can't trust them, no way," Tito said. "Martin never hurt a fly. And he didn't kill himself."

"Wasn't he a cartel member in Mexico?" she asked pointedly.

"Well... yeah, okay, but—"

"And you're telling me he never hurt anyone?" she asked with mild incredulity.

He looked defeated. "Okay... so he had some troubles when he was younger." He glanced sideway towards his son and grimaced, making it clear he didn't want to talk specifics in front of Sean. "But he loved God, sister. He didn't believe in suicide, and he would never have hurt Manny the door-man. I'm telling you, he was so broke, no way he could afford a piece, even illegal."

"He may well have a point," Bob interjected. "A trio of bruisers who work for a guy named Angel Herrera... visited. They wanted to discuss business in a less than cordial manner."

Sean shoved his hands into his pockets, a hangdog expression on his face. "You can say 'fight' in front of me, I'm not stupid, and I'm not a baby."

"Earlier," Bob continued, "a couple of cops stopped by and bothered the boy. It sounded connected."

Sister Eva didn't try to hide her surprise. She crossed her arms and began to subconsciously tap one forefinger. "Angel Herrera? That is not good. That is absolutely not good."

"You know about this guy?" Bob asked.

"Everyone who works in migrant resettlement does. His gang includes a series of 'coyotes,' men who charge exorbitant sums to bring Mexicans and Central Americans across the desert and over—"

"I'm familiar," Bob interrupted. "How bad is he?"

"He's a gangster, with all that entails. He's doubtless killed many people or had them killed, and that's discounting the likely hundreds of migrants who haven't made it across the Sonoran Desert under his men's watch. Once they're smuggled in, normally in the mountains around Nogales and Bisbee, he holds a debt over them that they can only pay by working for him, mostly small criminal tasks: drug dealing, theft and resale, prostitution in some cases."

"Shit," Bob muttered.

She pointed over her shoulder at the giant crucifix on the wall. "Bob... please."

He looked around, trying to get a sense of the layout. "Do you have somewhere you take visitors for a coffee or tea or anything? I imagine Tito and Sean would like a few minutes to rest and relax before we figure things out."

She read the cue to get them out of the room. "Sister Roberta, can you take our young friend here and his father to the dining hall for a soda and a tea?"

The nun behind the front counter rose and curtseyed an acknowledgment. She walked over to Sean. "Do you like Coca-Cola?"

Sean frowned, weighing the matter. "Is it Mexican?"

Tito looked over at Bob. "See? Smart kid. They use cane sugar back home, not the chemical corn syrup shit they put in here. Tastes much better."

Sister Eva rolled her eyes again.

The nun led them to the other room.

"Okay, now that we have a moment of privacy," Sister Eva said, her arms remaining firmly crossed, "what on earth are you *doing?* You're mixed up in a drug cartel dispute?"

He told her about the day prior and Tito's defenestration. "They were going to leave him to bleed out on the sidewalk."

The nun's cheeks filled with air like a trumpeter; she blew a gust out heartily. "Well! Well, well, well. I don't suppose you could have just left him there, and the ambulance wasn't coming. You had no choice. But... that doesn't help us right now. What are we supposed to do about this?"

"We?" Bob said.

She cocked her head, her eyes burning a hole through him. "Yes, we, Bob. You can't just bring them here and dump them on our doorstep. We have to—"

Bob held up both palms. "Hey! I'm not a nun, I'm not a migrant shelter worker, and I'm not a cop. I don't *have* to do anything. I stepped in because someone had to help an injured man, and I just happened to be there."

"But you wanted to help, clearly..."

"And I have, right? I've brought him to someone who can find him a place to stay until he deals with this shit, or it blows over, and the kid is protected. That's the important bit. That's me doing my part." He took a step backwards, both palms still raised in supplication.

"Seriously?"

"I told you that before I got here, I spent a lot of years trying to help people, and it always went to shit. What I didn't really stress is that most of the time, it was garbage just like this. And we didn't really discuss how shitty. I mean, like... *deadly* shitty."

"So... what would you like me to do in your stead, Bob?" she said, still looking unimpressed. Then her face softened, the implications to him becoming a bit clearer. "I don't mean to criticize. We can each only give what we have. But this isn't the type of thing—"

He pointed at the sign on the wall, the name of the convent in raised chrome letters like something from a sixties police HQ, as he once again interjected. "This *is* still a house of refuge, right? I mean, if someone requests sanctuary, you still have to help... correct?"

"Sure. I mean, within reasonable limits. It's been a very long time since anyone requested sanctuary from persecution here. We don't get many Russian spies or political dissidents in Tucson."

"Then I'd start by keeping them here. Me, I have to go find a new job. This guy has already cost me my driving gig, and we've all got bills to pay, right?"

"If I asked for your help?"

"You don't want it, trust me."

"If I asked for your help with this, would you offer it?"

Bob sucked on his tongue, his expression grim. "If you made it a personal request? Yeah, you know I would. After six months of you looking out for me here? Of course. Are you going to do that, to force me to wade into someone else's problem?"

Her eyes dropped to the stone tile floor for just a second. "No," she said with a firm, quick shake of her head. "No, of course not."

"Then I'm going to go," Bob said. He turned and took a

few steps, then turned back and kept retreating towards the exit. "I mean, if you really need me, or need to call me..."

"I'll keep it in mind," she said.

Bob let the convent's front double doors swing closed behind him. He took out his phone to call another hire car.

It's not your business. Just let it go.

12

C   ucho Lopez was having the time of his life, and making money doing it.

Ostensibly, he was involved in a manhunt. The man in question, Tito Agustin, was a noted gambler.

It just made sense to check all six casinos in the city.

And Cucho liked to gamble, too. Plus, the drinks were free.

By the time three days had passed, he was up six hundred dollars on the tables and had been at least a little drunk, for free, throughout. His boss, Manolo Marichal, had called a few times, but Cucho had ghosted him, because Manolo was a dick, and there was always a good excuse for ghosting someone.

He sat at the blackjack table at Diamonds and tossed a ten-dollar chip onto his showing double kings. He knew he was a handsome kid, and he played it up for the ladies. He wore a sixties-style V-neck golf shirt that showed off his tight biceps. He liked to think the waitress appreciated it.

"Player has twenty; player stays on twenty," the dealer said.

Luck like this, you ride it, he told himself. *Luck like this could mean a big, big win.*

Then he frowned through the boozy fog and remembered why he was actually there. *Haven't checked the room out in a while.* He turned on his stool and scanned the gaming floor, checking each head out in turn, being patient.

No sign. Tito would be easy to spot. According to the picture Manolo had handed out, he was short and stocky, with lots of tattoos. He'd stick out among the gringos like a house on fire.

But no Tito also meant no tall gringo accompanying him.

Manolo's admission that he'd been beaten down by some onlooker had prompted howls of laughter among his men. He'd smacked Cucho's friend Jose around badly as a consequence, to make it clear he wouldn't take any shit. But he'd also admitted the issue to Angel Herrera. They were all warned to look out for "Bob," whoever the fuck he was supposed to be.

Wait a second; was that...?

He turned quickly on his stool again, convinced he'd seen his boss near the doors. But there was no one there. He turned back to the game.

"Cucho."

He almost jumped, the voice coming from directly to his left. He turned. Manolo had sidled up to the table, which Cucho figured was a neat trick for a guy that big. "Boss!" he said in Spanish. "Kind of snuck up on me there."

"I've been here for a while. Angel wants to talk to you."

"Yeah?" That was never good. "What about?"

Manolo shrugged. "Fuck do I know? Come on, let's go."

"I've got a good hand..."

The dealer turned over his second card. "Dealer has twenty-one." He reached across the table and swept Cucho's chips closer, stacking them with lightning speed and depositing them in the bank next to him.

"*Coño*," Cucho muttered. That was bad, too. He'd been so lucky all week. Then Manolo had showed, and he'd lost on the flip.

That wasn't good. That felt like bad luck, which never came unaccompanied.

"Let's go," Manolo said, gesturing towards the front doors with a nod.

THE DRIVE WAS QUIET, which made it that much more nerve-racking.

Angel Herrera almost never spoke with foot soldiers. He always went through a lieutenant, like Manolo, or someone else he trusted.

Cucho had only been in Tucson for two years. Angel hadn't said more than three words to him in that time. Whatever he needed, it had to be important.

So maybe a good thing. Maybe he'd heard how tough Cucho was, how many times he'd beaten down a threat to their business, or who his family was. The booze was still affecting him heavily, and his bravado had risen accordingly.

At the club, they went directly upstairs, to Angel's office. Angel was sitting behind his desk, his dark suit and dress shirt worn with an open collar, like a businessman a half hour after work.

"Leave us," he told Manolo in Spanish.

He nodded and stepped out of the room.

"You're Cucho, yes?"

He nodded.

"We sent you to find Tito Agustin at the casinos on Monday."

"*Si*, Angel. I have been working hard. Very hard."

Angel acknowledged that. "Okay. You've been to all six casinos, yes? More than once, for more than a few hours?"

"*Si*, Angel, *si*."

Angel rose slowly from his seat. Cucho briefly wondered if his height – he looked about five feet five – was behind his notoriously ruthless history. *Got short-man issues, maybe*, he thought drunkenly.

The club owner crossed the room slowly and looked out the window, down to the nightclub below. "You've got family in the business, yes?"

"*Si, Senor*... my uncle in Mexico City recommended me."

"Yeah. Yeah, I heard that. I didn't have no one doing that for me when I got sent down here to this shithole. I had to start over from scratch. You know I built this shit, yes? This club, this life? I made this. Me. Not you. Not anyone else."

"*Si*, we all hear that, Angel," he replied, maybe too quickly to sound sincere. "It's banging."

Angel turned quickly, hands clasped behind his back, and fixed him with a stare. "Banging?"

"All the college kids think your club is dope, Angel."

Angel grinned wryly at that and continued to pace back and forth. "Banging," he repeated. "Banging!" Abruptly, he switched to English. "You like it a lot here, don't you, Cucho?"

"*Si*, Angel. Working for you has been good. I miss my mother in Juarez, but I speak with her every week by Face-Time. She is very happy that I am happy."

Angel stopped pacing for a moment. "Sure. Sure, that's very sweet. It's good; it's good that you still love your mother, show her respect. But that's not what I mean. I mean you like it here, America. You feel at home here, yes?"

Cucho wasn't sure where he was going with the conversation. Instinct was telling him something was wrong. "I... love Mexico. I mean... It's good, the money here, sure..."

"No," Angel said, shaking his head slowly. "No, no, no. No, I think you like the way the gringos live. You like their ways." He began pacing again, this time passing Cucho so closely the younger man could smell his cologne. "It's why you talk like one of these college kids: you say 'banging' and 'dope,' and you revert to English even though you're speaking with me."

But... he spoke in English first, Cucho thought. *Is he trying to trick me?*

"It's... it's nothing, boss. You know, I just..."

"You just want to fit in, do your job, right?" Herrera circled around him.

Cucho nodded. "I mean, yeah. Yeah, that's right."

Angel stopped pacing. "Is that why you decided to fuck me over?"

He resumed pacing again, walking back and forth behind Cucho, his movement slow, turning and going in the opposite direction every six or seven steps.

Why is he behind me, where I can't see him? The hairs on Cucho's neck stood up. It felt like Angel was almost daring him to get nervous and turn.

If I turn around, that will say I don't trust him?

"I... don't understand," he said instead. His heart had begun to thump in his chest a little, his breath shorter.

"Sure you do," the voice behind him insisted. "You come

down here, you take my money, you go to the casinos when I ask. But instead of finding Tito and his gringo friend, you spend the week gambling and getting drunk, hanging out with tourists. Rubbing shoulders with them like they were movie stars or something."

Just turn around. Just... turn around and keep your eye on him.

"You think they're special because they're white and have money, and we're just dirty Mexicans, is that it?"

You know he's dangerous. So why can't you turn around? "No! No... boss, I swear..." *Why doesn't he move where I can see him?*

"You think you can spend a week SPENDING MY MONEY, IGNORING MY DEMANDS, ACTING LIKE A RICH, STUPID GRINGO MOTHERFUCKER, IS THAT IT!" Herrera bellowed.

Turn around! Then you can defend yourself at least! But then he'll know you're scared and don't trust him.

"Boss, I..." Cucho began to turn his head to look, but the fist caught him in the temple before that could happen. It knocked him sideways, stunning him, and he fell to one knee. Another punch followed, a right cross, his legs lost as he collapsed to the office floor.

And then Angel was on him, Cucho trying to turtle, covering his head as the squared tip of Herrera's cowboy boots slammed into his body over and over and over. He winced in pain as a rib cracked, and tried to raise a hand in protest. "Angel... *por favor...*"

"*DIRTY... LITTLE... MOTHERFUCKER...*" Angel spat as he hammered the young man with kicks, a boot catching him in the face, Cucho's nose breaking, blood spattering across the carpet.

.   .   .

ANGEL KICKED Cucho for a solid minute after he felt the first rib break, his lips pulled back across dry teeth in an angry snarl, guttural rage emanating in every grunt of effort.

"FUCKING LITTLE FUCK, DIE! FUCKING DIRTY LITTLE MOTHERFUCKER, DIE, DIE, DIE!"

His leg was getting tired. He stopped momentarily, panting from exertion.

Angel looked down.

Cucho wasn't moving, but he was still breathing, barely. His eyes were swollen and closed, nose broken, teeth knocked out in jagged clumps.

Angel exhaled deeply, stood up straight and checked his suit jacket to make sure the blood hadn't spattered it. "That feels much better," he said out loud, his only guest barely conscious to hear the comment. Then he looked down at his boots and the mess. "Fuck. I love these boots."

Then he had an idea, something to make up for the mess. "Manolo!" he called out. "Manolo, get in here!"

The door opened. His lieutenant leaned into the room. "Boss?"

"Get in here."

Manolo complied, wincing visibly when he saw the broken man on the floor.

"Pick that piece of shit up and put him in the chair ahead of my desk."

Manolo looked puzzled. "Boss... he's probably dying—"

"Did I ask you for a fucking diagnosis? Put him in the chair. I want to try something."

Manolo crouched by Cucho, rolling his torso over just enough to get a hand under each armpit. The young man was muscular and heavy; he dragged him over to the chair ahead of Angel's desk and dropped him, slumping, down upon it.

Angel hurried around the desk and sat down, a blithesome, enraptured look on his face, like a boy unwrapping a Christmas gift. "Now put your gun on the desk in front of him."

"What?" Manolo's expression made it clear he realized the tone was too harsh. "Sorry, boss. It's just…"

"Just fucking do it."

He did as asked, laying the Glock 19 down on its side.

"Turn it so the handle's facing him," Angel commanded. "CUCHO! CUCHO, CAN YOU HEAR ME?"

Cucho's head slumped forward onto his chest.

"Boss… I think maybe he's dead…"

Cucho's head lolled back as he tried to make sense of consciousness, as well as what little of his surroundings he could discern from one half-closed eye, the other fully swollen over.

"Good! He can hear me," Angel said, leaning forward slightly, the anticipation clearly building in him. "CUCHO, I'M GOING TO GIVE YOU A CHANCE TO WIN YOUR FREEDOM. JUST GO FOR THE GUN ON THE DESK! I GIVE YOU A CHANCE TO SHOOT ME BEFORE I DRAW!" he bellowed, as if raising his voice twenty decibels would make up for the man's insensible condition.

Cucho's one functioning eye flitted from side to side, as if trying to translate what he was hearing. It peered straight ahead, locking its watery gaze on the pistol. He tried to raise his hand, to grab the gun off the desk, to take his one final leap at staying alive.

Angel's left hand came down on the red button. The

pistol popped out of its hole to his right and directly into his free hand. He yanked the trigger four times, bullets striking Cucho in the center of his chest, blood spattering Manolo's jeans.

The young man's head lolled backwards and remained there, unmoving.

Angel could barely contain his glee. "See!" he said to Manolo, grinning, excited. "Like I was James Bond or something! So fucking cool!"

In his peripheral vision, he noticed Manolo look away briefly, disappointed. The mess would have to be cleaned up, Cucho's remains disposed of in the desert. That was probably why, he told himself. Manolo knew he would have to take charge of the cleanup and didn't want to do a little work.

It couldn't have been over a cockroach like Cucho. Nobody would miss him, Herrera was certain, because he was a fuckup. He barely knew the man, just that he hadn't been in Tucson long enough to make himself useful.

There was a knock on the door.

"YEAH?" Angel's voice echoed from the other side of the office door.

Det. Carter Hayes pushed it open. "Jesus!" he muttered at the sight. Then he turned his head away. "I didn't see that."

"No?" Angel asked pointedly. "Probably better for you if you did. There's a message in that fucker's corpse, if you look hard enough."

"Point taken."

"Is it? Have you found Tito in the last half hour?"

"No."

"Then what are you doing here, eh? Get out there and find him."

Hayes smiled thinly. He was tiring of the gangster thinking he was in charge of a local cop. They had enough dirt on each other to assure mutual self-destruction. *The difference is, if I have to shoot you, Angel, I'll get away with it.*

It had occurred to Hayes eighteen months into his relationship with Angel Herrera that the gang boss was too emotionally unstable to be dependable. Eventually he would blow the kind of gasket that couldn't be sealed by a "friend" on the force.

At that point, as long as the cartel felt he remained an important asset, Hayes would still be in the picture, and whoever replaced Angel might be easier to deal with, less prone to angry flights of fancy.

Manolo ignored Hayes and nodded at Angel. "Boss, you got anything more you need from me this afternoon? I should go help with the search."

He knew better than to ask if everything was okay, or suggest Angel needed him in any way.

"Clean this shit up," Angel said, rising from behind his desk. He looked down at the floor. "*Ay, cabrón!* He stained my fucking boots with his weak-ass blood."

Manolo looked resigned to his life, Hayes thought, going through motions without choice.

"Cucho was okay," Manolo offered. "He didn't work hard, but he was a nice guy."

"He should have learned some fucking respect," Angel said. "Did I ever hide what would happen if someone pisses me off, Manolo? Did I do something wrong here? AM I THE ASSHOLE? EH? IS THAT WHAT YOU'RE SAYING?"

"NO! No... of course not, boss."

Angel puffed out his chest for a moment, then relaxed. "Of course not. Now, he can be a message to the rest. It's been nearly a week. I want that cocksucker Tito in my office by Monday, or more heads are going to roll."

He walked back towards his desk. Hayes glanced at the mess again, then at Manolo, who was frowning. Obviously, being given janitorial duty for his associate's remains wasn't sitting well with him. *Score some points, divide and conquer*, Hayes thought.

"Manolo's going to be way more use helping me find Tito," he told Angel. "Maybe get someone less valuable for cleanup duty... right?"

Angel leaned on his desk with two fists, as if the energy had drained out of him after a day of disappointments. "Eh? Sure, sure. Fine."

The detective nodded towards the other room. "Come on, Manolo, let's go find ourselves a snitch."

13

It was Friday afternoon, and it had been a quiet week after helping out Tito and his son. Now it was time to relax.

Some orange pekoe, feet up on the coffee table, a Jason Statham double bill, Bob thought as he parked the truck in the yard's last service bay, its backup alarm bleeping shrilly. *Party time.*

He'd found the new job on Tuesday, after one day of looking. Low-paying labor and delivery gigs were abundant. He'd vowed not to repeat the mistake of his first gig and not take a job unless it felt right; he'd gotten a good read on his new supervisor, a barn-door-sized Minnesotan named Mike Tardif: frustrated, a little bitter, but basically a good, hard-working guy.

He got out of the cab and headed to the dispatch room, where Mike sat behind his desk in blue overalls, talking on a mic handset to another driver, the room reflected in the giant, ornate "Harley-Davidson" mirror on the wall behind him. He had wavy brown hair and a Colonel Custer goatee and moustache, and he always seemed a little overcaffeinated to Bob.

"Just tell him you can't help, then, for crying out loud!" he barked at the handset. "No... no! Just tell him, for chrissake! We're not insured for that shit! If he won't sign, place the package on the floor in front of him and take a picture with your phone. Then leave. Okay? Jesus H double hockey sticks!"

Bob tipped an imaginary cap his way. "Heading out, boss."

Mike saluted him back. "Four days in, and you're already 'the Sane One.' Congratulations, Bob."

He headed out into the sunshine. Tucson never seemed to cloud over, and the temperature only dropped at night. At four in the afternoon, it was still 105F.

It was also the first time he'd ever lived anywhere so gated. Entire neighborhoods across the city were surrounded by privacy walls. It wasn't as bad as Phoenix, which could feel like a series of small army compounds strung together by roads until you got to the old section, downtown, and the houses were easily visible.

But it was all so planned, so grid-dependent, that people drove almost everywhere. Until they reached the university campus or the old part of downtown, that's just how the place worked: residential was residential, business was business, and rarely did they meet. It should've been quick and easy to get around, but somehow, the place you needed to be was always on the other side of the city.

So the sidewalks were often populated sparsely and, on occasion, would simply disappear, running out of real estate, that side of the road suddenly a green belt or divider. There were palm trees and white adobe homes everywhere; the yards that were visible were often xeriscaped with prickly cactus and saguaro.

Now, Bob knew, he needed to find some cheap wheels. The company's yard was a fifty-five-minute walk from his apartment, and as much as he enjoyed the exercise, the heat wasn't going anywhere.

Plus, he'd told Sister Eva he'd stop by the Youth Center every Saturday to work with Chico and the other kids. Suddenly, having a life was turning into a whole lot more walking.

He turned north, up Park Avenue and past a series of small restaurants offering barbecue and Mexican street food. Tucson was beginning to grow on him, to fascinate, even though the connection didn't feel personal. It really was a weird town, but in a pretty cool way, he figured. There were new age types and college types, an array of hucksters and criminals; there were surprising numbers of native Americans due to the proximity of multiple Apache and Yavapai tribes.

Most surprising was the number of Europeans and East Coast Americans, all drawn to the allure of the old west, with some of Hollywood's greatest westerns shot at Old Tucson Studios, just outside of town.

He passed an electronics store, a double lane of empty parking spots between it and the road. A bank of widescreen TVs in the giant picture window showed the same newscast. Reporters were doing an outro to a story, one in the foreground, more farther back, by a high school's front fence.

They were silent from the other side of the glass, but several had closed captions turned on.

Bob stopped walking. He turned and crossed the lot so that he could see what they were saying.

"The incident occurred as students at Challenger Middle School were walking to lunch. Tipped by other students that a twelve-year-old boy was carrying a gun, they confronted the student as he waited in line at a vending machine."

That was Sean Agustin's school.

"Police say the boy was taken into custody quietly and is being assessed. The pistol was confiscated, and classes are expected to resume Monday. The school says crisis counsellors will be made available. School officials have stressed there is absolutely no indication the boy intended to shoot any individual or individuals, but that he felt bullied and reacted poorly."

It cut back to the anchor so that she could ask the reporter questions. Bob had a sinking feeling in his gut. *There are probably hundreds of kids at that school. It could've been any of them*, he told himself.

The newscast cut back to the reporter, the closed caption spewing out another line of type. "Police are speaking with the boy's father today. He and his son have been staying at a convent, the Sisters of Benevolence, for reasons that weren't immediately clear."

Ah, hell.

He took out his phone, but stopped short of making the call. *It's none of your business anymore. You did your part. You found them somewhere to stay when they were in trouble.*

But he knew he'd dropped them into Sister Eva's lap. It wasn't going to take long for word to filter back to Angel Herrera and his men.

Ah... hell.

He scrolled to Sister Eva's number and hit "call."

. . .

THE CLOTHING FACTORY above South Euclid Avenue's line of family-owned shops was little more than an open floor space covered in wooden tables and sewing machines. But at nearly five thousand square feet, it was vast, each station manned by an illegal, each machine turning out a new piece of "fast fashion" every six minutes.

It wasn't quality; it was bulk business. Each seamstress cut out a pre-marked pattern from the cheapest material available, synthetic fibers, mostly polyester. They stitched two pieces together – or three if adding a collar or hem. Then they dropped them into a bin beside their station.

Angel Herrera watched from the supervisor's office, slightly raised and in one corner of the room, like a giant fish tank. The foreman was walking between the rows, keeping an eye on the workers' accuracy, berating them when they failed. He was a stern young man, more than willing to throw a scare into them.

"We're good on volume?" he asked the man at the desk along the opposite wall.

"*Si*, Angel, *si*. Everyone in Phoenix is very happy, very happy indeed. Your father... well, you know how he is. But he is as close to happy as I can remember in some time. The templates are perfect duplicates of this year's kids' lines at the biggest family stores. We have buyers in place. This is going to make them a lot of money."

"Good, good."

"One question: Cucho Lopez."

Angel felt his nerves twinge. Why did Santiago Obregon, a bookkeeper, have any interest in a lowlife like Cucho?

"What about him?"

"Well... you know he's the cousin of Hector Ramirez,

right? The Gravedigger? I mean, he's an idiot and a drunk, sure, but he's connected."

"Sure. Of course." *What? How didn't I know this? Mother of God! The Gravedigger? Hector Ramirez?*

"I guess Hector tried to call him last night. His girlfriend said he didn't come home."

"Huh." Angel prayed his face wasn't betraying anything. Ramirez was a cartel hitman based out of Mexico City, a *sicario* nicknamed the Gravedigger, utterly ruthless, brutal to sadistic degrees.

If he finds out you killed his cousin, he'll cut you into pieces and feed you to his dogs.

"Did he say what he needed? Maybe we can help him out before his cousin pisses him off by fucking it up."

"No. No, he didn't say." Obregon peered at him curiously.

Is he trying to figure out whether I'm lying?

"Are you okay, Angel? You look a little... you know... pale."

"I'm fine. Working too goddamned hard, is all."

He seemed to weigh that for a few moments. "Yeah... well, your people did great with this place. Sweatshops aren't what they used to be, income-wise, not with the Chinese cranking this shit out too. But it's still a decent stream for minimal fuss, extending the value of those debtors," Obregon said, waving a hand toward the window.

He rose and picked up his attaché case, opening it on the desk and placing the laptop inside. "I've got to drive back." He closed the case and picked it up, then walked over and offered a hand to shake.

Angel shook it, then returned his attention to the workers. "This is just one of the new income streams we'll have up in the next six months. You wait, Santiago: Papi will see the value I can build for them, with my police and immigration contacts."

The older man clapped him on the shoulder. "Good! Good, good. Just do yourself a favor and tell Cucho to give his cousin a call, okay? You know what Hector can be like when he's unhappy."

Angel felt his anxiety surge, but he held it in as Obregon walked out, his bodyguard joining him from his station outside the door.

You're being foolish. They know nothing, and you make them millions of dollars.

Ramirez was merely an assassin; Angel had an entire branch of the cartel to run in a major US city. He needed the matter to go away, not escalate.

Two mad dogs in Tucson would be one too many. Put up against a vengeful *sicario* with a predilection for explosive violence that made his own look insignificant, he didn't like his chances.

It all went back to Tito Agustin and Martin Guevara.

It seemed nobody believed the fool had jumped, even though there was no evidence to the contrary, and Tito had almost certainly been with him at the time.

Even if he knew nothing about Martin's work, he would have seen Hayes at the shelter; he might even blame the detective for Martin's death already, even though Angel's instructions, to just intimidate him, had been clear.

The truth was he had jumped. Hayes was adamant. But that did not mean the police would ignore Tito if he went to them. Even if he wasn't charged, Hayes would be investigated, his value as a contact on the force eliminated.

And Martin had known a lot. He had been a driver for the "intake" process that saw the illegals dropped at various warehouses, then educated on their responsibilities and given information on local work.

He'd had access to the staff at each warehouse; he'd couriered the books for them, dropped off payrolls.

In turn, the new arrivals were told how to handle police and immigration and how to keep from being discovered. Those who had no local family were also offered lodging, at a stiff price. Those who had family were forced to give over information on relatives, others with money who could be blackmailed to further guarantee the new arrival's safety.

By the end of their first few days in America, they were typically working in a cartel job, for minimal pay, building more debt than they or their relatives could ever pay.

If Guevara had passed that information to Tito somehow, and Tito had seen Hayes with Guevara, he could tip the authorities or even a rival cartel. It would be disastrous, even if dealt with, for Angel's reputation. A murder probe, properties seized...

The cartel would not stand for it. Hayes's insistence that the official book was closed on Martin did not imbue him with confidence.

Now there were two problems. He had to keep Hector Ramirez off his back, including calling Manolo to ensure he didn't mention Cucho to anyone, and he still needed to find Tito Agustin. "*Madre de...*"

A knock on the door interrupted his train of thought. Angel called for them to enter.

The door opened, and Det. Carter Hayes stuck his head through it and looked inside. "Am I interrupting anything?"

"Hayes! No, no, come in."

The policeman closed the door behind him. "Did I just

see a certain financier from Phoenix walking out the front doors?"

"You did. My father is happy."

"Good. My name come up?"

"It did not. Pftt! You think he gives a shit about you?"

"Even better. You watch the news at lunchtime?"

Angel checked his watch. It was past one. "Damn. I worked through it. Obregon was crunching numbers." He glared at Hayes. "I'm busy! I'm too busy to watch TV sometimes. If you had my responsibilities, you would fucking understand this!"

Hayes walked over to the desk and retrieved the remote control. He turned on the TV in the corner of the room. "Huh. Guess they're done with the coverage. A possible gun incident at a school and it only gets an hour? This country! Am I right? A kid actually has to shoot people these days to—"

"Hayes, what the fuck are you yapping about, eh?" Angel interrupted. "Why do I give a shit about this, huh?"

Hayes wore a smarmy grin. "Because I *did* watch the noon news. And now I know where Tito Agustin is."

14

The sun streaming through the leaded-glass window in Sister Mary Rose's office looked divine, bathing her old hickory desk in a soft white glow. The Mother Superior of the Sisters of Benevolence Convent felt a moment of serenity and bliss, as if she could've stood there and watched that glorious light all day.

She sighed... because it was not to be.

She turned her attention back to the room and the man across from her desk. Detective Carter Hayes had his hand in his suit-trouser pocket, and he had a pronounced slouch. He displayed no inclination towards faith or respecting that of others.

"I hate to disappoint you, Detective, but the sisters do not keep me up to date twenty-four hours a day. If they have had a visitor..."

"And his kid," Hayes interrupted. "And we both know a person of your stature isn't letting anything happen here that she doesn't know about."

"As flattered as I am at your view of my authority, Detective, reality disagrees. And besides..."

"Besides?"

"We both know that the church offers sanctuary to individuals in certain circumstances. Equally, I'm certain Sister Eva would not undertake to offer refuge to someone unless it were appropriate. Now... perhaps the best thing you could do, Detective, is have a nice chat with Captain Stevenson, your boss, and make sure he knows that you think sanctuary isn't to be taken seriously. He's a patron of the archdiocese, I believe."

He frowned at that and appeared to be thinking it over.

You wished for an exercise of my authority, Detective, she thought. *Perhaps it is best to be careful what you wish for.*

Then his gaze narrowed. Hayes looked her in the eye and cocked his head, nodding gently, a sense of discovery writ large. "You know what, Mother Superior? I suspect you're trying to pull a fast one on me." He waggled his index finger at her playfully. "But as I recall, from my brief review before coming out here, sanctuary is to be respected for political refugees. He's not fleeing another country or political persecution."

"Your point?"

"My point, Mother Superior, is that he's wanted on a charge of felony negligence for allowing a child access to an illegally obtained firearm, which is why his son is now in juvie. If you prevent me from arresting him and taking him out of here, you could potentially be charged with obstruction of justice. Now, I'm not saying I'd ever want that to happen. That would be unfortunate."

"Do you really think it wise..."

"To tick off your boss?" He leaned in conspiratorially. "By

which I mean the archbishop, of course, not the big guy upstairs. I don't think he'll make a deal of it. See, you're an optimist, and that's nice. We need optimists in this world; it keeps the square-deal Joe and Jane Citizen types from getting nervous. The Nervous Citizen is a skittish animal, prone to violence and rash impulsivity. Optimists like you make them focus on the good in the world. But I have to focus on the bad, Mother Superior. It's my job to decide who qualifies, not yours. And for all its concern for the lesser man, I don't think the archdiocese wants to get into a legal scrape protecting a lowlife like Tito Agustin." He sat down on the edge of her desk, like a professor mentoring a student. "That would be... well, that would be just stupid, wouldn't it?"

Is he right? She wasn't sure. But she did know her colleagues and that they'd do whatever they could to protect an innocent. "Well, Detective," she said, approaching the desk and picking up the landline's handset. "Let's call him and find out together."

SISTER EVA WAITED PATIENTLY, seated on an old pew that had been repurposed as a bench, just down the hall from Mother Superior's office. Bob had called as soon as he'd seen the news and was on his way.

She hoped he wouldn't be needed. He seemed a good man, and she enjoyed their conversations. There was someone good inside who needed her help, needed a path back to normalcy. But he kept hinting at violence in his past, a need to get away from men like Angel Herrera and Tito Agustin.

Somehow, she felt, knowing her had been problematic.

The people she advocated for daily had insinuated their way into Bob's life. If Tito were granted formal sanctuary, even a gangster like Herrera would pause before entering a church to take him.

The door to the office opened. Sister Mary Rose said something she couldn't make out to someone in the office, then closed the door behind her. She looked up and down the hallway quickly for prying eyes, then scuttled her way over to Sister Eva's perch.

"Mother Superior."

"Sister, it has not gone well. The gentleman in my office is a police detective named Carter Hayes."

Sister Eva rolled her eyes. "Yes, we're aware of him."

"Then you must be aware he intends to cause significant disruption if your guest is allowed to remain. I've talked to Father Pablo at the archdiocese, and he has most apologetically informed me that we have no legal standing in this matter."

"I don't understand. Legal..."

"Standing, yes. There is legal precedent for respecting church sanctuaries, but only in matters of political persecution and imminent risk of bodily harm. If Mr. Agustin were facing deportation to a dictatorship, for example—"

"We would be able to protect him. But because it's a local thug with lots of guns—"

"We have no legal standing," the Mother Superior confirmed. "He has to go, Sister. I am very sorry."

"How long do we have?"

"I shall bargain with the detective. How long do you need?"

. . .

BOB ASKED the hired car to stop a block before they reached the convent's front gate. If Hayes was at the convent, his partner or backup probably wasn't far off, he thought as he jogged past a row of single-family homes.

He reached the convent's block. Across the road, an unmarked sedan with speed hubs sat at the curb in front of public basketball courts. It was empty.

Behind it sat a black Mercedes SUV, nearly identical to the one they'd "borrowed" a few days prior. There were two men in the cab, but he could only make out their shape through the tinted windows.

Would they follow him into the convent? *Probably not.* That made them an issue to deal with once he had Tito.

He crossed the street corner and ran up the walk to the front door. He checked his shoulder. The two men were climbing out of the Mercedes. Bob opened the door and ran inside. Sister Roberta was manning the reception, as she had been when they'd first arrived.

"Sister Eva?" Bob said as he walked by her at pace.

She pointed to the hallway to his right. "She's with the Mother Superior, I believe."

"Thank you!" Bob said with a backwards wave.

He ran down the hallway. At the far end, fifteen yards before the final office door, Sister Eva sat waiting on a pew bench. "I got here as fast as I could," he said.

"He's still in there with her," she said as she rose. "She's going to delay him for as long as possible, but I imagine that he will soon become insistent. Bob... they won't let him stay. Tito has to go, or they'll come in and arrest him by force."

"Is there a back door out of the place of some sort?"

Sister Eva nodded. "Through the gardens. But visitors aren't allowed—"

"Is the back door unlocked?"

"It is."

"Then lead me to Tito's room, and after that... you didn't see us."

Tito and Sean had been staying in the residential wing. The guest room was sparse and undecorated, with just two small beds and side tables, along with a closet. Tito was lying down, playing a game on his phone when Bob opened the door.

"We need to go, *now*," Bob stressed.

"You heard?" Tito said as he rose. "Child welfare took my boy."

"Because he got hold of your pistol."

Tito hung his head. "He knew he wasn't supposed to touch it. Some kid at school has family who work for Angel Herrera. They were teasing him, telling him they were going to get a reward for turning him over. So when he left this morning, he went under the mattress..."

Bob was exasperated. The man was his own worst enemy and not doing his kid any favors, either. "Why didn't you just keep it...? Never mind," Bob said. "We'll get Sean back as soon as we can, right, Sister?"

She nodded enthusiastically.

"For now," Bob continued, "we need to get you out of here. A certain detective is in the main office, claiming he's going to arrest you."

"Hayes."

"Correct."

Tito grabbed his coat and a soft-sided carry-on bag that Sister Eva had provided from the donation bin. "He ain't taking me to no police station," he said. "He'll take me back to Angel, and pop, that's the end of Tito."

Sister Eva touched Bob gently on the forearm to get his attention. "That short corridor behind the main desk in the atrium essentially forms the top portion of a cross," she said. "The door to the gardens is at the end of it."

They made their way back down the long hall, jogging behind the reception area and taking the short, north-facing corridor. Bob pushed the metal fire-exit door open cautiously. He let its weight hold it back so that he could peer out the crack between it and the jamb but remain unseen.

The gardens were extensive, a xeriscaped central area of cacti and saguaros, along with other desert fauna, flanked to each side by greenhouses filled with flowers and fruit trees. Beyond them a long, low stone wall ran the width of the property.

They followed paving stones to its gate. Bob opened it and cautiously stuck his head into the lane.

The blackjack caught him off guard, a rubber cosh swung forcefully the moment his head appeared, catching Bob in the temple. He lost his balance and went over sideways, body thumping into the concrete alleyway.

15

B ob's head swam slightly as he lay on the ground, as if he might pass out.

He turned to his right and looked up. Tito had dropped his bag and was fighting two men, based on the two extra sets of legs. Bob wasn't sure what was going on, the blow concussing him, a foggy feeling taking over.

A man crashed to the concrete pavement beside him, unconscious. Bob didn't recognize him. He looked up again. Tito had squared off with the second attacker, his fists up in a boxing guard.

Oh, good, Bob thought absently. *Tito can fight.*

The second man took two steps back, then straightened up, using his left hand to draw a pistol from his waistband. *"Él no dijo que tenemos que traerte de vuelta vivo..."* He didn't say we have to bring you back alive.

Shit, Bob thought. *Shit. Need my brain to start working again. He's going to kill Tito.*

The second gunman worked the gun's slide, chambering a round. *"Adios, cabrón..."* he said.

The bag swung into Bob's field of view before the man could pull the trigger. It smashed into the side of the man's head with all the force Sister Eva could muster. He stumbled sideways and lost his grip, the pistol clattering to the ground. The gunman stooped and scrambled to retrieve it. His fingers closed on the cross-hatched grip, and he turned in one motion to fire.

Tito's boot caught him across the side of the chin, where the mental nerve resides. The man slumped onto his back, barely conscious.

Bob shook his head to clear the cobwebs, then righted himself. He retrieved the pistol and stuck it into his waistband. The first attacker was stirring, and he reached down, hammering the man's chin with a short, hard punch. The man blacked out again. Bob crouched beside him and took off the man's belt. He pulled his hands behind him and tied them with it. He skittered a few feet to the man's barely conscious friend. He measured the punch carefully, catching the gunman square and knocking him out. He repeated the procedure using the man's belt.

Then he dragged the second man over to his friend, who was beginning to stir.

"We need to go," he said, shaking his head to try to ward off the spinning sensation that had crept in. "Sister, I doubt he has any idea what hit him. I would head back inside. You didn't see any of this."

He closed his eyes and shook his head again twice, trying to clear the last of the cobwebs. Then he gestured to the block behind them. "We need to find a ride and get out of here before Hayes and the other two show up."

Sister Eva looked shocked and disturbed by the two prone men, the sudden outburst of violence. But she gestured away from the property. "Go," she said. "I will do what I can to help delay them."

She looked away as she said it, as if she couldn't even bear to look at them. Bob frowned. "Sister Eva..."

"Just... just go, Bob. Please. We cannot have this... this violence here. It isn't right."

Tito picked up his bag, and the two men sprinted for the gate. They turned the corner and ran down the laneway.

"We don't have long," Tito said. "We need to find some wheels—"

"Or..." Bob said, gesturing down the side street. Less than a block away, a taxi was making its way north, its sign unlit.

Bob waved at it, and the car began to slow.

THE DESERT COULD BE BLISSFULLY silent when no one was around, Manolo Marichal had decided.

He'd always liked the desert. His family lived in a small fishing village on the Gulf of Mexico, so those who knew him might have assumed he had a natural predilection for nature. But they weren't locals. His father had moved there from the Dominican Republic when he was an infant, and he'd spent most of his life in cities.

No, it wasn't heritage. It was just the stillness, the quiet. Most of the time, if he was on his own or with just one or two others, when everyone stopped talking, it was blissful. Parked off a trail to nowhere, nothing for miles but sandstone hoodoos and desolation. Just the wind, the dust and sand blowing gently, the occasional call from a coyote, or the screech from a bird of prey as it pirouetted across the cloudless blue sky.

But typically, he was there on business.

Business meant it never stayed quiet for long.

"Please!" Dennis King bellowed, his tone panicked. He was kneeling and stripped to his underpants, the sun beating down on three hundred and fifty pounds of pale white flesh. He had restraints on his wrists and ankles, one of Manolo's men standing just near enough to prevent him from toppling over if he lost his balance.

Two more men waited patiently thirty feet away, by the SUVs and the dirt track they'd created in their wake.

King glanced over at the giant saguaro to his left.

Manolo figured it had to be twenty feet tall.

"I figure there are at least one million needles on that one," the gangster said as he retrieved a cigarette from the soft pack of Camels in his breast pocket. "I figure we pick you up, hang you from that one like a coat on a thousand very sharp pegs. I figure you scream so loud, it's lucky Tucson is forty miles away, *cabrón*." He lit the cigarette, then looked at his phone. "It's... 5:20. By the time the sun goes down, you'll be cooked a nice dark brown, like a steak." He blew out a lungful of blue-gray smoke.

"I swear to God, I don't *know* anything else!" King pleaded. "I hired him six months ago because he could drive, and he took the pay. We needed people—"

"But there ain't no 'Bob Fleming' at the address he gave you, so that don't do us no good."

Angel had insisted on sending men to the convent, and those men had, once again, taken a beating at the hands of Tito's new friend. Hayes had wisely counseled tracking down "Bob's" home address; inevitably, they would wind up there, he'd suggested.

He didn't want to fail Angel again. His boss was difficult and sometimes stupid, but he had saved Manolo's life, got him out of jail and helped him beat a murder rap. He owed the man everything.

"I paid him cash, under the table. No need for benefits or insurance," King pleaded. "Please... I just want to go—"

"You want to go home, fat boy? You've got to give us something that helps us, eh?"

"Please..."

Manolo nodded towards the saguaro. "Go on, pin him to it."

The men grabbed King by his armpits and lifted simultaneously, carrying the bulky, terrified dispatcher over to the giant plant. King looked up at it, sweat smearing his glasses, the giant cactus's shadow covering his face like a deathly pall. "Oh God, oh God, oh God..." He began to plead.

"You'd better think real quick, gringo, because God ain't going to help you. We've got bets on whether you're too heavy to be suspended on that thing. I figure it's like Velcro, right? Those pins will just sink deep into all that fat, and you'll just hang up there until you cook to death or bleed out, whichever comes first."

King wet himself, a puddle of urine forming at his feet. He began to blubber, huge, wrenching sobs.

Manolo rolled his eyes. "*Ay, coño...* Fucking gutless! Do you want to die, stupid?"

King shook his head vociferously. "N-n-n-nooo," he blubbered.

"Then think! Don't cry! What else do you know about this man? His habits, his actions? Why did you fire him?" Whether he could lead to Tito or not, Manolo figured he owed "Bob" a beatdown.

"He... he gave a ride to a bum..."

"We know about that. How do you think we found you?

The bouncer at one of his regular bars gave us the name off the truck. The man he helped, Tito, did he ever mention him?"

"No! No, he never talked about anything!"

"Tssk..." Manolo dismissed him. "Go on, pin him up."

The two men began to drag King backwards, towards the saguaro.

"*No! Nooo!* Please, I'm begging you! I have cash!... my wallet..."

They reached the foot of the plant.

King wept some more, trying not to hyperventilate.

"One last chance, gringo," Manolo said as he strolled over to join them. He blew out a plume of smoke and tapped the ash off his cigarette. "Then we get to see you become the world's fattest pincushion. I think maybe all the air comes out and you just blow away like a burst balloon, eh?" He chuckled at that, his colleagues joining in.

A look of stark, sudden realization crossed King's face. "Wait! Wait... *pool!*" he screamed.

"What?"

"Pool." He was practically panting. "He mentioned once... that he plays pool at a bar..."

"Name?"

"I don't..."

The two men straightened him up again, lifting under his arms.

"The Third Act! Th-the Third Act Pub," King stammered. "He said he goes there after work sometimes."

Manolo smiled. Then he gestured to his helpers. "Amazing how fear can focus the mind, eh, you fat fuck? Let him go."

The gangsters began to make their way back to their cars.

King slumped to a cross-legged position in the dirt.

They began to get into the SUVs.

"Wait!" King yelled. "You... you can't leave me out here!"

It was 110F in the shade... had there been any shade. Manolo looked around quickly, once again appreciating the blueness of the sky. "It's a nice day, *cabrón*," he said. "You could do worse."

The SUVs departed in clouds of dust, leaving the mostly naked man in the rearview mirror.

BOB DOWNED two extra-strength ibuprofens and took a long drink from the kitchen tap. Then he splashed his face with cold water before turning the tap off.

A few feet away, he heard the click of a disposable lighter being used. He turned his head left. "Did it occur to you that maybe I don't want you smoking in my apartment?"

Tito took a puff and blew out a lungful of smoke. "Did it occur to you that right now, I don't give a shit? I'm stressed, *vato*. I've got to relax, you know?"

Bob kept his temper. Tito hadn't forced him to use his apartment as a hideout, or even to show up at the convent in the first place. The younger man was worried about his kid and their lives.

"If you're concerned about Sean, he's probably safer right now—"

"He's safer with me," Tito barked, illustrating it by jabbing himself in the chest with his thumb. "He's my boy, and we've got to get him back right fucking now!"

"If we show up at a juvenile detention facility, Hayes and Herrera's other flunkies will be down on us before you even see him," Bob said. "I get the sentiment, Tito. I understand where you're coming from. But the first priority is keeping you both alive. Eva's going to talk to Social Services and work on that end. Here..." He reached into the counter cupboard and took out a small juice glass, then placed it in front of Tito on the kitchen table. "Ashtray."

Tito glanced down at it. He flicked the long, drooping ash off his cigarette.

It missed.

"Figures," Tito said morosely. "It's like I'm cursed, you know? In Mexico... In Mexico, things were different."

"Better?"

His expression suggested some debate on the matter. "Different. I wanted to be a fighter."

"A boxer?"

He shook his head. "Mixed martial arts. I thought I had talent."

"But?"

"The cartel decided I was better suited to collecting debts for them. I was on the ladder, you know?"

"The ladder?"

"Like... the ladder to the top. When you're a full member, you can advance, like any job. But you start as muscle, near always, before they figure out what they want to do with you. My brothers, they were muscle before me. They moved on, moved up, became heavy hitters with the bosses in Mexico City. But I didn't want that, didn't want my wife and kid to be worrying about me coming home every day, or what bad shit I'd be doing. I just wanted to win fights and fix cars.

"They insisted.

"When I wanted to leave, the cartel was pretty mad. Gave me the same deal they gave Martin: you go, but you go with nothing but the clothes on your back. No money, no wheels, no gun. No chance. But we both made it. My brothers disowned me, said no more favors. My oldest, anyhow. I think he really meant it, too. He's..."

"Difficult."

"Frightening. I mean, he can be. The cartel is everything to him; I guess more than family, even."

"That's rough."

"Yeah. We haven't spoken now in nearly five years. He was so angry, I think maybe he'd shoot me if he saw me, let alone refuse to offer help. My middle brother, Ricardo, he's okay. He says I'm dead to him, but we still talk sometimes. But we never see each other 'cause I'm over here now and he's in Mexico City."

"So... you really did come here to get away from it all." That was something Bob understood all too well. Tucson was a damn sight nicer than an alley in downtown Chicago, but it was still Tito's escape.

You've been so busy seeing him as a criminal fuckup who needs you, you've missed the part where he was doing the right thing and deserves credit for it. Damn.

"Sure. Then we got here and... a different cartel, but the same old story. Still born to lose."

He had a bleak, distant expression, Bob thought, like a man who thinks his past has blotted out any chance of a future. *Yeah. Nothing disturbingly familiar there.* He'd seen the expression before: in medicine cabinets, in rearview mirrors, in crowded store windows, and in the smooth curve of a whiskey bottle.

"I don't want my kid's life to be like mine, understand? I don't want Sean around any of this old country bullshit. He's a good kid. We took my last wife's surname because I want him to have a clean break from the cartel. From it being about any of that."

"He'll be fine, Tito." Bob thought he needed assurance. He had that vacant gaze parents get when they can't think about anything except their kid and danger. "He's never been in trouble before; he was scared. Sister Eva will make sure they know why he brought the gun. He'll have to move schools, I'm guessing, but it won't end his life."

Tito shook his head. "It's my fault, man, leaving the piece where he could get it. Maybe, you know, if I'd talked to him about his life and shit... you know... he'd have told me he was being bullied."

"You can't watch him twenty-four seven, and you're not doing him any good wallowing in guilt," Bob said. "We need to figure out a way out of all of this." He used a tea towel to dab the moisture off his face. "You figured he came after you because of your friend Martin. Why, specifically?"

"Like I said, Martin knows... Martin knew all sorts of shit about his business. Herrera probably just figures he told me something I shouldn't know."

"So maybe he did," Bob ventured. "Did he talk about specifics when he was driving for Herrera? Locations, numbers of bodies, money... anything?"

Tito shook his head. "Man, no! Martin wasn't stupid, *vato*. He was careful. No! But we spent time together, so that's probably enough for Hayes."

Bob was puzzled. Something was missing. "Then what put them onto you in the first place? They had to be already looking for you the other day when you were waving around that pistol at the shelter. You hadn't been there long enough to prompt that response. And if you're right about your friend..."

"I am."

"Then it has to be because they think you have evidence of some sort."

The ex-gangster could only shake his head. "They want me dead, that's for real, Bob. But I don't got no idea why, *ese*... Whatever it is, I just don't know."

A ngel Herrera watched the phone on his desk as it shuddered, the ringer set to vibrate.

The display said the caller was unknown.

But the number was from Mexico City.

He knew plenty of people there, of course, and even had some family in the capital. But he had not talked to any of them in years.

If he answered it, Angel knew, and it was Hector Ramirez – the Gravedigger – he would want an explanation. *Whatever I tell him, he will expect to speak with Cucho sometime soon.*

The phone went silent.

Phew. Better for now I pretend I did not know he was...

The phone began to vibrate again.

What could he say? That they'd sent Cucho out on a job and he never came back?

That will not satisfy him. He will not believe it.

Sicarios were chosen to be assassins by the cartels specifically because they were ruthless. If he did not get an answer that satisfied him, he would investigate. He would demand to know where they'd sent Cucho. Then he would demand security camera footage, a witness, someone to confirm what had happened to him.

He will not give this up.

Ramirez would not care that his father was Aimon Mondragon Herrera, senior cartel figure. His father, for his part, would likely not get involved, certainly not if things were taking place in Tucson. Technically, it wasn't his place to deal with Tucson.

It was Angel's.

The phone vibrated again and again and again as he stared wide-eyed at it.

And then it went silent.

He waited breathlessly for a few more moments, exhaling with relief only when he was sure it would not ring again.

Angel knew he needed another solution, a way to shift the blame. If he could manufacture a story before Ramirez became so curious that he decided to visit, he could avoid any nastiness.

The phone buzzed again, and this time he nearly jumped out of his seat, his nerves beginning to betray him.

This time, the number was familiar.

He picked it up and answered it. "Manolo, talk to me. Tell me you've got Tito Agustin."

"Okay, but I'd be lying," Manolo said. "But we're getting closer."

"Closer? What the fuck does that mean, closer?"

"We think he's staying with some gringo dude named Bob. He helped him out a few times already. He's... He can take care of himself. I put a good scare into the dishwasher at a bar he goes to, and he says he drives truck for a local firm."

"So go down there, find someone, and beat the address out of them."

"They're closed. It's... nearly eight o'clock, Angel."

"Then find the owner, go to his house."

"If we do that, this guy Bob won't help, because he'll know it's a trap. It's a shit job; I'm betting they don't hang out. But if I go down to their office tomorrow morning, and his boss calls him in for a discussion..."

Angel hated waiting, but it made sense. "Okay. Okay, you do that. But the next time you call me, Manolo, I expect some good news, eh?"

"Yes, Angel, absolutely."

Angel ended the call. Finally, some progress. Things were beginning to break his way.

MEXICO CITY

HECTOR RAMIREZ STOOD next to the stretch limousine in the hotel parking lot and stared at his phone, perplexed.

Is he ghosting me?

Me?

Surely, he does not have the balls!

If he does... it will not be for long.

He dialed the number his assistant had provided again. The call rang through, but no one answered.

He put the phone into his pocket just as the driver climbed out of the car. The driver took his suitcase and placed it in the trunk, then moved to the back-left passenger door and held it open for him. "Señor."

"Thank you, Albert," Ramirez said as he got into the vehicle.

He hadn't seen Cucho – his second cousin – since the boy was twelve, nearly a decade earlier. He'd been a feisty kid, always in trouble at school, fascinated with boxing and football. It had been his wife's idea to contact him, make sure he was settling into his new life in America.

She wanted her cousin to be tough like her husband, to be a success within the cartel. She wanted Cucho to be a man whose name commanded fear and respect in equal measure.

He took out his phone again and stared at it momentarily, then put it away again. Everyone knew that Aimon Herrera's son was a sniveling weasel, a greedy man-child. *Would a cockroach like Angel actually dare ignore me? No. That makes no sense.*

Something is seriously wrong.

There had been no word from Cucho for a week, no sign from the few friends in Tucson his sister had been able to contact. Now, the man who employed him was ignoring calls from a man known to brook no interference.

He took the phone out again and called a number.

"Sir?"

"Miranda, book me a first-class ticket to Phoenix and arrange a rental car, please. Then book me a room in Tucson, somewhere comfortable and private. I'd like to head out tonight if possible."

"Yes, sir, of course. Would you like me to call ahead to our affiliates?" It was standard practice to smooth the way for a *sicario*, provide any equipment and assistance needed.

"No... no, I think I'll surprise them."

He ended the call. Miranda was efficient. She would doubtless email him an itinerary within a few minutes.

Ramirez did not want to travel to the States. In two days,

an antiques auction in Mexico City would afford him his best opportunity to own an Elizabethan writing desk, an elegant piece of engineering in walnut and tortoiseshell, with gold-leaf insets and hidden drawers. He had been looking forward to it for weeks.

But family and business came first. He would travel to Phoenix, where he would stop by one of the local gun dealers he'd favored for much of his thirty-year career as an assassin. Then he would drive to Tucson – never preferable, as he had family there – and he would have words with Angel Herrera, a provincial small-timer who evidently had forgotten his place.

And then, once he'd appropriately scolded his cousin, he would either bury Herrera for his insolence, or, in light of a reasonable excuse, leave him frightened enough that he'd never let a phone ring through to messages again.

A man was nothing without respect.

17

B ob spent the next morning in the delivery company's loading dock, working hard, helping other drivers prepare for the first shift.

He'd load a dolly with four crates, wheel it to a pickup or box truck, hand each crate to the man in the truck box, rinse, repeat. The crates were heavy, and he had a sweat going before nine in the morning.

The idea was Sister Eva's: the more he dwelled on his problems and choices, she'd argued, the less focused on the present he became, the more susceptible he became to depression and self-loathing, to letting his demons take over. "Try to stay 'in the moment,' appreciate and concentrate on what's going on around you," she'd said. "Focused hard work, regardless of whether it's complex, can be rewarding and distracting. It worked wonders for me."

Don't think, just work, he told himself repeatedly.

The trucks began to roll out at nine o'clock sharp. Bob watched the last pull out of the dim half-light of the loading dock and into the sunshine, then turn a corner and disappear.

"You're not even supposed to be here until two. I can't pay you overtime, you realize that, right?"

He turned to his right.

Mike Tardif, the dispatcher, was standing in his office doorway. "Feeling generous or something?" Mike asked.

Bob acknowledged him. "Yeah... something like that. I needed the exercise. I... just needed it to be quiet, is all."

Mike nodded knowingly. "Uh-huh. My ex-wife's got the ADHD, you know, so I get that. Be 'mindful and present,' " he said. "Something like that?"

"Exactly that."

"Whatever's eating you... any point in talking about it?"

"Not really." *Not with you. It's nice that you asked but... no.* It wasn't that he disliked Mike; but he was a stranger; there was no positive percentage in letting the dispatcher into his world.

Mike shrugged. "Fine, I guess. See you at two?"

"Uh-huh," Bob said as the other man disappeared back into the office.

AFTER A TRIP to the grocery store and paying some bills, Bob headed back to the apartment. Tito was seated on the sofa, watching the noon news.

"You okay?" Bob asked him. "You get something to eat?"

Tito nodded. "Had a bowl of Cheerios."

"You want lunch?" Bob asked. "I'll make us each a sandwich."

Tito shrugged. Then, after a pause, he said, "You got any idea what we do now? I can't stay here forever."

"We need to make sure Sean is safe first," Bob said.

"I know that. Don't you think I know that?" Tito was irritated. "He's my kid."

"I'm not suggesting otherwise. But before you go home or resettle, we need leverage. We need to figure out why Angel Herrera thinks you're a threat to him. Until we do that, every second you spend out in the open puts you and your son at risk. Okay?"

"Yeah, I guess," Tito said. He mumbled something softly in Spanish. Bob sometimes got the sense that Tito saw the world only in terms of winners and losers, and himself as perpetually the latter. It made helping him more difficult, if only because of the knowledge he might revert to form the moment Bob was out of the picture.

So he pretended not to hear the grumbling. "Ham and cheese okay? I've got some decent tomatoes I can slice on there, too…"

"Hmmm… Uh-huh," Tito said, his attention already back on the television.

It didn't bother Bob, the man's indifference. If he walked out without another word, Bob figured, it would be his right. Expecting gratitude from people just for doing the right thing had probably contributed to his own social disconnection. Trying to please everyone would always be doomed to failure.

He wasn't even sure Tito had the capacity to appreciate someone looking out for him, at least not fully. Years of being surrounded by amorality seemed to have left the gangster with his own level of disconnection, from social normalcy, advancement, dreams of better things.

Or maybe that was just losing his wife. You understand that part, Bobby.

That's a whole other level of emptiness.

His phone rang. The delivery firm's number flashed on the screen.

"Yeah..." he answered.

"Bobbo! How're you doing, pal!" It was Mike. He sounded weirdly chipper.

Bobbo? That's a new one. "I'm good. We just—"

"Listen, I know you're not supposed to work today, but we're short a man for the afternoon shift. Think you could come on in, work six?"

Not supposed to... he knows I'm in at two. What the hell...

Something's wrong.

Don't ask.

Assume they have him on speaker.

That's what you'd do.

But playing along could still prove helpful. "Double pay?" Bob asked. "I mean, since you need me on short notice."

"We can do triple if you can get here in the next half hour," Mike said. "It's kind of an emergency."

Three guys, at least, assuming he knew what I was going for.

Somehow, they'd tracked him to his workplace. Now Mike was in danger.

Like the nun said, Bob, don't think. Just live in the moment.

"Be seeing you," Bob said. He ended the call.

He walked over to the hook by the door and retrieved his light jacket. "I have to go out early. You're good?"

Tito tipped an imaginary hat his way without taking his eyes off the TV.

Bob reached up to the shelf above the coat rack and found the Sig Sauer P210 he'd confiscated from the thug behind the convent.

He didn't want to use it. It was built for competitive target shooting, the slide extra smooth, the sights ultra precise – although not as accurate as the FN 5.7 in his go bag. He'd managed to go nearly seven months without killing anyone, and that was the goal, to put violence behind him.

But Bob figured that if it became necessary, the 9mm Luger rounds would do the trick.

18

M ike Tardif leaned back in his typing chair and took as relaxed a pose as he could muster. The two men across the desk looked equally at ease: they wore long shorts and high-top sneakers, one in an Arizona Diamondbacks jersey, the other a black T-shirt. T-shirt had flashed his pistol as soon as they'd walked in with their friend.

"Okay, I called him. He lives right across the city, though, and it's midday. Traffic..."

The third man was standing by the picture window, watching the street. Manolo, the others had called him. He made Mike more nervous, although he wasn't sure why. Perhaps it was the "business casual" slacks and black short-sleeved dress shirt giving him an official air. Or maybe it was just the emotionless manner in which he spoke.

"If he doesn't show, we'll have to give him a reason to care," Manolo said. "He's helped out people he doesn't know before. That suggests he'll care if we hurt you to get to him.

He'll show up because he's confident, after beating us down once before."

Mike had kept his mouth shut. He wasn't sure what he could say that would help. But the notion of Bob Fleming, a guy he'd known for a week, showing up to save him seemed remote at best.

And good for the guy. If he's smart, he figured out he shouldn't be anywhere near this joint right now. Mike had never had much desire to be malicious to anyone else, or even much of a jerk. Yelling at the drivers occasionally was hard enough. For all he knew, Bob had a wife and kids, people he needed to protect.

"He's probably already on his way out of town," Mike said. "He probably read my voice as being nervous and took off. Heck, I know I would be. He doesn't know jack about me. He has no reason to help me, guy."

Manolo turned away from the window and towards him. "You got a wife? A kid?"

Mike shook his head. *Guy's looking for leverage. Uff da! Like the guns aren't intimidating enough.* "Nope. I got a mortgage, a decent team in the Tucson Men's Singles Five-Pin Bowling league, and some wicked bad gout in my left big toe. But no Mrs. Tardif, no."

Manolo's expression was rigid, his mouth a grim, straight line. "Did I ask you for your life story?" He turned back to the window. Then he frowned and cocked his head, like he'd just thought of something. "Is there a back door on this place?"

"There is, yeah. And the loading dock bay door is usually open as well."

"*Mierda*," Manolo muttered. He scanned the room. "You don't got no security cameras or nothing?"

"Yeah... but..."

"So how do I watch them from here?"

"You can't," Mike said. "They record twenty-four seven, but they're monitored by a company we hire, a subscription service."

"*Coño...*" Manolo looked up suddenly, struck by inspiration. "The back door, you can lock it up, right?"

"Sure." Mike realized where he was headed with it.

His associates didn't.

"*¿Quieres que entre por el frente?*" *You want him coming through the front door?* Diamondbacks jersey asked in Spanish.

Manolo nodded. "He thinks he's coming to work. But just in case he tries something, we close off the back route, make him walk in where we can see him. He normally comes in the front door, yes?"

"Or through the loading dock," Mike said.

Manolo kept up his stoic exterior. "Good. We wait a little longer; if he doesn't show, we make a show out of you. Then his conscience will do the rest. Either way, once we have him, we'll know where Tito is."

Mike scoffed at that. "Bob doesn't strike me as the kind of guy who makes things easy. I mean, I could be wrong, but..."

"Then let him try to make things hard," Manolo said. He drew his pistol and worked the slide, chambering a round before putting the safety back into place and securing it again in his waistband. "If he won't help us, we'll kill him so that he won't help Tito. Either way, eventually he'll turn up. But this guy Bob... this guy is a pain in my balls."

Angel expected him to interrogate Bob, use him to find Tito. But Manolo wanted payback. Whether he talked or not, he figured, the gringo was going down.

He looked back out at the street. Then another idea seemed to occur. He turned partially back towards the room. "The stairs by the front door—"

"They're to the offices above us," Mike said. "Empty. Used to be a call center, I believe."

Manolo took his phone out. "I've got an idea. Every time we deal with this fucker up until now, he handles us easy. This time... this time I figure we make his life a little harder. I got a friend lives real near here..."

He took out his phone. "Hey! *Hola*, Carlos! Hey, *carnal*, I need a favor. I need you to lend me that new arrival you just had. But it has to be quick, man, like, in the next fifteen or twenty. Yeah, with a big chain, like fifteen feet long, at least! All right, *carnal*, all right! Bring Arnold as well, and make sure you're both carrying."

BOB HAD the hire car drop him two blocks south of the delivery depot. They'd have eyes on the street, likely both front and back. They'd expect a casual approach, assuming they'd bought Mike Tardif's impromptu fiction.

Traffic had been heavy for midday, the ride across town taking nearly thirty minutes. But he saw no signs of police or squad cars anywhere nearby.

He followed the street for two more blocks, past Twenty-Ninth Street and Fourth Avenue, then turned right and covered the thirty yards or so to the rear alley, behind the depot.

There were no vehicles parked there. The back shades had been drawn. He peered cautiously around a dumpster propped up against the building's back wall, but there was no sign of anyone waiting to ambush him. He hadn't seen any camera monitors inside the business, suggesting it was done remotely.

He made his way cautiously to the back door. Instead of trying the handle, he crouched to catch a glimpse between the door and the frame at the hasp. The latch was on, but so was a deadbolt above it.

If they'd locked the back door, it was because they were expecting him to come in the front, but being careful. That suggested they were paying at least a little bit of attention. They'd leave the front door unlocked.

But they'll know I won't use it. Whoever has Mike is banking on me either strolling in for a regular shift, or...

The loading docks. Bob tried to remember if he'd ever seen the shutters drawn during work hours and couldn't. *They'll be waiting there, expecting me to sneak in.*

He thought about calling Mike's phone back, having him hand it to whoever the ringleader was. If he could bluff him into believing he didn't give a shit about Mike and wasn't coming, the element of surprise...

Nope. Mike's a witness. There's as much chance they kill him as me.

In fact...

It occurred to him, in the moment, that they weren't really after him. They were after Tito; they just figured putting another associate under pressure would draw out Bob... and Bob would lead them to the missing gangster.

That gave him an edge, Bob realized. *They can't shoot you, or they risk not finding Tito. They need to capture you... right?*

Or maybe they just figured they'd find Tito in good time. If that was the case, they would be armed and enthusiastic. Plus, they could kill Mike. Certainly they would use him as hostage leverage if confronted.

So how do I get Mike out of there before dealing with them?

He crouched by the back door and assessed the situation again. He took out his wallet and felt inside its pouch pocket, removing a lock pick torsion wrench, a half-diamond pick and a short hook, each the size of a hairpin.

The bolt was a common Master variety with five tumblers. Bob had seen it before many times, and it didn't take long. The weight of the deadbolt spring made the process tense, because the torsion wrench used to hold back the "teeth" inside the lock could potentially break off. But after about a minute, he was able to turn the lower handle and pull the door open an inch.

The back corridor appeared empty, half-occupied as it was by the stairs to the second floor. There was no one standing at the front door, either.

So they're either in the office or the dock or upstairs. The office seemed most likely, although Tito's opposition never seemed to work solo, which meant all three were possible. His eyes flitted the length of the corridor as he tried to determine how to draw them out.

They came to rest on a small red panel along the left-hand wall. *Worked in Memphis*, he thought. *What the hell, in for a penny, in for a pound.*

MANOLO's stoic exterior was beginning to crack. It had been more than thirty minutes since the dispatcher had talked to "Bob."

He should have been there already, Manolo knew.

"So you're telling me even if it stops me from blowing your head off, you don't got no kind of address on this guy?" he demanded.

"I have a PO box. That's what he wanted to use. But you've already said that's not what you're looking for," Mike said.

The gangster's associates had moved to the loading dock on his instruction, lying in wait.

"He don't get here soon, your ass is history, *cabrón*," Manolo said.

"You ever figure that if you shoot me, every camera on the street outside is going to pick up your image walking out of here?" Mike said. "I'm guessing you might have some priors, as the boys in blue like to say. They'll be able to identify you real easy."

Manolo leaned across the desk, pistol in his right hand. "I figure what I'll do is wipe my prints off the gun, then shoot you through the head at close range, then stick the gun in your hand, then let it fall, real natural, beside your chair. Then they just think you're another fat fuck whose life was useless, so he decided to end it all. How do you feel about that idea, smart man?"

"Not so hot," Mike admitted.

"Uh-huh. Shut the fuck up," Manolo insisted. "Besides... you don't got nothing to worry about. We get this guy and take him; he tells us what we want; we let you both go, no probs. And we will get him. I got my little surprise all ready to go for him."

"Is that the racket I heard a few minutes ago?"

Manolo grinned. "Uh-huh."

The sprinkler system gave no warning, kicking in a moment before the fire alarm began to sound, blaring shrilly on repeat. The room was immediately doused in water from six different outlets.

"*Coño tu madre...*" Manolo muttered, water beginning to

paste hair to his face. "Your friend think he's funny, eh?" He raised the gun. "Maybe I shoot you now, save us the bother."

"I don't think so, guy," Mike said. "You need me as leverage against Bob, or we wouldn't be going through this whole gosh-darn rigmarole in the first place. And the fire department will be here soon, maybe the police, too. You think they're going to believe I killed myself... and then pulled the fire alarm?"

"You can be real happy now, *cabrón*; but he still got to come inside to save you, right? Then I shoot him in the face, and I shoot you in the face. Then I'm the only one laughing."

Mike chuckled openly.

"What?" Manolo demanded.

"Eh... you'll figure it out," he said. "Or maybe you won't. Either way—"

Anger overtook the gangster. "Either way what?" he bellowed. He raised the pistol and placed the barrel against the middle of Mike's forehead. "Either way what, mother—" Then the realization kicked in. "*Ah, mierda...*"

"If he's pulled the fire alarm..." Mike said.

He's already inside.

BOB CREPT along the corridor between the main hall and the loading docks, the alarm ringing.

A split second after he'd pulled the alarm, smoke from the burning pile of Kleenex he'd wedged into a sprinkler head hit the detector, the emergency system kicking into high gear. Water showered down, soaking him quickly. He kept the Sig Sauer in his waistband, where he intended for it to stay unless absolutely necessary.

Halfway along the side corridor, he paused at the open

side door to the main office. He leaned left just far enough to get an angle through the doorway, to the giant Harley-Davidson-logo mirror behind Mike's desk.

Manolo Marichal was barking something at Mike, who seemed to be peering past him, towards the main office doors, which emptied into the main hallway by the front doors. He jabbed a finger in his direction, then waved his left hand, holding his pistol, towards the hallway.

He had to have other men with him, Bob knew. But the mirror image was fairly conclusive: for now, he was alone and isolated. He began to turn towards the hall, and Bob ducked backwards, out of sight and up against the wall.

Manolo stepped cautiously through the doorway. Bob hit him with a hard right cross to the jaw, the gangster's legs giving instantly. The gun flew out of his hand. He was half-conscious, dazed and trying to figure out what had hit him as Bob scooped it up.

He leaned into the room and tossed the pistol towards Mike Tardif. The surprised dispatcher caught it between both hands, like a child thrown a ball.

"What the fuck do I do with this?" Mike asked, wide-eyed.

"Nothing, just run, go! *Go!*" Bob bellowed.

For a big man, the Duluth native did a fair impression of an Olympic sprinter, Bob figured, and was out the door before Manolo had made it back to his knees. Bob knelt and hit the gang boss with a straight left, putting him down again.

At the other end of the corridor, the doors to the loading docks swung open.

Bob knew what was coming and turned to run, drawing the Sig Sauer from his waist as he did, chambering a shell, then turning and firing blindly back towards the door, emptying the magazine, keeping the two gunmen who'd been about to burst through the door hidden behind its frame.

He turned left at the main hall, the sounds of the dock doors crashing into each wall as they flew open somewhere behind him. A gunshot sounded a moment after the bullet ripped through the closet under the stairs. Bob ran towards the front door.

Hopefully, Mike's a block from here already, he thought. He had no idea who or what was waiting on the street. The chance that police had been called seemed high.

He was six feet from the front door when a man's frame filled it through the bug screen. He turned quickly towards the back door just as another man, smaller but also carrying a pistol, stepped through it.

Manolo brought in more men.

And now he was caught between them, all three exits cut off.

The stairs.

Bob took them two at a time, the sound of boots pounding the hall floor in his wake. He pushed open the first office door he reached. The men behind him were climbing steps, their heels clomping the worn wooden treads, just seconds away.

The office was massive, taking up two-thirds of the top of the building. It was empty and dimly lit by the sun, which pushed its way through grimy, soot-covered top windows. It was devoid of everything but some desks and a wastebasket overflowing with paper. There was a door opposite the entrance, on the far wall, thirty feet away.

Bob shut the door behind him and locked it.

He took quick, cautious steps as he crossed the room, half expecting one of Manolo's men to pop up from behind a desk.

Grrrrrr...

The growl was nervous and guttural, as if a lion had taken a small whiff of helium and its voice gone up an octave.

Fifteen feet ahead of him, a jaguar strolled out from behind the row of desks on the right.

Past it, he heard the other door's lock click firm.

They've locked me in.

Going back the way he'd come was impossible; there had been at least two men clomping up the stairs behind him.

The jaguar slowly turned its head and stared at him, its tail swishing gently from side to side, its tan and black mottled coat rippling with muscles.

Ah, shit. It's a trap.

Pretty good one, too.

The jaguar peered at him, slowly rolling back its lips to expose its fangs.

Looks hungry.

19

The big cat turned his way. It lowered its head slightly but kept its eyes on Bob, as if studying him. It began to lope towards him.

He's not going to ask you to pet him, Bobby. His hand went to the Sig Sauer in his belt... for just the split second it took to remember the magazine was empty.

Ah hell. Can't shoot it. Can't fight it.

The jaguar stopped fifteen feet short of him. It yowled, a short, throaty roar, then bared its fangs once more, followed by a steady, low growl.

A long chain was attached to its back-left ankle by a cuff. It looked like more than enough to reach anywhere in the room.

Make a decision. Can't go forward; can't go back.

Bob turned left and broke into a sprint in one motion. The cat's eyes widened, and it gave pursuit. He ran headfirst towards the back windows, covering his head and face with his arms as he hurled himself through the second-story pane of glass.

The fall was brief and hard, the contents of the giant dumpster doing little to cushion his impact from the twenty-foot drop. He took the brunt of the force to his right shoulder.

He was moving immediately, training and instinct kicking in, scrambling to free himself from trash bags and debris, ignoring the pain in his joints. Crashing through the window would've made a hell of a racket, Bob figured, and they'd be on him again...

He clambered over the side of the huge bin. He looked up. The jaguar was poking its head past shards of jagged glass, through the opening. It growled loudly, but seemed to have enough sense not to try the jump. That, or the chain was preventing it.

The building's back door flew open. Bob dropped down beside the dumpster in cover. He peeked quickly around its corner. It was the two men who'd chased him upstairs, pistols in hand. They looked around cautiously, aware the debris in the alley gave him places to conceal himself.

Manolo wasn't going to command a platoon anytime soon, Bob figured, but he wasn't a complete idiot. He'd thought ahead, prepared a trap, told his men how to lead Bob into it. That meant his threat was to be respected. *He'll have people around the front as well.*

That meant he'd be surrounded quickly. Bob knew he needed to even up the numbers. He scanned the ground around him and found a decent-sized shard of glass. He took off his T-shirt and wrapped it around the glass's base as an impromptu grip, then backed up to the end of the dumpsters, around the corner.

A circular chrome security mirror, its image a distorted fish-eye view, sat above the rear door of the building behind them. Bob watched the two men in it as they approached the dumpsters. *Walking side by side, always a bad idea.* If they'd been thinking, they'd have each taken one side of the dumpster, ensured anyone lying in wait was covered.

But they didn't. One of the guards took a single step beyond the end of the dumpster, and Bob acted, judging the two-foot gap between himself and his target, then slashing down hard across the man's Achilles. The gangster screamed and stumbled, falling face-first, his pistol flying loose even as his colleague tried to turn towards the source.

He raised his pistol, but Bob was on him before he could finish the maneuver, snagging him by the wrist with one hand, a flat-palmed punch from his right catching the gangster square on the chin.

He let go of the gun and staggered backwards, dazed. Bob spun on his left heel, a right round kick smashing into the man's chin, crushing the mental nerve and knocking him cold.

His friend was crawling across the cement towards his nine-millimeter Colt, clutching his bleeding heel. Bob scampered over and retrieved it. He flipped the pistol around and used the butt to whip the man across the back of the skull.

The click of a gun slide came from his ten o'clock. Bob saw two men rounding the corner and took off, sprinting south on Fourth Avenue. *Numbers are against you. Time to get out of Dodge.* He ran down the sidewalk, trying to put distance between him and his pursuers.

A black SUV rounded the next corner, a Mercedes. The side windows facing the pavement began to steadily lower.

Shit. I'm trapped. He looked left and right, but the adjacent buildings were businesses fronting Twenty-Ninth, with no way to get inside quickly – not that he had time. The SUV was less than a block away and getting nearer.

He looked back, towards the building. Manolo and two more men were making their way down the sidewalk towards him at a quick walk. Bob figured he had less than twenty seconds before the two groups met in the middle and finished him.

Options, options, options. Not seeing any.

His heart had begun to race. He closed his mouth to ensure he breathed through his nostrils, regulating it.

At the main intersection, to the depot's left, a police cruiser rounded the corner.

Bob's gaze veered back to Manolo and his men. As a unit, they concealed their pieces and watched the cruiser pass.

Shit. They're just going to drive right by this and not even notice, aren't they?

He looked south, the Mercedes about to roll up on him. A gun barrel inched its way out the back window, the man holding it turning it towards Bob.

Do something. Now.

Bob chambered a bullet in the Colt. He jogged out into the middle of the road, raised the pistol above his head, and yanked the trigger three times.

Ninety feet away, the police cruiser's siren and lights flashed noisily to life. Its engine revved as it sped towards him. Bob stayed in its lane, the SUV flashing past in the opposite lane as it headed north. He glanced past it to Manolo's group, which had abandoned its pursuit, the men now milling around the sidewalk, unsure of how to act.

The cruiser squealed to a halt, the front doors swinging open, the two officers exiting into cover behind each door, their pistols levelled at him through its open windows. Bob made a show of reaching forward and dropping the pistol. It clattered tinnily on the warm cement.

"*Down!* Face-first on the ground, now, with your hands behind your back! *Do it, now!*" the cop driver yelled.

Bob dropped and complied. The officers approached quickly but cautiously, the second wrenching Bob's right arm hard towards the small of his back, holding it there as he slapped on wrist restraints, then dragging his left arm up as well and securing it.

They lifted him to his feet.

"What was that supposed to be, exactly?" the older cop said, his tone a solid lecture. He had sergeant stripes on his epaulets. "You realize those bullets are going to come down somewhere, right? You'd best hope they don't hit anyone. It has happened, you know."

Bob shrugged. "A couple of guys who also have guns were chasing me." He nodded back towards the sidewalk, where Manolo and his men were awkwardly loitering. The police officer looked that way, and the men immediately all diverted their attention, with the tact of a wildfire in a hay barn. They began to drift around the corner of the depot building, out of sight.

"Uh-huh. You might be telling the truth about that." The cop turned his attention back to Bob. "Usually, people shoot at the guys chasing them," he said, with what seemed to Bob a resigned sigh. "Though often as not, they hit the wrong person, so I guess we can be glad you didn't do that. Any point in us chasing them?"

"Probably not. Gangsters trying to rob the depot on the corner. They're not going to give you shit, and by the time you catch them, their pieces will be gone. I didn't want to hurt anyone, and I needed to get your attention. But they had buddies in a car behind me, so I couldn't wait for you to drive two blocks. So..."

"So you fired in the air."

The cop looked back down the street. He had graying hair at his temples, a creased forehead, lines around his eyes. The badge on his breast pocket said "Glebe," and he had sergeant's bars on his sleeve. His expression suggested he'd dealt with a few Manolos in his decades-long career. "You fired in the air to avoid shooting an actual person."

Ahead of the car, from the corner of his eye, Bob saw the sergeant's partner picking up the pistol. He used a pencil, inserting it into the barrel to avoid smudging fingerprints, and placed it into an evidence bag.

"I needed to get your attention," Bob reiterated.

"Mission accomplished," the older cop said as he led Bob to the back door of the cruiser. He used his free hand to push Bob's head down as he stuffed their new prisoner into the back of the car. Then he reached under the corner of his protective vest and turned off his body camera.

Bob's hackles rose, the hair on the nape of his neck standing up.

The cop lowered his voice. "When we get to the station, you'd do yourself a favor by reminding me – and the detective who interviews you – that you accidentally discharged that firearm... as I will remind my partner."

Bob was suspicious. He couldn't remember the last time an authority figure had offered him help. "Why would I do that? It's a misdemeanor if I don't hit somebody, right?"

The cop shook his head slowly and methodically. "Not in Arizona, no, sir. In Arizona, one of those bullets came down a few years ago and hit a little girl, killing her. So here, it' s a felony... when someone does it on purpose. Right?"

"Right." Bob nodded.

"And we prefer that law-abiding gun owners, who are just trying to protect themselves from criminal scumbags, know all of their options."

Say a little prayer, Bobby. Thank whatever higher power got you a cop who's trying to be a decent dude.

"Glad we have that settled," the officer said, leaning against the still-open back door. "You have the right to remain silent. Anything you say can and will be used against you in a court of law. You have the right to speak to an attorney, and to have an attorney present during any questioning..."

20

T he bullpen at the police station was quiet, just three officers at nearly two dozen desks, each with a suspect sitting nearby in restraints.

Sgt. David Glebe finished tapping out his preliminary report on the desktop PC. He had reading glasses on, perched slightly down his nose by way of manual adjustment.

Bob watched him quietly from the seat by the desk. They'd booked him for a class-one misdemeanor, accidental discharge of a firearm in a public place.

The officer hit "enter" on the keyboard. The process took less than twenty minutes. "I've sent my arrest report to a senior detective, who is going to interview you, which is standard practice for a case in which a felony charge is possible."

"Which means?"

"If he disagrees with my findings – they never do unless it's obvious error, because they have to justify their take when they weren't on scene – but if he disagrees with my findings, he can attempt to lay the felony charge and then leave it up to the district attorney's office to decide whether to proceed. But if that happens, he has to give you access to a lawyer, as you will be placed in custody until arraignment."

"But... you don't expect that to happen."

"No, I don't. If this wasn't a gun charge, and people weren't politically correct about it these days, they wouldn't even review it, they'd just accept my take. The detective will likely issue you a citation. As a class-one misdemeanor, it will likely be an extremely expensive ticket."

"Ouch. Does that mean you can take this cuff off?" Bob pulled at the hard rubber bracelet attaching him to the chair. "My wrist is getting sore."

"The detective has asked me to ensure you are restrained for now, given that a weapon was involved," the officer replied. "But don't despair. It certainly beats where this could have gone for you, so I'd be grateful."

"Oh, I am, believe me. You guys saved me; I have no doubt. Five of them, one of me."

"Sure, sure," Sgt. Glebe said. He turned Bob's way and pushed up his glasses. "I... must admit, however, that it would look a heck of a lot better on the official record if we knew a bit more about you, Mr. Fleming. You have no fixed address – your driver's license is legit, but the address is a PO box – and you have no Social Security number that we can find. You say you took the gun off one of your attackers, and I'm sure the surrounding businesses have cameras, so we can follow up on that if necessary. But... your fingerprints appear to have been removed at some point. You have a number of prominent scars – including at least two gunshot wounds to your collarbone that are visible through your open collar."

He wants to be sure he's read me right, so he's double-

checking. "Okay. I have a recent burn scar on my ankle, too, if you'd like to see it."

"That's... no, that's okay. And it's deliberately not telling me much."

Bob had been staring at the man's shoes buffed to a decent shine. He got the sense that Glebe had been around a bit and was putting odd pieces together. "You double knot your dress shoes, and I can see the tube lights reflecting off them. Ex-service?"

Sgt. Glebe nodded. "Four years in the infantry. Old habits." The cop's eyes flitted back to his report. "The prints... we don't see that too often outside the odd Eastern European gangster or Mexican *sicario*. The only other guy I ever knew who had his prints removed was an 'adviser' to SEAL Team Six. He never really told any of us anything."

"Okay," Bob repeated. Mentioning the shoes had the sergeant thinking, which had been the point.

Glebe's eyes narrowed as he peered into Bob's, trying to discern what kind of individual he was really dealing with. "Does 'okay' mean, similarly, that you have nothing to say about why you have no fingerprints?"

Bob leaned in. The man had a fantasy narrative going already – albeit one that was accurate in his case – and it made sense to take advantage of that. "If I told you, I'd be breaking about six dozen federal laws, and it's possible no one would hear from either of us again after today. Does that sound like something I should be talking about?"

Glebe shook his head slowly again. "Maybe... maybe not." He rose from his chair. "The gangsters you mentioned? I could've sworn I saw Manolo Marichal near that corner. That's why I gave you a break. Or was that also some Washington weirdness?"

"No, that was as advertised. If you get hold of the dispatcher at the depot, Mike Tardif, he'll tell you they had him at gunpoint for a while. Might even ID that Manolo dude, if you want to pick him up. Mike managed to flee when I showed up and interrupted them."

Glebe seemed to weigh the veracity of that for a moment. His expression said he had unanswered questions, but the eagerness to raise them was gone. Bob got a sense he'd decided to extract himself from the entire matter, as quickly as possible, as soon as the implication of professionally removed fingerprints had hit home.

"The detective will be along shortly, Mr. Fleming." Glebe rose from his chair. "You have my card, if you need to contact me for any follow-up. I... hope you have a better day than thus far." The tone was slightly regretful, as if he'd rather not have stopped his cruiser in the first place.

Bob watched him walk out of the bullpen area and back towards the atrium.

He'd lied about one thing: offering "no fixed address" was necessary, even if it prompted more questions. At least one of the men chasing Tito was a cop. Noting his actual address would mean giving up the younger man's location.

At the opposite end of the room, a door opened, and the detective entered the room.

Well... isn't that just synchronicity in action, right there? Bob observed.

"Hello, Mr. Fleming," the man said, taking over the other seat. "I'm Detective Carter Hayes. You and I need to have a nice little chat."

21

Hayes leaned across the desk and rested on his elbows. He kept his voice low.

"Between you and me, this might qualify as a conflict of interest," he said, "seeing as I've been trying to find your boy Tito for weeks now. But here's the deal, Mr. Fleming: I have all the power right now. You have none. This isn't Manolo and his thug friends. You can't kick anyone's ass and somehow miraculously find yourself outside this detachment's front doors."

He leaned back, looking smug. He sniffed twice, then rubbed his raw, red left nostril with his thumb and forefinger.

Did he just...? It reminded Bob of a guy he'd met years earlier. He'd had a cocaine habit and was always pinching his nostril for some reason. *Well now; I wonder...*

"Maybe you'd like to start being a little more communicative," Hayes suggested.

"I mean... I can leave if you're not going to charge me with a felony, right?" Bob suggested.

"I can hold you for forty-eight hours before I make that decision, by law," Hayes said glibly. "A whole lot can happen to a man in forty-eight hours in remand. Or…"

"Or?"

"Or we could just be straight with each other. Maybe you start out by telling me why you're trying to protect Tito Agustin, a former cartel thug. If you knew some of the stuff he is alleged to have done in Mexico before he came here…"

"I can imagine."

"He's in the country illegally, as well. You know that, right? That he's an illegal?"

"It wouldn't surprise me."

Hayes pushed his chair back slightly and peered at Bob as if studying him. "You… don't really volunteer much information, do you, Bob?"

"Nope."

"But you're a delivery driver, correct?"

"Correct."

"You know Tito well?"

"What does this have to do with me firing off a gun accidentally?"

"About that: where did you get the gun? Its serial number has been filed off, so you were clearly in possession of an illegally obtained firearm."

"Which, as I mentioned to Sgt. Glebe, I picked up off the ground behind the depot on Twenty-Ninth Street, after a guy attacked me. There's probably security cam footage of them throwing me out a window, attacking me, and my picking up that piece. But… you don't need to go dig that up. You know all of this already… don't you, Detective?"

Hayes smiled but didn't respond, instead changing tack. He turned to the desktop PC's monitor to his right and tapped on its keyboard. "I noticed in Sgt. Glebe's arrest report that you've had your fingerprints removed."

"I'm incredibly clumsy around stove burners."

"Huh. Sure you are. And the sergeant's report says he witnessed the gun going off accidentally."

"I mean... he's your co-worker," Bob suggested. "If you have issues with him, maybe address them to him."

"Sgt. Glebe is an enthusiastic defender of the Second Amendment. Like several of the officers, he has... a history of leniency in matters involving the use of firearms for personal protection. He and I have a... strained relationship."

"He seems like a good cop. You seem like a bad cop. That might be part of it."

"Hah! Funny. You're a funny guy. But suppose I lean on him a little..."

Bob scoffed a little at that. "He didn't seem like the type that would work well on. But, like I said, he's—"

"My co-worker. Sure, sure." Hayes nodded but kept his pale blue eyes on Bob throughout. Then he leaned forward and lowered his voice again. "You can play this cool routine for as long as you like, Mr. Fleming. I don't know what your background is; judging by Manolo's description of the fight at the shelter, you have a history in either law enforcement or the military. But, as I stated off the top, you have no power here, no ability to intimidate."

"Okay," Bob said nonchalantly. "And you do, apparently? I mean, so far I'm not seeing or hearing it."

Hayes expression shifted from calm to irritated in an instant. He kept his tone quiet enough to be private. "I can drop a piece at my feet right now and kick it over to you, then shoot you through the head. There are two other detectives in the bullpen right now. Granted, they're on the other side of a large room; but I guarantee you – I *guarantee* you – not one of them will question whether it was a worthy shoot."

"Sure you can," Bob said. "But there are cameras in here, so you won't. Even if you do that, there will be a long, lengthy internal probe. Investigators will begin looking at your interest in my case. Glebe will swear they searched me and there was no gun. Even if all that isn't enough to inevitably sink you, it would lead to extensive inquiries into why you're after Tito Agustin."

"Mr. Agustin is a material witness in another case," Hayes said. "That's legit." But he sounded a little flustered, Bob figured, as if he hadn't been expecting a comeback.

"Well, if you're so sure I'm in your way and you can get away with it," Bob said, "go ahead: shoot me." He leaned back in his chair and crossed his hands across his stomach.

Hayes stared at him icily. "You really do think you've got it all figured out, don't you? Like I said before, forty-eight hours is a long time."

"During which, I'll be in remand, with cameras."

"For two days. And in those two days, do you know what's going to happen? No? Let me fill you in: I'm going to go down to the delivery depot with a warrant from a sympathetic justice of the peace, and I'm going to get the satnav and engine 'black box' data for your delivery truck. And it's going to tell us every single place you stopped in the last week. I'm betting you've stopped at home."

Bob tried to keep his expression neutral as he thought back to his time at the new firm. Had he...

Yeah. On day one, to grab lunch. But only once. That would make it difficult for them, but they'd find it eventually.

Shit.

"No snappy comeback on that one, Mr. Fleming? Maybe your gangster friend is holed up at an apartment somewhere. Of course, you're officially 'of no fixed address,' so if we found him there, I can still arrest you for lying to us and interfering with an official investigation."

Bob tilted his head a little and gave the man a derisive look. "Do you really think with you and half of Angel Herrera's gang chasing him, I'd take him to my home... assuming I had one?"

Hayes clearly felt the tide turning his way. It was his turn to lean back in his chair slightly and take on a relaxed pose. "I think dumb guys do all sorts of dumb things in the heat of the moment. So... yeah, I think that's exactly what you did." He rose suddenly, as if a telling notion had just occurred. "I'll tell you what: I'm going to make sure that warrant is coming, and then I'm going to step away for a few hours, and you can sit and stew. How does that sound, 'Bob'?"

The voice from the front of the room was booming, strong and confident. "I believe my client's constitutional rights would be violated under such a working arrangement, Detective. Don't you?"

Hayes turned towards the entrance. The lawyer wore a blue three-piece pin-striped suit, with a silk pocket square and matching club tie in a striped pattern. He was bald and stocky, and Hayes clearly recognized him immediately.

"Counselor," he said.

"I shall be representing Mr. Fleming, and all questions can be directed to me from here on in," he said as he walked over. He placed a large black legal briefcase on the end of the desk.

Hayes nodded at Bob. "And are you in agreement that Tony Deal is representing you, Mr. Fleming? Before you say yes, I should caution you that he costs about a thousand dollars an hour, and his client list is a who's who of the worst people in Arizona."

Before Bob could answer, Deal interrupted. "Should he accept, I shall be representing Mr. Fleming pro bono, Detective Hayes; and, as you're well aware, it can't be a who's who of the worst in Arizona. I don't represent you, after all."

What the fuck is going on? Bob wondered. "I didn't actually make my call yet," he said.

"A mutual friend alerted me to your needs, Mr. Fleming. If that's okay."

"Oh, it is. Very okay," Bob said. He gave the man a quick thumbs-up. "Super okay."

"Good. I've already talked to the arresting officer," Deal said, "and he confirms Mr. Fleming has so far only been charged with a class-one misdemeanor. As such, there is no reason for him to be in custody."

"I can hold him—"

"For forty-eight hours, yes. I'm well aware of all of the rules, Detective; the founder of our firm helped write some of them in his later capacity as a Supreme Court justice. Do you really think exercising that option without grounds is a legally sound option for your department?"

Hayes slumped back down into his chair. He leaned back, crossed his hands across his belly, and sucked on his lower teeth. He looked less than pleased, Bob decided. "Well, as I have nothing else at this moment to ask your client..."

"He's free to go. Yes, Detective, we know he is. I shall, of course, be filing a complaint with the Office of Professional Standards regarding his illegal detention for the last hour. I'm sure it will go nowhere, as you and your colleagues seem to have made it such a habit these days that no one even complains anymore. But for the sake of the record..." He nodded toward the door. "Let's go, Mr. Fleming. Detective Hayes is done."

Hayes rounded the desk and uncuffed Bob from the chair. "You and I will talk again," he said.

"Looking forward to it," Bob said as the lawyer led him out of the room.

I have no idea what just happened, Bob thought.

OUTSIDE THE STATION, a black Lincoln limousine was waiting at the curb.

"You got me a limo?" Bob let his surprise show.

The lawyer rolled his eyes. "He's my regular driver. No, I didn't get you a limo, Mr. Fleming."

"Please... it's Bob."

"We're not going to become familiar, Mr. Fleming," Deal advised as he opened the back door and gestured for Bob to get in.

Bob slid across the back seat to the other side. Deal climbed in a moment later.

"I'm going to give you a ride home, and then our business shall conclude," Deal said.

"I mean... assuming I pay this ticket on time. Twenty-five hundred is a lot of money."

"Very amusing. Even in that event, I will not be involved. I have a full caseload of clients who actually pay me."

The limo pulled out into traffic.

"So... why are you here, and why did you help me?" Bob asked.

"A favor was requested by an associate of Mr. Tito Agustin, and I complied."

What?

That didn't make any sense at all. Tito wasn't a high roller or heavy-hitting mobster. He was a day laborer, moving from job to job.

The limo rolled across the city.

Every twenty seconds or so, Bob took a peek through the back window, old work habits to ensure they weren't being followed. The stretch Lincoln kept to the speed limit. Deal probably didn't want any police attention, Bob figured. Police probably hated the man.

Eventually, he asked, "How on earth does a guy like Tito – or one of his friends, for that matter – know a dude like you? And if so, why the hell is he relying on me for help?"

"Our relationship is our business, Mr. Fleming, and I am not at liberty to say. He requested I have you released, and I have done so. Once I've dropped you off, our business is concluded."

They were less than a mile from the building. Bob did a rear-window check. He frowned. *Green BMW, not a normal color. Been with us for a whole bunch of turns now.*

He took out his phone and dialed Tito.

"Bob! What's happening, *ese*? My guy found you okay, huh?"

"He did. When we have time, you're going to have to explain that to me. For now... we're on our way there, but I think we've got company. Get moving. I'll get your lawyer friend to drop me off early."

"Company?"

"We're being followed by a green BMW. It must have picked us up at the police station in case they couldn't get an address from me. Whoever it is will flag Manolo and his colleagues to your location, if not directly, then close enough that they'll figure out which building it has to be. We're the only apartment unit on the block. Don't even pack; we're too close. Just go."

"*Guey*... I don't got no wheels, dude."

"Then run. Find a public spot where they can't touch you and they won't throw you out right away – a fast-food restaurant, a bank, something like that. Delay as long as you can and use that to get a hire car. You have any other places—"

"Nobody's going to hide me. Everybody I know is scared of Angel."

"Call Sister Eva," Bob suggested. "She can't hide you at the convent, but she might know somewhere else. Okay?"

"Yeah... but..."

"Tito, we don't have time."

"Yeah, but what about *you,* man?"

"What?" Bob said. The question momentarily confused him. "What about me?"

Tito's pregnant pause suggested he'd missed the obvious. "Bob, what about you? You can't take them all on, not on your own, *ese*; that's just stupid."

I have to, or you won't have time to get away. He couldn't remember the last time someone had worried about his safety. *Probably Nurse Dawn in Chicago.* Whatever his background and drunken bluster, all Tito had done so far was worry about his son and his new friend. He was a good person, Bob figured.

"Don't worry about that. They don't really care about me. It's you they're after, and I think I know why."

"Eh?"

"It's complicated. I'll explain when I next see you." Bob checked the back window. The building was just three blocks away. "They're still with us. Go! Go now!"

Tito ended the call abruptly.

Deal piped up, "There's someone following us?"

"The dudes who were chasing me when I fired the Colt in the air," Bob explained. "Let me out on the next block."

"Happily," the lawyer grumbled. "Jared, pull over, please."

The driver complied.

"Why here?" the lawyer asked.

"To give Tito time to escape," Bob said.

Deal sighed loudly. "You must owe Mr. Agustin some kind of loyalty."

"Barely know him."

The car pulled over.

Deal put a hand on Bob's shoulder. "Mr. Fleming... you barely *know* him?"

Bob stared at the hand until he removed it. "Sorry. I have a thing about being touched."

Deal's head sank slightly. He seemed to recognize that whatever was driving Bob, he wasn't in the mood for advice. "Good luck to you, sir. It is unlikely we shall meet again."

Bob opened the door and got out quickly, shoulder checking the BMW. A block behind them, it pulled over to the curb.

Time to move. Let them know they're going to have to work for it. He took off down the adjacent alley at a sprint.

Bob ran as quickly as his feet could carry him. He took a right at East Winsett Street, passing Mulcahy Soccer Stadium. They'd only be a block behind him at most, he knew. He ran south down Plumer Avenue, then across the street to the west sidewalk and along Seventeenth Avenue.

A pair of men rounded the corner ahead of him. They

quickly checked the street for people, then began to stride towards him.

They look purposeful.

Manolo's called in reinforcements.

He looked behind him, back up the sidewalk towards Plumer. His pursuers had gotten out of the BMW and were moving at a light jog, trying to close the gap while not looking conspicuous.

Cut off again. But this time, there was no dumpster to hide behind, no police cruiser to alert. He thought about running back across the street, but knew they'd just follow. *I need to lose them somehow.* To his left, a pet store door jingled as a patron left.

Bob headed into the store. The clerk looked up as he entered, then returned to the customer at the till. Bob moved towards the back of the store. There had to be an exit...

There. A short corridor led past a single bathroom.

At its end, the door led to another alley, vehicles taking up most of the space, parking for workers along the street. One end of the alley was blocked off by a mesh fence. The other end...

The other end leads out right by where the second group appeared.

I'm trapped.

They would have seen him enter the store, followed, and would exit it in a matter of mere moments, he realized. He checked his surroundings, then jogged over to the vehicles. He checked each in turn to see if anyone had left keys behind or a door open. On the third, a car alarm began to shriek.

Shit. This isn't good. He backed up a few paces to keep an eye on the store's back door.

It began to slowly swing open.

Bob's eyes scanned the asphalt for anything he could use as a weapon, but there was nothing.

From behind him, a hand grabbed his shirt collar and tugged him backwards, towards the building behind the store. He was half-turned by the time he realized they were going through a doorway, into a darkened corridor. The door slammed shut behind them, the area pitched into darkness.

"Stay cool, Bob," the person behind him whispered. "In case they can hear."

Bob reached into his pocket and retrieved his disposable Bic. He flicked the flint wheel, and a jellybean-sized flame sprang to life, casting a bare glow around him.

He had to squint to recognize the figure. It was the young man he'd agreed to train as a fighter. "Chico?"

Chico nodded. "But put that out, dude," he whispered. "It's still light out, so I don't think they can spot it. But in case. And be quiet."

Bob wasn't about to argue. They both stood in the black stillness, craning to hear what was going on outside. After about two minutes, Bob whispered, "Where are we? What is this place?"

"It's the back of my auntie's shop," Chico whispered. "She sells stuff for crafts, sewing or some shit. We come back here to smoke and roll dice sometimes. How long should we give this?"

"A solid fifteen minutes," Bob suggested. "They'll search around the block, maybe check inside a few stores. But they might come back for another look, so..."

"Okay. Fifteen minutes in the dark. I'm going to sit down," Chico said.

Bob heard the young man's clothing rubbing against the

wall as he took a crossed-leg position on the floor. Bob slumped down next to him.

"Didn't see you at the center this week," Chico said.

"New job, other side of town, is keeping me busy. But I'm still coming Saturday," Bob said. "You keeping out of trouble?"

"You know how it is," Chico said. "It's tough. It's difficult when you know everybody in the city, right?"

"Sure. You didn't have to help me, you realize."

"I know. But... well... like, you helped me, right? Dude... who's chasing you?"

Bob gave him the backstory.

"Damn... you're at war with Angel Herrera? That's fucked!"

"Yeah," Bob said, hoping he didn't sound quite as exasperated as he felt. "Yeah, I sort of figured that out when one of his men set a jaguar on me."

"A jaguar... *coño*... You need help?" Chico demanded, his tone all business.

"I need to make sure these guys don't hurt anyone else. Which means no, I don't want you involved in this. At all. Like you said, Herrera..."

"... is crazy. I got it." He sounded disappointed.

They waited a few more minutes. Chico seemed anxious to assist, but the men they were dealing with were far too much for high school kids to face. Eventually, Bob said, "I need to get out of here before they link us." He rose to his feet. "It's been" – he checked his watch – "what... ten minutes?"

"About."

Bob walked to the back door and opened it a crack. The alley was deserted. He opened the door and walked out.

He turned and nodded Chico's way. "I won't forget this. Thank you."

Chico shook his head. "You don't owe me nothing, homes. You help me fight... I help you fight." He crossed his arms, an imperious expression suggesting he felt emboldened by their success.

"I have another friend who might be in trouble. I have to go."

"We'll see you around," Chico said. "Count on it."

22

The man standing by the tee box at hole number seven was older, white, fleshy from years of overindulgence, his belly large and round in a red golf shirt. He leaned on his three wood and watched their playing partner tee off.

"Ho! That's a shot right there; get up there!" he yelled as the man on the box swung through the ball, driving it two hundred yards down the fairway. "Good shot! You see that one, Herrera? The one time we put money on a hole and suddenly his slice disappears."

Angel Herrera sat in the golf cart nearby and nodded placidly at the demonstration. He had nothing but contempt for his playing partners. But both men were heavy hitters in the Tucson Chamber of Commerce, both heads of local service clubs. They were his ticket to legitimate business, a place to reinvest his years of criminal earnings that would not only wash it clean, but maintain his veneer of being an up-and-coming nightclub owner.

He didn't care for golf. He wasn't bad at it – he was teeing off first because he'd won every hole so far, a legacy of years hanging around his father's club in Phoenix. And he was certainly not as bad as either of the two enthusiasts, neither of whom showed any signs of ever being an athlete. It seemed a waste of a day, walking around.

If every time they hit a bad shot, I was allowed to beat them around the head with my driver, this would be much more interesting.

He heard a rustling sound and checked his shoulder. A rotund young man in shorts and a short-sleeved dress shirt was huffing and puffing his way up the small hill to the tee box. Angel rolled his eyes. It was Daniel Delgado, the deputy manager of Legacies, his nightclub just down the road from the golf course.

Ay, coño... Exio que no haya disturbios. I said no disturbances.

He got out of the cart.

"What's up?" his fleshy companion asked.

"Just business. I'll be a moment."

He met the young man before he could reach the group, his tone hushed. "What part of 'don't fucking bother me today' was unclear?" Angel asked through gritted teeth. "These gringos are important men, you get me?"

"I know, sir, and I apologize absolutely," the young man said. He looked frightened, which Angel had come to consider normal. "I was informed that if I did not pass the message along... I..."

"Out with it."

"I would probably not be around to regret the consequences."

That took some balls in his town, Angel thought. "And who, exactly..."

"The message was relayed by a Ms. Echeverria from Mexico City."

He felt the blood drain from his face. Miranda Echeverria was a fixer for the Omega Cartel. She spoke with their authority, typically, and helped manage their daily business.

"I see. The message?"

"She said Mr. Ramirez has been trying to reach you without success for several days. Unable to do so, he has decided to visit and discuss the matter in person."

Be cool. Don't react.

"I see."

"He arrived in Phoenix late last night and will meet with you at ten o'clock at the Flaming Garter. He said to make sure you bring his cousin, Cucho, with you."

PHOENIX, Arizona

THE STUDY WAS AS MUCH a library as a place to do business, its walls lined with floor-to-ceiling teak bookcases, antique furniture in gold gilt strewn across the pile carpet. It could have come from another time and place, an era when men of means like Aimon Herrera considered knowledge a pursuit unto itself and not merely a route to more profit.

Aimon sat in the antique wingback armchair beside the picture window. Opera music – a Mario Lanza performance from the post-war era, the Grand March from *Aida* – swelled gently in the background. He leafed through the pages of *Love in the Time of Cholera*, by Gabriel Garcia Marquez, for the third time. He admired Marquez's wrenching prose, his spare use of language to produce emotional resonance.

He admired it, but he could not understand it, not

entirely. If he could admit it to himself, Aimon found the story frustratingly distant. He had never loved anyone so sincerely that it hurt, let alone so much that it caused him illness, not even his wife and children. Not even himself. It gave him a sense of fascination that bordered on confusion when two people could see nothing less than the entirety of the world in each other.

Such sentiment, such uncontrolled desire. It is made for a different man than me.

On the side table by his chair, his phone rang. He gazed over at the number, intent on ignoring it. As the head of the Phoenix Cartel, Aimon's word was outright law in the city, at least among the criminal element; and everyone knew that he was not to be disturbed when home in the evening.

His irritation increased slightly when he realized the number was his son's. Angel had always been a problematic boy, and now he was a problematic man, at least on the outside. Inside, Aimon suspected he was still very much a child.

Aimon took a deep breath, then picked the phone up.

"What?" he demanded.

"Papi! It's me."

"I know. My phone has a display, like every other phone on the planet, Angel. What do you want? I'm rather busy right now."

"I know, Papi, and I'm sorry about that. But I need your advice."

Aimon immediately wondered what his son was playing at. Angel was a disappointment, a dishonorable person. Unlike his father, he was emotional, selfish and angry. The boy's mother had been the same, which was why she'd rapidly become the third former Mrs. Aimon Herrera before

Angel reached age four. Nannies and housekeepers had largely raised him, which to Aimon's way of thinking should have made him docile and servile, at the worst.

Instead, as he'd aged, he'd become more self-centered. As a boy, he'd been the kind of child who emboldened himself by torturing small animals and insects. As a teenager, in an expensive private school, he'd been a bully. Sending him to run Tucson had kept the operation in the family, but after a decade of his behavior, his father had regretted the decision on a regular basis.

"What?" Aimon asked. "Make it quick."

"Papi, I have a real problem. A guy who works for me disappeared, and I can't find him. I think something bad happened to him."

"So?" It was a dangerous business. It happened.

"So... he is the cousin of someone respected in Mexico City, Hector Ramirez."

The Gravedigger? His reputation was demonic, but Aimon supposed it was just biological reality that the man had family somewhere. *Possibly buried six feet underground.* "Again, so what? Why are you bothering me with this, Angel? Tell them you can't find him."

"I... Sure, Papi, I can. But he called, and I was nervous, so I didn't answer. And now he is coming down here to meet with me tonight. He wants answers, and I don't have any."

"So... tell him that." What was he playing at? Angel was never straightforward with anyone. This was probably the business Obregon had mentioned on returning from his trip to check the books. "What do you want me to tell you, Angel? Or more to the point, what *aren't* you telling me?" There had to be more to it. Angel would never reach out for help unless trouble was brewing.

"*Nothing!* Nothing, Papi, I swear it," Angel said. "I sent him to look for Tito Agustin..."

"Achh! Not that mess, still."

"We found him, but he got away. It is complicated, Papi, but the point is, Cucho never came back. Now I think Ramirez blames me somehow."

If the Gravedigger thought Angel was behind a family member's disappearance, he would be out for revenge, Aimon knew. *Sicarios* did not let matters rest. He would also almost certainly be correct. That meant Angel was probably lying to him, as usual.

"You know the rules," he told the younger man. "I cannot interfere in his case. He works for Mexico City, and he's untouchable because of who he is."

"But... you could call them, Papi. Right? For me? They love and respect you. If you tell them I didn't do nothing wrong, that this guy is his own problem..."

"Absolutely not," he said. "Angel—"

"But it's not fair, Papi, it's not!" Angel whined. "He will think I had something to do with Cucho disappearing. They'll blame *me.*"

"Well?" Aimon demanded. "Did you?" *Let's get to the nub of this matter*, the older man thought. *Let's find out just how foolish he has been.*

"I swear I didn't do nothing! The guys you've got working for me, they are idiots! Useless sons of bitches! He should be talking to them, Papi, not me..."

"Coward!" Aimon barked, his temper frayed. "They work for you! Idiot! Sometimes I cannot believe we are related, you are so weak! Make them certain that they, too, will disappear if they fail you! Do your job, you sniveling weakling!"

"Ay... Papi, please..."

"No! Do not call me with this matter again, Angel. A *sicario* is his own man until the task is complete. If his task is to kill you because you cannot produce his cousin, I highly recommend you find his cousin or prepare yourself for a battle, one I highly doubt you can win. Either way, I am sure you will disappoint me."

"Papi..."

"No, Angel..."

"Papi..." He sounded half-broken, like he might begin to sob. "Don't you love me, Papi?"

No. No, I do not. I hate that you are my child. You are pathetic, an embarrassment.

But he didn't say what he was thinking. Instead, he did what he always did when Angel begged for his help, and remained stoic. "Angel, you will work this out for yourself, and that will be good for you. Respect Hector's status and do what he says, and I am sure you will be fine. Okay?"

"But Papi..."

"No! No buts, Angel. That is all there is to this matter. Do not contact me about this again."

He ended the call.

Aimon had bailed out his child countless times over the years. But Angel was a grown man in his forties; he had to stand on his own two feet, or be knocked off them by someone more deserving.

23

S ister Eva scanned the side of the road. Evening was setting in, the sun near the horizon, streetlamps beginning to take over.

Her headlights swept the sidewalk as she took the next left, briefly revealing the denizens of a small encampment of homeless. They covered their faces with both arms, turning their heads away from the glare.

He said halfway up the block, she thought. *So somewhere around...*

There.

Three men were sitting on old wooden pallets under Murphy's Overpass, the flyover on the South Kino Parkway. One of them rose as her car neared.

He pulled down the hood of his sweatshirt.

Tito.

She pulled the little blue Nissan alongside him. He climbed in.

"Seatbelt, please," she said.

He did as requested. "Thank you, Sister. I didn't know who else I should call."

"What happened?"

"Herrera. His men set a trap for Bob, figuring he'd lead to me. He bailed on them at the last second so they wouldn't wind up at his place, which is where I was. I saw this camp about a week ago, figured they wouldn't think to go this far south. Bob figured they'd tag the building eventually, so I had to get out. He said I should call you."

"Ah." She wasn't sure how to immediately react. She had no idea what she could do with the man, where she could hide him. "Did he propose, by any chance, where we might go? I can't take you back to the convent. I know you don't have other family…"

"Not here. I have two brothers in Mexico City, but we don't talk too often. Well… one doesn't often. The other… we don't talk at all."

A wave of nausea rose inside her. Sister Eve belched gently, a slight moan emanating along with it.

Tito turned her way, frowning. "You okay, Sister?"

"I'm fine. I… have an illness. A long-term thing. It's nothing."

"Ah."

They drove in silence for a few minutes, the nun guiding the Nissan south, towards the edge of the city. Tito seemed deep in thought. Eventually, he said, "I don't feel real good about you two helping me."

"It's what we do," she said simply.

"Yeah, but—"

"It's our way, Tito. Just accept it for what it is. We like helping people. It gives us a sense of purpose."

It hit her right then, saying it out loud. *That's what Bob hasn't figured out. He's busy helping people while he looks for his purpose in life. But helping people is his purpose. He just doesn't believe it, doesn't have faith in himself.*

It's why he volunteered at the shelter. I didn't even have to ask him.

She slowed the car. "We should head for the youth center. It's closed after nine. By the time we get there—"

"The kids will all be gone." Tito nodded a few times, the implication hitting home. "You can lock us in there."

"They won't have any reason to suspect it," she suggested. "They know I volunteer at Sacred Heart. They don't know about Pima Youth."

She flicked on the car's turn signal.

"What about Bob?" Tito said. "Last I heard, they were still chasing him."

"I have a feeling he's more worried about us than we need to be about him. Don't worry about Bob," she said. "He's a surprisingly resilient man."

MAIN GATE SQUARE was busy around dinnertime, the rows of restaurants and bars on University Boulevard teeming with students and older patrons, neon casting an extra glow over the sidewalks.

Det. Carter Hayes leaned on his unmarked cruiser, parked in a lot along adjoining North Tyndall Avenue, and watched the pair of black Mercedes SUVs pull into spaces thirty feet away.

Manolo got out of the first, alone, and began to walk over. The tinted windows weren't giving much away, but Hayes knew his usual crew would be occupying both vehicles. But Manolo knew Hayes's rules: in public, he met with one person at a time, in a highly visible place. He had no reason to doubt Angel Herrera still needed him; he just knew better than to take it as certain.

Once Herrera no longer needed someone, they tended to disappear. The desert was an unforgiving place, full of bones bleached by the sun.

"Good job on Bob Fleming," Hayes said, crossing his arms. "Angel's going to have a fit if he hears you had him cornered on the top floor of that depot."

"Ptth! You had him under arrest! Right in front of you! What the fuck?" Manolo countered. "What happened?"

"If I had to guess, Tito pulled in a favor of some kind. You know Anthony Deal?"

Manolo nodded. "Of course."

"He showed up and sprang him. The arresting officer – a continual pain in my ass over the years, I should note – decided that Bob 'accidentally' fired that gun in the air."

Manolo shook his head. "Tony Deal? Tito don't have that kind of money. Man... can't even trust cops to arrest people properly no more."

"But after that, you were supposed to pick up his tail."

"We followed the limo, but he must have spotted us. He bailed out in the middle of the road, took off on foot."

He had a morose expression, the closest Hayes had seen to Manolo exhibiting self-doubt. As unhinged as Angel had been recently, he wasn't surprised. Everyone who worked for the man was nervous.

I can use that. "Without sounding too sentimental about it, I've noticed Angel doesn't treat you very well. Why do you put up with it?"

Manolo peered at him as if trying to read his actual

intent. "You never cared much about any of us before tonight, Hayes. Why now?"

Hayes shrugged. "I don't care, Manolo, I just... I don't know." He made it sound just a little exasperated. Nothing desperate. "I've worked for him for four years, and this is the first time I've thought he could just blow at any moment, at any one of us."

Manolo looked down and away. Hayes had been taught to read expressions, body language. He knew it was reluctant agreement without a word being said.

"So what you want me to do about it, huh?" Manolo eventually said. "He's the boss. That's the way it is and always will be."

"Always? Come on! We both know ten different men have run this city in the last twenty years. He's the latest."

"He's been the man for half of that. You know who his father is. So... my question is the same, Hayes. What the fuck you expect me to do about it? He's angry. So... keep your head down, *cabrón*. Don't expect me to do you no fucking favors."

He's getting to the meat of it. "I'm not asking you to help me or even like me, Manolo," he said. "I'm just thinking that as the two he relies on most, we're closest to him, which means we're also closest to the short-fuse bomb that could go off. So maybe we look out for each other a little."

Manolo drank the offer in with a wide-eyed, unbelieving shake of his head. "*Coño*... Hayes... you're the most hated fucking cop in Tucson, you know that, right? I mean... I don't want to be the first person to break this to you, man... but you're a dick. Most people figure you'd rather kick an old lady into traffic than help her across the road."

The detective sneered at that. "Oh sure, and you're Mr.

Sweetness and Fucking Light! That lump of fat they recovered along I10 near Southlands this morning... Danny King... Something like that..."

"Dennis," Manolo said.

"Yeah... that was your handiwork, right? Dead with his gigantic tighty-whities bunched up his ass crack, cooked damn near to a crisp, covered in dirt. Yeah... you're a real sweetheart, Manolo, a real soft touch."

"So we fucking hate each other, but you want me to help you?" The gangster crossed his arms, his face suggesting he was tiring of the detective. They were less than a foot apart, like two boxers posing for a hype shot.

"I suggest we're both a great deal saner right now than Angel and should help each other. A working arrangement, that's all. If I hear he's lost the plot and is coming for your scalp, I give you a jingle before it happens. You do the same in return. He'll almost certainly go for one of us eventually; he fucks up too much. Eventually, his father will lose his patience, or he'll do something he can't hide, and he'll try to pin it on one of us. Given that I'm a cop, it'll probably be you. But I wouldn't put it past him to try to take me on, either. So..."

"A working arrangement." Manolo glanced over his shoulder quickly, at the SUVs. "Those guys in the car, they're my brothers. Two of them literally. But if they heard me agreeing to that, they'd still put two in the back of my head instantly. I mean, like, in the moment, *ese*. Right then and there."

Hayes looked past him briefly to the SUVs. "That's why they're not in charge and you are. That's why you're the one cutting the smart deal. You can see it coming, Manolo, admit it. You know Angel's time isn't long."

Manolo's eyes flitted away. "He saved my life once. A long time ago, before he was the boss here. When he worked for his old man in Phoenix. I was stupid, tried selling some dope on the side, got picked up. He knew the cop, had him on the take for a little taste here and there, got the guy to divert the cruiser. The cop got all riled up, started talking about taking us both in."

"So Angel shot him?" Hayes could see where it was going.

"No. No, he made me do that. But he wasn't wrong. It had to be done. And if he doesn't intervene, I'm going down for a dime, at least. So... you wanted to know why I take it? That's why. But I know he's a mad dog." He glanced at the SUVs one more time, this time wistfully. "Don't feel right, but... okay. A working arrangement."

Hayes nodded reassurance. "Hey... if it were up to me, I'd be retiring from a lucrative NFL career right now. Bum knee decided otherwise. We don't always get dealt the hand we wanted. We just play it as best we can."

Manolo flashed a grim smile at that. Then he frowned. "We still have to figure out where the fuck Tito went."

"I've been thinking about that. If there's one thing this last week has exposed, it's that neither Tito nor this Bob dude knows a lot of people in Tucson, at least not the type of people they can turn to for help. So far, only one person has been willing to help both of them repeatedly."

"The nun," Manolo said. "But they can't take him to that convent, we know that. So how do we find her?"

"That part was easy. She's in a career based on devotion to duty. So where does she work when she's not at the convent?"

"The shelter on Park Avenue."

The detective shook his head. "I thought about that. Tito is barred, and with the trouble they had over Martin Guevara, there's no way they head there. So I called her Mother Superior, told her I had some follow-up questions for Sister Eva. When she's not at the shelter, she volunteers at the Pima Youth Center."

"They'd be closed at night," Manolo said. "It's a pretty good hideout."

"Go," Hayes said. "I'll call Angel, talk him down over this afternoon's events, tell him we have a lead."

The street around the center and possibly the building itself was rife with cameras, Hayes knew, from other security systems, from webcams.

The last place he needed to be was wherever Manolo killed Tito, especially with a nun on hand for the festivities.

He turned and headed back towards his unmarked sedan. Bob would meet up with Tito, and Manolo's men would take both out at the same time.

Two shitbirds with one stone, and Manolo worried about Angel Herrera. This could turn into a productive night.

24

M anolo watched as four of his men stood outside the youth center's doors and prepared to try to force them open.

He looked over the small group. "Anybody been in here before?"

A hand went up tentatively, stopping halfway. "I was, boss." A smaller man near the back stepped forward. "I used to go here after school when my mother was at work."

"What are we looking at?"

"There's, like, a café sort of area just inside the doors by the lobby desk, looking out the front windows. Then there's a big room behind it, like a rec room with a lounge and stuff. That's what I saw."

"What about cameras?"

The younger man nodded. "I think so, yeah."

The gangster considered it for a moment. "Terry, go around back, make sure no one comes or goes that way. Use the black spray paint on the external camera if there is one; we'll do the same inside. They're probably carrying, so keep your heads down. They try to make it out the back door, you pin them down. Don't get cocky and empty a clip on them or nothing. Just keep them inside."

BOB'S FRIEND WAS NERVOUS, Sister Eva recognized. It wasn't exactly imbuing her with confidence.

Tito Agustin sat on the arm of a sofa at the Pima Youth Center, hunched over, staring past the café seating near the lobby and towards the front window.

"Would you like a bite to eat?" Sister Eva said. "We have a small kitchen with—"

"I'm fine." He didn't take his eyes off the window. "I thought I saw something."

"What?"

"Just... a shadow by the door. Shadows. Nothing, I guess." He swayed a little in place as he said it, clearly nervous.

She drifted over to one of the vending machines. "A coffee, then?"

"No, I'm good."

She made one for herself. He'd been on edge since their arrival, twenty minutes earlier. "There's really no need to worry, Tito. Bob's barely ever here. There's no reason to think anyone would search here for him."

He glanced back at her briefly. "Yeah... but I know the guy looking, Manolo. He don't give up." Tito reached behind him and drew the Colt pistol from his waistband. He checked there was a round in the pipe, made sure the safety was on, and put it back.

She frowned. In her limited experience, those expecting violence usually found it, whether required or not. "Is that really necessary?" she asked.

He looked at her matter-of-factly. "With Manolo? I wouldn't get within a hundred miles of that fucker without a piece... excuse my language, Sister. But..."

"I understand what you mean. I just don't think we have any reason to—"

The sound of car doors slamming interrupted the thought. Tito got up quickly and scampered over to the doors to the lobby. "Shit!" he hissed. "Two black SUVs. They're here!"

"Are you sure—"

He ignored her doubt, striding past her brusquely, his head on a swivel as he checked out the back of the building, the gym area, the lounge. "Is there another way out of here?"

"There's a back door by the offices."

Tito jogged towards the back corridor. He followed it to the main office, turned right, then followed another short passage to the back door. He put his eye to the old-fashioned spy hole. A bulky figure stood ahead of it.

Shit. They've surrounded us.

He jogged back to Sister Eva.

"We need somewhere secure. If we can hold them off until Bob gets here—"

"I'm calling the police," Sister Eva said. She took out her phone.

"*No!*" Tito demanded. "You know what'll happen; they'll turn me over to ICE. My boy's still in detention!"

"We don't have a choice, Tito, and we don't have long." She dialed 911.

"911, what is your emergency?" the operator said.

"Hello? Yes, I need to report a crime in progress. Men with guns, at the Pima Youth Center on North Warren. Please hurry!"

"Just try to stay calm, ma'am. Are you in danger right now?"

"Yes! We have to hide—"

"Tell them they surrounded the building," Tito urged.

"They've surrounded the building," she repeated.

"Ma'am, what I need you to do is find a hiding spot until we get there. I'm going to dispatch the nearest unit we have. Until they arrive, stay in a hidden place and remain quiet, okay? Do you have any kind of weapon in the building?"

"We have a gun. But... I'm a nun. We don't want to shoot anyone."

"You're a *nun*?" The dispatcher sounded skeptical in the extreme.

"We do exist, you know."

"Okay. I'll make sure our men know to identify themselves. When they find you, they're going to be very careful and ask you to lie facedown so they can wrangle the weapon and ensure they're helping the right people. Okay?"

"Yes. Yes, all right."

"How many are with you?"

"It's just me and Tito... I mean a friend. One man."

"Okay. You stay put, ma'am; we'll be there as soon as we can."

Across the room, there was a loud rattle as the locked double front doors shook. "I have to go," Sister Eva said. She ended the call.

"They won't get here in time," she said.

Tito nodded towards the back of the building. "You got a secure area of some sort?"

She nodded. "The main offices. There's a security door, metal."

He gestured that way. "Then let's go."

• • •

OUTSIDE THE YOUTH CENTER, Det. Carter Hayes sat in his unmarked cruiser and watched as Manolo's men began to put shoulders to doors.

He had no intention of sticking his own neck out by joining them. With the number of businesses and apartments on the street, it wasn't going to take long for them to be noticed or recorded, for someone to call—

The radio beeped. "All units, CODE 2; all units, CODE 2. Be advised we have reports of a 10-30, possible 10-39, on North Warren Avenue at the Pima Youth Center. Be advised, firearms have been reported, and we have two individuals who say they feel threatened, looking for nearest units to respond. Please advise. Over."

A 10-30 was just a disturbance; a 10-39 was a possible "serious incident." That would require a large response. Hayes snatched up the mic. "Roger, dispatch, Unit 327 on CODE 7 right now, but I'm less than a block away and can check it out."

"10-4, Unit 327. We'll have you a Patrol 10-84 momentarily—"

"Negative, dispatch, negative. Will advise on backup. I've been on North Warren and around the area for nearly an hour and haven't seen anything. I suspect this is a 10-42, kids messing with us. I'm going to circle the block a few times, see if I can see anything worthwhile. Over."

"10-2, Unit 327, let us know. Over and out."

He held onto the mic and waited thirty seconds, watching as one of Manolo's men circled the building. He'd cut off any attempt to flee out the back, Hayes figured. The gangster was gathering the remainder out front.

Jesus H, how many guns did he bring? There had to be ten guys waiting to pile in through the front doors.

The clock on the dash kicked over to eight forty. He depressed the mic's call button again. "Unit 327 to dispatch, unit 327 to dispatch, come in. Over."

"Dispatch to Unit 327, go ahead, 327. Over."

"Yeah, you're going to want to cancel that call, dispatch," Hayes said. "I saw some kids giggling as they ran south on Cherry. You know what they're like these days; they're going to be a pain in the ass for at least the next hour, I figure. I'll see if I can track them down. Over."

The dispatcher sounded tired. "Yeah, 10-4, Unit 327. I should've known better. Thanks for the check. Over and out."

Hayes hung the mic receiver back on its cradle. That would keep his co-workers out of Manolo's hair for at least an hour or two, more than enough time to get the job done. Legit calls got missed all the time, after all.

What was one more?

He dialed Manolo's phone and watched through the windshield as he answered it, standing next to the doors. "What?"

"They're in there. They just made a call to dispatch, which reports two individuals inside. A hundred percent, it's Tito and Bob."

"Understood."

Hayes ended the call. He put the unmarked sedan into reverse and backed out of the slip. When the deed was done, he wanted his car's radio beacon at least halfway across the city. Blowing a call was one thing; being present for an ensuing shoot-out was quite another.

It wouldn't be long. Once they were inside, their

numbers would overwhelm Bob and Tito. They would kill both men and dump them in the desert, and any question of what had happened to Martin Guevara would die with them.

THE FRONT DOORS WERE STURDY, reinforced with metal. But the deadbolt and latch weren't designed to keep out nearly a dozen men.

It rattled and buckled and rattled some more.

Manolo hung up on Hayes's call.

"What if they're not there, *carnal?*" his brother Cesar asked, a Sig pistol in his right hand.

"They're there. One of them just called the police dispatch line, and the bastard intercepted it for us."

The bastard, or "El Cabrón," as Manolo's men had come to know Detective Hayes, was the man they all trusted least, even less than their mercurial boss. But when it came to avoiding police attention, he was useful.

"On three: one, two, three!" The men smashed shoulders into the doors a fourth time, wood around the hasp cracking and splintering, the entry giving way.

Manolo held up a hand and shushed his men. "See?" he told Cesar. "No alarms. They turned them off because they can't stay inside with them on."

Both men nodded and headed towards the corner of the building.

"Cesar, you guard the front doors with Max, make sure we aren't disturbed. The last thing we need is their nun friend or some other innocent walking in on this shit, adding to what we've got to do. Ethan and Mike, you search the café and lobby area. Saul, Artur and Nacho are with me in the rec room. Everyone keeps their earpiece in and the channel open, you got me? Let's go."

The men drew their pistols and chambered rounds. Ethan cautiously pulled the left-side door open, and they began to file inside.

25

Heading back to the apartment was out of the question, Bob had decided.

Bailing out of the limo meant they wouldn't be able to identify the building. But Manolo would have men around the neighborhood, looking, keeping an eye out for anything out of the ordinary.

He needed to assess the situation, figure out what happened to Tito, and...

Mike. Shit.

He walked briskly to a family restaurant a few blocks ahead and got a booth table, away from the windows. The sun was low, night beginning to set in. The restaurant was nearly empty, a man on a stool having lunch at the counter, a short-order cook-cum-server behind the counter, paying all his attention to the hot grill; a foursome sat in a booth along the far wall.

The place smelled of chili powder.

He dialed Mike's number. The man behind the counter

noticed him and brought over a menu, tossing it casually onto the vinyl tabletop, then retreating to his station.

The call rang twice before it was answered. "Bob. Jeeeeesus Christ, Bob. Jeeesus Christ," Tardif said.

"Mike... I'm sorry, man. I swear I had no intention of bringing this to your door. Where are you?"

"I'm home. I had a cop call me, a guy named Hayes—"

"Yeah. Yeah, he's a hard case."

"He says you're making up some shit about those guys robbing the depot. I told him that's what happened. But I figure we both know that's not true, right?"

"Mike—"

"Bobby... I can't have that kind of trouble around. I got a call from head office that the landlord had to call animal control to remove a jaguar. A *fucking jaguar,* Bob! From the second floor! What the hell?"

"They're gangsters. They hurt a friend of mine, and I pissed them off in return. That's all this is."

"Can't happen," Mike said. "I'm sorry, bud—"

Don't say it. Please. It wasn't like he needed the money, not anytime soon. But Bob liked the job and was tired of always moving on, tired of being the problem.

"—but I've got to let you go. Assuming this other dealie all works out for you and such, come by on Friday, and I'll see if I can cut you a check for some severance. It won't be much because head office is a son of a bitch, but—"

"Mike... It's okay. I get it," Bob said. He couldn't blame the man.

"Like I said..."

"Assuming it turns out okay. Thank you for warning me when they were holding you. That took guts."

"Yeah."

It had become awkward. "I'll see you on Friday," Bob said. He ended the call before Mike made it any worse.

He dialed Tito.

A waitress stopped beside Bob's booth table and poured him a coffee.

"Appreciated," he said.

She carried the pot back towards the counter as his call rang through.

"Bob! Where are you, man?"

Tito practically hissed it through his teeth. Bob recognized the sound of someone under immediate threat. "What's going on?"

"We're at Pima Youth Center," he said. "The office has a steel door, *ese*, but Manolo's got two carloads of his boys here. I don't know how long we can hold out."

"I'm on my way. Don't leave the secure area under any circumstance, you hear me?"

"Yeah, yeah, of course!"

"I'll be right there. Bye." Bob ended the call, took out his wallet, and tossed a five on the table.

He ran outside and dialed a hire car, his eyes peeled for a cab on the street. There were none. He looked down at the app on his phone. The nearest car was more than five minutes away.

Fuck. If ever there was a time when you needed your own wheels, Bobby...

A younger couple approached a brand-new Tesla parked at the curb. Bob jogged over to them. The man fumbled with his key fob and looked nervous.

"I need your car," Bob said.

The young man was small, but brave. He reached inside his jacket as his girlfriend backed away in fear. Bob saw the chrome of the pistol before it cleared the coat. He grabbed the man's wrist and forced it straight down, then reached up and grabbed him by the back of the hair. "Hey!" Bob shook the gun loose even as he pulled the man's head backwards by the scruff. "I'll leave it intact, undamaged." He snatched the gun from the man and stuck it in his own waistband. "With your gun and some money for your troubles. Give me the keys."

The man held his hand back and up, his reluctance obvious.

"I have your gun. I'm stealing your car. Think about what comes next," Bob said.

The young man handed over the keys.

26

Tito sat leaning against the wall of the rear main office, surrounded by empty chairs and desks, the room bathed in the faint glow of the emergency lights. He had the pistol in hand, hanging suspended between his raised knees. He looked despondent.

Sister Eva occupied a typing chair behind the last desk. She'd rarely felt helpless in her second life as a woman of God, but the situation was growing more dire by the minute.

"They're going to get that door off, and then I'm going to have to shoot back," Tito eventually said. "I... I just don't want you all shocked, like at the convent, when things get violent."

"Nobody has to be shot," she said gently. But she wasn't sure it sounded convincing, or that she even believed it herself.

He raised his head and looked over at her. "You think I'm just another criminal." He made it sound like a statement.

"I don't think that of anyone."

"Anyone?" He scoffed at that. "Please, Sister... you're

telling me you think the guys on the other side of that door have some sweetness and light in them?"

"I think anyone can redeem themselves in God's eyes. Maybe not always in humanity's. But even the worst of us has someone they loved, something that mattered to them. Something other than themselves they'd fight for. It's too easy to just think in black-and-white terms, good and evil, right and wrong. Everyone has more or less of either, but I don't believe I've met a soul who couldn't be saved. And in my experience, people appreciate being saved."

"Huh. Like Manolo."

He sounded almost wry, she thought. "Manolo?"

"Angel's enforcer, the guy who's probably out there leading them. He has this thing... He always tells his men about how he owes Angel for saving him."

She studied him. He looked grim most of the time. It made sense in the circumstances. "They're your friends."

"They were, some of them."

"And Manolo?"

"I barely know him."

"But he cares about his boss because he figures his boss cared about him."

"In a sick sort of way... yeah," Tito said. "Like me and Bob. I don't know him, either, you know that, right? *Es verdad!* He just showed up one day, picked me up off the street. Acted like people should act, you know? Why'd he do that? Why'd he take that chance?"

"Maybe he wasn't thinking about it," she said. "Maybe he's decided his default stance is to just be the good guy, even when it costs him. I think he's... well, he's tortured by a lot of things in his past, and he wants to make it right. And to him, that's helping people out. I can relate to that."

Tito looked skeptical. "No, *I* can relate to that. But *you*? How so?"

"I wasn't always a nun, Tito."

"No?"

She chuckled. "No! Of course not. We don't come out of the womb dressed as penguins!"

He smiled broadly at that, revealing big, white teeth. She hadn't seen Tito smile before. It was good.

"So... what did you do before this?"

"Before this? Before this, I ruined lives. Many, many more than you, Bob and every other person out there put together. I was a corporate executive in Silicon Valley and, prior to that, on Wall Street."

Tito looked shocked. People usually did, although she hadn't shared the story many times.

But maybe Tito needed to hear it.

"I was a very fortunate, very privileged young woman. Yes, I worked hard in school. But I also had a family with money, who could pay for an Ivy League education. I had a stable home life, generous parents who left their children to their own devices. We had a summer home on Nantucket. So it was a lot easier for me to do well in school, to take chances. I always had family to fall back on. But at that age, I didn't see any of that. I just saw a path to success, making even more money than my father."

"You were a corporate asshole," Tito ventured.

"Of the worst order. I saw everyone as a product of their own efforts, with no understanding at all of the pressures most people face, people in poverty, people with mental illness or mentally ill parents, people with developmental challenges. I saw people like you as beneath me, Tito, because you hadn't acquired the life I had. I had an immature perspective, poor emotional growth. By age twenty-eight, I was making nearly a million a year, had an apartment in the city that I owned, trips overseas, weekend cocktail parties, a boyfriend with a Ferrari."

"Sounds like the American Dream," he said.

"Sure. A dream. And then three days before Christmas, twenty-seven years ago, I laid off nearly five thousand employees. I did it before the end of the year so that the company could benefit by paying out less under their benefits package as part of their severance. By doing it at Christmas, I saved the company – a company with more than three billion in revenue the year prior – a spectacular twenty-three thousand dollars."

Tito's mouth had fallen open, his tongue probing his front teeth, a distant expression on his face. "Damn... you were... Damn..." He couldn't quite find the words.

"Yeah. Yeah, I was." She sighed bleakly and wide-eyed just then, the weight of it hitting her again, pinning her down like a mythical rock rolling down a hill. "I... heard about the first suicide on the local noon TV news the next day, while out Christmas shopping. There were a few others. By the time I got home, I could see the people around me, the other shoppers, the normalcy of their lives. Some happy, sure, some caught up in the holiday. But so many tired and pained and weary. And I could see the absurdity of my own life, the emptiness of it. The cost. What I'd done."

"Damn," Tito intoned again. "That's cold, sister."

She nodded gently. "Yes. It felt so."

"No... not how you felt. What you did. That's the coldest shit I ever heard."

"It was. My father, as distant as he could be, always gave to charity. He always talked about how he'd been poor in

Mexico and how lucky he'd been that his employer – he was just a gardener originally, cleaning backyards in Hollywood – how his employer helped him pay his way through college, helped him get his first job. So he gave to charity and was quietly generous, even though he was too emotionally restrained to talk to his own kids. For a long time, I saw caring for others as his one great weakness. But just then, I thought the one lesson I could take from his life to fix mine was that we always have more to give."

"You made it your life."

"Uh-huh. I'll never just look at you as a criminal, Tito. I see you with your boy, I see you trying to make it without the parasitic behavior of Angel Herrera, and I admire you."

Tito looked away quickly, and if she'd had to guess, Sister Eva supposed he got a little emotional at that.

And that felt right, too.

On the other side of the room, the handle turned. There was a dull thump as someone tried to open the locked steel door.

The handle began to rattle rapidly back and forth.

Tito rose to his haunches. "They've found us."

MANOLO STARED at the steel door, his arms crossed, his scowl unrestrained. "You're joking."

Saul shook his brown, shoulder-length locks. "No, boss. Steel-reinforced hinges. And I'm pretty sure it's a steel-reinforced wall, also. So cutting around it is out. They probably had a safe back here at some point when the building was—"

"I don't need no fucking history lesson, Saulie. I need that fucking door off."

The other man shrugged. "I've got my acetylene gear in the back of the SUV. I can cut through the hinges, but..."

Manolo tried to resist letting his head drop. He knew he needed to show leadership. "But what?"

"Like I said, inch-thick, reinforced steel. It's going to take a long time, boss. Like, an hour maybe?"

"You've got thirty minutes," Manolo said.

"But, boss, I'm not estimating, not really. I mean, that was already optimistic. It's going to take at least that."

Madre de... Can't they show any initiative? "You got another one of those blowtorch rigs?"

Saul nodded. "Hmmm... Sure at my nephew's shop. It's, like, five minutes away."

Again, Manolo restrained himself, biting his tongue. "Two hinges. Half the time. Math, *idiota!*" He turned to Nacho, Saul's usual working partner. "Nacho, go to the fucking shop and get the fucking torch. Do it in under ten minutes total and I may not shoot you."

Nacho nodded effusively. "Yes, boss!" He ran for the front doors.

"Wait!" Manolo called out. *Mother of God, he is stupid.* "Stop!"

Nacho stopped in place, confused.

"Saul, give him the keys."

Saul frowned. Then his eyebrows rose as he realized they'd almost blown it again. "Oh! Oh yeah." He fished the keys out and tossed them to Nacho. "Side door. It sticks a little. Alarm code is one-three-three-one. There's a little white panel just inside the door."

Nacho set off.

"Sorry, boss," Saul said. "I need to think more."

"You're damn right," Manolo said. "Forty minutes beats an hour. Let's go!"

Tito craned his ear to the crack of the doorjamb. The gap was almost imperceptible. He listened for about ten seconds.

"They've got a torch to cut through the door," he told her.

"You're sure?"

"I've welded enough body panels to know the sound of a blowtorch, so... yeah, I'm sure. They'll try to cut through the hinges."

He didn't want to scare her. For whatever she'd done in her earlier life, Tito had seen Sister Eva care for the poor of Tucson, for illegals and addicts, for the mentally ill. The idea of Manolo hurting her...

He chewed on his lower lip slightly to contain his rage. He hadn't shot anyone in a long, long time, not since Mexico. And as far as he knew, he'd never killed anyone. But the hour was drawing near.

"How long?" Sister Eva asked, her eyes tracing the contours of the room, looking for some advantage: a delay, a way out.

"I didn't look at the hinges when we came in. If they're bank-vault thick, a few hours. If they're office-security-door thick... I don't know, maybe an hour, maybe two."

"We can buy ourselves some time. These desks don't look that heavy on their own."

"Heavy enough to take two of us to lift," Tito said.

"Yes... but much heavier if they're stacked, weight working down—"

"In front of the door, along with the filing cabinets." Tito nodded. "It's a couple more minutes maybe. Worth trying."

The nun rose from her chair. "Let's get to work, then."

IT TOOK twenty minutes to get to the youth center, even with the electric car breaking every speed law with abandon.

Bob parked it two blocks north. The neighborhood was familiar to him; his first visit had effectively been recon, an exercise in knowing how to get away in the event of a visit from old friends.

He hadn't heard a peep from Washington, from Eddie Stone or Team Seven, in nearly seven months. It had been nice, putting all of the trouble behind him. Life had almost seemed normal.

And then Tito Agustin got himself thrown through a window.

Jesus H, my frikkin' life.

The building directly across the side road from the center was four stories, with a wrought-iron fire escape up one side. It offered a good overview. Bob pulled down the bottom ladder and climbed it to the second level.

One in the alley, two in front. But also two big SUVs, which could mean eight men, maybe more. Manolo wasn't with either group. Bob didn't recognize the guards, which meant at the very least, the two who'd chased him up the stairs at the depot were probably with him. The two men they'd fought in the alley were missing, also.

So... figure five more inside, maybe six.

The odds weren't good.

Time to even things up.

27

What is that?

It was the barest glint of light superimposed on stucco, a white circle about the size of a jar lid.

Little Terry – ironically nicknamed at six five and two hundred and eighty pounds – had been paying attention to both ends of the alley because it was full of debris, and that meant places for people to hide.

He'd been back there less than five minutes when he'd spotted the glare off the old pane of glass leaning against the opposite wall by the garbage cans. He'd also seen two rats, as well as a bum who'd stared down the alley from the east before deciding against the excursion. But there was no sign of police, the only presence that worried him.

In truth, he was happy, because he'd seen what Tito and Bob could do in a close-range fight. They'd be overwhelmed by the crew, that he did not doubt, but they'd do some damage first.

The alley, conversely, was sedate and safe.

Then he'd spotted the light reflection. It hadn't been there before. But that meant something had moved in the alley, and he hadn't noticed it.

They told me to stay by the door.

But...

I should just stay by the door.

He thought about calling it in, getting advice. But chances were good Manolo would just yell at him, tell him to shut the fuck up and order him back to his post.

It's nothing. I just didn't see it before, that's all. It was always there.

But he was pretty sure it hadn't been.

He looked both ways quickly again to be sure none of his colleagues were watching. Then he trod down the steps to the alley. He walked over to the spot by the trash cans and leaned down. He tried to follow the light back to its source.

There.

Beside a pile of debris – trash bags and crates, mostly – something was catching the streetlight from the other end of the alley, fifteen yards away, and bouncing it back across, through the old pane of glass and onto the wall.

It must have been there. It's probably just broken glass. You just didn't notice it.

Better be sure.

He crept fifteen feet over to the pile of refuse. He readied his pistol and moved to its edge, quickly swinging around the pile.

But there was no one. A roundish, jagged piece of glass had been propped against the wall at just the right angle...

He followed it back to the other side, turning his head just in time to see the elbow flying in, but unable to react and stop it. It crashed into the side of his chin, his legs giving way, everything fading out.

BOB CROUCHED beside the guard and removed his earpiece, putting it into his own ear. He recovered the man's pistol and pocketed it.

He stripped off the man's belt and used it to tie his hands. He took off one shoe and sock, then stuffed the sock into the guard's mouth just as he began to wake.

Forty seconds, or thereabouts. Not bad.

The man's arm jerked slightly, the autonomic nervous system playing catch-up as his brain tried to drag him back to consciousness. His eyes fluttered open, then widened when he saw Bob.

Bob leaned down on one knee and hit the man in the chin again with a short right. His eyes rolled back, and his lids closed once more.

He took off the man's remaining shoe and sock, using the latter to bind his ankles. Taking out one guard quietly was one thing. If he had multiple others inside, gunplay became a factor. He'd avoided it scrupulously and for too long to want to lean into it in the moment.

Then again...

Bob took the Smith & Wesson .45 revolver he'd confiscated from the Tesla owner out of his pocket. He opened the cylinder and emptied all six rounds into his hand.

He crouched beside the man and waited until he woke again, about forty seconds later. He looked confused for a moment as he came back from dreamland. Then his eyes widened, and he yelled through the sock, the sound utterly muffled.

"That's not going to work. The sock is blocking the sound waves before they even leave your mouth, for the most part." Bob held up the revolver, letting the dim light from the streetlamp glint off the chrome. "Nice gun. Let's play a little game." He reached into his pocket and took out a bullet. He held it up for the guard to see, then popped the cylinder on the revolver again, flicking the gun to one side so that it came open. He slid the round into the chamber. He tilted the gun and let the bullet slide back into his palm behind the cover of the grip, out of Terry's sight, gripping the hidden round with his little and ring fingers as he swung the cylinder closed again.

"You ever play Russian roulette before?" Bob asked.

The man's eyes widened like he'd just seen conjoined triplets. He shook his head vigorously.

"First time for everything," Bob said. He unlocked the cylinder and spun it manually, the perfect mechanism clicking gently as each chamber passed the hammer. He moved to Terry's side, dropping the loose round out of sight behind him in the process. He placed the barrel against the guard's temple. "Man... I hope this goes well for you because I need you to answer a question or two for me. Still, here goes attempt number one..."

The man's muffled protests sounded through his gag. Bob closed one eye and squinted theatrically, then squeezed the trigger. The hammer came down on an empty chamber. Terry bellowed through his gag, a heavily muffled scream, and squirmed in place like he'd been hit with a jolt of electricity.

Bob smiled broadly at him. "That was pretty thrilling, right? Like, you really relish the importance of living after that! Man... I don't know about you, but *I* was on the edge of my seat."

"Hnh-*mnnh*-mmh!" the guard protested.

"You want to try again?" Bob took a big breath, exuding a fatherly look of concern. "I don't know, sport. You're already up waaaay past your bedtime, champ. Kiddo. Slugger. But... okay!"

This time, he cocked the pistol, raised it and pulled the trigger in one smooth motion. Terry struggled and yelled, tipping over onto his side, kicking like a dying fish out of water. Then, quite suddenly, he stopped squirming and looked down at his jeans, where a darkening puddle was spreading across his groin. "Mmmmh..." he protested, almost forlornly.

Bob grinned at him and bobbed on his haunches. "This is fun! I'm telling you... wait a second; I don't know your name. Hang on... I'll take your gag out for a second, and if you scream or make any other sound other than telling me your name, assuming you might get another empty chamber... I'll pull the .45 you just dropped and blow your fucking brains all over the wall behind you. Got it?"

He took out the gag.

"Terrance. Terry," the man said, defeated.

Bob stuffed the gag back in. "Good boy. Terry, I can understand how, from your perspective right now, I might not seem a likable or personable fella. But the truth is, I'm actually the height of fairness. So I'm going to offer you a square deal, Terry, the kind you'd never get from a car dealer or a lawyer... or Angel Herrera. What are the names of your two friends out front?"

He removed the gag again.

"Gah... Cesar and Max."

Bob stuffed the gag back into his mouth. "I'm going to take this earpiece off and place it back on your head. When I do, you're going to call your two friends and ask them if they've seen anything. If they ask you in return, you'll confirm all is quiet. Got it?"

Terry nodded, his gaze burning a hole through Bob.

Bob took out the gag and placed the earpiece back over Terry's left ear. He removed the gag once more.

"Cesar, you got anything going on? Uh-huh. Nah, it's quiet here too," he said.

Bob tapped the earpiece to mute the mic. "Well?"

"He says it's all quiet."

"How many inside?"

Terry shrugged and stared at him with contempt.

Bob moved the gun from the big man's temple to his mouth. "This is chambered in .45 caliber, and I do sort of wonder how wide the hole in the back of your skull is going to be from this range. Or... we can play another game of Russian roulette. I didn't spin the cylinder again... so your odds now are down to one in four. I mean, you *probably* won't die immediately because even a headshot can take its time, but..."

"Seven! Seven. Manolo, his brother Cesar on the door, five more guys."

"Names."

He looked puzzled, but muttered, "Uh, Ethan, Saul, Nacho, Cesar, I think I said him already..."

"That's probably enough. Thank you." Bob stuffed the gag back into Terry's mouth. Then he flipped the pistol around and clubbed the guard across the side of the chin with the grip. He slipped back, unconscious.

Bob took the earpiece mic back and put it on. He rifled Terry's pockets.

He withdrew a set of keys with his right hand. He took another look at the back door. It was steel, reinforced, with a peephole, like the door he'd noticed in the office area. Getting through it would prove difficult.

But now I have other options.

28

Bob crossed the side street and headed a block east before circling south and west until he was on the block just north of the youth center. There were restaurants nearby, but it was a hot night, the patios empty, patrons opting for air-conditioned comfort.

The sidewalks were empty, deserted as nine o'clock approached.

He hugged the shadows of the three-story building across the street until he reached the corner of Seventh Street. He peeked around the corner.

Two men. The one in front of the doors has a shotgun, although he's trying to hold it behind him. The other guy...

He smiled and leaned back into cover. *Old operational habits kicking in.* The other man was wandering slightly, undisciplined. When guards weren't properly trained, they didn't understand how slight position changes could undermine them.

A steady chatter of guys talking in rapid-fire Spanish filled the earpiece. Evidently, Manolo had them on an open channel. Bob listened as he barked at two men who were cutting through something.

A door?

The steel door to the offices.

From Manolo's excitement, it sounded like they would be through the door before too long. Then it wouldn't matter how many of them he could take out; they'd kill Tito before Bob even reached him.

He checked the corner again. The two guards were about fifty feet away and clearly overconfident. The wanderer was occasionally strolling in front of shotgun guy, blocking the other man's view for a split second.

Nearer, parked on a slant at the opposite curb and just twenty feet from Bob, sat the two SUVs. *And they've even parked them facing the road for me. Having a nun for a buddy is starting to pay off in the luck department.*

It had occurred to him as soon as the back-door guard had told him how many were inside that he needed to even up the odds. But he was trying to maintain his pledge to not kill anyone, at least not deliberately. If they go as collateral, given the circumstances...

He wondered how his conscience would handle that.

Probably too easily.

And that was its own source of worry.

For now, he needed a distraction that would allow him to enter the building safely.

He backtracked up the block, to the next alley. An idea was forming, but he needed the right tool.

Time to give Manolo a serious headache.

·   ·   ·

TITO AND SISTER EVA stared at the jet of blue flame as it peeked through the upper hinge.

"They're almost through the first," Tito said. "Second won't be long. The furniture won't delay them much beyond that." He drew the pistol.

"Please," Sister Eva implored. "Don't just start shooting when they come through the door. Perhaps there's still a way we can resolve this without violence." She studied the room again, looking for any sign of another way out, seeing nothing. "Maybe the police will still get here."

"They're not coming," Tito said. "It's been a half hour, maybe more. If they were coming, they'd be here already."

"I don't understand—" Sister Eva began.

"Hayes," Tito explained. "They have a cop on the take. He probably heard your call go out from their dispatchers, and he shut it down."

She stared at her shoes as she contemplated the possibility. "There has to be another solution than guns," she said. "Maybe something just went wrong somewhere else. Perhaps they were sending a car, and it was distracted by another call."

"Sister—"

"I should try, at least," Sister Eva insisted. She took out her phone and called back.

"911 Emergency, go ahead, please."

"Hello, I called a few minutes ago. From the Pima Youth Center—"

"Stand by, caller..." The line went silent for a moment. "Ah. Yes, there's a note here. The 'nun,' " the dispatcher said sarcastically. "Miss, you should know it's a felony offense to call the police with a prank call—"

"But I'm not—"

"We've had an officer look this over already, and we are far too busy for your nonsense, miss. We have people with real emergencies who need help. Govern yourself accordingly. Bye-bye now."

The call dropped.

Sister Eva stared at her phone.

"Told you."

She glared at Tito, then looked worriedly at his pistol.

"Sometimes, it's the only way," he said, feeling its heft in his right hand. "It's the only thing people like Manolo understand. If we had another choice, Sister, I think we'd have seen it by—"

He stopped mid-sentence. Tito looked around the room. "A moment..." He held up one hand, deep in thought. Then he swiveled quickly. "Where is the AC coming from in here?"

"I'm... not sure," Sister Eva admitted. They both looked around. There were no floor vents, no ceiling units. But the room was cool.

Tito walked to each corner of the room. He wet his index finger with saliva, then held it up as he moved to each area. Near the refrigerator in the corner, he stopped. "There's a draft here."

Sister Eva joined him. Tito reached behind the refrigerator and tried to pull it forward.

Behind it was a large air vent.

"Could we fit through that?" Sister Eva wondered aloud.

Tito nodded. "I think so. We just need to move this beast, then find a way to get the screws out."

A look of recognition crossed the nun's face. "Hold on a sec." She opened the refrigerator door and withdrew a dinner plate covered in plastic.

"Leftovers?" Tito queried, confused.

She pulled off the wrap. "Butter knife." The nun retrieved the dull blade and set the plate down on the nearest desk. "Think that'll do it?"

Tito shrugged. "We're going to have to try. The mag on this piece only carries seven; that's not enough bullets to go around."

She moved to the other side of the refrigerator. Together, they began to shuffle the heavy object out of its spot.

MANOLO LOOKED AT HIS PHONE. By his rough count, the forty minutes were almost up. Saul and Nacho worked on the lower hinge, both torches trained on it.

He tapped Saul on the shoulder. "How much longer?"

Saul lifted his face shield. "It's going good. Any minute, boss. Maybe five, tops."

He called through to the men at the front of the building. "Ethan, you seeing anything?"

"Still quiet, boss man."

"We're going in in about five minutes. When you hear that door come down, I need you and Mike back here right away, you got that?"

"Uh-huh."

His phone rang. He checked the screen.

Angel. "What's up?"

"Is it done?"

"Not yet. But not long."

"Good. That thing the other day in my office—"

"With Cucho?"

"You didn't see or hear any of that. Got it?"

"Of course."

"Call me when it's done."

29

The twin flames were slicing through the second hinge rapidly. Tito checked over his shoulder as he worked on the half-dozen screws surrounding the vent cover.

"I think they're almost through," Sister Eva muttered. She hoped he would hurry up.

"So do I," Tito said. The last two screws were proving difficult, one possibly cross-threaded, the other immobile. He turned the butter knife around in his hand so that the thicker edge would fully engage the stripped thread.

He smacked the handle forcefully. The stripped screw's head broke off, leaving the thread behind. "*Fuck!*" Then he looked over at the nun. "Sorry."

"What's wrong?"

"A screw broke. But it's okay. As long as I can get the other one off, we can force this one."

The hissing sound at the door loudened. There was a clunk of metal on concrete, part of a hinge tumbling to the ground. The door dropped off the bottom hinge, clanging loudly as it hit the polished concrete floor.

Almost as quickly, light appeared around its edges, a big enough crack for fingers to begin grasping it, to move it away. The stacked furniture leaned against it, making the work difficult.

Tito pushed down with all his force, feeling the butter knife begin to bend.

The screw's tension gave. He reached down and finished the job with his thumb and forefinger. Tito pulled the screen away from the vent.

"Go!" Sister Eva said. "They don't care about me. They won't hurt me."

Tito looked horrified. "Sister, I'm not leaving you."

She reached down suddenly and grabbed the gun, forcing it from his hands. "I shall delay them while you get out. We don't even know where that leads, but it's better than here. *Go!* I'll be right behind you."

"Sister—"

"Go, or I shall turn myself in with you, and we can both face whatever fate Manolo has for us."

Tito shook his head vigorously, but it was clear she would not budge. He grasped the edge of the chest-high vent and pulled himself up. Sister Eva helped push his legs up and inside.

Behind her, she heard a crash as the topmost desk was pushed off the pile in front of the door. She looked back. Tito had scrambled ahead a few yards, but his feet weren't yet even at the T junction just visible at the end of the shaft.

A thought occurred to her. She looked up and smiled.

Ah. That's it, then; that's why I'm still here, even though the cancer should've taken me months ago. You're an odd sort, you know, Lord...

She calmly reached down and picked up the vent cover, then put it back into place over the end of the shaft, hastily sticking the screws back in the holes just enough to hold it in place. She took a few paces back, then leaned into the refrigerator with all her weight and strength, managing to slide it back so that it was at least straight, if not flush with the wall.

A boot crashed through the doorway and into the next desk and filing cabinet, sending them crashing to the floor. A man's arm appeared, trying to hold the doorjamb for leverage. It wouldn't be long now.

BOB STOOD at the corner and waited until the wanderer was careless once more, drifting in front of the guard with the shotgun. He darted around the corner to the first SUV, crouching below its roofline until he was by the door.

He tapped the earpiece's call button. "Ethan, you guys should see this shit out front," he said loudly. He closed the channel and shifted his attention to the two guards.

Bob watched as one guard wandered a few feet right, waiting until he'd returned and the shotgun carrier's view was again blocked. Then Bob opened the driver's side door just wide enough to reach in and start the SUV.

He knew he only had seconds. The SUV's headlights flashed to life. Even thirty feet away, the men would notice it quickly. He reached across the seat and slipped the automatic transmission into neutral, thankful the street was flat. He reached down in front of the driver's seat, a length of rusting pipe from the alley in his left hand. Bob wedged the near end against the front of the driver's seat, its other end against the gas pedal. He angled it down until the engine was revving heavily.

He looked up and around the front end of the SUV. Sure enough, both guards had taken an interest and wandered a few steps towards the road. Bob reached across the seat and depressed the lock on the shifter. He slid it into drive and yanked his arm out as the vehicle shot forward, momentum slamming the driver's side door as it careened towards the rec center.

Bob ran behind it.

The two men realized quickly that the vehicle was heading straight for them, as did the two others who had moved to the front window on request.

One of them would be Ethan, then.

The guards dove in different directions as the SUV crashed through the front plate-glass window, a hail of glass splinters and broken wood flying as it ground to a halt, the pipe having popped loose.

The first man was struggling to get up, almost to his knees. Bob reached him and threw a straight right while still moving, the guard stunned.

He picked up the man's shotgun just as his colleague peered cautiously around the SUV. He saw Bob, and his eyes widened. He looked around for his pistol lying ten feet away on the pavement.

His hand was grazing the grip when the shotgun butt caught him flush, laying him out. Bob circled the SUV and looked through the hole it had created. He saw the flash of a pistol and ducked just as a pair of bullets shattered the SUV's windshield. Bob crouched and circled the vehicle clockwise. The shooter was three feet from the front left bumper, his gun braced with both hands as he tried to peer through the half-lit room to his adversary.

Bob used a forward roll to close the distance, staying below the man's line of sight for just long enough to gain a positional advantage. He shot out a hard side kick, his attacker's feet swept, the gun going off again as the man slammed to the ground, back first.

He crouched and hammered the man once in the jaw. Not using a gun was proving difficult. *The two guards will be conscious momentarily. And this guy right after them. This isn't going to work.*

There were too many, he knew, to just knock them cold for two minutes. By the time he reached Sister Eva and Tito, they'd be back in the fight, and he'd be overwhelmed.

In his ear, he heard Manolo. "WHAT THE FUCK IS GOING ON OUT THERE? WE'RE ALMOST THROUGH, GODDAMN IT!"

Near the back of the building, Bob heard a loud clang, as if metal had been dropped onto the concrete.

The security door. They're through the door.

To his left, he saw a flash of movement from the area of weight machines. He threw himself sideways just as a fourth guard popped out of cover and opened fire. Bob scrambled along the floor, between overturned café tables, as the gunman tried to sight him, bullets pinging off the tile. Just ahead, a glass salt shaker rolled slowly in front of him.

Bob grabbed it and jumped sideways, turning in mid-leap and spotting the man. He hurled the salt shaker sidearm, doing his best impression of a shortstop. It slammed into the man's forehead with a disturbing crack, his assailant slumping over onto his side.

He clambered to his feet, not seeing the fist until it was

too late, the punch catching him square in the jaw, his legs instantly rubbery as he crashed backwards into a table and collapsed to the ground.

30

The last desk was being shoved out of the way, two men clambering past the broken furniture in front of the door, when the massive crashing sound rang out, an unmistakable chorus of broken glass and splintered wood.

Gunshots sounded towards the front of the building.

A figure tried to reach around the remnants of the final filing cabinet, a gun protruding into the room.

That would be Manolo.

It had only been a few seconds since covering up for Tito. They would realize immediately that he had escaped somehow, begin scouring the building and surrounding area. She had no idea if he was even free and clear yet.

I need to buy him some time.

She raised the pistol and fired twice in the general direction of the two men, making sure her aim was well above their heads.

They ducked out of the doorway.

"*Tito, pequeño hijo de puta sucia... es mejor que te rindas, hombre. Tu amigo gringo no va a salvarte...*" Give up, Tito, you dirty little motherfucker. Your gringo friend can't save you...

Gringo? Sister Eva felt vaguely insulted, even though she realized they meant Bob. But she kept quiet; the longer it took them to realize Tito was gone, the better.

"What you got there, a Glock?" Manolo called out. "You've got maybe five more in the mag. That ain't going to be enough, *cabrón*. You might get a couple of us; your buddy Bob might get a couple more. But the rest will still kill you, homes. Or, you could give yourselves up, come quiet."

From the same spot, she could hear the faintest chatter, as if two men were arguing in Spanish. Something was irking them, big time.

The crashing sound?

Bob.

He's come to save us.

But... he was terribly outnumbered, she knew; it would have been better if he hadn't come.

THE GUARD WAS over him in a second, the gun pointed down at his face. Bob reacted with instinct, rolling sideways, sweeping his right leg around in a semicircle halfway, tripping the man.

His attacker, the guard named Cesar, slammed butt-first to the ground. He tried to right himself, but Bob was quicker, turning sideways and hammering the man's chin with his elbow. Bob righted himself, snatching up Cesar's pistol as he climbed to his feet.

A figure was pushing past the debris by the SUV. *Enough of this. "Gunplay" doesn't have to mean "fatal."* He raised the pistol, chambering a bullet in the same motion, and shot the oncomer in the left thigh. The man bellowed and collapsed clutching it.

Training was to always aim center mass, take the target down quickly. But the circumstances were unorthodox, his methods restricted.

Works for me. He turned and shot the prone attacker on the floor through the same thigh. A few feet away, Ethan was shaking off the concussive blow from the salt shaker. Bob shot him twice in the legs for good measure. He screamed loudly and collapsed again, clutching the wounds.

Now where's...

The thought had only just occurred when Cesar rounded the SUV, a butterfly knife in hand. He charged at Bob.

Bob didn't move an inch until he was within eight feet, for the sake of accuracy. The pistol spit fire, the guard collapsing next to his friends on the lounge floor.

From the back of the building, he heard two shots. He sprinted towards the offices, past the pool tables and the gym area to the rear corridor. He peered around the corner in time to see Manolo and two other men leaning into the room, pistols raised.

A shot rang out from somewhere ahead of them. All three men reacted in tandem, raising their pistols again and peppering the room with bullets. Bob ran at them, raising the pistol and opening fire, trying to draw their attention away from the room beyond.

Manolo turned and spotted him, firing twice. Bob ducked behind the corner of the corridor into cover.

Behind him, a police klaxon blared its arrival, followed by a second.

"Shit!" The shorter man next to Manolo was trying to get

his attention. "It's not Tito in there," he said, just loudly enough for Bob to hear at the end of the hall.

"*Ay, coño!*" Manolo exclaimed loudly. "Back door, now!"

Bob leaned around the corner and took another shot, catching the smaller man in the shoulder. "Ay!" he screamed. The force carried him into the doorjamb. Bob dropped back into cover. He peeked around the corner quickly. Manolo was leading his men off to the right, to where the corridor wound around the offices and to the back door.

So much for loyalty. The men up front will be surrendering to the cops right about now... He waited a moment until they were out of sight, then ran for the door and climbed through, over the office debris.

"Eva!" Bob yelled.

The nun lay in the middle of the room on her back, the front of her blouse stained crimson from her wounds. He ran over and knelt beside her. She'd been hit at least three times, one near dead center, another catching a lung, blood pooling at the corners of her mouth. She was barely conscious, her eyes narrowed, breath short.

"We have to get you out of here, to a hospital..."

"No time," she muttered. "It's okay, Bob. It's okay. Tito got away..."

"Eva..." Bob cradled her head in his hands. He was supposed to be operational, he knew, but for the first time he could remember, he was filled with panic, his hands trembling, tears beginning to fill his eyes. "Please, Eva, I need to get you up..."

"Won't be long," she said, her eyes fluttering. "Knew He needed me..."

"What? Please... don't... Eva..."

"Needed me for one more save." She smiled serenely as

she said it. "That's... that's why the cancer didn't take me. Wasn't you; it was Tito."

"Please, no..." Bob could feel more tears coming, streaming down his cheeks, frustration a white, explosive heat.

It was the impotence of watching her leave him.

"It's okay! It's okay, Bob," she said. "God loves me! He'll look out for you, even when you don't. He knows how worthy you are."

She reached up with what he knew must have been great effort, her fingertips gently stroking his cheek.

"Accept it. Accept..." She took a sharp breath, her eyes suddenly dazzled, or perhaps just opened to a newer truth, her hand drifting from his face, falling back down beside her. Her eyelids fluttered. "Accept you are loved, Bobby. Be happy for me."

Her lids stopped fluttering, the light behind her eyes gone in a moment. Bob reached down and closed them, his soul scalded.

There was a bang behind him, towards the front of the center, a crash of objects being moved.

I can't do anything else for her. I can't stay here with her.

I can't bring her back.

I can't do anything.

He got up and ran out of the room, following the corridor around it to the back door.

Police cruisers sat at either end of the alley, blocking it off. Bob ran across the lane to the fire escape on the building due south and began to climb it. It wasn't the most direct route of egress, but it would keep them off his back until he could clear the scene.

On the rooftop, he wandered to the other side of the

building and the other fire escape. On the first wrought-iron landing, he stopped for just a moment, using his T-shirt to wipe the tears from his eyes.

There would be time for mourning later.

Now, somebody had to pay.

31

Angel Herrera stood in his office and stared, wide-eyed, at Manolo Marichal, an aghast expression on his face.

"Don't tell me that, Manolo! Don't say that again! *Don't you fucking say that!*"

"It's true. We thought it was Tito. She shot at us first, Angel, I swear."

"You killed a fucking *nun*? What the fuck have you done!?"

Manolo's eyes sought out the ceiling in obvious frustration. It had been a difficult night. "Don't worry, Angel..."

"Don't worry? *Don't worry?* I sent you to take out Tito Agustin, and you *shot a fucking nun!*"

"Hayes says he can fix this, make it look like our guys at the scene were trying to protect her from Tito. Then he can turn that warrant into a priority for the cops, because it's not just 'unsafe storage' anymore."

Angel looked away for a moment and exhaled a measure of stress. How the fuck was he always so calm? "So what you're telling me is you didn't get Tito; you didn't get his dude helping him..."

"Bob. I think he was the dude shooting at us when we were working on the door, but it was dark; he was in cover..."

"Bob... And you shot a nun. Not just a nun, but the saint of the fucking sewers, for all intents! You know, if I wasn't expecting a very important individual to walk through the front doors of this place in less than ten minutes, I would be sorely tempted to shoot you myself, Manolo, our history aside, eh?"

"I know, Angel." Manolo stared at the carpet. "I'm sorry."

It was worse than Manolo knew, though, Angel thought.

He'd planned on pinning Cucho's murder on Tito, serving him up to Hector Ramirez.

But if he did that, Ramirez would either kill Tito, removing Hayes's scapegoat for Sister Eva, or he'd believe that Tito had nothing to do with it... and tell the Omega Cartel that Angel sanctioned the murder of a holy person.

As ruthless as they could be, they were old-fashioned, outward benefactors to the church.

I would not last the week.

Fuck.

Then, a thought occurred. He waggled a finger as the idea settled in. "Ha! Yeah, yeah, that's what we've got to do."

"Boss?" Manolo asked.

"I figure maybe tonight didn't go so bad after all." He gestured to the door with a nod. "Go on, get out of here for the night; keep your head down. We'll work on the story with Hayes tonight and get the boys out on bail tomorrow. In the meantime, I have a very important meeting."

. . .

ANGEL TRIED to project his broadest, most welcoming smile. He'd chosen a sharp suit and a string tie, his favorite gator-skin cowboy boots. The idea was to make an immediate, striking impression.

He held both hands wide in a welcoming gesture as the figure crossed the room, from the front doors to the base of the stairs. "And who do we have here, eh?" he said cheerfully.

Hector Ramirez was tall and wide-shouldered, wearing all black, the dress shirt under his tightly tailored suit open at the neck. His expression didn't change as he crossed the room, followed by Nick the doorman. It was a look of utter indifference, as if he occupied a different plane of existence from the smaller man he approached.

His eyes drifted briefly up and down Angel Herrera. Then they flitted away, taking in the nightclub's entirety. Angel had prepared for the evening by closing it to the public, yet a dancer continued to swing around the pole on the central stage, in increasing undress.

Ramirez's attention returned to Angel. "Where is my cousin? Where is Cucho?"

Angel had spent nearly two hours that afternoon practicing every required facial expression in the mirror of his private bathroom.

First, solemn. He looked down at the floor, his hands ahead of him, tips pressed together in an inverted arch as he nodded solemnly. "I am most distressed to tell you that we still do not know, Hector. We have been chasing every lead, following every possibility for nearly a week, and we have not found him." He looked Ramirez in the eye as he concluded, holding the *sicario*'s gaze.

Solemn, sincere, grave.

Ramirez stared right back, unblinking. His pupils danced up and down as he took the measure of the man ahead of him. "Explain."

"We sent him to look for a man who has been bedeviling our operations here for two weeks, a man named Bob Fleming. We do not know why, but he has taken to interfering in our efforts to collect tribute, scared our dealers and girls... He is some sort of crazy gringo vigilante, a friend to illegals."

Sheepish, slightly embarrassed, like you know you need to do better. "I... confess, for the first day he was gone, I did not take it seriously, Hector. I did not believe anyone would be so foolish..."

"Yes, foolish," Ramirez intoned bloodlessly, staring right through him.

"But after two days, I sent my man Manolo and his crew looking. They turned the city over until this week. A few people think maybe he skipped town..."

"Are you calling my cousin a coward?"

"No! No, Hector, no, of course not. But perhaps he met a girl, or..."

"Or? Perhaps he met a girl?" Ramirez peered at him suspiciously. "I do not know what this bullshit you are trying to sell me is, but I know goddamn well my sister's boy would not walk out on his people. What aren't you telling me, Herrera?"

You expected this. Surprise, mild indignation, frustration. "Nothing, Hector! We are doing what we can! We are doing everything we can... we're just..."

"Failing," Ramirez intoned. But that was fine to Angel. It meant he was buying the narrative.

Prideful, responsible, respectful. Match his expectations. "Not failing!" Angel insisted. "We just have not succeeded yet, for which, I assure you, men will make respectful amends to Cucho when we find him. Hector... I am not stupid. I know exactly who you are and what can happen if we fail you... but I also must back my men, support their efforts. We are fully aware of and respect your power."

"Think hard on it," Ramirez suggested. "Let it guide your hand to steadiness, not shake it. Because I'm not leaving Tucson until I talk to my cousin."

32

The apartment had been out of the question. With most of its block occupied by businesses, it wouldn't have taken long for Manolo's crew to narrow down where they'd been staying.

Bob had turned up the collar of his jacket and headed south on foot instead, walking briskly. He took a brief break at a convenience store, using the pen at the lottery ticket counter to mark down a few phone numbers before dropping his phone in the store's wastebasket.

The store had burners, but he'd ignored them. People mistakenly thought pay-as-you-go phones were safe from surveillance unless the SIM card was cloned. In fact, law enforcement could track a phone just off its mobile identification number and tower triangulation, narrowing its location to less than 500 m in seconds.

If they found his first phone, they might assume he bought another at the store, check store tapes, demand serial numbers to match to MINs. His burner would then become a homing beacon. Better to wait until he was well away from the area.

A half hour later, he was several miles south, halfway along residential South Vine Avenue, dialing Tito's number.

It rang through, but he didn't answer.

Bob texted the number.

> We need to regroup. Had to get a new phone. Eva didn't make it.

His phone rang ten seconds later.

"Bob... fuck..."

"What happened? Why weren't you with her!? What happened!?"

"She had a plan. We were going to crawl out – there's a vent in the staff room, behind the refrigerator. Bob... she made me go first, insisted. Then she shut the vent behind me."

Bob wanted to scream at him, but he knew it wasn't Tito's fault, not really. He hadn't asked for Angel Herrera's deadly attention.

And screaming wasn't what Tito needed to hear. *Do right. Be the good guy. Tell him.* "She was already dying," he said instead. Tito deserved to know that. "She had terminal cancer and was already 'past due,' as she liked to put it. None of this was your fault, okay?"

"What did they do?"

"They shot her. From the gunshots... I think she was trying to delay them so that you could get clear. She fired first, I think. When they barged in, they probably just unloaded at the general position of a shooter. She took three to the chest."

"Acchh..." Tito made a sound like a dying, crying animal. "Bob... Bob, what have I done? What did I do?"

"Like I said..."

"Yeah... but I *left. I left her!*"

"She was a nun, but she wasn't a doe-eyed innocent; she was nobody's fool, Tito. You didn't force her hand. She told you what she needed you to hear to get you out of there, because she wanted the end to... she wanted her death to mean something. When what it mostly means is we'll never see her again."

Both men fell silent. The warm evening air rustled the handful of trees in yards along the street. Eventually, Tito asked, "What now? What the fuck do we do now, Bob? You can bet with Hayes involved, they're going to try to pin that shit on me."

"Did either of you think to call the cops?"

"Sister Eva. I figure Hayes called them off."

"That might work in our favor. The only way he can blame you is if he claims the guys after you were trying to protect her. The only way they identify you is after he's questioned all of them and cooked something up."

"So?"

"So... the only four he can officially question are all going to be in the hospital for at least a night with gunshot wounds to their legs. I didn't have any other quick way to restrain them."

"If I'm being real with you, you held back, *guey*. You could have just shot those fuckers. No one would miss them, not even their families. Maybe especially."

"I... yeah... Not an option for me, not right now. I have a difficult past."

"Uh-huh. It's going around, I guess. Ain't helping no one, now."

"We need to meet up, figure out how we handle this from here on in. Okay?" Bob didn't need an angry, vengeful Tito riding around Tucson.

"Where at?"

"You tell me. Your town. I'm near Vine and Manlove."

Tito thought on it for a second. "Okay, okay. There's a ball diamond nearby, Cherry Field. It's about five minutes' walk from you. I can be there in a half hour, tops."

"I'll meet you there."

THE SEDAN WAS a thirty-year-old rebuilt beater, but it functioned. The owner, plucked from an online classified ad, was willing to take cash for no paperwork. They drove south, both men staying silent until Tito began to worry that they were running out of city.

"Bob?" he asked eventually.

"Yeah?"

"Where the fuck are we going? I told you before, man, I can't leave the city. Not without Sean."

"We no longer have that luxury," Bob said. "Sean's in state care. He's safe. The only way you're going to be able to get him out after all of this is if we prove Hayes is dirty and works with Herrera. If we do that, Sister Eva has a friend at the police department who can show you had a reason to have a firearm, even an illegal one, and that Sean's fear was also at least justified. It won't get you off a charge for the gun or prevent him being expelled, but it'll get rid of the mounting felonies Hayes is going to try to pin on you, and explain Sean's actions."

Tito wasn't sure what to say to that. They were heading
down I19 on the city's western edge, the night sky a blue-
black carpet of stars, the desert around them dark and still.
"Okay. I mean, I guess if we don't got no choice."

"I don't see one. Your face is going to be all over the news.
By the time I showed, I suspect Hayes was long gone. He'll
have no evidence I was there. He can guess based on
Manolo's say-so, but Hayes will know that if he puts me out
there as the shooter, he risks me having an alibi elsewhere in
the city."

"True."

"But you? You're the guy hiding out, and she's your only
way to get inside the building. That puts you in the room
with her. So he'll try to pin it on you alone once he's figured
out a story with Manolo's injured men. They'll have you on
the noon news tomorrow, guy. I'm sorry, but... no. Tucson is
not your friend right now."

Tito went silent again. After a few more minutes of
driving, he lit a cigarette.

Bob rolled down his side window.

"Sorry, but—"

"Don't sweat it. But *two* windows open would be even
better."

Tito obliged, the low-bass rush of wind noise greeting
them.

"Got any idea where we're actually going?" Tito asked
after another few minutes, the borders of the city rolling past
them as they headed south.

"I only know one other person from Arizona. She used to
live in a town called Bisbee..."

"Yeah, everyone knows it," Tito said. "In the mountains,

big former copper mine there. Mostly a hippie tourist town now."

"My friend moved to New Orleans years ago, but she mentioned she and her husband lived there. I looked it up; it's far enough away, and small and weird enough, that I figure we can hole up in a motel there or something. They probably won't be thinking about your kid keeping you here, so they'll expect you to flee the state."

They drove on silently. Bob kept a close eye on his distraught companion; stress could make people do dangerous and stupid things, as he'd learned from personal experience.

"So how did you convince that lawyer to bail me out?" he eventually asked when Tito was beginning to look a little twitchy again.

"Tony Deal, yeah... too big a hitter for me, *ese*. I called my brother Ricky in Mexico City. He's the one who still talks to me. He's the one who won't kill me on sight."

Bob glanced sideways at him. "Really? Your oldest brother would kill you on sight?"

"That's how he made it sound last we talked... five years ago. I mean... he never really threatened it or nothing, but he don't talk to me; he don't talk about me. He don't offer me nothing."

"I suspect that, like most family, you may be worrying a little too much about how angry he is. He could be a bad dude, but..."

"He is that. Cold as ice."

"But he's still your brother."

"Hmm. Maybe. Maybe he don't see it that way."

"But your middle brother..."

"He was pretty goddamned pissed, I have to tell you."

"Does that mean you now owe his cartel a favor?"

"Nope. I told him if he helped me, it was because I'm his brother and he loves me... and I'm asking, and that's it. No tradeoffs or bullshit."

"And he went for that?"

He nodded. "Sure. Ricky's pretty easygoing, even though I pissed him off by leaving Mexico. It's my oldest brother who's the hard-ass. Him you don't mess with."

"I can see why you left."

"Yeah, it's true. My old man wasn't much better. Ricky... he's like the compromise position between my old man's violence and my mother's good nature. He's more the first than the second, though, so calling him wasn't easy."

"Well... thank you, anyway. Hayes was going to hold me in there for two days, use my truck's satnav to locate the apartment and you. Then I would've suffered a nasty fatal accident in remand."

The drive to Bisbee was just shy of a hundred miles and took them nearly two hours. Bob used a phone app to rent them a room for a night, until they could find something longer term.

The beater's engine chugged as it traversed the twisty, inclined road that led through the Sierra Vista mountains, past the massive, abandoned pit of the older copper mine.

Bob had read up on it before they left. Bisbee had once been the richest town between St. Louis and San Francisco, back in the days of the telegraph. It even had its own stock exchange, later converted into a nightclub, as well as a copper-roofed hotel with an old hand-crank elevator. The old courthouse was 1920s stark-white art deco, like something out of pre-war Los Angeles's boom. Most of the local businesses seemed to be antique stores, galleries, studios and other arts-related tourist traps.

The guesthouse was just a three-bedroom family home with a cabin in the backyard, the owner a jovial retired German national who loved the old West. He showed them to the cabin and left them with a key and fresh towels.

Bob closed the door behind them. "Pick a bunk and settle in. I'm going to head back at dawn."

"What?" Tito turned abruptly. "Are you kidding? Bob... man... think, like you told me! They're going to be looking for both of us, and you shot his guys, man; you fucked up his plans. Manolo wants your ass dead even more than me, I guarantee it."

"He's not the first. My track record in the matter is pretty good. Gerhardt, the German guy, says he has the next five days free, so you won't even have to move if all goes well. I'll leave you some cash to get food delivered. And besides, it's like I told you on the way here: we have to pin Hayes down on this, for Eva and your boy."

"How?"

"Well, I figured one thing: when he arrested me, he made a point of saying that coming after you was legit, because you're a 'material witness'... which raises the question—"

"Witness to what?" Tito said.

"Uh-huh. My guess is he thinks you saw him throw Martin Guevara off that roof, that maybe Martin gave you something right before, evidence of some kind. But he's got the wrong guy."

"So..."

"So I'm going to go find the actual witness. If he's sure there was one, there probably was, but we know it wasn't you. If I find that person, we have leverage."

"Then we get revenge for Sister Eva and Martin," Tito said.

"Not revenge. Justice," Bob said, "or maybe the closest we're going to get."

He needed to get some sleep, Bob knew.

He'd promised to return the Tesla driver's revolver, but circumstances had taken over. It weighed down his right coat pocket, the Sig Sauer nine mil he'd retrieved from Little Terry in his waistband. When he got back to Tucson, he'd drop it off at the Tesla, assuming it hadn't been towed yet. The owner had left his insurance papers – and home address – in the sun visor pocket. The least he could do, Bob figured, was try to get it back to the man.

Then he'd get down to business. If he couldn't get dirt on Hayes or Herrera, Bob knew what would inevitably have to happen.

It had been seven months since he'd had to kill anyone.

But some things in life were inevitable.

33

Sister Mary Rose closed the door to her apartment, at the far end of the convent property, and put on the safety chain.

Her trip to the store for cat litter had been a chance for a nice morning walk. She was typically up before dawn, and it had passed an hour earlier. In a half hour, she would cross the rear garden and go to work.

Before she could turn and face the living room, the sensation of someone else being there stopped her cold. For one, the room was too dim, as if someone had drawn the blinds while she was out.

"Sorry it's dark," a man's voice said from somewhere behind her, in the living room. "I didn't want anyone thinking someone was here when you weren't."

The voice was familiar, but she didn't immediately place it.

"I don't have any money," she said. "I'm going to turn on the light."

She switched on the overhead by the door and turned

around slowly. A strong-willed woman who brooked little nonsense, her fear gave way to annoyance almost as soon as she saw who it was.

"Bob."

"Mother Superior."

She crossed her arms. "Sister Eva," she said simply.

He didn't need any more of a prompt.

"I'm so sorry," Bob said. He rose. "I didn't get there in time. She was protecting Tito and sacrificed herself so that he could escape from Angel Herrera's thugs."

She pondered that. "I'm not surprised." She wandered over to the living room, arms still crossed, discomfort obvious. She nodded to his perch. "It was a difficult night. Police called us after ten to tell us. Please... sit down."

She sat down in the armchair opposite. "She didn't tell us about the cancer until a couple of months ago, you know. I suspect she was rightfully afraid I would try to limit her duties."

A single tear ebbed out of her right eye, tracking its way down her cheek. She wiped it away as if it didn't exist. "I was up late last night, making arrangements and informing her friends and colleagues. She was very special to us."

"I suspect she was to everybody who knew her," Bob said. "I can't let it go unchallenged, Sister Mary Rose. The men who did this—"

She wagged a finger. "I will *not* have you making this into a matter of revenge!" Her nostrils flared as she interrupted him, and he half expected her to leap out of her chair. "Not when there are innocents like that young boy involved, or the sisters! Not under any circumstance! Do you think Sister Eva would have considered that acceptable?"

"No, but—"

"It was a simple question."

"No," Bob continued, exercising his own semblance of patience, "but that's *not* what this is about. I have to go after the people who did this because they have no intention of stopping. Not, at least, until Tito and I are both dead."

"This is *not* your job or responsibility," she insisted. "The police—"

"The police can't keep one of their own from helping Angel Herrera, and they *know* he's dirty! Do you really think they're going to stick their necks out for the likes of Tito Agustin, an itinerant illegal migrant laborer? Come on!"

She took a moment to think about it. Eventually, she said, "Did you come here to argue with me, Bob? What do you want? Tell me. Tell me what I can do to help make all of this end."

"I need access to Sacred Heart."

"Absolutely not. Those men—"

"Would you wait until I've made the point before shooting me down? Please?"

She took a deep, cleansing breath to lower her stress momentarily. "Fine. Proceed."

"I need access to Sacred Heart because I believe one of the men there witnessed Martin Guevara being thrown off the roof by Detective Carter Hayes. They're trying to kill Tito because they think he is the witness."

"But he isn't, I take it?"

"No. And whoever it was may have more information Martin shared on Angel Herrera's operations. They're also in incredible danger. Once they realize it wasn't Tito…"

"The actual witness will be next."

"Exactly. And prior to falling off the wagon and winding

up at Sacred Heart again, Guevara drove for Herrera's coyotes."

A contemplative expression crossed her face. "Now I see. So, this entire time, you've been protecting the wrong man from being murdered."

"*Yes!* Yes... that's it exactly."

Her eyes narrowed as she peered at him, hands on her lap like a grandma about to knit something. "And you became involved in this... why? What was your motivation, Bob?"

He looked impatient with that. "I don't really have any. He was lying injured in the street. No one else was helping him. Someone had to."

"So you followed the parable of the Good Samaritan on the road to Jericho."

"Okay... sure. Not really a Bible guy."

"We're all Bible guys, Bob. It's His world, not ours."

He sighed, probably too loudly. "Okay."

"And after that? Why are you still the only person helping him? You're not a policeman or bodyguard or anything."

"I used to be in... ah, hell, let's call it law enforcement. Just... overseas, in mostly lawless situations. I have specific training and experience, and he has a young kid. I thought I could bail him out, and things escalated from there."

"Oh." That caught her by surprise. She looked mildly distressed. "But... you're one person. Angel Herrera has a large criminal organization in this city... you are aware of that?"

"Yeah... yeah, he's made that pretty clear."

"But... that's suicidal, Bob. Who are you going to help if you're dead?"

You'd be surprised. Officially, I've been dead for a long time. "Nevertheless... someone has to," he said instead, because her perception of the risk made it more likely she would help. "If I get the information I need from the shelter residents, I can maybe rig a solution that skirts all of that conflict... and me getting my head blown off in the process."

She looked distant for a moment. "I don't know. I'm not sure. Anything of this importance... the archbishop would have to make the call, I should think."

"And is there a chance they'll look at this not from a humanistic perspective, but from one of political expediency?" Bob asked. "Because if there is, you already know the answer."

She nodded and thought about it some more. She rose from her chair. "Would you like a coffee while I consider this?"

"Just a water would be nice," he said. "But we can't waste time. Tito's hiding, and I don't know how long—"

"When?" she interrupted as she walked over to the kitchen door. "When should we—"

"When are most residents at Sacred Heart? Early? Late?"

"Late," she said. "Most look for work during the day."

"Then late it is," he said. "But you're not coming. I can't risk it."

"Oh pish!" she said as she entered the kitchen. She leaned back to be seen through the doorway. "You don't have a choice in the matter."

34

The drive to Sacred Heart was quicker in the early evening, the rush-hour traffic long gone. Sister Mary Rose had a steely sort of focus, Bob had decided, even when driving.

She eventually broke the silence. "She asked for a cremation in her final wishes," she said. "I noted you hadn't asked yet."

"I sort of figured," Bob said. "She told me she hated the idea of her body decomposing while her spirit was soaring."

The Mother Superior showed a rare, personal moment, looking down for a brief second, a sly smile crossing her lips. Then her attention was back on the road. "She'd like that: her spirit soaring. She had more than most, I think. A truly good soul, happy with her time here."

"She didn't see herself that way," Bob said. "She was hung up on the past, just like the rest of us."

The nun glanced over at him, then returned her gaze to the road. "Tell yourself that if you want, Bob. I'm sure it will allow you to continue to wallow in whatever self-pity she was trying to help you abandon. But it will do you no good, and she wouldn't have approved."

Ouch. Mother Superior got barbs. "Don't be so shy and retiring, Mother Superior; tell me what you really think," Bob suggested dryly.

She looked at him again, and this time Bob felt more of a glare than curiosity. "You really are quite a typical man, Mr. Fleming," she said. "You're so certain you have it all figured out, yet you're unhappy. Those two don't really seem to fit, do they? Do you know what she did when she was younger?"

"Corporate type, sort of heartless. She didn't really get into the details."

"She wasn't proud of what she'd been. But she was so, so grateful to have been given another chance. A chance to lead a different sort of life, to start over and find respect, for herself and others. Does that remind you of anyone you've helped lately?"

"Tito."

"Tito Agustin, yes. Has he ever discussed being in a criminal organization in Mexico with you?"

"A little. No details, again."

"And again, it's because he's glad to have put it all behind him. Despite his alcoholism, for which we were trying to find him help before his friend was killed, he is a lovely, hardworking man with a nice boy. He learned to push back against the darkness, walk to the light."

"He did."

"But you? You, Mr. Fleming, are a coward."

What? Where the hell did that come from? "Excuse me?" He turned to look at her. She concentrated on the road. "I just waded through a firefight with ten gangsters to try to save our girl..."

"Ptth! Right there, you begin by fictionalizing things, adding the drama of Sister Eva being just a 'girl,' just someone else frail you need to save. Building a persona, the expendable hero, so that you can feel secure you know your-self, that you're doing all you can. Yes, yes, you were her 'sav-ior.' Of course, that didn't happen."

"But I sure as hell tried! What am I missing here? How am I the coward in this?"

"Because you can't bear to do what she wanted you to do: truly forgive yourself and rejoin society! If you do, you're giving up your de facto role as the underdog outlaw hero. Oh sure, it's really brave for a trained ex-military man to wade into a fight when he places little to no value on his own life! I'm sure you don't want to die, Bob, because you're a survivor. But the very reason you can take such chances, despite being so personally lost, is because you don't really want to live. You don't want to do what the rest of us must do every single day: take chances with our feelings, not our lives. Expose ourselves to the harshness of humanity, the insecurity, the rejection. You won't let yourself be hurt inside, so you let it happen on the outside."

Bob wasn't sure what to say. He wanted to tell her to shut up, to fuck off, even though she was a nun. Who was she to judge him? To judge his real motivations and feelings?

But he couldn't. A gnawing sense at the edge of his consciousness, a voice he didn't want to hear, was telling him that she was right.

You know it's fucking true, he finally said. Civilians, civilian life... it terrifies you. You'd rather fight maniacs like Angel Herrera and Alexi Pushkin, take a chance they'll finish you and solve the problem for you.

"You know... there's nothing wrong with fighting for

what you believe in and for yourself," she said. "You're allowed to love who you are, to be happy with yourself for becoming a better person, enjoy the company of others. No one is trapped in permanent penance by the passage of time. What's past has passed. It's what you do moving forward that matters."

He let out a lungful of air, letting his tension recede slightly. "She told me something similar. It's—"

"Difficult, I know."

"Even for a Mother Superior?"

"We all have a past, Bob. We all have reasons to fear being vulnerable, trusting others. But we only really lose when we give up."

SACRED HEART SHELTER WAS DARKENED, the front window blinds drawn, the doorman the only real acknowledgment that anyone inside it existed.

They climbed out of Sister Mary Rose's car. The Mother Superior locked it with an electronic key fob, to a reassuring beep. "Now please remember: you are to be respectful in all of your dealings. Our clients are human beings who have been unfortunate, not animals who can be—"

"I know," Bob interrupted. "I know, Sister, believe me."

The doorman recognized her. "Sister Mary!" he said, surprised. He pushed back greasy black shoulder-length hair. "We weren't expecting you. It's..." He fumbled for his phone. "Nine o'clock."

"Good evening, Joe. We waited until after dinner to ensure as many people were in as possible," she said.

"Full house, or just about," Joe said. "Father Bernard from the archdiocese came over before supper and gave a talk on drinking, how he quit." He nodded his head slightly in affirmation. "Good dude."

"He is. He is indeed a 'good dude,' " she said. "Joe, this is my friend Bob Fleming. He's going to be talking to some of the boys about Manny and Martin."

Bob reached out a hand. The doorman studied him warily but shook it. "We don't say his name around here no more," he said. He frowned, as if pained. "You think you know someone."

"It surprised you," Bob suggested.

Joe shrugged. "I mean... yeah, of course, dude. I'm from Bakersfield, and we've got our share of, you know, social problems and what have you. But Martin was... I mean, he wasn't the type you think could do something like that. But I guess who knows anymore."

"He didn't have any violence in him?"

"Nah. Nah, he was a peaceful dude. Really. I mean... I know I shouldn't say that now, what with what happened."

"Did you doubt the official story?"

The doorman looked down and away. "I don't want no trouble."

Well, that's an interesting reaction, Bob thought. "From Detective Hayes?"

Joe kept his eyes on the sidewalk. "Like I said, I don't want no trouble."

Bob looked past him to the door. "You mind if I take a look at something?" he asked the doorman.

"What? Sure." The man stood aside at Bob's gesture towards the handle.

Bob opened the door. He looked down at the gunshot damage. "So the story is that Martin Guevara came here with a piece, shot your doorman Manuel to get inside, then jumped off the roof."

"Yes," Sister Mary Rose confirmed.

Bob rattled the handle slightly. "This has been replaced."

Joe nodded. "Yeah, they figure he shot the handle because it was locked."

"Didn't Manny have a key?"

"Sure."

"Then... why didn't he just take the key off Manny's body, assuming he'd already shot him to get past him in the first place?"

Sister Mary Rose frowned. "That's a fair question. The official version provided by the police did not mention it."

Bob opened the door and looked at the inside panel. "The backplates were replaced as well," he said. "Why?"

"A bullet hole," Joe said. He reached down. "Right... about here."

Bob craned his neck and tilted his head, peering at it studiously. He looked over at Sister Mary Rose. "Does that make sense to you?"

"I'm... not sure I follow."

"If Martin was standing right in front of the door, how did one of his rounds manage to miss the door handle and mechanism by nearly three inches."

Joe shook his head slowly as he pondered it. "Maybe he was drunk? I think the cops said he was drunk, right?"

"He had a high blood-alcohol level, as I recall," Sister Mary Rose. "Why? What are you thinking, Bob?"

"Well... people have an odd view of pistols, from the movies. They think they're much more accurate than they are, when in fact most people, over about ten or fifteen feet, would have a hard time hitting a small target. But... from a foot away? I don't know how he misses by three inches, even if drunk. If it was a misfire, it would've been at an oblique angle, and the exit point would've been above the backplate. But the fact that there was a bullet hole in the inside plate means the shot was relatively lateral... which means the person who missed, the actual shooter, was probably solidly ten feet away when he unloaded."

"That... doesn't fit the narrative," the Mother Superior said.

"Not to mention the suicide no longer makes sense," Bob said. "If he had a gun to shoot the door lock off, he could've just blown his brains out. Instead, he chose to fall to his death? Makes no sense at all."

"But... he had the gun on his body," Joe said.

"Uh-huh."

Sister Mary Rose recognized the implication. "Detective Hayes shot Manny, then planted the gun on Martin Guevara," she said.

Bob nodded matter-of-factly. "The only part I don't get is why. Why shoot Manny the doorman when he could've just ordered him to let him in? I think Hayes marched Martin up to the roof and pushed him off. It's a shelter; he's a bum to most people. Who's going to check? But Manny... that I don't get yet."

"Maybe Tito does. Tito was here the night it happened," Joe said. "He was hanging around the back of the men's billet with Martin and Don Ambrose. Donny had some cards or something, and he was showing them. I was gone by four though, which was when Manny came on shift."

"Don Ambrose?" the Mother Superior questioned. She turned Bob's way. "I'm not here as often as I'd like, so some of the newer clients—"

"Donny Legs," Bob said. "I met him when Tito came over all liquored up."

Joe raised a hand by way of notification. "Look, Tito's not really like that," he said. "I mean, he may come across as a crazy Mexican dude and all, but he's really solid. Like, I know that sounds like bullshit from some drinking buddy or something, but he's actually a good guy."

Bob held in a broader smile than the bare straight line he chose to display. If there was one thing he'd learned to count on while living on the streets of Chicago, it was that poor people were better to each other than rich people.

"I know," he said instead. "That's kind of why we're here." He nodded to the ajar door. "Is Donny Legs here right now?"

THE INSIDE of the shelter was cool as a cucumber, air conditioning keeping the excess of bodies from overheating in the Tucson sun. The main client room consisted of twenty bunks, each with a small lockbox at its foot for personal belongings. Most of the beds were occupied, some sleeping, some reading books or texting, others sitting up and chatting with their neighbor.

But Donny Legs was nowhere to be seen.

Joe frowned. "I don't get it. He was just here, back corner to the left."

Bob's head swiveled that way, only to find the corner of the room empty, two cots without users. He scanned the room. "Where else could he go from here?"

"Upstairs, to the roof... I mean, it's locked, so there's not much risk of him trying, but there's a window in the bathroom down the hall that—"

The sound of crashing glass interrupted him.

Bob took off running, heading for the latrine.

35

B ob shoved open the swinging washroom door with his shoulder and ran inside.

The window was broken, tiny teeth of glass remaining around its outer edges.

A jean-clad leg and a sneaker were disappearing over the bottom of its frame.

He didn't follow, instead sprinting out of the bathroom and to the front door. He was just in time to see Donny Legs hightail it across the street and down an alley.

Bob gave chase.

Halfway along the lane, Donny tipped over a trash can, then another, trying to delay his pursuer. Bob hurdled each obstacle easily.

The shelter client turned the corner to his left at the end of the alley. Bob was just a few yards behind him, Donny's never-trained body no match for his fitness. He dove and grabbed the man by the collar, bringing them both crashing to the alley's concrete floor, Donny's blue ball cap flying off.

Donny tried to right himself, scuttling backwards on all fours, like a crab, towards the brick wall. He cowered beside a half-empty dumpster. "I didn't do nothing, I swear!" he pleaded. His teeth were rotten, a giant callus on his lip giving away years of using a crack pipe.

Bob rose to his feet. He towered over the tiny, terrified man. Then he crouched just ahead of him and retrieved the LA Dodgers cap he'd been wearing. He handed it back to the man. "I'm not here to hurt you, Donny, I promise. But I need your help."

Donny stopped pleading and looked puzzled. He snatched the cap out of Bob's hands and put it on. "My help? Me?"

"Uh-huh."

"You want *my* help?"

"You were at the shelter the night Manny and Martin were murdered." He made it a statement of fact. People were always less inclined to deny something the other party might already know was true.

Donny scoped the alley both ways, looking for options. "I... Like I said, I don't know nothing. I don't see nothing," he said.

"But you know it wasn't Martin who shot that front-door lock, don't you?"

Donny looked away abruptly. Then he said more softly than before, "There's nothing good comes of this, chief."

"Because? Doesn't Martin deserve justice?"

The younger man scoffed at that. "Justice, for street people? Are you joking? There's no justice for us. Nobody cares about us. The politicians are all millionaires; the public's tired. No one wants us to get ahead, have a life. No one cares how we feel. No one wants us to... I've... I've been on the pipe a long time..." His voice drifted at the end, his mind distracted, his ire forgotten in a moment of dazed self-reflection. Then he looked up again, his eyes flashing with indignation. "Average Joe doesn't give a shit about us. Nobody does."

"That's not true and you know it!" Bob insisted. He knew he probably sounded more exasperated than would help. Maybe it was just a day for people to hear hard truths. "Every person in that place works their ass off to try to help you, Donny! Sister Eva died yesterday trying to help Tito, trying to help a guy who already got off the street and out of Sacred Heart. He can do it. So you can do it."

"Now you're blaming me."

"No, I'm telling you they believe in you! She believed in you! She believed in pretty much everybody. And she's dead! And I need your help catching the person who did it! Or you could shit on her memory, tell her she's wrong, tell her you weren't really worth it. You could go back to being someone people like Hayes see as nothing but a bum. Is that really you? Really? Dig deep, and tell me who you see? Are you nothing better than a bum, Donny?"

Donny's nostrils flared, his jaw tight with umbrage. "N-n-no! Fuck you! Fuck you, I am not! Fuck no!"

"Then prove it. Help me. Just answer my questions. Tell me what you really know. That's it. It goes no further than this alley, and I won't ever ask you again unless they arrest the fucker and you're needed to keep it that way. Can you do that? Or am I still asking too much? Should I just give up fighting, Donny? Because... fuck... I don't want to. It's not me. Is it you?"

Donny Legs composed himself. He pushed himself up onto his haunches and accepted Bob's help getting to his feet.

"On the night Martin died," Bob asked, "was Hayes inside the shelter?"

Donny nodded affirmatively. He reached into his side pocket and withdrew a pack of Winstons, then lit one. He put on the ball cap. His hand shook as he raised the cigarette to his lips and took a drag. He exhaled and momentarily closed his eyes, stress subsiding somewhat. "Yeah... Yeah, he took him up on the roof. We were in the other room, playing cribbage. I beat Tito and won this cap... he loves the fucking Dodgers. Me, I just liked the hat."

Bob tried to get him back on focus. "So, Hayes... what, just comes in and grabs Martin by the arm?"

"Yeah, didn't even pause, just dragged him back towards the hallway."

"And did you go upstairs after them?"

Donny shook his head. "No... Uh-uh. I didn't see... you know."

Bob's eyes narrowed. Was he lying? "Then why does he think someone witnessed it?"

Donny shrugged. "I was coming out of the bathroom when he took him up the stairs. He sort of glanced back, but I figured he didn't see me. You can't really see the stairs from the main room."

"And you were wearing Tito's Dodgers cap."

"Yeah."

"So he mistook you for Tito and thinks Tito can put him on the roof, and maybe that's enough to prompt an investigation. But it was you."

"But I didn't see him do it, I swear. I... I'm sorry, man... I don't know what else to say..."

"And when he left?"

"He walks up to the door and from, like, ten feet away unloads with a gun. Fired... four shots, I think."

"It probably didn't occur to him until he was inside that he needed it to look like Martin forced his way in, so he destroyed the handle. Did you see the pistol type, the model?"

"Eh? I... don't really know that shit, dude..."

"And there was no struggle when he arrived?"

"Why would there be? He's a cop. You think Manny's barring a cop from entering a homeless shelter?"

Bob weighed what he'd been told. *Manny was a mistake, a moment of stupidity.*

"Tito was barred, right? For fighting?"

"Yeah, but he and Manny were tight, so he let him come in for a few hours, just to see Martin."

Hayes, probably a little high on coke, had decided to set up Martin for Manny's death. He'd tried to make it look like a forced entry. Only Manny was sitting in a wooden school chair outside the door.

Bob figured he knew enough. He gestured the way they'd come. "You should go get your stuff. I'll talk to Sister Mary Rose about finding you a place to stay for a few days until I can clear all of this up. Okay?"

"Sure."

They walked to the alley's entrance. The pieces of what had happened that night had begun to come together. But it still didn't quite make sense, Bob figured. What made them go after Martin in the first place? His experience as a driver?

If that had been enough, surely they'd have killed him before then.

Or maybe he took something.

He stopped walking. "Martin didn't leave anything with you, did he?"

Donny stopped. "Why?"

"That wasn't a no."

"Well... nothing that you'd care about."

"Not... like, a USB drive or a folder or something. Pictures, maybe? A binder?"

"Eh?" Donny peered at him, confused. "No. No!"

"Then what?"

The shelter resident sighed. "I have his cards."

"His..."

"Playing cards. He loved gin rummy and crib. He loved this deck, in particular, because the pattern on the back of the cards reminded him of his mother's place mats at dinner or some shit."

"And he gave them to you."

Donny looked a little puzzled. "Yeah. Yeah, he didn't really explain why."

"I don't suppose you're carrying them?"

Donny took a dark-blue box of cards out of his pocket. "I'll get these back?"

"If possible."

He handed them over. "Probably the best you can do, all things considered."

"Yep." Bob pocketed the cards. It seemed a stretch, but also the sort of deliberate act that might lead him somewhere. "He didn't say anything about them? Like maybe they had a purpose, or..."

Donny shrugged. "No. He told me to hang onto them."

But he stared at his feet for a moment as he said it, like a kid caught in the cookie jar.

"Donny... now, we're being honest about all this shit, right?"

Donny nodded balefully. "He told me to give them to Sister Eva or Father Pablo from the archdiocese."

"Anything else?"

He seemed plaintive. "I just wanted something to remember a friend by. There's no harm in that, is there?"

"No. But I need to know if he said anything else, Donny. A lot is riding on this."

He sighed. "Martin said, 'Tito knows where I get my mail.' I figured he was really drunk... and besides, it didn't matter much once he was dead, right?"

Had he mailed himself something? Bob wondered. *Maybe to a post-office box?*

The two men crossed the street to the shelter. Joe the doorman held the door for Donny. Sister Mary Rose came out to meet Bob.

"You caught up with him."

"He was helpful. He's a good guy; he's just really messed up. Hang on a sec: I have to make a call."

Bob dialed Tito's phone.

"Bob! Man, I'm getting bored as shit sitting here, *guey*..."

"No time right now, okay? Your friend Martin. Where did he get his mail?"

"Eh? General delivery, the main office, like most at the shelter. I mean, I think. Why?"

"I'll get back to you, thanks, man," Bob said. He ended the call.

"Now where to?" Sister Mary Rose asked.

"Nowhere. We need to settle in for the night, and you

need to find Donny a place to sleep. One of those nifty guest rooms at the convent should do it. Tomorrow morning, I go see a man about some paper and then head to the post office."

"The post office?" Her confusion was evident.

"A great American tradition, Sister," Bob said. "Tito says Martin used a little thing called general delivery."

36

The biker bar was self-evident, the kind of place that was its own warning.

A row of chopped and rebuilt Harley-Davidsons sat outside a log-cabin-style longhouse, along with a solitary, dented old pickup truck, its eggshell blue paint faded by the relentless desert sun.

The neon sign said "The Wasted Wench" in cartoon script, a pair of aces finishing things off.

Two men sat on a tiny outside porch as Hector Ramirez approached the front door. He wore the same all-black suit, shirt and tie that he favored for most work trips.

"Heeey, *cabrón*, nice threads!" one of them called out as he approached the door.

Ramirez ignored them both. Had either risen from his seat in threat, Ramirez would've shot him dead before he took a step, such was his dwindling patience with Tucson's criminal element. Instead, he paused briefly and fixed them with an icy stare before opening the door.

Inside, the room was boisterous. A jukebox was cranking

out Los Lonely Boys, Henry Garza's baritone growling a cover of The Doors' "Roadhouse Blues." Pool balls clacked in one corner while a stripper spun around a pole in the center of the room, bikers in denim, T-shirts and bandannas whistling at her as they lazed around low-slung white plastic tables.

Ramirez gauged the men inside, their body language. Along the left wall were booth tables. At the back corner, two men sat in relative quiet, a garishly dressed woman hanging off each of their shoulders.

He headed directly towards it.

He was ten feet away when two men stood up at nearby tables and moved to block his path.

"This club's private," the first said. He had a shaved head and arms covered by ink, as well as six inches and at least a hundred pounds on the *sicario*.

"*¿Eres el hijo de puta más grande y peligroso de aquí?*" *Are you the biggest, most dangerous fucker in here?* Ramirez asked.

The man said nothing, his sunglass-clad head barely nodding as a response.

"Good." Ramirez's foot came up with blinding speed, catching the man square in the testicles.

He doubled over in pain. Before his friend could react, the Gravedigger dropped to one knee and struck the outside of the bouncer's knee joint with a flattened palm, full force, the joint buckling inwards, ligaments tearing. "Aaaaayyy!" he exclaimed as he collapsed onto one side.

His friend looked down at his prone friend, then quickly returned his attention to Ramirez, his hand going into his coat, towards his waistband. The pistol came out smoothly, a practiced motion. Ramirez pivoted to his left, fluidly balanced on his right heel, then slammed the man's gun arm down and across his knee, the pistol flying off and clattering. He shot a side kick outwards immediately, anticipating fight-back and catching the bigger man in the solar plexus, his wind driven from him.

The two bouncers lay side by side, trying to recover, their guns lying on the floor.

The entire sequence took less than twenty seconds.

More men rose from their tables. Ramirez walked slowly towards the corner booth.

Pistols were cocked, raised in his direction from around the room.

The man at the table held up both hands. Then he silently motioned downwards with both, telling his people to calm down. "Everybody sit down and shut up. This is an important man, an honored guest."

The metallic clunk of a dozen guns being put away simultaneously rounded the room. Ramirez sniffed ever so slightly, the smell of burning weed and stale beer assaulting his nostrils.

The obvious leader approached his new arrival. He was smaller, in a fashion-cut jacket, with a head of curly tight black hair. His deference bordered on groveling. "Señor Ramirez." He held out his hand, and Ramirez accepted it. "It is an incredible honor to meet you, sir, of course."

"You are Eric Ladrón, the coyote?" Ramirez demanded.

"I am, sir, yes."

"You were not expecting me?"

"No. No, sir, we were not told, or I would have ensured a more respectful approach from these idiots."

"It is fine," Ramirez said. "It is better for me this way. Where is Cucho Lopez?"

The man's eyes widened. "Señor Ramirez? Why... he is

not here." The man's eyes were dancing around. Ramirez had seen it plenty of times, a nervous individual weighing his options.

"But you do know where he is. I can see it in your eyes. I've looked into many men's eyes; I've seen the light disappear from them time and again. Now, I will say this once, Eric the Coyote: I know exactly who you are. I know who your mother and father are. I know who your little sister is. I know about your newborn nephew in Nueva Leon, and your grandfather, the ex-Don, in Merida, with all of his retiree gangster friends, on their 'protected' turf. But no one is protected from me; no one. If you hold out even a word of the truth from me, I will execute every one of them. And then I will come for you. And I will ensure the Earth is scorched of your existence, your name and line forgotten. Am I being entirely clear?"

He nodded vigorously. "Yes... yes, Señor Ramirez, of course, sir."

"Where is my cousin? Where is Cucho?"

"Cucho is your..." The man had begun to flop sweat; he was practically twitching from anxiety.

"Cousin, yes. Out with it."

The man looked like he was about to vomit.

"If you are wondering," Ramirez added, "whether your best option right now is to be quiet or to talk, I should explain that regardless of what you tell me, you had best say something, Eric the Coyote... or I will castrate you in front of your men and feed you your supper."

Ladrón had turned a greenish hue. "Cucho... Cucho is dead, Señor Ramirez. He... I mean... I heard..."

"You heard what?"

"I heard... I mean, we all heard he got in a fight with the boss over something. And... that's the last we heard."

"The boss. You mean that weasel Angel Herrera?"

The coyote glanced around nervously. The entire room had fallen silent, his men rapt with attention. "Everyone, go back to what you were doing!" Ladrón yelled angrily. Clearly, Ramirez thought, he did not want to be seen as a snitch.

But no one was stupid enough to take on a *sicario*.

Ladrón reverted his attention to the taller man. "We heard Cucho made him angry. Then we heard he had some guys drive out in the desert with him. And... that is the last we heard."

"Where was he on the day they took him?" Ramirez didn't need evidence to make his decisions; Mexico City trusted him implicitly. But he knew they would prefer it.

"He was looking for one of Herrera's guys who wanted out. I heard Manolo Marichal picked him up at Diamonds Casino about a week ago, and..." He held up both palms, signifying the end of Cucho's story.

"What about this 'Bob'? The gringo who is supposedly making Herrera's life so difficult?"

The coyote looked puzzled. He looked over at the two humiliated bouncers, but they both shrugged. One of them was sweating profusely, a leg extended to cope with the swelling of a torn knee joint. "Señor..."

"Call me Hector. It's okay," Ramirez said calmly.

"Hector... I am honored—"

"Only if you cut it out with the honorific bullshit, though. I am a working man, just like you. Only much more dangerous to lie to. Who else carries out his orders? Who else does he rely on other than Manolo?"

"He has a cop on his payroll. He tells him everything, I think. Hayes, a homicide detective."

"Which of them will speak most openly, Hayes or Manolo?"

"Manolo thinks Angel saved him years ago," Ladrón said. "I do not think he would betray him, no matter what. But Hayes? Hayes would betray his own mother for a taco."

Ramirez nodded thoughtfully at that. The frightened young man was proving most helpful. "So... this 'Bob' Angel mentioned to me..."

Ladrón stared at his boots again. "I am nervous again because I must admit I do not know who you are speaking about, but I do not wish to upset you or have you think I would hold back—"

"Shhh!" Ramirez cautioned. "Shhh... Slow down. As I said, I am not here for you, Ladrón."

"I have never heard this name, Señor Ramirez. I mean... of course I've heard the name 'Bob' before, but not in the context—"

"Shhh..." Ramirez calmed him again. "Let me think."

Herrera had claimed "Bob" was disrupting his local trade, that he was Cucho's killer. But this man was an important cog in Herrera's operation and had never heard of him.

Angel is trying to serve me a scapegoat, trying to get me to take care of a problem for him. But not so big a problem that the story holds together. If Angel was not truly responsible, he would not bother to do so.

He had heard about as much as he needed. A stop by the casino would doubtless net him the security footage he needed to confirm Ladrón's story.

Not that he doubted it.

Nobody lied to a *sicario*.

Not if they expected to continue breathing.

THE STEREO at the Viper Lounge strip club was blaring, bass pumping so hard that the floor vibrated in time with each beat.

Det. Carter Hayes sat in the front row by the stage, watching a young dancer remove her already scant clothing in slow motion. She was clearly skirting being underage, he figured, and she looked half-terrified.

He liked that.

Hayes had his knees spread wide, and he was slouching down, a glass of rye whiskey and ice in one hand, his collar unbuttoned and his tie loose. The rest of the room was practically empty. The manager was aware the detective didn't like to be bothered, patrons keeping to themselves on the other side of the club, separated by a three-quarter-length wall.

The dancer moved to the corner of the stage, by his seat, and squatted low, gyrating on her way down. She beckoned to him with a crooked finger.

"No, baby," he yelled. "I just like to watch." She just wanted money anyway, he figured, and he didn't come to the club to supplement whores' incomes. He waved a hand for her to go away.

She crawled back towards the pole center stage, a sad expression on her face.

"Carter Hayes!" a voice bellowed from the front of the room, behind him.

He didn't recognize it.

His hand found the butt of his service Glock 21, in a

speed holster clipped to his belt. He turned and looked back towards the entrance. "Who's asking?"

A figure stood ahead of the door, half-blended into the club's shadows. He stepped out of them and approached, the overhead tube lights casting a dull glow across his face. The man's eyes were black as pitch, and at least as dead as Hayes felt inside.

"You have information I require," the man said, his voice still raised above the music.

Hayes scoped out the man's clothes. The suit looked expensive and tailored. His shoes were newly shined, almost glowing under the neon. He had rings on his fingers, a gold watch – a Rolex? He couldn't be sure from a distance.

Probably the dude I've been getting free drinks off here for six months. Hayes rose to his feet unsteadily, feeling the drink. He'd only been off shift for two hours, but the whiskey had gone down easily.

"*Hola, amigo!* What can I do you for?" He kept his right hand down and behind him, ready to draw his piece if necessary. "Would you be Sid, the owner of this fine dive bar?"

"I would not," Hector Ramirez said as he neared. "Would you be the corrupt cop who sucks Angel Herrera's dick for his lunch money?"

Who the fuck...? "That's a pretty ballsy thing to say to me," Hayes said. "Or maybe just stupid. You know who I am, right?"

"I know who you're supposed to be, a homicide detective." The man continued to wander slowly towards him and was now just ten feet away.

"Ah!" Hayes reached into his pocket and took out his shield to flash, then used his right hand to lift his coat and display his gun. "You might want to think about adopting a slightly more respectful fucking tone, okay, pal?"

"Why?" Ramirez said as he slowly drew closer. "Because you might shoot a man you don't know, who just walked into a club?"

"Hey, now!" Hayes's nerves kicked in. He went for his gun.

His hand had just cleared his coat when the man ran forward. Hayes leveled the Glock, but Ramirez was on him, locking up his arm and yanking it towards the ground, the gun flying loose. Hayes scrambled to his knees to retrieve it.

Ramirez didn't bother, instead stepping into a goalie kick to Hayes's ribs. He felt something crack.

"Gnnnhh!" Hayes grunted as he went over onto one side, clutching his fractured ribcage. He tried to scuttle on one side towards the gun. Ramirez took two long paces and kicked it, the gun sliding across the hardwood floor and under a booth.

The *sicario* drew his pistol and stood over the prone detective. "Go ahead. Grab it. Snatch your gun from the floor and victory from the jaws of defeat."

Hayes glanced over at the gun, three feet away, then up at his attacker. He remained still. "You're making a big fucking mistake, pal," Hayes said. "You know who the fuck I am in this town? Do you *realize* that? *Do you know who the fuck I am!?*"

"I know everything about you, Carter Hayes," the man said, his expression unwaveringly intense. "I know you were a high school football star, and a college football failure due to your bad knee. I know Angel Herrera pays your bills, and with your cocaine habit, it is no small amount. I also know that, whether you realize it or not, that means you work for my employers."

Hayes's eyes widened. "You're cartel."

"Where is Cucho Lopez?"

"Do you mind if I get up?"

Ramirez gestured "up" with his free hand.

Hayes clambered to his feet slowly. "So... you fellas are sort of big on the drama..."

"Answer the question. My patience is waning."

"Why do you care? Cucho was just some small-time—"

"He is my cousin."

Hayes dusted off his suit jacket. "He *was* your cousin."

The *sicario*'s expression did not change. "Who pulled the trigger?"

"Oh, I think you've figured that out already."

Ramirez's eyes closed for a split second, stress washing over the assassin. "Angel Herrera. Where? When?"

"In his office, last week." Angel's time had come, Hayes had decided. That was his cue to get out of the way, pick up the pieces later. "Manolo took the kid in to see him."

"Manolo was present?"

Hayes was about to shake his head no, tell the cartel man Herrera's right hand had left Cucho with his boss, per their mutual protection deal.

Then a thought occurred.

Two shitbirds, one stone. "Yeah, he helped."

Ramirez's fingers shifted, his hand flexing tersely on the gun's grip.

Hayes's eyes widened. "Hey! Hey now! I didn't have shit to do with that. And last I checked, I'm still a detective in this town. My value to your people doesn't change just because Angel Herrera fucks up, right?"

"Where did they take his body?"

"I don't know, man! I swear!" Hayes held up both palms. "They did what they always do: took the remains out to the desert somewhere."

Ramirez holstered the Glock. He turned and headed for the doors.

"Wait... what about me?" Hayes demanded.

Ramirez paused and glanced back at him. "What about you? Go back to work. You are correct: a corrupt police officer has value. Be thankful, Carter Hayes. Today, no one digs your grave."

The *sicario* walked out the door.

Hayes took two steps sideways and slumped to a seated position on a booth bench. Angel didn't have long, it seemed, maybe Manolo, too.

Herrera's men would need new leadership. They'd see the benefits of having a white guy in charge, especially a cop, he figured. Maybe they'd even want a new boss who didn't bend his will to Mexico City.

He'd always seen himself as a winner... and believing it was half the battle.

GERARDO "NACHO" Garcia sat in the air-conditioned comfort of the Range Rover's cab and watched the club across the street. He'd been there since just after supper. He'd stopped at the front door and looked in, briefly. The place was nearly empty.

Hayes had eventually shown, just as Manolo suggested he would, because the detective was grooming some eighteen-year-old stripper to be his new piece on the side. But an hour later, a guy in a dark suit had entered.

Nacho had crossed the street again a few minutes later, peeked inside to see the two men standing near each other. He looked a serious player of some kind. He looked Mexican to Nacho, but that was a guess.

Either way, he had not stayed long, ten minutes in and out, at most.

Hayes had remained, his unmarked police car parked a block down the street. Manolo had made it clear he didn't trust the detective, that he seemed to be planning something, working an angle. "Keep eyes on him. I want to know who he meets with and when."

The two men probably deserved each other, Nacho figured. Sure, Manolo made a big deal of being honorable. But he'd killed more men than any of them.

That also made him too dangerous to mess with. He'd want to know about Hayes's meeting, if that's what it was. He took out his phone.

Manolo answered before the first ring. "Yeah?"

"He's still there. I checked in an hour ago, and he was just watching the girls, waiting for the brunette to go on."

"So why the call?"

"Some dude came in and out. Too quick to be a customer, and the suit looked too expensive to be a cop. I took a glance at the door, and he was talking to Hayes."

"Black suit? All black? Mexican?"

"Yeah."

"Shit," Manolo muttered.

"What? Who is this dude?"

"Never mind. You don't want to know. But I have to do some thinking."

Manolo ended the call, while Nacho stared, puzzled, at his phone.

37

The shop just off North First Avenue was as discreet as it gets, a dry cleaner with a small counter and a store that couldn't have been more than fifteen feet wide until you reached the back door and the cleaning racks beyond.

Its door chimed as Bob entered.

"Good morning! All orders today ready tomorrow, yes?" The smiling man behind the counter was southeast Asian, older, maybe seventy, with a frail, slouched-over frame. For the barest moment, Bob wondered if he'd opened the wrong door.

"I'm here to pick up my mustard yellow tuxedo," Bob said.

For everything that had gone wrong in the year prior, Bob knew, meeting John Butcher in New Orleans and tapping his network of black-market suppliers had been one of the wins.

John had written the code below the store's address on his helpful list.

The man's demeanor changed. His slouch disappeared. So did his accent. "You got a reference?"

"John B., back east a ways."

The elderly man held his gaze for a moment longer than normal. Then he nodded curtly. "Good. I'm Han. I haven't seen that little shit in many a moon."

"Your obsequious Vietnamese accent was particularly uncomfortable," Bob said. "Congratulations. I take it you also act?"

Han cocked his head, as if suddenly aware of a distant sound. "You know what? You are literally the first guy to come in here and notice that I am, indeed, a quite exceptional actor. I've done okay."

"Really?"

"Sure. Two episodes of *Magnum* – the original good one – back in '83, a Pat Morita movie in '94. Did stunt work, too, on *The Fall Guy, Remington Steele, Simon & Simon...*"

"All the latest hits."

Han wagged a finger. "Don't be insolent, like your mouthy friend John," he said. "Come! Follow!" He began to walk towards the back. "I retired from acting in '95. Doctor said my arthritis needs a dry environment."

"Drier than Los Angeles?"

"Too close to the ocean." Han flinched as he said it, unhappy memories settling in. He opened the back door and led Bob past a rotating rack of clothes that filled most of the corner-store-sized back room. He opened another door and gestured for Bob to enter.

His normal instinct would have been to defer to his host, but that felt insulting. *If John Butcher trusts him... I won't let the fact that I barely know John affect things.*

Han reached past him and flicked on the light as Bob

entered. The room was small but functional, a jeweler's counter on one side, the display cases filled with a bizarre array of loosely scattered goods: freon cans, lockpick sets, night-vision goggles, pitons and climbing axes.

On the other wall was a display case filled with handguns. Bob counted twenty, all different makes, models and calibers. *Neat. One-stop shopping for a bank robber, I guess.*

Between the two counters sat a raised table with a computer, a jeweler's loupe and a powerful lamp. Han hiked himself up onto the tall stool behind it. "Now, if John B. is your boy, you're here for paper."

"I am indeed." Bob nodded back to the entrance. "You don't lock the door?"

"Someone wants in here bad enough, lock on the handle ain't going to cut it," Han said with a shrug. "Better to be careful who I talk to. You too. No recommendations unless I ask. You dig?"

"I do indeed," Bob said. "Careful is good. You mind if I ask how you know John?"

Han snickered like a teenage girl. "Yeah, funny story: during the war, I was in charge of the POW camp his father was in. He was a remarkably forgiving man."

"The Vietnam War?"

"Sure. How old do you think I look? I mean, I think I'm doing pretty good, right? I'm eighty-four."

"We should all be so lucky."

"So... what do you need?"

"I need a complete new workup: new Social Security and corresponding name on something with a picture, but not a driver's license. Nothing that can be run on a police network; age of majority, some shit like that."

"Can do. It'll take a couple of days."

"Good enough. How much?"

"Twenty thousand."

Bob's mouth practically fell open. "Twen... For *one* set of papers?"

"You want it good enough to fool government and get you real government paper?"

"I do."

"That's the going rate. At least, that's the going rate at the back of my shop in south Tucson at nine on a Monday morning."

"Okay, done," Bob said. It was almost half his stake. *Damn you, Tito, if you turn out to be a waste of my time.*

But he knew he couldn't really complain. Sister Eva had given up a lot more.

"Throw in one other ID? Doesn't have to be your best work, just something for use at the post office."

Han shrugged again. "Sure. You're helping put my grand-child through college, in case you're wondering where the money goes for an eighty-four-year-old."

"Good to hear."

"That and baseball cards. Got my eye on a Cal Ripken Jr. Topps rookie."

"Swell."

MANOLO KNOCKED three times in rapid succession on Angel Herrera's office door. It was not even ten o'clock in the morn-ing, and the men downstairs said his boss was already "excit-ed," which usually meant coked to the gills.

"Yeah!"

He opened the door and leaned in. "Boss? Got a minute?"

Herrera was seated behind his desk, leaning forward slightly on it. He had a pistol in his right hand and used it to gesture an approach. "Yeah, yeah, come in!" he said. "I'm keeping watch for that crazy fucking *sicario*, in case he figures your man 'Bob' isn't enough to satisfy him."

Manolo nodded and kept his eyes squarely on the man. Herrera made him nervous at the best of times. Lately, his paranoia had pushed him to the brink. Hayes wasn't wrong.

But he was wrong to think he'd betray his boss.

"Angel... you need to know, your boy Hayes was talking to Hector Ramirez last night."

Herrera let the tip of the pistol rest on the desk. "What?"

"For ten minutes, easy. I heard Ramirez was over talking to the coyotes, too. I think he's checking out your story about Cucho."

"*Ay, maricon!*" Herrera's distress grew. "You think—"

"I think someone's going to have seen me bring Cucho in here. After that, he's going to put two and two together and come up with a dead cousin. We need to deal with this."

Herrera fell silent, his eyes wide, expression bleak. He was clearly racing through whatever options he could bring to mind, but nothing was resolving the Gravedigger's threat.

"If he wants to kill me, he'll kill me," he said, his voice flat. "You too."

"So we kill him first. Or we feed him someone else responsible. Like maybe Hayes."

That caught his attention. Herrera broke from his daydream. "Hayes? No, Hayes is too valuable..."

"Hayes gave you up, boss. I fucking guarantee it."

"He doesn't have the balls."

"Angel... I swear... *carnal*, you know how grateful I've always been to you."

"Yeah, I know."

"So listen to me now: whatever you tell him, he's going to assume you are lying. He will come over here once he has confirmed you are in your office, and he's going to kill you and anyone who gets in his way. So you have to leave, now. Pass word back through one of your father's people that Hayes killed Cucho, played us against each other. That's a story everybody in Mexico City and Phoenix would want to hear."

"No! No, I don't like this. Hayes keeps the heat off us, but he's in deep, and he's scared of me. He's not going to help Mexico City with nothing."

Filla de puta... why do you even want to save him, Manolo? Because he helped you once, so now he's... what, family? Fuck this guy.

Manolo ignored his inner voice. "He probably wants it to be someone else as much as they do! He takes care of Hayes, maybe Bob too; you stay in Phoenix for a while..."

Herrera's glaze disappeared. He stared at Manolo bloodlessly, his eyelids drooping slightly, his mouth a grimace. "I know what I need to do," he said finally. "Go home, Manolo. He will be here before long, and you do not want to be here when that happens."

"But boss—"

"Just... do as I say."

"You can't face him alone. You saved me once in Phoenix. Let me..."

"Just... just *go, chingón*. I can take care of this. Go home, pack a bag, and get ready to get out of town once I call you." He waved the pistol again, this time motioning Manolo towards the door. "I still need you here. I need you to handle this place tomorrow night."

For once, he is trying to do the right thing by you. Don't fight it.

Manolo doffed an imaginary cap and closed the office door behind him.

HERRERA WAITED until Manolo had gone down the stairs to the club proper before picking up his landline. He needed to arrange to stay a few weeks at the family house. His father would not be happy, but he would not turn him down.

But first, he needed to make another call.

It rang twice.

"Who is this?" Hector Ramirez demanded.

"Señor Ramirez! It's Angel Herrera. One of my men said you were looking for me."

"I know where you are. I shall be stopping by."

"That's good, that's good. I think I have some information for you. I was confused, at first, with what I was hearing about Cucho."

"Oh? And what were you hearing?"

"That people thought I'd ordered him brought to me or something, which is not the case. It seems he had some sort of personal dispute with one of my men."

"Oh really."

"Yes, really. You met him, the tall guy, Manolo Marichal?"

"He has my cousin?"

"I... I am not sure how to tell you this, Señor Ramirez... I think Manolo may have killed him. I saw him briefly today, and he blew me off. His men said he was nervous, that he was muttering about packing his shit up and getting out of town. I ordered one of them to go back down and grab him... but he had already gone."

The line was silent. Herrera felt his heart pounding in his chest.

"Hello?" he asked. Perhaps Ramirez had already heard enough, perhaps...

"I'm thinking. You're in your office, yes?"

"Yes."

"And you have Manolo's location?"

"I do." He read out the address. "He is also managing the club tomorrow night."

"Very well. Stay there," Ramirez said.

He ended the call.

He bought it, Herrera told himself. *The idiot. He thinks I would allow Manolo to make such an important decision.*

But one thing was certain: staying in Tucson to find out how satisfied the Gravedigger was with his explanation seemed a fool's errand. It was time to call his father's house-keeper and make sure a guest room was ready. His father did not want to help, but he could not turn down his son's friendly visit.

38

Sister Mary Rose sat with her arms crossed, a stern expression suggesting growing impatience as she watched Bob, seated on the other side of her desk, shuffle through the deck of playing cards.

"What on earth are you up to?" she asked.

"Don Ambrose gave me this deck of cards he got from Martin. He didn't want to give them up, as they're the only thing he has to remember his friend, but..."

"And now you're... attempting a game of solitaire, perhaps?"

"I'm attempting to figure out how Martin marked the cards and what the message is. There has to be something; the timing, handing them over to a guy he gambled with right before he died, seems more than coincidental."

"Ah... so that would be why they're face down, then? I'm not sure I've read or heard too much about how people actually 'mark' cards."

"There's no definitive method," Bob said. "But there are some tried-and-true favorites, like filling in some of the tiny white dots on the back of the card, with different positions signifying different suits and values."

"Oh! But they're so small, it would be almost impossible to notice!" the head nun said.

"That's entirely the point. Most of the people who mark cards plan to cheat with them at some point, after all."

"Well!" She seemed delighted to have learned something both new and naughty. "That is clever! And do they also mark the fronts?"

Bob found her naivete charming. "They can't see the fronts when someone else is holding up their hand, so..."

"Ah. Of course. You must excuse me, Mr. Fleming. I have no real expertise in vice, other than the guidance of our Lord, of course."

"Ah."

"And... are you finding marked cards?"

Bob sighed wistfully. "On that front, I have to admit defeat so far." He gathered up the deck into a pile and squared it off. "That's... irritating. I was sure Martin had tried something with these." He put the deck back into the box and pocketed it, then got up from his chair. "I'm going to the post office. According to Tito, he had stuff mailed to general delivery at the branch on Thurber."

"And you think he might have been expecting a package or letter or..."

"An envelope, from himself. If we're lucky."

THE POST OFFICE was busy at lunch, and it took fifteen minutes before Bob's place in the line wound its way to the only manned station.

"What can I help you with?" The clerk was tall and aging, with 1960s black-framed spectacles.

"I'm expecting a general delivery package." Bob handed him the fake driver's license in Martin Guevara's name.

The clerk looked at it, then punched something into his computer terminal. "I'll be right back," he said. He turned and headed to a sorting area behind the main counters. He rifled through a mail slot for a moment, withdrew three items, and walked back.

"Just junk." He put the three restaurant flyers down. "I'm guessing you were expecting something a little more important."

It didn't make any sense. Donny Ambrose had been adamant Martin had no fixed address and had all his mail sent to the Thurber depot. But his cryptic comment about the cards telling all had to mean something.

He left the post office and walked up the block. Bob knew he had to figure out what Martin had been trying to tell his friends. The coffee shop on the corner seemed as good a place as any to go through the deck again.

At the restaurant, he ordered a green tea and took a high, round table near the back of the room, with a clear run to the back door and good sight lines.

He took the cards out of the deck and riffled through them. Nothing obvious was jumping out at him, front or back. *Martin, if you ever felt like offering some inspiration from beyond, now would be the time.*

He spread the deck out again.

Nothing.

"Order three-twenty-two!" the counter clerk announced. "Large Americano!"

The numbers?

He took the deck apart again, breaking it down into suits, then putting the cards in order.

Nothing. What am I missing? His gaze flitted to the pile of cards. Then he looked at the box they'd come in. He picked it up and turned it over. *Nothing obvious.*

He opened the top flap and looked inside. *Empty.*

Bob put it back down. *What am I missing? Or maybe I'm just overestimating this guy, maybe...*

His eye travelled back to the box. *Maybe I just need to turn this on its head.* He turned the box upside down and opened the bottom flap.

In ballpoint, someone had scrawled "568" followed by "479."

He looked through the front window of the café, to the post office. His mind drifted back to being there, looking around, taking the place in, seeing...

Post office boxes. One wall had been covered in private mailboxes, rentable by the month.

He got up and returned to the post office, the line down to just a few people, the lunch hour gone. The box numbers ran from one hundred to six hundred.

So it's probably either four-seven-nine or five-six-eight. But... how do I open the damn thing? He turned towards the counter. "Excuse me..." he called out to the clerk.

"Sir?"

"Do you rent lockers, or are there any around here?"

He pointed across the road. "Mail & Such, private company. They have lockers. But... if I could suggest, there's no substitute for a proper post office—"

"Thanks," Bob interrupted him and headed out the door.

He checked the street both ways for traffic, then crossed. He pushed open the door to Mail & Such. It felt like a cheap high school drama version of the post office across the street, but the counter was tan particleboard, and the lockers lining the walls were half-size versions of the plain steel gym lockers he'd seen so many times. With combination locks, not keyed locks like the ones across the street.

He walked over to them and found locker 479.

It had a three-number combination lock.

Worth a Hail Mary...

He rolled the dials to five-six-eight.

The lock popped open.

Martin, you sly dog.

He opened the locker.

It was empty save for a key. The number "568" was etched into its head. *Familiar territory. I'm betting if I walk back across the street...*

Five minutes later, Bob climbed back into the old beater and tossed a brown envelope onto the seat beside him.

39

His second stop of the day took a little longer.

Bob waited behind the wheel of the rusty sedan for four hours. It had no air conditioning.

He'd been wise enough to stop on the way to get a thermos and a bottle of cold water, along with a sandwich. The sandwich had been gone by the time the first hour was out, and the cab was sweltering.

But he needed eyes on the exit from the police station's parking lot. After two hours, he'd gotten out briefly to feed the meter another two dollars. Now, his back was sticking to the cheap vinyl car seat, his T-shirt soaked through with perspiration.

You know, Sarge, if you could do me just one more favor, it would be to show up sometime in the next—

Movement across the street interrupted the thought. A black Trans-Am pulled out of the lot and turned left, passing him on the other side of the road. Sgt. David Glebe was behind the wheel.

Bingo.

Bob checked his mirrors and made a U-turn. He kept the Ford back a few car lengths, letting in cars from the outside lane, keeping his pursuit as random in appearance as possible.

The Trans-Am led him across the city into a planned neighborhood, Northridge. The homes were new builds on tiny lots, each a picture-perfect clone of the next. The sports coupe took a right, then another, leading to a long cul-de-sac.

Bob pulled up at the curb outside the first house, watching as the Trans-Am travelled the length of the street, a garage door opening ahead of it, seven houses down.

Okay, now we know where he lives. Let's find out just how reasonable Sgt. David Glebe really is.

He got out of the car with the envelope in his right hand and hiked the length of the street. If he'd picked up a tail at any point and missed them, he knew he'd have seen movement before he reached Glebe's house. But the block was quiet.

He used the door knocker.

After a few seconds, a voice muttered loudly, "Just... Just wait a sec. Geez, I just got home..."

The door opened on the safety chain. "Yeah... holy shit!"

"I know," Bob said with a shrug. "Probably not the most pleasant surprise in the world."

Glebe just stared at him, the chain on. "Are you expecting me to open the door to you right about now?"

"The thought had occurred."

"Yeah... this is Arizona, at a private home, in a cul-de-sac, where company is not expected. You're lucky I haven't shot you already."

"I actually put that down to character, Sergeant. Now...

can we talk for a few minutes? Please? I have something to show you."

SGT. DAVID GLEBE finished pouring the second cup of coffee and walked over to the kitchen table.

Bob had spread out a handful of document pages: photocopies of lease agreements, what appeared to be a corporate hierarchy chart for a numbered company, photos of a half-dozen familiar faces, including Angel Herrera and Manolo Marichal.

In his two years working for Angel, Martin had apparently been busy.

"Sorry, again, for bothering you at home with this."

"It's okay," Glebe said, though he didn't sound happy about it. "I've got four days off right now anyway. Better to get this shit out of the way right off the top."

"Thank you."

"So let me get this straight: Martin Guevara figured he needed some insurance, in case his repeated trips off the wagon got him into Angel's bad books."

"Correct. Martin had been a driver for Herrera. Obviously, if a guy develops a drinking problem, that's not going to last long. But he'd been through hell to get here, paying off coyotes to take him across the desert. He didn't trust his employer as far as he could toss him."

"And you're telling me you've got more of this?"

"Safely stashed. Once I get what I need, I'll tell you where you can find them. You'll find the last two binders particularly interesting. A certain pain in both our butts features quite prominently."

The police sergeant developed an immediate gleam in his eye. "Hayes."

"There's enough in there to have him under investigation for a long time. But I'll go you one better."

"How so?"

"Well... that's where I need your help. I need to know where he lives."

"Whoa." Glebe leaned back in his chair. "Now, that's another thing entirely. You want me to give you a fellow officer's home address?"

"In exchange for enough information to shut down Herrera's entire migrant network."

"Yeeaahh... that's not really my point. If there's one thing you're never going to get out of law enforcement, it's a co-worker's home address. I mean, I'm already working off an assumption in accepting that all of this isn't just made-up bullshit..."

"But... are you? Are you really?" Bob stressed the "really," leaning into it. The man wasn't an idiot.

Glebe was clearly torn. "I know what he is, but... Suppose you fill me in on what happens when you go to his place."

"I'm going to tell him Herrera's going down, and him with it. I'm going to give him a chance to turn himself in for the murder of Martin Guevara."

"And how do you figure you'll make that stick? He was the lead on that one. Are you telling me we sent a killer cop to investigate his own victim?" Glebe shielded his eyes. "Jesus H."

"There was a witness."

"You're kidding."

"I've got him stashed."

That puzzled the veteran officer. "So why not just hand over the witness and have us pick up Hayes?"

Bob knew he had to weigh his words carefully. He needed the sergeant's help, but if he was completely honest, he wouldn't get it. "He won't come forward unless Hayes is already under arrest. He's terrified." Telling the cop Donny Legs hadn't actually seen the murder wasn't going to help.

But Glebe was already shaking his head. "I just can't do it, Bob. I... I think you're legit, if that helps at all. But I can't take a chance like that on the word of a guy I just busted on a gun charge and nothing else. And this stuff..." He gestured at the table. "It looks like it is what you say, which is great. But until we can be sure..."

He let the thought hang.

Bob nodded. He'd sort of expected that. "Okay, I get that. I kind of figured that might be a bridge too far."

"I'm sorry, Bob, really, I am. But we deal with a lot of cases, and sometimes, that's—"

"Do you know where he drinks?"

DET. Carter Hayes was drunk.

Fortunately, he'd decided, the cocaine was propping him up.

But he had to go home. The clock on the wall above the faux-neon Budweiser sign had been stuck on seven since the late nineties. His phone, however, told him it was nearly one in the morning.

He had a shift at noon the following day.

Hayes pushed off the stained vinyl tabletop and staggered to his feet. He patted himself down until he found his soft pack of Marlboros, in his shirt's breast pocket. He shook the pack upside down until the last cigarette appeared. He used his lips to draw it, then realized the cigarette had snapped just above the filter. He tore the filter off and lit the rough end, then jammed the burning cigarette between his lips.

The detective wandered unsteadily past the bar.

"Hey! Hey, man, you can't smoke in here!" the bartender said.

Hayes turned his way. He took a puff and took the cigarette out. "You know who I am?"

"Yeah... but you still can't fucking smoke in here, man."

His expression darkened. He took out his shield and flashed it. "See this? You would be fucking astounded what this lets me do. Now... gimme a bottle of rye."

"Hey, man." The bartender looked distressed. He lowered his voice. "Hey, man, I can't just give you a bottle, okay? I've got to—"

Hayes drew his pistol and chambered a round. Then he stuffed it back into its holster. "You were saying?" He took a long puff off the cigarette, then blew out a plume of smoke.

"Rye." The bartender nodded twice, his eyes flitting to the bottles behind him, then back to Hayes, uneasy about taking his eyes off the man.

Hayes walked south from the bar, along Craycroft Road. It had been a strange and difficult week. He had the sense Angel wasn't long for the world, maybe Manolo, too. The dude at the strip club the night prior had scared the shit out of him. That hadn't happened since junior varsity, staring down a big, mean linebacker intent on ripping off his head.

At East Twenty-Sixth Street he turned left, walking another few blocks until he reached South Jefferson, then south until he was at the apartment block.

He took out his keys and opened the front doors.

The man behind him came up silently, slipping an arm around him and into his coat before he could react, the pistol stolen from the speed holster clipped to his belt. Drunk as he was, Hayes realized a split second too late what was happening. He was already raising both hands before he'd finished turning around.

"Pretty slick, chief... you!"

"Evening, Detective," Bob said. He swiveled his head either way to make sure the sidewalks were still deserted. Then he gestured forward with the gun. "Let's head on in and – to borrow your words – have ourselves a nice little chat."

HAYES'S APARTMENT was surprisingly spartan, Bob had decided. For a man on the take, he had cheap tastes: a ratty old furniture set, a newer flat-screen, no art on the walls other than an Arizona Cardinals flag above the TV.

"Nice place you've got here, Hayes. You get kicked out of a dorm room recently or something?"

"Yeah... well... I don't get much company. Am I allowed to sit down?"

"Please." Bob said, motioning towards the sofa. "Just don't pull a piece from behind the cushions or nothing like that."

"Oh yeah? You going to shoot a cop, Bob? That seem a wise play to you?"

Bob shrugged. "Irrelevant. I know how it'll seem to you.

It'll seem like you're dead. So... back to you, Detective. Got any loose firearms in the vicinity?"

Hayes weighed that, his head bobbing. "My backup piece."

"Ankle?"

The cop nodded.

"Take it out, slide it over on the floor."

Hayes did as ordered.

It was a snub-nosed revolver, a .38 Police Special. Bob scoffed a little as he pocketed it. "Huh! Really trying to cement the image, right?"

"I have been known, on occasion, to actually arrest criminals."

"But only the competition, right, Hayes?"

The detective didn't reply, instead seemingly just studying his opponent. His eyes narrowed, his jaw suggesting tension, grinding teeth.

"You look like you'd just love to kill me right now," Bob said. He shook his head mockingly. "Tsk, tsk, tsk. Such a piece of work. What were you again... college football star, somebody said?"

"All-American. Would've made the NFL Hall of Fame if my knee hadn't torn in my sophomore year." Hayes leaned forward, just about spitting the words out. "Let me tell you a little secret: without that gun, you're just a guy my size who wasn't a star athlete. A delivery driver. A fucking nobody. I would eat you for lunch and have enough left in the doggy bag for supper."

Bob smiled. *Well now, what would Nurse Dawn or Sister Eva say about this? They'd probably tell me to let him wallow in the self-delusion.*

But I need this idiot to talk. I wonder when the last time was that he was afraid of anything?

Bob uncocked the pistol and put it down on the old telephone table, by the front door. "Well now... I have no gun; you have no gun. Why don't you just give me a good old demonstration of that old-college-football-star power? Come on over, Hayes," Bob beckoned, cupping his hand and gesturing for him to approach. "After all, I'm just a delivery driver."

Hayes rose from the sofa, swaying slightly. He was still drunk, evidently, his expression sullen, almost dead. He sniffed hard. "I've seen shitbirds do some stupid things over the years, but *you* getting into a fight with *me* has to be right up there."

He strode over towards Bob. He'd just begun to raise his hands in a boxing stance when Bob took a step forward onto his left foot, swung around on the ball at lightning speed, raising his right leg, crooked at the knee, then whipping a spinning kick that caught the detective flush on the side of the chin.

His legs folded, and he collapsed to the ground. He looked shaken, confused. "Wha...?" Hayes muttered. "What hit me?"

"Humility," Bob said. "You're not even going to warm me up, are you?" He snorted derisively. He leaned over the man and offered him a hand to get up. "Come on, get up."

Hayes grasped the offering and began to rise. Even drunk, the speed of his other hand was surprising, the blade glinting just enough for Bob to see it a split second early. He snatched Hayes's attacking arm at the wrist and leaned in, head-butting the man in the bridge of the nose, bone breaking, blood streaming from both nostrils, the detective's eyes tearing up.

Bob shook the blade loose with his left hand, his right foot coming up in a short front kick that caught Hayes mid-chest, his solar plexus depressed, air gone.

The detective fell onto his back, wheezing.

"Pathetic," Bob said. He kicked the blade under the sofa. "You had about as much chance at the hall of fame as I did of winning Miss Tucson." He stood and waited while the man regained his wind.

Hayes climbed to his knees. He used his sleeves to wipe the blood and snot clear.

"You're going to fucking regret this, Fleming," he said.

"Yeah... you're a regular harbinger of doom. Take a seat on the sofa, there, buttercup. You've got a few things to explain, officially. For the record." Bob took the digital recorder out of his pocket. He walked over to the living room and put it down on the coffee table but remained standing. If Hayes had any more tricks, he wanted to shut it down quickly, make it clear to the man what he was risking.

"I'm... I'm not telling you shit," Hayes panted.

"Oh... I think you will. If you think that beatdown was uncomfortable, it's going to be a really long and terrifying night for you. Because I can do shit to you that would turn Jeffrey Dahmer's stomach. Fascinating exercises in applying nerve pressure that'll make it feel like your heart will explode. Crushed testicles. You name it. You see, I'm *not* a cop, Hayes. This confession isn't going to count for shit, officially. What it will do is tell your badge-wielding brothers where to start looking. We're going to give them a road map, to guide them through the darkness in your soul."

He reached down and hit "record" on the device.

"So what do you think you know?" Hayes asked.

"I know that if Tucson Police Internal Affairs go back through your homicide investigations, they're going to find a vast number of unsolveds that seem, surprisingly, to be Angel Herrera's rivals. I know there's a black-and-white picture of you meeting with Herrera at one of his migrant depots in a file I've got. And I figure if they check, they'll find you waved off police help called by Tito Agustin and Sister Eva, right before she was murdered."

Hayes's mouth was hanging open, but he still managed to contort his lips into a rictus grin, teeth glossy with saliva. "So... what you're really telling me is you don't have shit. Do you, 'Bob?' What you've got is barely even circumstantial. Half the detectives in town get accused of bad shit at some time or another. I'm a local hero, remember?" He looked vaguely giddy, the booze and the beating combining to daze him.

"You're a local hero who missed a witness."

The expression disappeared. "Nobody's going to believe an ex-cartel alcoholic like Tito Agustin, especially when he's already wanted for gun offenses, child endangerment and questioning in a murder. So... nice try again, 'Bob.' I didn't do shit. And you can record that. Or, you know, do any of that nasty shit you threatened, to force a confession out of me for something I didn't do. But I bet you won't record that part."

"Tito wasn't the witness." This time, Bob allowed himself a smile. *I know schadenfreude is a weakness*, he told himself. *But damn, sometimes...*

Hayes's mouth had once again dropped open. "Fuck off!"

"Nah. He lost his hat in a game of cards. You saw a hat. But the guy in the hat saw you, jagoff."

"You're lying," Hayes said. "You have to be."

"He followed you up those steps, Hayes. He watched as you pushed Martin Guevara to his death." Bob said it coldly, without inflection, a supposed statement of indictable fact that he'd just made up. "Why? Why push him off a roof?"

The question was whether Hayes would bite.

C'mon, idiot, admit it...

Hayes's expression shifted again, a sudden lucidity kicking in, confidence. Knowing. He wagged a judgmental index finger in Bob's direction. "Ah! Ah, ah, ah, Bob!" He shook his head gently. "That was a bridge too far, my convincing shitbird friend! You almost had me with that witness shit... then I remembered, it couldn't be true because I didn't do shit to your friend."

"Hayes, there is a witness."

"Sure. Sure, to me being there. That's not a secret. It's in my shift report that I stopped by looking for a CI who... that's a criminal informant, I should explain... for a CI—"

"I know what a CI is, Hayes. Jesus H, get to the point."

"You know—" Hayes looked puzzled. "What the fuck are you, exactly, Bob? Ex-cop? Ex-military? Some weird fucking ICE militia with a fetish for illegals? I mean... who the fuck are you?"

"I'm guessing you don't really mean that in the profound, larger sense."

"And I'm guessing you didn't bother to actually go up to the roof at the shelter."

I missed something. That's why he's suddenly become cocky. "Why's that?"

"Oh, I'm sure you'll figure it out, chief. But what it tells me is you haven't done your due diligence. Some shitbird has sold you a story about the 'corrupt' cop, and you've bought it." Hayes's eyes flitted over to the recorder for a moment, then back to Bob.

Bob thought back to what Joe had said at the shelter. The door was always locked. Somehow, Hayes had obviously commandeered a key. But... that meant he could've locked it behind them as well.

I told him he saw the push. That has to be it. He knows that can't be true.

"Whether he was on the roof or not, he can put you going up there with Martin and accidentally killing Manny the doorman," Bob said. "This is going to get ugly no matter how you slice it, Hayes. You think you can survive this? Even if you did, all the questions that will be asked... all the cases reopened."

"So what are you suggesting, Bob? That I turn myself in for some fairy tale you've made up? That you'll torture me until I crack? I've got news for you: one, you're not a cop. I don't think you're even a real person, just a string of stolen IDs, like any number of other shitbirds who've rolled through this town. And two, anyone who had done all the heinous shit you're trying to pin on me... well, if he talked to police or the feds, or even just to you, a certain criminal organization in Mexico City would make his life incredibly, incredibly nonexistent. So... do what you will, asshole. I ain't saying shit."

He's right. I've blown it. Bob knew he had to retreat. He still had to deal with Angel Herrera somehow, or Tito would never be safe. But Hayes was in so deep, even evidence wouldn't prompt a confession. *If he figures he's going down, he'll probably book out of town.*

He won't do it until the very last. Which means I still have time to come back for round two.

He picked up the recorder. "We'll be having another nice little chat real soon, Hayes," he said as he walked over to the door.

"Looking forward to it."

Bob retrieved the pistol from the telephone table. "I'll just hang onto this until I'm out of range," he said as he slipped out the door. "Not that you'd ever shoot anyone in the back... right?"

40

BISBEE, Arizona

Tito stared out the front window of the tiny wood cabin as the German tended to a flower bed, kneeling on a plastic sheet, his gloved hands and trowel dipping into the dirt.

He seemed nice enough. He'd come by right after Bob's departure and offered Tito breakfast, which he'd taken gratefully, only to discover the man liked to eat at least two pounds of sausage with every meal.

The rest of the day had been so placid as to seem inert. The quietness in the cabin felt like an assault, as if empty air were a bludgeon. He wanted to run outside – to run all the way to Tucson, snatch his son from the people who did not love or know him.

But that was impossible as long as Angel Herrera wanted him dead.

The barest thought of the man enraged him. Now, he had to live with the knowledge that a man he barely knew –

a true friend who was nonetheless a stranger – was out fixing his problems, his choices.

He'd flipped on the television to discover the cabin had no cable TV, just apps built into the set to watch streaming services he didn't have. The wall shelves were lined with books, but he had no confidence in his reading skills. And the books were old, yellowed paperbacks by John Steinbeck, Ernest Hemingway, D. H. Lawrence. Old people's stuff, he figured.

He'd ordered a pizza, eating half a large on his own, as much out of boredom as hunger. The German had come out after supper to finish his peaceful gardening. Watching someone move around freely had done nothing to quell his growing sense of impotence, of having no say in his own future.

He took out his phone and checked the time. It was seven twenty in the evening, the sun beginning to hang low over the Mule Mountains. He dialed Bob.

"What's up?"

"A whole lot of nothing, *ese*," Tito said. "A whole day of a whole lot of nothing. I'm going crazy here, dude. What are you doing?"

"I'm making progress," Bob said. "You just need to be a little patient, okay? Watch some TV or something."

"He don't got TV here! Just Netflix and shit."

"So read a book. I saw a bunch on the shelf there."

Tito stared at them anxiously. "Yeah... I already read them all. Seriously, Bob, when the fuck can I get out of here and start helping?"

"You can't," Bob said bluntly. "Tito, Angel Herrera has men all over this city who are looking specifically for you. Most of them have never even seen me before, and the ones

who have are mostly in the hospital. But they would probably spot you within minutes."

"I can't just sit here."

"Coming back to Tucson is suicide. You have Sean to
think about. You can't care for him – you can't be his dad – if
you're dead. Just... relax, okay?"

"Relax? You want me to relax? You think I don't know
Sister Eva is my fault, Bob, that you sticking your neck out is
my fault? They're chasing me because of who I am. They're
threatening my boy because of me. But everyone else is
taking the risk. This is bullshit!"

"That's *not* true." Bob barked the words pointedly. "The
only person to blame for any of this shit is the guy in charge,
Angel Herrera. If you want to extend that to flunkies like
Carter Hayes, feel free. But this isn't on you. Don't drag your
ego into this in an attempt to regain some 'control' over a
situation you never had control over to begin with! I've made
that mistake too many goddamn times, Tito, and it never
ends well. Just... please, after everything we've been through
over the last few weeks, trust me to handle this."

A question had occurred to him since Bob's departure.
He'd been reluctant to ask it before, but his ire was up.
"Yeah... about that? *Que pasa?* What the fuck are you doing
in Tucson in the first place, and who the fuck are you? We
don't even know each other, yet I feel like I'm going to owe
you until we're both old and fucking gray, assuming we live
that long. I don't even know... I have no control, Bob. This is
all happening because of me and to me, and I have no
fucking control over any of it. And I fucking hate it. It sucks. I
don't even know who you are, dude."

The line was silent for a moment. Tito felt a swath of
guilt crawl over him. "I'm sorry, I didn't mean it like—"

"It's okay," Bob said. "I get it. I'm not from your world, and I appear and stick my nose in."

"Well... yeah, kinda..."

"It's... complicated," Bob offered. "When I was younger, I did a lot of bad things. I mean cartel-level bad, probably worse."

"That's... that's bad."

"Yeah. I thought I was doing the right thing, but I was working for the wrong people. I owe many more debts than I can ever repay, mostly to people who aren't around anymore to benefit from it. So... if I see someone who needs help, I try to help. That's all it is, really."

"A conscience can be dangerous in the wrong company," Tito said. "I get that. I just don't want you or anyone else getting hurt because of me. You get that, yes?"

"I get what you're saying. Just... hang tight for today. I'll call you tomorrow and tell you where we stand, okay?"

"Sure," Tito said.

"We'll talk later."

"Okay."

"Okay. Bye."

Tito wandered over to the edge of the bed and sat down. Bob wasn't going to let him get involved at all. That much seemed clear. He was going to go after Angel on his own.

Plenty had tried in the past. Most hadn't gotten close. When they had, a call from Angel's father in Phoenix had ended even base consideration of a new regime. Ultimately, Angel was protected from upon high. That was what really gave him his power: his own men couldn't really stand him.

So maybe Bob isn't the only one who can resolve this. Maybe there's a tactic he hasn't thought of.

He rose from the bed and collected his jacket from the

back of the cabin's front door. The Sig Sauer pistol Bob had left him was in the left side pocket.

He needed to steal a car. The drive to Phoenix was just over three hours. If he was smart and lucky, he figured he could resolve the entire matter before Angel hurt Bob or anyone else.

Lives for a life. My friends and family for his father. Time to show Angel what it feels like to be on the receiving end, for a change.

41

Manolo Marichal approached the front doors of the Flaming Garter at a brisk pace, as if he had nothing to worry about. It was eight o'clock on a Monday night, and usually the place would be busy with "industry night," with drinks and buffet food discounted for hospitality workers.

But the parking lot was empty save for one car, which he assumed belonged to Reb, the doorman.

He'd stayed away from his modest apartment the night before, sleeping on Nacho's pull-out sofa bed. He had a feeling Ramirez was cleaning house. That meant they all had to look over their shoulders, find safe ground.

Angel had left him a message to come by the club at eight. But when he'd tried to call him back, it had rung through to voicemail immediately.

He wondered what the man was up to; normally, his boss was in his office at eight. Manolo had told him to go to Phoenix, hide out. Instead, Angel had waved him off, made vague references to having an answer.

Manolo wanted reassurances; he'd warned Angel about Carter Hayes and about the Gravedigger. If his boss valued the mutual aid in their past, he would offer official protection against the *sicario*, maybe even call his father and see if the assassin could be recalled to Mexico City.

Either way, he figured, his best bet was to be with Angel when the man showed. Beyond the strength of numbers, it would sound more convincing if they both pinned Cucho's death on Hayes.

He looked around as he neared the bouncer. "Where the fuck is everybody?" The club's neon "OPEN" sign was turned off.

"Boss closed us up. He headed out."

"He say where?"

"Nope."

"He say when he would return?"

"Nope. Looked motivated. Had fire in his eyes, sort of."

Ramirez would show there. Manolo was certain of it. Had Angel fled?

It would be in his nature to lie to me.

He clapped the bouncer on the shoulder. "He didn't tell you to lock up, go home?"

The bouncer shook his head. "He just said, 'We're closed. Tell anyone who shows we'll reopen later in the week.' "

Later in the...

Manolo felt a sinking feeling in the pit of his stomach. Angel was only away from his office for that long when he left town for a trip or vacation. It had been consistent for a decade.

He gestured towards the lone other car in the lot. "Go home. Take a couple of days off and call us after. I'll lock up."

"Ok, boss, you got it. Thank you."

Reb headed for the lot. Manolo opened one-half of the double doors and went inside. He waited until the door had swung shut before turning the deadbolt. He could leave through the back door, which was secured with a coded lock, once he knew what was going on.

If it was some sort of trap, Angel would've had men waiting for him. But the club was empty, the loop of background dance music the only presence, albeit at a subdued volume. He looked around the vast room carefully.

Nobody.

So... not a trap. But why here? A trap had made sense if he was going out of town. But if no one was there to greet him? *Maybe he does plan to meet. Maybe he's coming back.*

What had Hayes said?

He'll do something he can't hide, and he'll try to pin it on one of us.

And you just assumed he meant the gringo, Bob. But... maybe that's not who's coming.

I need to get out of here.

From outside, headlights swept across the front windows.

Manolo jogged over to them. He didn't recognize the car.

Shit. That might be him.

If it was Ramirez, it would take him time to get inside, to force the lock or knock the door in.

Make sure the back is locked, idiot.

He sprinted across the vast room, past the stage and pole, to a back exit corridor. He ran its length and tried the back door.

Locked.

The back door had a backplate over the handle, a coded

number pad and mechanism that would make it difficult to get through. The front was just a standard lock.

He'll come through the front. Manolo drew his pistol and jogged to the main doors. He peered through the block-glass insert. The car was blurred by the glass's distortion but was still parked, headlights on and illuminating the side of the club.

Come on, you son of a bitch. Come show me how special you are.

The car continued to sit, idling. Manolo considered what he'd do in the same circumstances. *I wouldn't come alone. Maybe he's waiting for reinforcements. If so, that would complicate matters. It would mean—*

"Don't move unless you wish to die immediately." He felt a barrel pressed against the back of his head. "Do you know who I am?"

Manolo nodded cautiously. "You are Hector Ramirez, a *sicario*."

"Gun, please. On the floor ahead of you. Good. Now slide it to one side, out of reach."

Manolo complied. "Is this it, then?"

"No," Ramirez said. "And if it were, I would not tell you. I have no intention to cause you suffering, Manolo, but right must be done by my cousin. Nod gently if you understand."

He did.

Ramirez turned him around, then nodded over his shoulder towards the vast open room. "You're going to tell me everything you know, but not here. Tactically unwise. You have an office somewhere?"

Manolo gestured towards the stairs. "We can use Angel's."

Ramirez waved his gun to direct him. "Walk."

BOB WATCHED from the driver's seat of the rusting compact. The man in the suit got out of the Audi, leaving the car running, exhaust still drifting from its tailpipe. Its running lights spotlighted the front corner of the strip club.

Without Hayes's confession, he still had plenty of information that Sgt. Glebe could use to shut down Herrera's properties and his people-smuggling ring. Ultimately, he was willing to bet, none of it would legally belong to the gangster. He would have fronts, covers forced to act as proxies in case of just such a circumstance.

The only solution was to take out Herrera. He'd mulled it over for hours; in two weeks of helping Tito survive, he technically hadn't killed anyone. He'd stuck to his pledge, his goal of removing killing from his life. There had been too many already for Team Seven, too many of whom he no longer trusted even deserved it.

With Angel, there was no such concern, just the principle. And that principle had eaten at him, the ambiguity of it all, the need to put aside a code almost as soon as he'd adopted it. He wasn't supposed to be judge, jury and executioner of every criminal scumbag who made someone's life difficult.

Now a third party had entered the proceedings. Whoever he was, he moved with languid ease, rounding the club via its side path as if he hadn't a care in the world. A protector, maybe?

That didn't seem likely. Angel had plenty of guns already.

Towards the back corner, Bob could just make out the man reaching into the back waistband of his suit trousers, drawing a pistol from a speed holster.

Well now... he doesn't look like he's here from the security company. And if he's on Angel's side, he wouldn't be going in there with a piece drawn. The Audi is way too pricey for him to be a cop unless he's as corrupt as Hayes.

That leaves opposition.

A hitter.

He'd come there to end Angel. But maybe this guy was going to do it for him.

Bob frowned. Why had he gone around? *Element of surprise, probably.* But that didn't make much sense. Surely Herrera had a private office, another bodyguard with him. And why wasn't the club open? It was five after eight on a Monday night.

What, exactly, is going on here?

He got out of the recently purchased beater and closed the door gently. Bob crouched and stayed low as he covered the thirty yards from the road to the other arrival's car. He looked through the side window. The engine was idling, but there was no one inside. He moved over to the front window and peeked through it, the lack of light in the parking lot leaving it glare-free.

He could barely make it out, but two figures were climbing a set of stairs near the back of the club.

It was the man who'd just entered, with...

Manolo.

Bob had expected Herrera. Now he wondered if he'd underestimated the gangster. Because it looked a lot like Manolo had been left there as bait for someone.

Just who has this guy pissed off, exactly?

He took out his phone. If anyone knew who the third party was, it might be Tito. He dialed his friend's phone.

"Bob!" It sounded noisy, like he was in traffic.

"Please tell me you figured out the TV, and it's just turned up too loud."

"I'm on my way to Phoenix, *guey*. Going to go fix this shit once and for all."

Phoenix? "Tito, I told you..."

"I know what you told me. But Angel's old man is in Phoenix, and he runs everything in the state. We need leverage, right? Something to bargain with. So I'm going to get us some."

Jesus H, this is the last thing we need. "Turn around, *now!*" Bob ordered. "You can't walk onto this guy's turf on your own!"

"What? Bob, I'm getting a bad signal, *ese*... it's all scratchy..." Tito made scratching sounds with his voice that wouldn't have fooled anyone. "No bars, got to go, bye!" He ended the call.

Well... fuck. Bob dialed him back.

"Yeah?"

"It's me. Don't hang up on me again! I'm trying to help your ass! Who's the heavy hitter who just showed up at the Flaming Garter? He's in a suit, driving an Audi, big pistol. Looked like he was coming for Angel."

"You got me, *ese*," Tito said. "A hitter maybe? A *sicario*? Maybe he pissed off the wrong person. If he's cartel, I'd get out of there if I were you. Those dudes are lethal."

"But... where's Angel? I haven't seen him yet, and there's only one car around back, Manolo's Mercedes."

"Again... you're asking the wrong guy. Maybe he's hiding out in the office, waiting for backup or some shit. But if I'm in his shoes and I have to flee for my life from a *sicario*, I'm running straight back to daddy."

"Great." *That's the last thing I need, a pro here and Tito in Phoenix, possibly with Angel.* "Tito, Angel's father probably has a compound, a mansion. There will be armed guards, cops on the take they can call. It's suicide."

"Kr-ssh-t!" Tito said. "Reception's going again, *carnal*. Later, I guess..."

The call dropped.

AS THEY APPROACHED THE STAIRS, Manolo could see down the back corridor. The rear door was slightly ajar. "How...?"

"Your boss gave me the combination," Ramirez said. "He clearly thinks I am a fool. I will deal with him eventually."

Hayes was right.

That bothered him almost as much as the prospect of dying.

Manolo led the man up the stairs. He glanced sideways halfway up, hoping Ramirez was close enough to surprise him, boot him down the stairs or something. But the reflection in the glass under the railing suggested he was keeping a safe distance, several steps back.

"Why would you work for such a dishonorable man?" Ramirez asked as Manolo opened the office door.

"He saved my life once, a long time ago."

"So... you felt indebted. That is a shame. It is a shame that you should pay for his dishonor."

They entered the office. "Sit down." Ramirez gestured towards the desk and chairs.

Manolo saw his opportunity. For once, Angel's bragging would be of some use.

He sat down behind the desk.

"You want the seat of power for the short time this will take? I suppose I can understand that. You figured it would be you sitting there eventually, eh? But your boss is an ignoble fool and has dragged you both down."

The red button hovered to the left of his left hand. He'd been there when Angel had installed it, giddy with joy over his childish new toy. *Do not rush. Do not move too quickly. He is fast and lethal. Wait until he sits down.*

Ramirez rounded the chairs ahead of the desk, his pistol still trained on Manolo.

Wait until he lowers it for a split second. Then you have your opportunity.

Ramirez sat down. "Tell me about Cucho. The truth, this time."

"Boss sent him to look for a guy. Cucho... man, your cousin didn't want to be a gangster, not really. He just liked the money and the women."

"So?"

"So he spent the week gambling and drinking, and did not take the job seriously. Angel was mad at him. He asked me to go and get him."

"And you killed him."

"*No!*" Manolo barked. "When I left this office, he was still alive. That was on Angel."

"But you covered up for him."

"I did not. We left, me and the cop, Hayes."

"And he had someone get rid of Cucho's body. So you do not even know where he is buried."

Manolo shook again. "No."

Ramirez nodded. "I think I know what I need to know."

He let the barrel of the gun drop slightly, his elbow on the chair's armrest.

Manolo slapped the red button, the pistol popping out of the slot in the desk and right into his hand. He yanked the trigger once, twice, three times...

But the trigger just clicked uselessly.

Ramirez took a deep breath, then sighed with resignation. "I suspected your boss was a duplicitous jackal the first moment I laid eyes on him. So to be careful, I came by last night and removed the magazine from his little 'toy.' " He rose to his feet. "It's too bad. I thought perhaps you had avoided involvement. I gave you a chance to explain. And instead..."

The gun boomed from a very close range. Manolo felt the hot sting of the bullet as it pierced his chest, the chair rolling backwards, his body crashing to the carpet.

BOB HUNG his head for a split second and stared at the phone in a moment of incredulity.

Idiot.

Tito means well, but he's an idiot.

There was nothing he could do immediately to help Tito, except maybe find out from Herrera – or his hitter – where his father lived in Phoenix.

Priorities: deal with the hitter, deal with Angel, then go save Tito.

He jogged around the building. The other man had clearly found an easier route in.

The back door was ajar.

By design? Are they trying to funnel me in that way? Does he even suspect I'm coming?

It was a dead entry, no intel, no idea of what lay beyond the door. For all he knew, he was walking into a kill zone of unavoidable crossfire. Angel could've had twenty men inside, hidden and ready.

I need a distraction.

He jogged back to the car. He opened the door.

From somewhere nearby, he heard a muffled gunshot.

He climbed in and slammed the door. Either Angel was holed up in his office and these two were there to protect him, or he was already gone. But the only way to find out was to head inside.

Time to get this show on the road.

Manolo lay on his side. The pain was intense, overwhelming. His strength was instantly gone. He raised a hand to his chest and felt only warm slickness.

Ramirez rounded the desk and stood over him. "You have my sympathies, Manolo, such as they are."

"You got to do it, huh? Can't... can't let it go even once?"

Ramirez shook his head. "Matter of principle. You know the rules. *Sicarios* are untouchable. If I let you live, you go around telling people I gave you a break, even though you drew down on me. Then they start thinking maybe I've gone soft. Maybe they can exploit that."

"If it matters... I always liked your cousin," Manolo wheezed. "Not a gangster, but an okay kid."

"It doesn't. But thank you. It's nice to think he was not a complete idiot when his time came."

"So... this is it, then."

"It is. I'll make it quick."

He aimed at the man's head. Two more usually did the trick.

Manolo closed his eyes tightly, expecting one last moment of pain.

The crash was explosive, a screeching mesh of broken glass, wood and flying concrete from the first level that shook the building.

Ramirez turned and ran for the door.

42

The *sicario*'s pistol was raised a split second after he exited the office.

On the landing, he dropped into a slight crouch, the pistol braced for accuracy on his left palm.

The rusty sedan had barreled through the front doors, knocking them off their hinges and buckling the frame. It stalled a few feet later, the grille bent in, its headlights cutting twin beams across the darkened room.

He kept his aim trained on the driver's side door. The glass was tinted, and he couldn't see whether the driver was still inside. He swept the room visually, the Sig Sauer tracking left, past the stage, to the tables and washrooms beyond, then back to the right, past the car to the bulk of the tables and the buffet stand along the right wall.

No movement. That meant whoever had interrupted them was still in the car. Its front end was badly damaged. *Enough to pin the doors closed? Perhaps.*

He took careful aim along the Sig's rail and squeezed the trigger three times, the kick smothered by his bracing palm, the bullets piercing the windshield in three tightly grouped white dots of splintered safety glass. *If he was behind the wheel... he's not going anywhere anytime soon.*

He leaned over the upper rail and checked the periphery of the stairs. Then he crouched again as he slowly followed them down to the first floor.

He swung around the corner to his right, checking the corridor. It was empty.

Ramirez traced a semicircle, moving left with his back to the stairs, circling the tables, checking for movement behind them. The room was empty.

And that means he is behind the wheel... or perhaps in the back seat, trying to get out through the trunk?

The tinted glass clearly wasn't bullet resistant – the old Ford was rusty and cheap, something driven by a teacher or bank teller – which meant anyone inside could shoot through its body panels as easily as he'd done with the windshield. That required caution; he stayed low and used the round four-person tables for cover until within ten feet.

He popped out of cover, braced the pistol, and fired four more shots, two through the side window, two more through the door panel. He remained in the crouch as he quickly scurried over, under the wing mirror. He reached up and over and pulled the door handle. The car's open-door warning beeped softly.

Ramirez looked around the door.

Empty. He stood and peered around the front seats. The back seat was empty, too. He peered down into the driver's well. A cinder block lay loose next to the pedals.

Someone wedged the accelerator. But that means—

He was turning to his left before finishing the thought, the move coming a moment too late, a man's leg flying towards the door in his peripheral vision, the boot landing hard, slamming it closed on Ramirez, his gun thrown from his grasp and into the car.

The figure didn't pause as it closed on him, around the door, then reaching down to grab at him. Ramirez shot out a hard side kick, catching him in the midsection, knocking him off his feet. He turned to face his attacker, who rolled effortlessly backwards, coming up standing.

He was a gringo, taller, thin, his features angular and chiseled.

"You would be 'Bob,' then?" Ramirez asked.

"I would. And... you would be?"

"Busy, and you are interfering. Now, we fight."

The man charged towards him, Ramirez reaching back to pull the butterfly knife from his suit coat pocket, a flick of the wrist opening its razor-sharp, double-edged blade.

43

The assassin's hand flew up from his side, scything a sweeping cut at Bob's throat. He bobbed out of range, feet spread for balance, two hands instinctively blocking the arm down and away.

He followed the momentum of his block, twisting to his left, his right elbow sweeping around to smash the tall gunman across the jaw. Ramirez stumbled backwards, the knife clattering to the ground a few feet away.

Bob surged forward, throwing a straight punch to the solar plexus, trying to drive the wind out of his opponent. Ramirez used a cross-arm block, the punch deflected. He thrust a forward kick out, not pausing as Bob blocked it downwards, dropping low into a kneeling groin punch.

Bob anticipated, turning just enough to take the blow to his thigh, a Charlie horse numbing it, his balance thrown slightly to his left.

The *sicario* realized his advantage and threw himself forward from his kneeling position, his momentum and body weight taking them both down to the ground. He rolled over and onto Bob, trying to pin his arms with his knees. Bob raised his right leg, wrapping it around Ramirez, using it to pull him off.

The two men rolled away from each other and came up on their feet.

"I was expecting less," Ramirez said. Bob noticed he wasn't even breathing hard.

"You stay fit. A little bit of... I don't know. Mixed."

"Maeda jiu-jitsu mostly. You are military."

"It's that obvious?"

The Mexican nodded. "So precise, the angles, the motions, like a machine. It... lacks elegance. But efficient? Yes! Before we continue, a question..."

"Shoot. I mean... don't shoot me, but... go ahead."

"Why are you involved in this? Why are you trying to protect these men?"

"These... you think I'm here to protect Angel?"

"Angel's not here. I was thinking more of Manolo Marichal."

"He has information I need."

"Did you assist in Cucho's death?"

"What?" Bob squinted at him. "Who the fuck is Cucho?"

The *sicario*'s expression shifted immediately, the intensity giving way to surprise. "You... don't actually work for him, do you? I thought he had thrown me your name in the same way as Manolo, as a sacrificial lamb. But... Angel was telling the truth. You are after him also."

"I am."

The *sicario* stood up straight. He pulled down hard on both lapels, straightening his suit jacket, a small cloud of dust drifting away. "My fight is not with you." He nodded towards the stairs. "Manolo is in the office. I shot him in the chest. It may already be too late for you to get what you want. But I will not stop you."

"Damn straight you won't." Bob remained in his stance. "What are you playing at?"

"I am a professional, like yourself. I am not being paid to kill you, and I have nothing personal against you, as long as you stay out of my way." He nodded towards the stairs. "Go. Now. Or we can waste both of our time continuing this until one of us drops."

Bob circled his opponent, keeping his back to the stairs until they were directly behind him. Ramirez carefully strolled around the front of the car, keeping his hands at chest height, palms out. "I am just going to retrieve my pistol from the car..."

Bob reached down to the Colt in his waistband and slowly shook his head. "Uh-uh. No deal. You want out, you leave as is, and I watch you go. I don't want any nasty surprises in two minutes' time."

Ramirez backed up to the shattered doorway. "You have a gun. You could have shot me when you had the drop on me."

"I'm trying to turn over a new leaf. Your timing is just really good."

"I shall take your word for it." Ramirez stepped around the door frame and disappeared.

Bob turned and took the first two steps.

"Bob!"

He turned quickly, his hand going for the nine-millimeter, drawing and bracing it.

Ramirez leaned around the door frame with a phone and snapped his picture. "For posterity," he said.

He disappeared from sight again. Bob kept the pistol trained on the doorway for another ten seconds. He'd gotten no sense of duplicity from the assassin, just the pragmatic notion that a fight benefited neither of them.

Bob turned and took the stairs two at a time. He pushed the office door wide, leaving it open behind him for situational awareness. Manolo was lying on his back by the desk. He had a gaping chest wound.

He crouched beside the wounded man.

He was barely conscious, his eyes swimming. "Manolo!" Bob slapped him gently. "Manolo, can you hear me?"

Manolo looked up at him. "Eh... oh. You. I think I'm dying."

"You're bleeding, but he missed your lungs, or you'd be coughing up blood by now. Wounds are relatively smooth. Bullets passed right through, I'm guessing. If the ambulance gets here in time, you'll probably make it. But... that's a big if."

Bob took out his phone and held it up.

"Call," Manolo said weakly. "Please."

"Tell me how to find Angel."

Manolo smiled and gently shook his head. "No. I owe him—"

"Your life. He fucking betrayed you, man! Wake up!"

"No. A deal is a deal."

Now? Now I get a gangster with a sense of honor? And it's this idiot?

"You want an ambulance..."

"I'm... I'm no snitch, gringo."

Bob knew he couldn't just leave the man to bleed out. But he could still make something of the situation.

"I'll call you an ambulance. But only after you talk to a friend of mine. You're going to tell him how you gunned down Sister Eva Morales, and a little more helpful information. You do that, I'll call for help."

Manolo's eyelids fluttered. "Feel... dizzy."

"You're down a couple of pints. Take much longer, cardiac arrest and stroke become issues due to your dropping blood pressure," Bob said. "What's it going to be, Manolo? Confess and live, or I leave you to save yourself."

Manolo could barely nod.

Bob smiled. *That's job one.* He reached down and searched the gangster, finding his phone in the front right pocket of his jeans. He took it out. "Password," he demanded.

"Six... four two four."

Bob punched it in. He scrolled to the phone app and checked recent calls until he found the two most-used numbers. He copied them into his own phone. Then he returned to Manolo's.

He dialed Sgt. David Glebe's number. Manolo was going to help him with problems two and three, as well.

44

Tito checked the rearview mirror of the old '79 Thunderbird one more time, but the highway behind him was empty. It faded to black as it stretched away from the glow of the stolen car's taillights. Ahead, the pop-open headlamps cast pale white spotlights on the concrete as it flew by, the car's big 302-horsepower V8 rumbling happily.

The German had kept the car in good condition, Tito had noted. He'd left his host tied up in his kitchen. Once in Phoenix, he planned to call the Bisbee police, tell them the man needed untying. The car would be safe in impound until claimed.

It wasn't ideal, but Tito figured he was running short on time. Angel was too powerful, too connected in Tucson to face without leverage. A man of Aimon Herrera's magnitude would never expect someone to snatch him from his own home.

On the bench seat next to him, his phone rang. He looked down and checked the number.

Bob.

He let it ring through to voicemail. That would worry the older man, but it couldn't be helped. He would call back eventually, when everything was handled.

For now, all he needed to do was stay within the seventy-five-mile-per-hour speed limit, avoid police attention. Finding Aimon hadn't been hard. He had his fingers in every criminal pie in Phoenix... but he was also anonymous, despite his power, unknown for years to the police. And that meant he could live openly, as a wealthy, expatriated Mexican. One of his wives had been featured in a home design piece in *Phoenix* magazine, a socialite showing off their impressive mansion.

The phone rang again. After four rings, it kicked over to voicemail once more.

Bob was going to be pissed. But Tito knew he had to do something, take control of his own destiny. It was time for Angel and his loved ones to start worrying.

HECTOR RAMIREZ HAD his foot down, the Audi R8 coupe rocketing down I-10 at over a hundred miles per hour, shooting past the exit to Marana, once a tiny village, now a bustling suburb. The twinkling of thousands of lit homes was a white blur in his peripheral vision.

He had his phone on hands-free, controlling it from the steering wheel.

A voice came over the car's speakers. "We have a hit." Miranda Echeverria, the cartel's efficient assistant, had run the man's image through their system just ten minutes earlier.

"That was quick."

"Yes, sir, thank you. It helps that he was so prolific."

"Was?"

"According to our source with the US National Security Agency, he worked for the CIA at one point, although it's unclear whether he was on the payroll or freelance. And he's supposed to be dead. He had an 'expedient demise' order placed on him in 2012. His file was dormant for a decade but picked up again about eight months ago, after a shoot-out in Chicago."

"Who is he, exactly?"

"His name is Robert Singleton. He's a former Marine who served in Iraq and also spent time seconded to the US Navy SEALs as a sniper in Afghanistan, then showed up on the CIA's payroll for parts of the following decade."

"Fascinating. A real spook," Ramirez said. "I wonder why he would be here, now."

"That's where it gets interesting. He had an open contract on him for most of the time since resurfacing. The firm offering the payment is a known CIA front."

"Whatever he did to upset them a decade ago is still a problem."

"Potentially, sir, yes. About six months ago, they pulled the contract. My suspicion is they've decided to deal with him in-house or through a particular mechanic."

Well, well, well, Ramirez thought. Now it was Bob's turn to have good timing. If they'd left the open price on his head, it would have made for a lucrative diversion. And the irony of the US government paying a Mexican cartel *sicario* for his help would've been irresistible.

For now, however, it was neither here nor there. "Thank you, Ms. Echeverria. I shall be in Phoenix within two hours. Call me with my room details when you have them. And...

sniff around on where he stands with them now, if you could. Tap our Washington connections. I don't want any surprises in dealing with him, like a third party on the hunt."

"Yes, sir, of course."

He ended the call. If Angel expected his father to protect him, Ramirez surmised he would be sorely disappointed. In fact, he intended to call ahead, ensure Aimon knew he was coming. The fewer people caught up in collateral damage, the better.

BOB WATCHED the road fly by from behind the wheel of Manolo's Mercedes-Benz GLE. The gangster had done as he was told and would doubtless be in custody and the hospital before too long.

He tried Tito's phone again.

No answer.

Damn it.

He'd turned the tracking app on, so it was clear the phone still functioned. It was parked somewhere in suburban Scottsdale, it appeared.

Up ahead, a blue-and-white road sign glowed in the beam of headlights. The exit to I-10 was just a few minutes ahead.

I guess I'm going to Phoenix.

45

Tito slept in the car overnight, parked in an abandoned lot just off Prairie Avenue in suburban Gilbert.

Just past dawn, he drove north to Desert Camp Drive, following it for a few miles to Iron Rings Drive, where he turned off.

At the end of the road, a private roadway twisted and coiled like a snake through the hills, leading another hundred yards to a secluded block of three properties, each enormous.

The property and mansion occupied the vast middle lot, surrounded on three sides by a white adobe privacy wall and fronted by a massive wrought-iron fence topped by spikes. All around it was nothing but desert and scrub for at least a half mile, a golf course just visible in the distance. But despite its desert location, Tito could tell the grounds were lush and green, hedges and ivy growing over the top of the wall as if rain was not hard to come by.

He stayed outside the gates for nearly two hours. He sat

behind the wheel of the stolen Thunderbird, parked just far enough down the street to allow him visibility through a gap in the fence rails. He could keep sight of the mansion and the main gates, the car's tinted windows partially concealing him.

He was trying to be patient.

Need a drink.

It had been nearly two days, he realized in the moment. His hands felt shaky, and his mouth had been dry for most of the day prior. But it hadn't killed him to go without. Maybe it was because he hadn't been a drinker until his late twenties, he figured. Maybe it had been more ease than addiction, a quick dose of comfort when he needed it – not like Martin, who'd seen heaven in every drop of bourbon.

Now, what he really needed was information, a break. He'd tossed the phone Bob had given him, aware it could probably be traced either by his new acquaintance or, worse, by the police. The fifty dollars Bob had left him hadn't been enough to replace it, so he'd stolen one off a café table downtown, while crossing the city. But an internet search had given him little on the property other than Herrera's ex-wife's taste in furniture, from a magazine layout, and overhead views.

He'd walked around it several times, taking care on the second and third pass to do so from across the street, in case staff were monitoring security cameras.

The place was large, four or five acres of land in a massive garden that mixed both traditional grass – difficult and expensive to maintain in the desert – and traditional desert fauna like cacti and saguaro. There was a guard post at the gate, another two men on the front doors. At least two others patrolled its perimeter constantly.

Beyond them, the mansion was a behemoth, five or six thousand square feet of Parisian-style white concrete with a Mansard-style gray slate roof.

Somewhere inside it, he figured, was Aimon Herrera.

Getting past the guards was most of the problem, Tito supposed. Once he had the big man at gunpoint, his people would back off, and he'd walk him out the door. None of them would risk harm to a Don with the Omega Cartel. That was insanity.

Pero también lo está agarrando el bastardo. But so is grabbing the bastard.

There were just too many men. He had no desire to try to shoot his way through them. Tito had never killed anyone; he'd beaten a few damn near to death in Mexico and shot another in the leg. But that wasn't the same thing, and he didn't feel good about them, either.

If they called his bluff with Herrera, he knew, he would be a dead man.

He took a deep breath. He hadn't had a cigarette in hours; Bob's endless nagging about it had finally gotten him thinking maybe he could do without, that it would be better for the boy once he got home to not be around secondhand smoke.

But now, his hands were shaky, and his breath was becoming a little ragged, and a nervous tension was making him tap his index finger on the steering wheel as if playing a tiny drum.

He pulled out the pack of Camels and lit one, letting the nicotine rush wash over him, his nerves suddenly calmed, the addiction assuaged.

Thirty yards ahead of him, a gray van slowed as it approached the mansion's gates. It turned right. "Amazon" was scrawled across one side of the vehicle in an orange stencil and cartoonish script.

Taking deliveries. Maybe that's something.

He started the car.

Through the gap in the fence, he watched as the delivery driver got out of the van, jogged up the steps, and handed a small cardboard box to a man at the front door in a butler's tails. Then he got back into his vehicle.

With less than three minutes gone, the van was pulling back out onto the street.

Tito put the car into gear and followed it. A delivery van was allowed in with minimal fuss, which meant he could use one as a route in. But not right away; they'd be suspicious if another showed up within an hour or two.

Instead, he needed to find out where the vans' depot was, what their security was like. Mostly, he knew he needed to ignore the past, his snap decisions and the rage he felt whenever he thought about Martin lying lifeless in the street.

He needed to be patient.

AIMON HERRERA SAT at the head of the long conference room table and stared at ten empty chairs. Ahead of him, a laptop spewed back reams of text, a long argument between two of his captains, each representing one of two rival families.

It was depressing, watching a fight by text. The other eleven chairs around the conference table were all empty. In the old days, they would have been filled by his captains, lieutenants and legal advisors, avoiding the risk of a wiretap for the monthly meeting, their views and competitiveness echoing around the room.

Now, they used an encrypted chat application that erased

itself at the end of the meeting, leaving no trace. Video was nowhere near as secure, so they typed.

It was not the same. There was no passion in the room, no sense that men were forging their destinies together. Aimon hated the modern world and what it was becoming: disparate, dissociative, men sheltering in place as if trapped on islands of their own construction.

The only other presence was Elvis, his driver and personal bodyguard, who sat on a stool by the door, dutifully ready to cut down anyone who interrupted.

The doors burst open, both pushed wide in angry unison. Elvis was off his seat in the blink of an eye.

But it was just Angel, his self-absorbed, fearful son. He rushed into the room, both hands in the air, as if he'd been imploring God to make it all better. "*Why?*" he asked. "Why, Papi? Why do you tell Ernesto to move my things to the guesthouse? *The guesthouse!* Like this is not my home anymore, like I am just some flunky you have spending the night..."

Aimon motioned downwards with both palms, twice, quickly. "Angel... please! I am in the middle of a very important meeting. Can this not wait?"

Angel stopped, planting a fist on each hip, as if a four-year-old were about to scold his mother. "No, this cannot wait, Father! What is this?"

Exasperated, Aimon typed *Please hold a moment, gentlemen, while I tend to an issue.* He lowered the laptop's lid in case Angel decided to draw any closer. Phoenix business was not his business. "Your old room is going to be renovated into a sewing room for Mrs. Sanchez, the retired seamstress who worked for Don Eduardo. Her son, Henry, was one of our best lieutenants, but was killed in a car accident last month. She has no other family and is nearly eighty and will be staying in the room next door. I wish for her to be happy and comfortable. So..."

Angel looked agog, as if someone had told him the Pope had just died. *"What?"*

"You heard me. Now, I must—"

"That is *my* room! I grew up in that room."

"Angel, there are fourteen bedrooms in this house, and the guesthouse is nicer than all of them, a self-contained—"

"It's my room!" he barked. *"My* room! Not some old crone whose family cannot care for her! I just... I cannot believe you sometimes!"

Aimon stared at him bleakly. He was forty-two years old, yet the Don was convinced his son had the temperament of a spoiled child of twelve. Eventually, he growled, "It is a fucking room, boy! You are a grown man, running your own city! Or you should be. Still, you cannot even be honest with me about this sudden 'visit' and the fact that something else is clearly at play..."

"I told you, I just needed a break, that's all! But I can't even come to our house and—"

Aimon rose to his feet suddenly, slamming his fist on the table, his rage obvious. *"It is not your house! It is my goddamned house!"* He felt a sudden swell of annoyance that the boy had made him lose his temper. He lowered his voice. "It is my house, and you are a grown man. You are fortunate, indeed, given your behavior since your mother left, that I even allow you on the property."

"Father—"

"Even then, I must trust that you are not somehow neglecting your duties to the cartel in Tucson while you 'hide' here from whomever... Ah." A moment of realization struck him. "That's it, isn't it? This is the same nonsense from ten days ago, the dispute with the *sicario* Hector Ramirez."

"No. I don't—"

"Don't try to bullshit me, boy! I know when you are lying, and you know I am never wrong about it."

Angel looked away quickly, obviously feeling exposed. "He is a madman. He thinks I killed Cucho Lopez and did away with him somehow. All of my men have told him this is not true; all of them support me! But he has put the fear of God into them, and whoever is actually responsible has made him blame me."

I don't believe him. I am incapable of believing him. He lies with the same ease the rest of us breathe, but with the skill of a lobotomized chimpanzee.

But Aimon had promised his ex-wife he would always take care of him. *¡Vaya marrón!* "Why? Why would they tell him you were responsible if you are not? That makes no sense. They fear you, yes?"

Angel shrugged. "Sure. I mean, of course, yeah. I lay down the law."

"But they fear lying to him more," Aimon said. "Why? Why would that be if you were behaving?"

Angel looked down at his shoes and shook his head. "I do not know. Truly."

Sure. And pigs will fly to the moon. "The guesthouse will have to do," Aimon said instead.

"But Papi..."

"No! Enough!" Aimon gestured for him to move away. "Go! You will find it's a lovely place to stay. Enjoy the pool. Stay out of my way while you are here. Now, I have business to attend."

"Father, please..."

Aimon drew in a lungful of air and counted back from ten silently, allowing his anger to settle before he did something regrettable. It had been decades since he'd lost his temper with homicidal results; he didn't want a return to the rage of his youth meted out on his son, even if he was worthless. "Elvis, take him to the guesthouse. Make sure he's settled. If he tries to move back into the house, shoot him in the leg. Am I clear?"

"Yes, Don Aimon," the bodyguard said.

"Shoot me in the..." Angel was wide-eyed and shocked that the old man would even suggest it. "Papi..."

Aimon spread his hands wide, a plea for thoughtful consideration. "All you have to do is lie low quietly and not bother me, and he won't have to shoot you."

"In the leg," Angel said with dry incredulity.

"Exactly."

Elvis draped a hand over Angel's shoulder. "Come on, Mr. Herrera, I'll make you a smoothie." He led the stunned younger man towards the door.

"Yeah... yeah, okay," Angel said. "In the fucking guesthouse, I suppose?"

"The pool really is lovely," Elvis said as he opened the double doors.

BOB ROSE EARLY. He'd gotten into Phoenix at just after midnight only to find Tito's phone lying in a deserted lot just off I10. With no sense of where he was going or whom to talk to, he'd gotten a motel room for the night.

Now he needed to do some research.

A fifteen-minute drive took him to the Acacia Library. Extensive searches of periodicals, the name Herrera and "organized crime" had borne almost no fruit, such was the man's obvious caution.

But after two hours and a rejigged search using "gangster," he'd found it.

It was a clip from a newspaper gossip column written nearly thirty years earlier, in the *Arizona Republic*. The accompanying photo featured a young man who looked like a more handsome version of Angel Herrera, his beard cropped tight, shirt collar open to display a thick gold chain. On his arm was a pretty young woman with dark hair.

A small subhead in bold caps read:

YOUNG LION LAUGHS OFF LOUSY LEINSTER.

"This columnist's heart goes out to poor Aimon Herrera, the young starlet of the Phoenix real estate scene, seen here with wife, Angela, at the Heart Fund Gala, and the latest to suffer a slur at the hands of Councilor Joe Leinster. While we won't dignify Greasy Joe's scurrilous statement by repeating it, suffice to say the city councilor accused young Aimon, a principal investor in the new Valley National Bank building, of skirting the law in his sudden rise to local wealth and prominence. Once again, Greasy Joe – whose grandfather was from Sicily and would be ashamed – chose to raise his victim's ethnic heritage, in a city where being of Mexican origin should be a source of pride, not an epithet. Take a vacation from being a sleaze, Joe: Aimon Herrera is no gangster."

Aimon Herrera. The picture was so old, he had to be either Angel's father or uncle. The similarity was too close to ignore.

He headed back to the desktop reference computer and typed in "Aimon Herrera."

The list of articles it returned was much shorter, just a few dozen pieces. Nearly all were business stories, acquisitions and new construction projects, the purchase of a casino, then another, then a nightclub, then a partnership in a golf course.

There was also a magazine layout from the eighties, an interview with Herrera's wife, Angela, about her choice in home decor.

He's been busy. This is not a small player.

Bob leaned back in the library chair. If Angel was in charge of Tucson, it made sense that perhaps his old man ran Phoenix.

Tito's going after the big prize.

He probably figured Aimon Herrera was the ultimate in leverage.

IT HAD TAKEN MOST of a day, but Tito's patience had finally paid off.

He'd noticed it during his perimeter tour of Aimon Herrera's property, taking a chance to boost himself up just high enough to see over the six-foot back wall: a rear entrance that staff used to come and go, as well as to bring in food and take out waste.

But taking advantage of it, and the fact that familiar delivery trucks were granted access, had taken a little longer.

Eight hours had passed, some of it seated in his car across from the depot, watching men load and unload a small fleet of gray vans, the rest spent following vans.

Eventually, they'd loaded one up with something large and square enough to be a refrigerator.

Perfect. Tito started the Thunderbird.

Two minutes later, the van pulled out of the depot lot. He put the car into gear and followed it.

Following the trucks had told him how they worked, each had more than one delivery, but they seemed to all be destined for the same zones or zip codes, maximizing the amount they could carry while minimizing necessary travel distance.

He waited until the van's second stop before acting. The moment the driver unloaded a small box and began to carry it to the home's front porch, Tito jumped out of the Thunderbird. He checked the road in both directions to ensure they weren't being watched. It was empty.

He crossed the street and crouched beside the van's driver's side door. A moment later, the deliveryman returned to the vehicle, walked to the back and checked that the door was fastened as a matter of habit, then rounded the vehicle.

Tito held the pistol at face height, for maximum effect. "Give me your keys! Now!"

The man complied.

"Get in the truck!" he commanded. "Don't touch the radio; don't ring any alarms. If I see a cop or another one of these trucks before we get where we're going, I'll fucking kill you. Do you understand?"

The driver's eyes were wide with fear.

"You got a piece in the van?"

"A... piece?"

"A piece. A fucking gun, *cabrón!*"

"We're not allowed."

"Good. That's just asking for trouble, driving around all day with a piece. Go on, get in."

The man climbed into the cab. Tito rounded the vehicle, opened the back doors and climbed inside, then closed them behind him. Past the refrigerator box, the truck had twin shelves against either wall, each stacked with boxes. Between them, a narrow path led to the front seats.

Tito secured himself behind the driver.

"I don't have any money," the driver said. "We don't carry cash."

"I don't want your money. I just need a ride. And the place we're going, the guy who owns it, he's way more dangerous than me. So if you make this trouble, if you try to get help from them, or warn them about me, or any of that shit, just know and understand that they will shoot us both dead on the spot. And if they don't kill you, I will. You feel me, homes?"

"I... please: I'm really scared."

"You should be. But the only way this goes bad for you is if you let it. Just drive in, I climb out at one point, and you drive back out. Okay?"

"Okay."

"You're delivering a new refrigerator. That's all you need to tell them at the gates. You got that."

"What if they ask why? What if they're not expecting it?"

"The house has staff handling things, and an owner they fear. They won't ask questions. Just... drive. I'll point the way for you until we get there."

Tito knew the man had a point. The gate would be easy, accustomed to deliveries coming and going. But the back door was also guarded, and the man there would check before letting anything in. He'd thought about hiding inside a large cardboard box, literally letting himself be delivered to his target. But if the driver was right and the back-door guard got suspicious, he would also be trapped.

Instead, it made more sense for him to slip out of the van at that point, tell the driver to give the back-door guard an address off by one digit. They would send the man on his way, but he'd be inside, at least in a position to find cover behind the bushes and flowerbeds around the building.

Bob figured that Tito couldn't do stuff for himself, or that he was always too angry and drunk to manage. But Tito knew he was a survivor.

If he had to walk through hell to make sure Angel Herrera couldn't hurt him or Sean, that was what he would do.

The truck pulled away from the curb.

46

The gate went smoothly, the van slowing but not stopping, waved through by the guardhouse.

"What now?" the driver asked. "I don't know where I'm going."

Tito peeked out from between the seats. They were on the main driveway, directly ahead of the house. "When you get near the house, you'll see the driveway curves around it on both sides in a circle. Go right, follow it to the parking area just ahead of the rear service entrance."

The driver nodded rapidly. The kid was nervous, Tito knew. The guilt over scaring some dumb gringo wage slave was eating at him. "If it's any consolation, you were just the first guy carrying a big box," he told the young man. "And like I said, I don't got no reason to hurt you so long as this goes smooth. Okay?"

His captive nodded again, just as vigorously. *Damn it. He's scared to death.* It was the part Tito had hated about being a gangster, the knowledge he could only achieve what his bosses wanted through fear and intimidation. Making someone else feel like shit. Being a gangster was no business for someone with a conscience.

"Okay, we're here," the driver said. "What now?"

"Park in the third bay, with the bushes ahead of it."

He felt the vehicle pulling a hard turn into the parking space.

"Okay."

"Get out, head up to the guard at the top of the steps, and repeat what I told you. I'll be gone by the time you get back. Raise an alarm, and I will shoot you where you stand. Better to just play it cool, a delivery gone to the wrong address like so many others. Okay?"

"Yes! I mean... yeah. I got this."

The tone sounded like the kid was trying to convince himself. Tito moved quickly to the twin back doors as the kid climbed out of the cab. He turned the handle as gently as possible, not fully allowing it to click open until the young man slammed the driver's side door.

He opened the door rapidly and climbed out, closing it gently behind him. He could hear the kid talking to the guard as he rounded the van to the bush and crouched behind it.

"... wrong street entirely," he could hear the guard saying. "You want Hideaway Lane. That's back nearly a mile from here."

"Ah, heck. Knew I should've just punched it into the satnav at the depot," the kid was saying. He was acting up a storm, Tito figured. He looked to his right. The row of bushes stretched right to the far corner of the massive home. If he was right, there would be accessible windows at the very end of the building, away from either parking area.

He began to follow the hedges, keeping his head down. If

another car had driven around the building at that point, he knew, he'd have been discovered.

Tito was twenty feet from the end of the building when he spotted motion through the foliage. He glanced over the top of the topiaries for just long enough to see a guard in a tan sport coat round the corner, an MP5 slung over his neck.

Shit. He ducked low and glanced back in time to see the delivery truck pass him, the driver keeping his eyes straight ahead. As it cleared his view, another guard popped into view, strolling from the other end of the mansion.

One coming one way, one coming the other. Nowhere to run. He peeked both ways. The men were following the hedge line, on the green belt between it and the house. A regular patrol of some kind? The hedges weren't high enough to be sure he'd stay hidden once they got close. From nearby, his body would stick out, catch the eye.

Think, cabrón, *think!* He couldn't shoot them and didn't want to, anyway. He had no quarrel with Aimon Herrera's men, or even the big man himself.

They were getting closer, each man just twenty feet away, eighteen, fifteen...

Out of time. Have to try something... He dropped onto one side as if taking a nap, then rolled over backwards, wedging his body as well as he could under the lowest hedge branches. Twigs jammed into his skin, one pushing against the soft flesh under his left eye, the sudden sense he was about to accidentally blind himself prompting near panic, every ounce of restraint required to keep from rolling back out again.

The footsteps converged behind him. "What was the van?" one of them asked the other.

"Amazon."

"Yeah, I know that! I mean, it's on the fucking side of the vehicle, guy! What was he delivering?"

"Ronny says wrong address. Kid wanted Hideaway Lane."

Tito held his eyes closed tight and tried to hold his breath but somehow couldn't, his heart pounding. If they even just looked down, he realized, his T-shirt was white. They would see it through the top of the bush.

Just go. Stop fucking talking and just go, please...

"Fucking drivers, man," one guy said, waxing solemn. "Tough gig in summer. Then again, Phoenix is never fucking cold, is it?"

"See, you say shit like that, and people know you're not from here," the other guard said. "We get all sorts of weird weather come winter. Snow, flooding, baking heat at Christmas. It's nuts."

Tito felt a brushing sensation on his nose, like a hair trapped against soft skin. He opened his eyes.

The wasp seemed much larger from its forced perspective.

Shit.

His eyes widened. The wasp wasn't moving except to probe his skin for its next meal. It was bent at the midsection slightly, as if a moment of anger might cause it to plunge its tiny stinger into the tip.

"Well..." one of them said.

"Yeah."

The wasp turned to face him. *Please not now,* Tito begged. *Please.*

It considered him for a moment.

Then it buzzed away. Tito let out a breath slowly.

The two guards began to pace away.

Tito waited until they'd gone silent, and rolled out from under the hedge. He stayed on his haunches, following the line quickly to the right side of the rectangular building. He checked around the corner. It was clear, a giant weeping willow on the lawn twenty yards ahead blocking off the view from the road and guardhouse.

As good a guy as Bob was, Tito figured his new friend would've expected him to fuck up by then. *If he didn't think I needed help, he wouldn't keep helping me.* But he'd have been proud of this, Tito figured, some genuine planning paying off.

As he'd figured, there were windows: four in a row. But they had to be a dozen feet off the ground. There was no way to reach them let alone figure out how to open them.

Shit. He felt like smacking himself on the forehead. There were grand stairs ahead of the front doors... so obviously the first floor was well above ground. *Should have thought of that. Stupid!*

Movement to the right caught his eye. Past the giant weeping willow, at the very periphery of the property, was another small house, invisible from the road. A maid was exiting its front door, turning to close it behind her. Tito retreated a few feet to the end of the hedgerow and secured a spot behind it. He watched her walk away from the cottage, following the path he supposed eventually led back to the front entrance.

He needed a way to reach the mansion's windows, Tito figured. Even an extra foot or two would put him close enough to jump up and grab the lower ledge, pull himself up. He looked up at the imposing structure.

Two men on the gates, two at the front door, probably more inside.

Man, Tito, you've lost your damn mind, trying this.

There was nothing nearby obviously high enough to use as a boost, just rocks and scrub. He glanced back at the guesthouse. If she was changing sheets or cleaning, that meant someone was using it or had used it recently. That meant there was furniture inside, including chairs.

His vision swept over the fifty yards between the end of the house and the guest cottage. The willow would prevent the guardhouse from spotting him. But someone on camera duty might well do so, even if the guards on the front steps didn't.

But he knew he had little alternative. Once he'd gotten inside, the option of quitting had been taken away from him; he'd never make it back to the street alive.

So... better be quick. He turned to face the cottage and crouched low, bracing against his back foot like a sprinter.

Go.

47

Angel Herrera lazed in the lounge chair by the pool, his white bathrobe loosely draped around him, Ray-Ban Aviator sunglasses on, lenses glaring, a margarita in his right hand, a joint in his left, the tip smoldering as gray smoke wisps climbed towards the rich blue sky.

Perhaps his father was right. Perhaps this was better, a place of his own on the family compound. He was not a boy anymore, as the old man was so happy to point out.

Repeatedly.

Coño, *he disrespects me so. He thinks nothing of me.*

But I built Tucson without him, me! He is old, out of touch, too accustomed to having everything go his way. Me, I have to deal with crazy ex-gangsters, crazy gringos, angry sicarios. He drifts around that mansion like a ghost, reading his books, sipping his expensive French brandy like a king.

He glanced over at his phone. It still hadn't rung despite nearly a day passing since he'd fled Tucson, leaving Manolo to his fate. It was unfortunate, he told himself, but could not be helped. The younger man was weak, too easily swayed by a few kind words. People like that eventually always became cannon fodder for the strong. Yes, he had been loyal, but so was a dog. Shooting stray dogs was practically a kindness.

Once again, you do him a favor just by letting him help the cause. He is a hero, even if it comes because of his weakness.

He will be remembered as such by someone, surely.

Angel reached over to the side table to retrieve his cigarettes. The box felt light. He flipped the top open.

Empty. He threw it back onto the table.

He gently shook the margarita with his other hand, judging how much crushed ice he had left in the last ounce. *Need a refill, too.*

Angel rose, using the lounge chair's wooden frame to pull himself upright. He wandered back to the patio door and pulled it open. It swung wide silently.

Then he froze in place.

There was a man at the bar in the corner of the living room, his back to the patio doors, picking up one of the high-backed stools. Angel looked to his right. He'd left his pistol on the coffee table, ten feet away.

The man began to turn.

Angel's eyes widened.

Tito.

Tito looked up and saw him, then froze in shock for a moment.

Angel darted towards the table, falling to his knees, grabbing the pistol as Tito darted towards the front hall.

He swung the gun around. "*¡Alto! Detente o ayúdame Dios, te volaré la cabeza!*" *Stop! Stop, or so help me God I'll blow your head off.*

Tito ground to a halt, the stool held aloft in one hand.

"Put it down."

Tito was shaking his head almost imperceptibly. "You, here. My luck—"

"Your luck is terrible. But we already knew that, you fucking traitor."

"Ptth!" Tito scoffed at that, even with a gun to his back. "I paid my debt. I owe you nothing, and you send your cop flunky Hayes to kill me anyway."

"*Cállate!*" *Shut up!* "The fact that you talk back to me like this in the first place is why you're going to die, Tito. Stupid fuck! Always with the attitude! You stick your nose in my business and this is what you get. Stupid!" Angel peered at the stool on the floor. "What the fuck were you planning to do with that, hit me over the head?"

"I'm sure you can figure it out."

Angel's expression soured. "It doesn't matter. Fuck you, Tito Agustin. Now I finish your ass. Then I go for..." He paused. "Where's your gringo friend?"

He saw Tito's body relax slightly, as if he'd just heard something amusing. "What? Where the fuck is he, you useless piece of shit!"

"I figure you'd want to know that because you know what he's going to do to you when he finds you, especially if you kill me. We're like..." Tito held up his left hand and crossed two fingers. "Like this. You kill me, he'll make your death last even longer."

Angel shuddered down to his toes, a streak of raw fear. He liked to think he had always been careful, always had reason to be confident in his security. And here, he was surrounded by his father's property and men.

But try as he might, he believed Tito. "Turn around," he commanded.

Tito did so. He was expressionless, as if studying a pile of trash that needs to be cleaned up.

"Get... get over onto the sofa," Angel said.

He waited until Tito had complied. "I figure he knows what you're up to. He hasn't done shit these last two weeks without you around, according to Hayes. So he's somewhere near. Take out your piece... Careful! Do it slowly; slide it across the floor."

Tito reached behind him and took out the pistol, then slid it across the parquet floor. Angel picked it up and put it in his waistband. "Take out your phone and call him; tell him where you are."

Tito shook his head. "Don't got one. Dropped it on the way here."

"You think I'm stupid?"

Tito sighed. "I don't have his number. I replaced the phone, but I didn't write it down."

Angel didn't believe him, but it probably didn't matter. "I don't care. He's come to save you multiple times already. I have no reason to think this one different. We're going to wait for your friend Bob to show, and you'll make a convenient hostage. He will realize he can do nothing without you paying the price; my father's men will capture him. And then I'm going to kill you both and end this farce once and for all."

48

Don Aimon Herrera watched as the cigar's end flared to life, clouds of smoke gushing outwards as he puffed on it, drawing air through the cylinder, pulling the match flame close.

"Don Aimon." The man's voice was unfamiliar, which meant it could only be one person. He shook out the match and tossed the matchstick into the ashtray on the desk ahead of him.

"I do not recall asking for company. And yet the guard post is most apologetic in informing me that they had let you pass without even calling the house first."

"I intend no disrespect, Don Aimon. Your legend and stature within Omega continue only to grow. But we must talk."

The mob boss blew out a plume of blue-white smoke and looked up to see who was addressing him. "You would be Hector Ramirez, I take it?"

"You are correct, sir. My apologies for intimidating your guards."

"They got a call right before you pulled up. They know what an order from Mexico City means. Please..." He gestured to the seat ahead of his desk.

Ramirez sat down. "You have a lovely home."

"Thank you. But clearly you are not here to list the property or write an article in *Phoenix* magazine. One of those was quite enough."

"You know why I've come."

"I do. Angel insists he has done nothing and is being framed."

"By one of his men, yes, I've heard this story already. I do not believe him."

Don Aimon puffed on the cigar again. It tasted vaguely of sour cherries. "You will question him?"

"I will."

"And if he did what you believe he did?"

"He will pay with his life."

The Don studied the man across from him. Ramirez was a top man, a contract killer for Omega Mexico City, with hundreds of targets eliminated across a nearly three-decade career. If Aimon ordered him killed by the guards, there was a chance even a half-dozen men would fail. But...

"He is my only son."

"I know. I am sorry it has come to this."

"Who did he kill?" He didn't bother to phrase it as unlikely. He fully believed Ramirez. Angel was a fool, after all. Even if he was his only boy.

"My second cousin, Cucho Lopez. He was... not a bad boy. He knew his family's reach, and he probably thought Mexico City made him immune to something happening to him. So he was lazy, not a good worker. They sent him to work for your son's crew because Tucson runs itself; it's small change."

"And yet you believe Angel would nonetheless—"

"May I be frank, Don Aimon?" Ramirez interrupted. "Your son strikes me as a vainglorious and arrogant man. He makes many mistakes; he abuses his people. They fear him, but they do not like him or respect him."

The Don drew in breath sharply at that. "I know. Get to your point."

"I think he was unaware that Cucho had family who would look out for him. I think he lost his temper and killed him, and now, like a coward, he is hiding somewhere in this house so that your reputation and men can protect him. But..."

"Those are not the rules," Don Aimon anticipated. "The rules say that a *sicario* has free passage against anyone but the leadership. That's how they maintain their distance, mete out the cartel's justice. Even when it is personal."

"Even then. Where is he?"

"You will give him a chance to explain?"

"I will."

"And if he offers you an alternative that may be true, you will check it out first, yes?"

"I will... within reason. If he can hand me someone he can prove killed Cucho... I will spare him."

Don Aimon gestured towards the west side of the house. "He's in the guesthouse. I shall call ahead to tell him you're coming. If he runs, I will not stop him. He..." He glared at the top of his desk, briefly wondering if he could reach the pistol in the top drawer before the assassin cast him to hell. "He is my boy."

"I would expect no less." Ramirez rose. "That must have

been difficult. The numerous stories of your exploits in building your operation here are legend... but they do not do justice to your honor."

"Go, Gravedigger," Herrera said. "And I pray that in doing so..." He could not find the words. "Just... go."

Ramirez headed towards the door.

ANGEL HERRERA ENDED his father's call and put his phone back into the pocket of his robe.

He'd turned pale, Tito thought. "Bad news?"

"My father just called. A man is coming over to the house to kill me. That means you just acquired a new skill, Tito: you get to be a human shield."

"A man? What man?"

"A *sicario*, from Mexico City. You know what that means?"

"Of course. I also know if he wants you dead, a hundred and fifty pounds of me ain't going to stop him, *cabrón*. Maybe what you need to do is give me a piece as well, and we have a truce until—"

"*You think I'm stupid!?*" Herrera barked. "You think I was born yesterday? I know what you want: revenge for your lost drunk friend. I give you a weapon, you kill me, end of your story, right, Tito? What... then you shoot it out with this man, maybe make it out alive, maybe talk him into..."

He stopped, a notion occurring. Angel nodded gently, the possibility of his redemption staring him in the face. "I will not give you a gun, Tito. What I *will* do is give you to him, as the man who shot his family member. That's what he wants: revenge, nothing more, nothing less, a foolish matter of so-called 'honor,' just like your stupid pursuit of me. But I am not stupid, Tito. I am not some drunk at Sacred Heart, or

Manolo, or one of his idiot friends. I am the son of a great Don, and the better man also."

"He won't believe you. They're not stupid."

"Maybe. But I would bet that my father's price for letting him take me was to give me a chance, an opportunity to hand over the actual killer."

Angel's phone began to buzz once more.

BOB STARED at the pair of guards by the gatehouse. They were indolent, undisciplined.

One was overweight, the MP5 submachine gun slung around his neck afforded a sort of shelf on his rotund belly. The Terminator shades and goatee didn't make him look any tougher. He was big, but in the way that meant he had to catch you to hit you.

His friend looked more the part, six feet plus, a neck like a tree trunk, worried eyes under ginger hair, a little loop earring betraying the fact that he had at least some under-lying character.

Neither man looked like they'd moved in hours, and it was nearly three in the afternoon. If Tito had been there already, he hadn't been successful.

That means he's either dead or captured or holding off for some reason.

Tito had had most of a night and the day to make a move. But maybe he'd been careful, Bob figured. It wasn't his stock in trade, but he'd been sober for days, worried about his son more than anything. And Tito was nobody's fool despite sometimes playing it.

Bob had rounded the building several times, getting the lay of the street, the scrub desert around the wall, cover, potential angles to get in over the wall unseen, the layout of external and obvious cameras. There had been no visitors.

A car passed the borrowed SUV. Bob's eyes widened as it turned to enter the compound.

The Audi from the Flaming Garter. The assassin.

Shit.

Through the open side window, he thought he heard a telephone ring, somewhere around the area of the gates.

A moment later, they opened electronically, the Audi rolling inside and towards the giant home.

They just let him in, Bob realized. That meant he'd either gotten Aimon Herrera's permission to enter... or he effectively outranked the Phoenix boss.

Maybe he goes in there and finishes Angel off, does everyone a favor.

But... if Tito's there, maybe he finishes him, too.

For all he knew, Tito was already dead. He had no way to contact him and could only rely on his friend calling him if he needed help.

Or...

He took out his phone and dialed the number he'd retrieved from Manolo's phone.

A nasal voice answered after three rings. "What?" Angel Herrera said angrily. "What do you want?"

"Angel Herrera?"

"You have my number, which means someone is in deep shit for giving it to you. Now, you've got ten seconds to tell me—"

"I'm Bob. I expect your friend Manolo has mentioned me."

A stream of epithets spewed down the line in Spanish.

Bob pulled the phone away from his ear for a split second until the yelling subsided.

"Yeah... well, I'm not your biggest fan either," he suggested. "You have Tito?"

"Not for long. He's going to die, *maricon*! A *sicario* thinks he killed one of my men, and he's on his way here right now. I tell you what: you want to stop him, you got some work ahead of you, gringo."

"Okay. Where are you?" Bob demanded stoically.

"Where—" Angel paused as if incredulous. "*Madre de Dios*, you've got some balls, man. You know what? You make it this far, you can take your best shot. We'll be in the guesthouse. Asshole."

The call dropped.

Bob put his phone away. His patience was waning.

He got out of the car and crossed the street, approaching the guard post.

ANGEL ENDED THE CALL. He began to pace back and forth, occasionally darting a look towards the front hall.

"Bob's here, isn't he?" Tito asked. He looked smug, Angel thought, like he really thought one man could make such a difference.

"It does not matter. It takes less than three minutes to walk here from my father's office. He will not arrive in time to help you... and he would not defeat a *sicario* even if he did."

Angel allowed himself his own smug little smile in retort. This man was about to find out what real power was.

"You think the *sicario's* going to believe your bullshit?" Tito proposed.

"Why not? It fits, doesn't it? I am an important man, not a brawling, drunken fool like you, Tito. And I am the future of the cartels. Where my father contented himself with one city, I will one day run all of the cartels, from wherever I choose, united under my firm hand. My father is weak, old-fashioned. He kowtows to his 'honor' system as foolishly as this assassin, letting the man speak with me even as he calls to warn me like some pitiful, cowed dog barking at a stranger. But there is no sentimentality in what we do. There is no time for honor when the killing starts."

Tito sniffed a little, the air humid, the slight waft of chlorine drifting in from the pool area and the open patio doors. "You sound real sure of yourself... for a grown man hiding in his daddy's guesthouse," he said dryly.

"What I am sure of is that you have delivered yourself to me at precisely the right moment, a sign from God if ever I saw one that I am destined to survive and thrive, and you are not. You are like so many of them out... there," he said, waving a hand limply towards the city. "You are just... like fuel for my fire. You are useful... and then you are not, and I get rid of you, like anyone. So when he arrives here, he will hear a terrible story. A terrible story about how you killed his cousin, brutalized him with your fists and feet, then tossed him into the desert, to rot in the heat, unsuitable even for carrion. And he will believe me because I am Angel Carlos William Herrera, and I am a god in this city."

To his right, the patio door swung fully open, the slender and imposing figure of Hector Ramirez stepping through it.

He had a pistol in his right hand, slung casually to one side.

49

The guards weren't accustomed to seeing any action. That was obvious from the lack of urgency as he jogged up to them.

"Oh... hey!" Bob said, waving at them. "Hey, glad I saw someone out here... I'm sort of lost!" he said.

The impression he intended was goofy white-guy tourist, just some dude in a light jacket and sneakers, idiotically running up to the home of the city's most powerful criminal boss. Judging by their puzzled expressions, it was working.

He was within five feet when the standing guard turned his considerable bulk Bob's way. "Fuck off!" he said bluntly.

Bob's eyes widened in feigned shock. "Excuse me? Did you just tell me to... to eff off?" he said.

The guard scrunched up his face, as if both annoyed and puzzled. He looked down at his MP5, then back at the tall dude he'd clearly just offended. "*Chingón*, you got balls walking up to a man with a machine gun around his neck," he said. "You stupid as fuck, but you got balls."

His friend chuckled at that.

Bob took out the silver cross around his neck. "Ah, but I have the power of righteousness on my side," he said as he approached the man, standing just a foot away.

"You think that'll stop a bullet, homes, you be my guest and get all up in my face," the guard said, his friend still chuckling. "But like I said... I got the machine gun."

"It's actually a submachine gun," Bob said. "The optional longer stock doesn't actually make it—"

The guard lost his temper, his hand grasping the gun's grip as he swung it to bear on the stranger. "You think I give a—"

He didn't finish the line, Bob's left hand grabbing the MP5's stock, twisting the gun a quarter-turn and shoving it into the man's gut even as he leaned in and head-butted the bridge of the guard's nose, bone snapping. Bob's fingers hooked the MP5 strap as the man stumbled backwards. His foot came up quickly, a side kick slamming into the guard's gut, his already compromised momentum toppling him over, the gun staying behind.

His friend was already up, turning to sight his target as Bob ran towards him, covering the space in three steps, arms swinging the MP5 like a cut-off baseball bat, the front hand-guard his handle, the wide stock the barrel, catching the guard flush in the side of the skull. It hammered home with a dull thud, the man's head caroming off the guardhouse.

The first man was up to his knees despite his considerable bulk. Bob turned and kicked him hard in the jaw, the man crashing to the dirt, unconscious.

He needed to restrain them before a camera gave him away to other guards or someone called in. He checked the perimeter, the bench ahead of the guard post.

Nothing.

The second man had a bulky webbing belt on under his vest. Bob laid down the MP5 and rifled the pouches.

Bingo. Stupid guards win stupid prizes. The second contained three sets of rubber wrist restraints. He took them out and used them on each man's wrists. *Gag them? No point.* They had to be close to fifty yards from the main house and the property huge, guards likely spread out.

That would be advantageous. He looked inside the guardhouse. A small red button sat by the light switch near the door. He held it down, and the gates began to open. *He's probably got someone manning security monitors, which means I'll have company soon.*

Angel had announced he was in the guesthouse with arrogant, smooth certainty. He didn't have the patience or cleverness to spring a trap spontaneously, Bob figured.

He ran across the main lawn. An array of ornamental topiary bushes and cacti dotted the green space, each just about large enough to provide some visual cover.

The house ahead was huge, with perhaps a dozen double windows across each of two levels. To its right, the driveway led around it circularly. There was a wide gap between the house and the six-foot-high privacy wall. To the building's left, a giant weeping willow followed by a row of trees blocked much of the view except...

Is that the end of a wall?

The guesthouse. It was perhaps thirty yards farther back than the house and a solid hundred yards away wide, towards the far-left privacy wall.

The trees were natural cover. He checked his sight lines, then stayed low as he sprinted towards them. The guards were packing serious heat, which meant caution was required. As he reached the treeline, he drew the Glock 17 from his belt.

He caught the barest glint of sunlight on chrome from a pistol barrel as he stepped into the trees, from his left. Bob hammered down with both fists, catching the guard's forearm as he strode out of cover, blocking out the man's aim, the gun firing wildly and away.

The instinctive move worked, but Bob lost his grip on the Glock, the gun tumbling into the low-lying shrub and ground cover.

Before he could spot it, his attacker recovered, turning back to him, pistol still in hand. Bob snatched at the man's wrist, pulling the gun up and away even as he turned, tossing the man over his hip, the judo throw allowing him to wrest the gun from the guard's grasp. But his opponent was adroit, recovering as soon as he hit the ground, reaching back and lashing out with a low kick to Bob's ankles, his foot kicked out from under him, balance lost.

Bob crashed to the ground, the gun falling away. Before he could recover, the guard rolled his way on the ground, not bothering to right himself, using his spinning momentum to try to throw a backwards elbow to Bob's face. Bob spotted the arm at the last second, catching it in both hands, reversing the man's move by spinning over and rolling on top of him, yanking his knees up to pin the guard's arms. Before the guard could struggle free, Bob hit him with a flurry of crosses to the chin, the "ground and pound" maneuver knocking him unconscious.

There were voices near, a rustling of leaves as more men approached. Bob's eyes scanned his surroundings quickly. A tree to his left was older, wide-trunked. He stepped behind it.

The men were aggressive, careless. They walked past the tree without slowing. He turned side-on, the high kick catching the first guard square, driving him dazed to the ground. His partner tried to turn to face their attacker. Bob hopped forward one step on his balanced back leg and repeated the motion, the high kick with his front leg catching the man square across the side of the chin, the mental nerve crushed, all strength gone from legs that practically wilted to the turf.

He picked up one of the MP5s and slung the strap around his neck. He didn't bother restraining them. It takes the average man less than a minute to recover from being knocked out. But by then he'd be close, and they'd be irrelevant to the mission.

He pushed through the trees. On the other side of the tree line, a low-slung brick wall surrounded an elegant cottage, with neatly manicured rose bushes.

Christ, the water this place must go through, he thought, in a brief loss of focus.

He followed the wall around the house. Behind it, a swimming pool occupied most of a large back patio. Bob hurdled the wall and approached the corner of the house, wary of cameras, the back patio door just twenty feet away.

50

Hector Ramirez closed the patio door behind him as he entered.

His eyes widened when he saw the two men.

"Señor Ramirez, sir!" Angel said breathlessly. "My God, your timing is perfect, sir!"

"It is, is it?" Ramirez said.

"It is, Señor! Right after my father called, I caught this man, Tito Agustin, attempting to break in here and assassinate me. This man... this is the man who helped Manolo kill your cousin. This man is the reason you have come to Arizona, and I present him to you, sir, so that you can deliver the deadly justice he so deserves."

"I see," Ramirez said. He was nodding, but he had an oddly placid, almost romantic look on his face, as if he'd just walked into a high school reunion. "This man... this man here, this... disheveled, underweight little man—"

"Hey, that's a little much," Tito grumbled. Angel glanced over at his captive quickly. Tito also looked strangely happy.

"I... don't understand," Angel said. "Shoot him, Señor Ramirez! Kill him now! I tell you, this is a dangerous man, and not to be trusted."

"Yes, yes, of course, very dangerous," Ramirez said, almost nonchalantly. He walked over to Angel's side. "Give me your pistol."

"I..." Angel hesitated, unsure of how to act. But he knew he could not turn down a *sicario*. And he needed this to work, to sell Tito as the guilty party. He handed over the gun.

"Good," Ramirez said. The Gravedigger looked him up and down again, without emotion, the way a butcher might study a new cut of beef.

Outside the home, from somewhere nearby, they heard two gunshots, then a third. "We have company, it seems," the *sicario* noted.

"His associate!" Angel blurted. "The man called Bob I mentioned to you in Tucson."

Ramirez looked at him quizzically. "But... I thought you said this Bob was the real culprit."

"I did. I mean... yes, but that was before—"

"And then you changed the story without explanation, and it was your man Manolo who was to blame. Right?"

"I mean... yes, but—"

"And now, it's Manolo... And it's Tito... And it's Bob."

"Uh... yes, Señor."

The Gravedigger walked over to Tito, a pistol in each hand. He raised both of his arms... and threw them around the smaller man, hugging him. Both men began to chuckle.

Tito patted Hector Ramirez on the back twice, heartily.

"*Mi hermano*," Ramirez said.

"Brother," Tito responded.

Angel's mouth dropped open.

He felt pale, a sickly sensation, a bead of sweat escaping his left temple, tracing a path to his jawline. "Wha-what?" he stammered.

Tito looked at him, his face stony. "I always tell people I have two brothers in Mexico City: Ricardo, my middle brother, he is the amiable one. But my oldest brother, Hector... man, you don't want to mess with him."

Angel felt dumbstruck, his mouth hanging open, the shock of his miscalculation rendering him mute. Ramirez flipped around one of the pistols and handed it, grip first, to Tito.

"But... but your last name is Agustin," Angel said.

"So? It's no secret. I tell everybody I took my wife's name when we got here."

Ramirez glanced over at his younger brother. "You're an idiot. You know that, right? And I'm still really goddamned angry with you."

"I know."

Angel glanced back and forth at them. This couldn't be happening.

Not to me. Not to Angel Herrera.

What was it he'd told Hayes?

Everybody knows somebody; everybody's related. You've got to know who you're dealing with to survive in the cartels.

"Oh..." Angel muttered aloud. "Oh God. Oh God, Papi... I think I fucked up."

The two brothers raised their pistols and opened fire in unison. Angel's body contorted, hung up by gunfire, before collapsing, bullet-riddled, to the ground.

. . .

THE GUNSHOTS WERE RAPID-FIRE, the muzzle flash glaring through the cottage's side windows. Bob sprinted to the back door of the patio and yanked it open, turning the corner, his eyes sweeping the room even as he raised the MP5.

"Whoa!" Tito said. He stepped in front of Hector, making sure there wasn't another sudden, violent death.

"*¡Se necesitan explicaciones rápidas!*" Bob demanded. *Quick explanations are needed!*

"Bob..." Tito stepped to one side so that the two men could see each other. "Bob, this is my eldest brother, Hector."

"The one who doesn't speak with you—"

"Because he has dishonored us by leaving the cartel," Ramirez said, finishing the thought. "But he is still my brother, idiot or not. And I know he did not kill Cucho."

Tito frowned. "Cucho? Cucho Lopez? Rhonda's Cucho?"

Ramirez nodded. "He is dead. This..." He gestured to Angel's corpse with his pistol. "This piece of shit killed him, or his man Manolo."

Tito shook his head gently. "I did not even know he was in Arizona."

"That," Ramirez said grimly, "is because you walked away. That was your choice."

Bob looked confused. "Excuse me... but that's the second time you've mentioned that name. With all due respect... who the fuck is Cucho?"

The *sicario* raised a finger and wagged it at him, as if restraining himself from losing his temper. "Do not... Do not regret the things you do not learn in this life, Bob. Be thankful for the things you do not have to. This is a family matter and none of your business."

Bob shrugged. "I'll take your word for it."

Ramirez took out his phone. He dialed a number. "It's

done," he said solemnly. He ended the call. "I have told his father. We shall receive no opposition in leaving."

He turned back to Tito. "You are still in my bad books."

"I know."

He glared at Bob. "And you have strange taste in friends."

"Without doubt."

"I'm right here," Bob said dryly.

"Yes, you are," Ramirez said. "You spared me in Tucson, and I was not sure whether to kill you out of pride or thank you. As you also saved my foolish brother, I shall opt for the latter and tell you this, Bob Singleton..."

Tito's eyebrows rose. "Singleton?"

"My real name. How do you know it?" Bob asked.

"We have a great many associates. Not as many as your CIA, mind you. But good information. They still want you dead. A man is looking for you, a private contractor. I do not know who, just that they have engaged him to find you and kill you."

"There was an open contract," Bob said, watching the blood puddle grow around Angel's lifeless form.

"CIA?" Tito said, overawed. "CIA?"

"It was a long time ago," Bob said.

"Not long enough, apparently." Ramirez walked over to Tito and hugged him again. "I shall go. I would not stay here long. Aimon Herrera is honorable and follows the rules, but he will also be grieving soon."

He walked over to the rear exit. "Tito, call me sometime and we'll talk. Mr. Singleton, I trust we shall not meet again. It might be fatal for both of us."

And with that, the Gravedigger disappeared through the patio door.

"We need to go," Tito said.

"Damn straight," Bob said. "I'm driving. And when we get back, you're going to do me a little favor for helping you with all this mess. And no, we're not going to talk about the CIA."

51

It was nearly one o'clock in the morning, and once again, Det. Carter Hayes was slightly drunker than he'd planned as he mounted the stairs to his second-floor apartment.

But it didn't matter. The club was shut down, Angel having fled the city. Manolo Marichal had inexplicably confessed to killing the nun. His immediate paymasters were effectively out of the picture.

There was, however, great opportunity in change. As long as no one could tie him to the bum's death, he stood to come out of the mess unscathed. He reached the apartment door and slid the key into the lock.

Unlocked. It wasn't a mistake he'd normally make, and even intoxicated, his hackles went up. He retrieved his service weapon from the speed holster clipped to his belt. He pushed the door open wide, but stepped back and away from it.

Nothing.

The room ahead was dark. There was no sign of movement. He quickly stepped across the doorway, to the other side, glancing inside the apartment as he did so, but seeing no one.

You're getting paranoid, bud.

He holstered his gun and walked inside, flicking on the light, then turning back to the entrance to close the door.

"Evening, Detective."

He spun around, hand going to his gun. Bob had appeared from nowhere – or perhaps just the nearby kitchen door – and stood behind the sofa.

"You know, just the trespassing alone gives me plenty of reasons to draw down on you and shoot your ass," Hayes said, his hand resting on the pistol butt.

"And you know you wouldn't even clear the holster before I took it away and spanked you with it, like the naughty boy you are."

Hayes gestured towards the street with a nod. "Manolo Marichal. Was that your handiwork?"

Bob shrugged. "The Lord works in mysterious ways. A friend of mine really believed that."

"Ah. The nun." Hayes nodded, a small, knowing motion. "So this is... what, revenge? You're here to kill me because Manolo's a fucking idiot with an itchy trigger finger? That it?"

Bob relaxed his posture and sat on the top edge of the sofa. "If I wanted you dead, Hayes, we wouldn't be having this conversation. Hell, you wouldn't have made it up the stairs."

"Pretty confident in yourself, aren't you, Bob?"

"We've done this once already, remember. And you're less drunk this time. The smell isn't quite as wretched."

"Ah... let me guess: one of those pussies who can't handle his liquor."

"Something like that."

He didn't seem easily flappable, Hayes thought. Certainly, insults weren't doing it. He considered going for his gun again, how quickly he could draw and fire. The Glock 21 didn't have a safety, and he'd had the trigger pull loosened, a mere flick of the index finger enough to fire it.

"Right now," Bob predicated, "you're probably assuming I'm lying, and that I'm here to hurt you or kill you. But that's not it at all, so you can just relax."

"Sure," Hayes said. "I'll relax. I'll fucking relax when you're on the other side of that fucking door."

"Okay," Bob said. He gestured with one hand. "Move aside, and I'll let myself out."

"Just like that?"

"Sure."

The detective turned side-on and waved an arm dramatically. "After you."

Bob rose from the sofa perch and walked past him to the door, keeping his eyes on Hayes throughout. "Oh... I should mention a couple of things in passing."

"Yeah? Like what?"

Beyond Bob, from somewhere outside and near the building, a police siren wailed, followed by another.

"Well, for one, those guys are probably pulling into the front entrance of the parking lot just about now, so I'll be going out the back. As I'm not the guy they're looking for, I kind of imagine they won't stop me. They probably want the rest of the building as clear as possible."

"The guy they're looking for?"

"Oh, yeah... that would be you, Hayes, naturally."

The detective's eyes narrowed. "Fuck you. Fuck off. They're not here for me."

"Yes and no. First, they're going to want to find that brick of cocaine you've hidden and that Manolo helpfully supplied to you. Or at least, that's the version he already told the cops."

He didn't look like he was full of shit. It was a hell of a story if it was, Hayes figured. "Why would he do that?"

"Same reason he confessed. It was that, or no ambulance, and he had multiple gunshot wounds at the time. Maybe the two of you can try working together and try that as a story in court. Either way, I have to go now. If I were you, I'd spend the next few minutes trying to find and flush that brick."

Hayes looked around the apartment quickly, trying to see anything obviously out of place. "You fucker. They'll never... I mean..."

"Oh, but they will, Hayes. You see, they already know you're dirty. They have a bunch of other paperwork and photos of you with Angel, and that doesn't look good. Plus, they have a witness to you shooting wildly at the shelter door, and might even be able to match the slugs they took out of Manny the doorman to your spare piece, so you might want to find that, too. But the coke..." Bob shook his head as he walked out the door. "Naughty, naughty, naughty."

"*Fuck!*" he heard Hayes scream from inside the room.

Ahead, on the front staircase, he heard boots beginning to climb the steps. Bob turned and strolled towards the back stairs.

"Bye now, Hayes!" he called back. "Enjoy prison!"

"*Fuuuucck!*" Hayes bellowed as Bob turned the corner and headed down the apartment block's stairs.

. . .

A<small>N ARMOR-CLAD</small> officer had just opened the back door, pistol in hand, as Bob arrived.

"*Sir!* I need you to stay clear, please!" he bellowed, gesturing with his free left hand for Bob to leave the building. "We have a police scene here and require you to stay clear."

"O-of course, sir," Bob stammered as he jogged past the man and out. "How long—"

"Unknown at this time, sir. Please stay clear until we've cleared the scene or advise you otherwise."

Bob nodded frantically. A second officer passed him on the step, followed by a third.

He shoved his hands into his pockets and strolled across the back lot, past the second group of staging police.

From the corner of his eye, he noticed Hayes's gray Mustang parked partly across two slots, taking up both. He'd hidden the brick of coke from Tito's friend under the spare wheel well, along with the pistol he'd confiscated on his last visit.

Right about then, Bob figured as he strolled down the street, they would be slamming him to the ground and cuffing him, Hayes's time wasted searching the apartment. Sgt. Dave Glebe would be suggesting to someone that the warrant extended to all of Hayes's property, including his vehicle.

Between a kilo of coke, Manny, a murder weapon and the photos placing him with the late Angel Herrera, Bob suspected, Det. Carter Hayes was going to prison for a very, very long time.

And they were going to love him in there.

EPILOGUE

Tito Agustin stirred the pot of macaroni and cheese vigorously. Cooking was new to him, but he figured he almost had the easy stuff down... or at least the stuff Sean liked, which was the important part.

He scooped two big portions into two bowls. "Okay!" he announced with gusto. "Two bowls of the Magnificent Mac for two magnificent fellows."

He carried them out to the living room. Sean was ignoring him completely, his head immersed in a video game. "Sean! Time to eat!"

"Yeah, yeah... just a minute!" The boy waved him off without turning away from his game.

"Now!" Tito intoned. "You need your strength. Summer school starts Monday."

The boy tilted his head back, and Tito thought he heard a sigh. He didn't have the heart to push discipline, though, or the need for manners. He'd only had his son back for a day, Sgt. Glebe helping to smooth over the gun charge, but not the expulsion. He needed to find a new school for next semester... once he'd done some catching up.

It had been two weeks already since...

He caught himself mid-thought and took out his phone. Had it been...?

Yeah, two whole weeks already. That was what the man said.

He dialed a number.

"Tito."

"Bob." Tito smiled. "It's good to hear your voice, *carnal*! You said wait two weeks, then call. So... where are you?"

"Yeah... nowhere near Tucson. I had to go. Too many questions, too many people wondering how I play into things."

"So... you just left?"

"Yeah."

"And... what? You're not coming back?"

"I'm not, no. I'm sorry, Tito. I wanted to stay. I liked it there. But I also liked people there, and some of the people looking for me... they don't seem inclined to stop, if you get my drift. I made a lot of noise. Word gets out."

He did. But it didn't seem right. "You show up, save my ass – three times, no less – deal with Angel and Hayes, and then you just disappear?"

"Yeah. I don't like it either, bud. But... it is what it is. We'll see each other again at some point, though."

"Yeah?" He sounded sincere, but somehow Tito wasn't convinced. For whatever reasons, Bob's job there was done. "Now what? You go off, help some other dudes with lousy choice in friends?"

"Something like that," Bob said softly.

"Don't seem fair. I owe you so much."

"You want to do me a favor?"

"Name it."

"There's a kid named Chico who's going to show up tomorrow for a boxing lesson at the Pima Youth Center. You said you trained MMA when you were younger?"

"Yeah... but I ain't no trainer! Me? Teaching someone?"

"You did okay with your kid. Same deal, just a few years older. Well? Can you do it?"

"I mean... until I don't know no more. Yeah, of course, *carnal*. Name it, it's done."

"Hey... what happened to Hayes?" Bob wondered.

"Trial set for this fall," Tito said. "Murder, conspiracy, drug trafficking. They're pinning it all on him. Your cop friend Glebe is the happiest motherfucker in Arizona."

"Well... good. Look, I should go. Long calls attract attention. Your boy—"

"He's home." Tito looked over at his son seated at the table, oblivious to most of it as he dug into his mac 'n cheese. He felt a tear roll down his right cheek. "He's perfect."

"Hang onto that feeling and remember it when he does something stupid, okay? Everyone needs to be loved."

"You know it," Tito said. "Thank you. Thank you for what you did here. I... I can't even tell you what he means to me."

"You don't have to. Goodbye, Tito."

"Goodbye, Bob."

The line went dead. Tito stared at the phone again for a moment, the notion of something ending, a moment of sadness settling in.

"Dad? What's the matter?" Sean was looking over, noticing his tears.

Tito just smiled and shook his head gently.

"Nothing. Absolutely nothing."

BOB ENDED the call and leaned back against the diner booth's velour bench seating. The plate in front of him had featured an egg-white omelet and chicken sausages, but it was empty now, the food demolished in a perfunctory five minutes.

An elderly waitress at the other end of the restaurant peered its length to see if he was finished. She glanced at the lone other diner's plate as she passed, twisting the side locks of her strawberry blonde beehive.

She snapped her gum as she leaned over to remove Bob's plate. "You want anything else, darlin'?" she asked. "We've got a fine raisin pie if you like. Owner gets them from the bakery just down the road."

"I'm good, thank you."

She smiled briefly. "Another green tea, then?"

"Sure."

"I'll be right back with a pot," she said.

Bob glanced out the adjacent window. The diner was in North Vegas, well away from the famous Strip. But there were still game rooms on every other block, and splashes of neon color dappled the sidewalk.

He checked his watch. It was just after eight o'clock. It had been good to hear from Tito, but there was no future in Tucson. Vegas, on the other hand, held the promise of some answers. Nurse Dawn had called him just after he'd left Arizona and offered him a name: a prominent psychiatrist who dealt in hard cases, men who'd done terrible things.

Most of his clients were mobsters, apparently. Bob tried

not to dwell on that. He needed help, he knew, figuring out who he really was, and who he wanted to be.

Answers weren't guaranteed.

But he figured it was worth rolling the dice.

THE END

ABOUT THE AUTHOR

Did you enjoy *Hell Bent*? Please consider leaving a review on Amazon to help other readers discover the book.

Ian Loome writes thrillers and mysteries. His books have been downloaded more than a half-million times on Amazon.com and have regularly featured on the Kindle best-seller lists for more than a decade. For 24 years, Ian was a multi-award-winning newspaper reporter, editor and columnist in Canada. When he's not figuring out innovative ways to snuff his characters, he plays blues guitar and occasionally fronts bands. He lives in Sherwood Park, Alberta, with his partner Lori, a confused mostly Great Dane puppy named Ollie, and some cats for good measure.

ALSO BY IAN LOOME

A Rogue Warrior Thriller Series

Code Red

Blood Debt

Dead Drop

Hell Bent

Hard Country

Snake Eyes

Body Count

Dark Cargo

Made in the USA
Monee, IL
11 June 2025

19236447R10225